FATE DEMANDS SACRIFICE

THE SIRIANS SERIES
BOOK TWO

K.M. DAVIDSON

Copyright © 2024 by K.M. Davidson

All rights reserved.

No part of this publication may be reproduced, stored, or transmitted in any form or by any means, electronic, mechanical, photocopying, recording, scanning, or otherwise—except in the case of brief quotations embodied in critical articles or reviews—without written permission from its publisher.

The author expressly prohibits using this book in any matter to train artificial intelligence (AI) technologies for the purpose of generating text, including works in the same genre or style as this book.

This novel is entirely a work of fiction. The names, characters, and incidents portrayed in it are the work of the author's imagination. Any resemblance to actual persons, living or dead, events or localities is entirely coincidental and not intended by the author.

K.M. Davidson asserts the moral right to be identified as the author of this work.

Cover and Interior Map Design by Brian Andersen
Edited by Wonder and Wander Editing Co.
Proofread by Brittany Bookworm Editing

DEITIES & THE GODS

DEITIES

KUK
The Darkness, the Abyss, Dark beings

KHONSA
Choice, Magics, the Light

GODS (CHILDREN OF KUK & KHONSA)

DOLA
Goddess of Destiny & Fate

MORANA
Goddess of Death & Magic

DANICA
Goddess of Nature & the Energy of All Things, The Morning/Evening Star

ROD
God of Family, Birth, & Humanity

DEMI-GODS

CHILDREN OF MORANA

SYBIL
Magic, Founded House of Echidna

CHILDREN OF DANICA

PHOEBE
Sirian – Gravitational Energy Manipulation

TARANIS
Sirian – Lightning Manipulation

ASTERIA
Sirian – Heightened Energy Manipulation, Stars & Galaxy

DIONNE
Sirian – Heat Manipulation Variation

CHILDREN OF ROD

BRIGID
Magic, Founded House of Argo

BODHI
Immortal Human

ENKI
Immortal Human, The First King

GARUDA
Magic, House of Nemea

AVEESH ROYAL FAMILIES

MARIANDE
HESPER
King Darius
Queen Lucia
Crown Prince Tariq
Princess Eloise
Prince Clint

RIDDLING
CITLALI
King Seif
Queen Raya
Crown Prince Ruhan
Princess Naja
Princess Numa
Princess Thana

THE NORTHERN
PIZI
GRAVES
King Amos
Queen Olena
Crown Prince Garrick
Prince Anton
Prince Nazar

TESLIN
CORVUS
King Wren
Queen Keitha
Crown Prince Lang
Prince Horne
Princess Jenae

THE CLIPS
ALDRAM
King Silas
Queen Atalia
Crown Princess Linore

ETHEREA
KORBIN
King Ciar
Queen Mela
Crown Prince Keiran

Content Warning

This adult fantasy novel contains mature themes and content that may not be suitable for all readers. Readers are advised that the story includes depictions of violence, graphic imagery, explicit language, and scenes of a sexual nature. Additionally, the narrative explores challenging subject matters, including but not limited to death, betrayal, and psychological distress. Please exercise discretion and know that the content may trigger or be unsettling for some audiences.

★★★

To all the cinnamon rolls out there,
May your kindness never go unnoticed, your jokes always land,
and your awkward moments be forever endearing.
Keep being your charming, dorky selves because the world
could use more of your wholesome vibes.
Remember, nice guys finish first in our hearts…

Even if they might not in this book.

PROLOGUE

Their daughter's birth had been extremely difficult for both parents, but especially for the Mother, who had lost a large volume of blood in labor. It did not help that when the child arrived into the world and the Mother beheld her, she sobbed as her worst nightmares came true.

The Father stared at his daughter in trepidation as she whimpered restlessly in the nurse's arms, her little fists flailing.

His instincts took over instantly, and he ripped the child from the nurse's hands, placing her into the arms of her sickly, paling Mother.

Without hesitation, he lunged for the nurse when her back was turned and snapped her neck with a deafening crack.

The Father knew the nurse had to die, the first of many unnecessary deaths to occur. Most nurses were taught to kill the child upon observing the Mark or report it at the very least. A nurse of the castle would relay what she assisted in delivering to the world and take that information to the king.

The Mother flinched at the sound but remained

focused on reveling in her child before acknowledging the reality of their situation.

Their child looked just like the Mother, with raven-black hair of which the blue sheen was already noticeable. She stroked her baby's face, trailing a finger down her full cheeks and brushing her tiny, bow-shaped lips.

The child stopped squirming and whimpering at her touch, falling into a gentle silence filled with serenity.

The Father peered over his wife's shoulder, marveling at the sight of their child. She was the most beautiful thing he'd ever seen; his heart now belonged to her.

"The Mark," the Father breathed, addressing the truth before them.

"He told us this would happen," the Mother said, panicked, her grip tightening on the bundle in her arms.

They knew if anyone discovered their child was Sirian, they would have to hand her over. The child would be dropped in the middle of the forest in the north, left with the Goddess Dola to decide her fate.

The parents of the Sirian child both stared warily at the lifeless body on their bedroom floor before locking eyes. The Mother's gray-blue eyes flickered to the armoire before landing back on the Father's frantic hazel ones.

He moved quickly after their unspoken agreement, gathering all the belongings they would need and all the money they had before helping his wife clean the blood and gore from her body.

FATE DEMANDS SACRIFICE

While they only had a general idea of where to go, it was better than staying in their homeland, where their daughter was at risk.

They set out north to Outsider Land, hoping for a chance to raise the child not to fear herself.

Their travel took a toll on the enfeebled Mother in a short time. The trauma her body endured, coupled with the lack of proper medical attention after blood loss, quickly deteriorated her.

They stumbled upon a rickety inn far from Main Town, somewhere quiet and shoddy where they knew they would find the folk to help the Mother.

The Father positioned a winter cap on their unnamed child and swaddled her as best he could, silently thanking the Gods that the early fall of Eldamain was cold enough to warrant layers for an infant so small. He held his frail wife in his arms, the child dangling in a basket on his elbow, and rushed into the inn to discreetly request a *real* nurse for his wife.

The innkeeper produced a Magic to inspect the Mother and child. The Father was able to offer jewelry in exchange for secrecy, and the Magic did not startle when she spotted the Mark.

Carefully positioning the hat back over the child's forehead, she examined her to ensure good health. Fortunately, the infant girl could not have been better for a newborn.

But the Mother and baby were in disparate conditions.

She lost too much blood to recover. The Magic expressed that the distress endured during birth caused internal damage to the Mother and, if there had been a Magic at her birth, her fate would have been different.

The Father looked upon the child in the basket, willing himself to be angry with her, but he could not find it in him. His heart only melted at her parted lips as soft breaths released from them.

He gathered her in his arms and lay by his wife's side, assuring she was comfortable. They whispered to each other, reminiscing of their life together, confessing their unyielding love for one another, and desiring a better life—a better world—for their forsaken daughter.

The Mother passed long into the night, whispering a name for their child.

Reva.

Months after the Mother died, the Father spent what little remained of his life trying to care for the child, Reva. He hopped from inn to inn, avoiding onlookers who despised Mariande and the Sirians and, coincidentally, wanted him and his daughter gone.

Night after night, dreams and nightmares plagued the Father, replaying in his mind: a strange oily substance swimming through mountain peaks, a stone tower shrouded by mist, the shouts of men and women in battle, a young woman who looked strikingly like his wife, and an eerily familiar crown on top of dark blonde hair.

Yet the one constant in every dream was a woman with ebony skin and marigold eyes, beckoning him with

FATE DEMANDS SACRIFICE

her finger before he woke.

He knew who it was. The woman had assisted in his own birth, and his parents made him memorize a code in case he would ever need to call upon her again.

How the wheel of time goes round...

The Father stood before the rugged wooden door, the cold winter sneaking under his worn-out coat and biting at his cheeks. He swallowed the swelling emotions in his chest, bending down to place his daughter before the door, bundled up tight with every layer they owned.

He retrieved the three letters he had written that night from his coat pocket, tucking them between the child's small body and the side of the basket he always carried her in. He gently laid the Mother's gold and hematite necklace on the rise and fall of Reva's chest, resting his hand over her little belly and admiring her.

She resembled her Mother in so many ways it pained him, especially when she giggled and her eyes and nose crinkled. He allowed himself some pleasure in knowing that, underneath her eyelids, her golden-hazel irises were the same color as his.

Maybe the people they once knew and called family would recognize her one day.

The Father sniffled, wiping the back of his nose against his sleeve. He leaned over the baby and placed a fleeting kiss on her Mark.

Without another glance back, he left his daughter and his reason for living behind him forever.

CHAPTER 1

The orb of Light hovers between my hands, thrumming with the beat of my heart and quivering as I struggle to hold it in position. Barely bigger than a melon and as bright as a fire, the contained Light threatens to expand, grow, and jerk around the room.

My jaw clenches, a bead of sweat cascading from my hairline and tickling the side of my face. I blink, trying to open my vision beyond the tunnel, narrowing by the second. Even my arms tremble in front of me, from my fingers to my shoulders.

You'd think I'd been doing pushups for *hours*.

"Hold it there, Reva," Lightning warns, her tone throwing me back into memories of training with Remy.

The orb pulses, growing an inch in diameter.

"You have to learn how to maintain control with distractions," Lightning lectures, her voice dropping low. I train my eyes on the ball between me as the sand crunches beneath her boots, closer to me this time as she says, "When you're in the middle of a battlefield, others will be fighting alongside you. You can't get distracted and lose control. The enemy will always try to throw off

FATE DEMANDS SACRIFICE

7

your focus."

"I'm not learning how to battle," I force out between clenched teeth. "I'm learning to help Clint."

"One and the same, Healer," Lightning whispers, her breath tickling my neck and startling me. Despite the ball flaring briefly, I reel the Light back to a steady glow.

Her boots crunch again as she slides into my peripheral with her arms crossed over her chest.

"Good save." Lightning nods her head once. "Let's snuff that out, but don't let it snap back into you like usual. Just let it go… Whatever that means for you."

Only a week ago, Lightning agreed to train me under the agreement that she'd help me learn to harness my powers enough to heal Clint, but it's clear she's not given up the belief that I'm meant to be leading the Light Sirians who have been gathering. I've spent every morning working on generating and releasing the Light. Still, my weakness has been maintaining control while distracted and releasing it without cracking back into my body like a whip against my skin.

I know I need to learn faster, especially before I start flinging things around underneath a castle, particularly one with inhabitants completely unaware there are two Sirians training below.

I press my eyebrows together, breathing.

I've been trying to imagine the power absorbing back into my skin, but that never seems to diminish the strength of the recall. I try something new this time.

Just like I absorb the power *into* me from all around

me, I give it back to nature. I refrain from closing my eyes, watching the orb slowly dim as I replicate the vision in my mind.

The ball breaks apart into smaller orbs, like stars scattered in the night sky, before they fade out of existence.

I've never felt lighter after extinguishing my power. There was no snap to make me unsteady on my feet.

"That was—"

Lightning is interrupted by a deep, velvety voice from near the doorway as it calls out, "Whimsical."

We spin on our heels toward the archway, my heartbeat rising.

Tariq rests against the wall, casually leaning on one leg with his arms crossed over his chest. Fin stands underneath the doorway, feet planted shoulder-width apart and his arms mimicking Tariq's.

My heartbeat doesn't slow. Instead, it hammers in my chest.

"Like a puff of glitter," Tariq continues, demonstrating his metaphor by splaying his fingers out in front of him and letting his arms arch away.

I suck my upper lip between my teeth, biting.

"Gods above," Lightning grumbles, glaring. "You can't just sneak up on us during practice."

"In theory," Tariq begins, pushing himself off the wall with his hips. The movement flexes his chest muscles, stretching against his black dress shirt. "I can do whatever I want."

FATE DEMANDS SACRIFICE

He struts across the floor until he plants himself before Lightning and me. He slides his hands into his pockets and bends at the waist, aligning his burning amber eyes with mine. Two strands of dirty blond hair fall from his half-bun.

"But I understand." An inviting smirk tugs at the corners of his lips. "I didn't mean to startle you *too* much."

"I could've hurled the Light at you," I warn him, the threat not coming out as confident as I would've liked.

He instantly catches that, which only brightens his smile. "I think you have more control than you give yourself credit for."

"You figured that out from a week of knowing me and sneaking into a handful of sessions?" I question, crossing my hands over my chest and tilting my head to the side.

Tariq's smile diminishes, but his eyes are still alight with excitement. He straightens, shrugs, and purses his lips. "What can I say? I'm a fan."

My gaze flickers momentarily to Fin, who's still lingering in the archway but switched up his posture to stand like a proper knight with his hands clasped behind his back. Our eyes lock, and his shoulders lift slightly as if to say, *What are you gonna do?*

"Well, I hope you enjoyed the show," I sneer, stepping into Tariq so there's only an inch between us.

His scent engulfs me at this proximity, so I hold my breath. I made the mistake of inhaling a few days ago, and *Gods,* it was intoxicating.

Like being submerged in a hot spring during the dead of winter, the warmth seeping into my bones as an icy breeze kissed my skin.

"I have a younger prince who needs my attention," I finally manage, sidestepping him to walk past. His arm snaps out, and his hand wraps around my forearm, halting me.

Both of our heads bow to where his skin brandishes mine. We simultaneously raise our gazes at each other, and I can't imagine what he sees in mine as every sense narrows in on the firmness of his grasp.

His face is a perfectly trained mask with just a touch of amusement as he says, "I came to let you know that my father requests your presence at dinner with us this evening."

"Just me?" I clear my throat around the slight grumble, averting my gaze.

"I'll be there, too," Fin announces from the archway, still standing at attention.

Tariq removes his hand from my arm, shoves it back into his pocket, and faces Fin as he adds, "We'll all be there."

I trudge across the room towards Fin, using all my willpower not to look over my shoulder and check if Tariq or Lightning are following behind me. I level my focus on Fin, whose dimple is slowly peeking out from underneath his auburn-tinted stubble.

By the time I'm standing in front of him, those emerald eyes are twinkling.

FATE DEMANDS SACRIFICE

11

"He's not wrong." Fin tilts his head to the side, wincing. "That was whimsical, and you had way more control than when you first expelled the Light with me."

I side-eye him, falling in step as we journey up the stairs.

"I need to get faster." I roll my shoulders as the extra feet shuffle behind us. "Today was the first time I've released my power like that."

"Reva," Fin chuckles, shaking his head. "It's been barely over a week since you started training with Lightning. You said so yourself: you have a lot to rethink about how you wield the Light and firepower."

"I am not touching *that* yet." I point my finger at him. "I don't want to risk it popping up when I'm trying to work on the mass for Clint."

"Don't you think it would be helpful to be comfortable with it, at least?" He twists his head to look down at me. "You want to have control to dampen it, too."

I steadily inhale through my nose, rolling my eyes. "I hate it when you're right."

Fin laughs a little then, his eyes crinkling at the corners. I can't help the small smirk that sneaks onto my lips.

Fin's laugh has always brought me joy, no matter what's happening around us.

Or between us.

We emerge from the hidden stairwell one after the other, lucky no one sees the four of us suddenly appear in the hallway. The fewer there are of us, the less suspicious it is, and we don't want to draw unnecessary attention to our secret training room, considering we're wielding the forbidden Light.

"I'm going to the library," Lightning announces, adjusting the strap on her shoulder. "I'll see you at the same time tomorrow, Reva."

"Ass-crack of dawn," I grumble under my breath, but Lightning lifts her chin with a ghost of a grin.

"I'm going to take my leave as well, unfortunately." Fin extends his hand towards my arm, but his eyes flicker to Tariq standing perfectly straight beside us with a tightlipped grin.

He pulls his arm back behind him, and my heart cracks, swelling around itself.

"I have some rumblings I need to check on in Saros, but I'll see you both at dinner." Fin's eyes connect with Tariq's.

I frown. "Rumblings?"

"We'll debrief you and Elly sometime tomorrow," Fin assures, returning his attention to me. His smile barely reaches his soft, downturned eyes.

I nod, waiting for him to make it down the hallway before I twist on my heel and start towards my room to prepare for another day with Clint…

Then, steps follow behind me, and my heart races.

I press my lips together to keep myself from doing a multitude of stupid things. Fin's sad, puppy-dog face flashes in my mind, and that seems to encourage me.

FATE DEMANDS SACRIFICE   13

"You know, Reva," Tariq begins, walking in time beside me with those damn hands shoved into his pockets. "I'm a very observant individual—"

"You and your sister both," I mutter, staring straight ahead.

He lets out a breath of a laugh. "We are twins, after all. But as I was saying before you interrupted, I'm a very observant individual, and a week of knowing you has allowed me to observe quite a bit about you."

"Oh, Gods," I groan, my stomach twisting in a knot and anxiety rising into my chest.

I can't imagine what he's getting at since he already knows I'm a Sirian, but I truthfully don't want to know.

"I know you're dying to know," he says, reflecting the opposite of what I'm thinking. "So, I'm going to tell you."

"I figured you would." I twirl my head towards him, squinting.

He's smiling like a fool, and my heart flutters in my chest like a bird's wings.

"The first matter of business is Finley," he starts, clicking his tongue against his teeth. "I'm well aware of his—"

"Don't go there," I snap, balling my hands into fists at my side.

"Calm down, Reva." Tariq chuckles to himself. "I mean no harm by it. It's just I know how smitten he is by you, and I was going to say that you—"

"There is nothing to discuss about me and Fin," I

explain, staring straight ahead again, hoping he can't read how complicated it is on my face. I clear my throat. "We've been friendly since I got here, and all of this," I wave my hand in the air above my head, "has only made us closer."

"I hear a *but* at the end of that," Tariq pushes, his voice low.

"But nothing." I shrug, and the guilt crushes my chest. "That's where we are, and that's where we can be."

"And why is that?" he questions, and I silently thank the Gods as the view of my door grows larger down the hall.

"You stick your nose in places it doesn't belong, don't you?" I divert, allowing myself a glance at him. He stares at me intently, his face momentarily void of emotion.

"I'm just a curious man." A mischievous grin creeps up the side of his mouth. "See if there's a spot for me to play the game you're playing with Fin."

I stumble in my stride, nearly choking on my own spit.

He walks for a moment longer before realizing I'm not beside him anymore. He straightens, twisting to the side and waiting with an eyebrow raised.

"Something I said?" he asks with a small smirk, eyebrows slightly lifted.

I resume my pace, continuing right past him and not waiting to see if he follows. "There is no game to be played, Prince."

"How many times…" He scratches his eyebrow with

an exasperated sigh. "You can call me Tariq. I've heard you refer to my brother as Clint and my sister as Elly, so why am I still *Prince*?"

"You're different." I shrug, fumbling with my key.

I stand in front of my door, and Tariq leans against the wall beside the frame, his shoulder pressing against it and his hands *still* in his pockets. I pause with the key in the lock, turning my head toward him with an eyebrow raised.

"I'm different," Tariq repeats slowly, craning his head to the ceiling. "Is it because you're trying to maintain a level of professionalism between us to keep that distance my sister mentioned or because you like taunting me?"

Both.

Without another word, I twist the key in the lock and step through my door, closing it swiftly behind me.

I wait with my back pressed against it, taking four deep breaths in and out.

It takes nearly a minute of steadying my breathing before Tariq's footsteps retreat from the other side.

***

I shuffle through the vials in my crate while peering at my notes on the experiments I've been testing to treat Clint. The dose differs daily depending on how he's feeling, which means I don't get a single day off until I start using Energy to rid his body of the mass.

"Wait," Clint blurts from his bed. "*Levitation?* You're telling me you could make yourself *float?* In the *air?*"

"Don't make me regret letting you read that," I lecture, throwing my gaze over my shoulder.

He sits upright with the book from Jorah on demi-gods wide open in his lap. His gaze is glued to the text as he continues, "It says you could even make *me* float if you wanted. Does that mean you could make the mass float out of me?"

"I don't appreciate the visualization that just came into my mind." I scowl, returning to my mixture.

"Maybe not the best use of that particular gift," Clint grumbles to himself.

A light chuckle floats from my mouth as he continues reading to himself, a few awestruck whispers sneaking out here and there…

Until he suddenly blurts again, nearly shouting and startling me. "You can create *clones?*"

"Gods, Clint," I yelp, checking to make sure none of the liquid sloshed over the sides of the vial.

He bursts with laughter that rings like bells through the room.

"I just like to rile you up." He reclines against the headboard, slipping a piece of paper into the book before shutting it in his lap.

"I'm glad you find amusement in my life crisis," I scold, extending the vial to him. He curls his lip but accepts it. "Besides, we don't know what I can do. Lightning believes we'll be able to identify whether I

FATE DEMANDS SACRIFICE

17

descend from Asteria or Phoebe once I have more control over the normal Sirian Light."

He downs the liquid, smacking his tongue against the aftertaste, wincing, and then clearing his throat. "Well, I am anxiously waiting to find out which one, so I can have you either lift me into the air like a bird or make duplicates of me so I can be in two places at once."

"Again," I smirk, glaring at him. "Amusement at my life crisis. You don't see me amused by your pain."

"Some of those experiments we've done would suggest otherwise," Clint mutters under his breath.

Just as I pick up the quill to write down his dosage, there's a knock on the door. I snap my head over my shoulder, shifting my eyes from Clint's book to the space between his mattress and headboard. He nods as he shoves it into his favorite hiding place.

"Come in," I call out, quickly scribbling my notes. I lift my eyes from the paper as the door creaks on its hinges.

I stiffen when my gaze meets Pax's dark brown eyes.

Contrary to his usual demeanor, he casually rests one hand on the doorknob and the other flat on the frame. He leans his weight into both arms with a slight hunch to his shoulders.

"Pax?" Clint asks, just as confused as I am. Pax barely acknowledges Clint, though, as he intently stays locked onto me.

"I'm Prince Clint's new post," Pax announces, his eyes momentarily flickering to Clint before falling back on me. He steps into the room and shuts the door behind him.

"New post?" I question, laying down my quill. "I saw both Fin and Tariq this morning. Neither of them said anything about Clint getting a new post."

"We were just released from a morning debrief," Pax explains, but his tone is stiff like someone is pulling the words from him.

I frown, pouting as Clint and I wait for him to elaborate.

He awkwardly rights himself, adjusting his uniform before settling with his normal stature. "There have been a few disturbances in town. Until we can figure out who and why, Prince Tariq wants to avoid a repeat of the last attack. He has increased the Saros patrol and wants to increase watch over the Hespers." He pauses. "And you."

My heart backflips despite my best efforts to ignore that the protection couldn't mean anything more than a Crown Prince guarding one of his kingdom's best assets: an undercover Sirian Healer.

"Why were you chosen as Clint's guard?" I narrow my eyes, shrugging. "No offense."

Pax returns my expression.

"All the offense," Clint interjects, frowning and folding his arms over his chest.

I swear Pax flinches before clarifying, "Since Sir Finley is the Lieutenant General until further notice, he will be patrolling in Saros frequently, so he was unavailable. Due to more personal circumstances, El…

FATE DEMANDS SACRIFICE   19

Princess Eloise has been assigned another knight. Thus, I am here."

"Wouldn't your aversion to Magics demonstrate that you shouldn't be assigned to this post?" Clint interrogates, his voice hard.

I keep my eyes on Pax as I blink, astonished yet proud of the young prince for his astuteness. Pax presses his lips into a tight, thin line, shifting on his feet. His eyes bounce between Clint and me, lingering on me just a little longer each time.

As if I'd come to his rescue.

"Prince Tariq believes it would be best if I spend time with you, Prince Clint." Pax bows his head. "He also believes it would be... healthy if I spent time with the Royal Healer."

"Reva," Clint corrects, balling his fists into the sheet beside him. "We call her Reva in this room. We don't use titles here unless necessary, like when my father is present. In that case, it's *Miss* Reva."

Pax bows at the waist, his head trained to the floor until he stands straight again. He positions himself in front of the door, which means closer to me. I fixate on him for only a moment longer before I resume writing in my journal, a million thoughts racking my brain.

Like, is Tariq doing this on purpose? Why would Fin let this happen?

I know Tariq is the Crown Prince, but the relationship between Fin, Tariq, Elly, and even Pax is different from that of other knights and generals and what-have-yous.

But I also recall Fin having a problem with challenging leadership. Then again, I don't know if Fin put up a fight in this instance.

I pause my quill mid-stride, twisting my head to Pax.

He's already watching me with hesitation, leaning away like I'm a caged animal that might lunge at any moment.

"What did you mean by…" I hesitate. "The *Prince* believes it would be healthy to spend time with me?"

Pax eyes me with a clenched jaw and resentment glowing in their depths, which I can't even blame him for.

Ever since Tariq came home last week, there's been a noticeable distance between Pax and the others. Elly's eyes may linger, but interactions end there. Her brother must have dealt a missive to limit engagement with the man she's clearly in love with—even if I can't understand why yet.

Not to mention that Fin has all but taken Pax's position in the Mariande army.

From his point of view, I've effectively replaced him in his friend group.

Part of me finds it hard to believe such a juvenile matter would hurt someone with Pax's station and morals, but if Elly loves this man, I wouldn't be shocked to learn there is substance and warmth underneath the hard exterior.

Pax finally answers quietly, "I have made it clear to

FATE DEMANDS SACRIFICE 21

you and the others plenty of times that I don't trust you." He stares towards the lone window in Clint's room. "I have vehemently argued against blindly trusting you while the rest of them have doled out their faith without question. The Crown Prince believes the only way to understand why they've decided to do so would be to spend some time with you and Prince Clint."

I swallow against the tightness in my throat and chest as Pax glares at the window like it may reveal his savior. While Tariq has a point about Clint needing protection, this puts my secret at risk.

What happens when it's time to use the Light to help Clint? Or worse, while I have Clint's illness under control for now, what happens if I'm *forced* to use the Light and Pax is just here?

I exhale, dragging my attention back to my notebook. "Well, we may hate each other, but Prince Tariq has a point."

"I said no formalities," Clint snaps, peeking over the top of a different, more Pax-friendly book.

CHAPTER 2

I gawk at my reflection in the full-length mirror in my bedroom. "So, it's this type of dinner," I drawl, fidgeting with the long bell sleeves.

"You're being dramatic." Elly waves me away, rolling her eyes. She stands behind me, securing strands of my hair to the side of my head.

Other than the pieces pinned back, my raven-black hair falls in curling ringlets down my body, nearly blending in with the color of the dress made entirely from black velvet. Silver beading extends from the collared neckline to mid-bicep. Beaded lilies are perfectly perched on either shoulder, broadening them and accentuating my natural but usually subtle curves.

The neckline also complements my shape. The collar is pulled up, resting just an inch below my jawline. As it drops to my collarbone, it flares outward, meeting the top of a sweetheart neckline. My hematite necklace is on display, hanging directly in the center of my chest above the peak of my cleavage.

Cleavage that is rather exposed, I might add. It's not overly scandalous, but this is where Elly and I disagree.

FATE DEMANDS SACRIFICE   23

"This." I gesture around my breasts in a circle. "Can't be appropriate for dinner."

"You are exuding power," Elly insists, double-checking her handy work. "You need to start making an impression when you're around higher authorities and those who could doubt you."

"And showing my boobs exudes power?" I lock my eyes onto hers through the mirror's reflection. "I thought it was just a few of us at dinner."

She avoids eye contact as she clears her throat, fussing with rogue hair pieces. "It is, but you never know who will step in. It's not often you can get an audience with my father and his right hand."

I purse my lips, my eyes lingering on my cleavage.

"No matter how much you stare at it, you're not going to burn it off—" Elly pauses, tilting her head to the side. "On second thought, don't even *think* about burning it off."

"Elly." I stretch out my arms, and the fabric on the ends of the sleeves hangs down like twin waterfalls. "There's nothing under this. Why would I burn it off?"

"You're naked?" Elly squeals.

A knock on my door has us freezing, my hand poised to strike. She wiggles her devious eyebrows at me and yells to the door, "It's unlocked."

I roll my eyes, flicking my wrist. The Light slides the latch to the right, effectively unlocking it for whoever is on the other side.

The door cracks open, and Fin peeks his head in,

eyebrows raised in hesitation. His eyes swing left and right before snagging on Elly momentarily. Those green orbs find me, and his face slacks.

"Reva," he whispers, just above a breath. He opens the door the rest of the way and takes one step in, dressed in his official knight uniform. The maroon coat decorated with gold embellishments makes his auburn hair and green eyes pop, and the matching pants hug parts of him I'm trying too hard not to look at.

His eyes dip to my chest fleetingly before meeting my gaze. My chest warms and my body relaxes more into the fabric as I let out a deep breath I didn't realize I'd been holding.

"See?" Elly mutters into my ear. "Show stopper, Reva."

She gathers her gown in her hands, the tulle fabric the same deep maroon color as Fin's knight uniform. Her sleeves are similar to mine, except they hang off her shoulders instead of reaching up her neck. Dark green leaves woven from lace stretch down her left side to the hem.

"Come along, Reva." Elly stands at the doorway, beckoning me. "Finley is escorting us ladies to dinner."

"Escorting the Royal Healer, once again," I tease, smiling up at him and accepting his elbow. I slip my hand through it, nestling it into the crook.

"Escorting lovely ladies." He straightens his shoulders. "This is the best responsibility in the castle. I get to walk into dinner with two women on my arm."

FATE DEMANDS SACRIFICE

He winks at me, biting back his own smile. I snicker under my breath, following his lead down the hall, past the stained-glass windows, and into the formal dining room.

"Ah," King Darius exclaims as we step through the propped double doors. "Last but certainly not least, our dear daughter and Royal Healer."

"You expect me to arrive on time when I'm responsible for dressing myself and Reva?" Elly removes her hand from Fin's arm. "A thank you would suffice. She would've showed up in her normal, boring garb without my help."

"Thanks, El—" I stop short, locking eyes with the king. He smiles kindly, but his eyes have a knowing glint.

"Don't worry." Queen Lucia picks up the wine glass in front of her, tipping it towards me. "Despite the attendance and the dress code, you can be more informal around this company."

My eyes scan over the table, thankfully recognizing everyone but one woman. Clint sits beside his mother in a matching wheelchair, spritely thanks to today's medicine combination. Across from them is Eamon, Fin's dad, and beside him is the woman I'm unfamiliar with. She turns her head over her shoulder to look at me, and I know without a doubt she could only be Fin's mother.

Her hair is the same shade of auburn, and I see something within her face that reminds me of him. Unlike Fin, though, she has a spattering of freckles across her nose and cheeks, endowing her with a young spirit as she smiles warmly at me.

"Anya Wardson." She waves. "I'm told you've already met my husband."

"It's nice to meet you," I say, nodding once. I adjust my gaze to Eamon. "And nice to see you again."

"I'm glad it's under better circumstances this time around." He flashes me a bemused grin. Fin tugs gently on my arm, guiding me to my seat.

Across from Tariq.

I stop beside my chair as Fin pulls it out. Tariq's eyes are bolted to me, the deep gold shining through the orange tint of his irises. I hold my breath, my heart slamming against my ribcage to get out.

His eyes trail painfully down my neck and chest to where my hands are clenched in front of my stomach. They keep traveling further until they're settled on the floor before tracking back up at the same agonizing pace.

Tariq fastens onto my eyes again, his lips twitching slightly at the corners.

"You look…" Tariq tilts his head to the side predatorily. "Regal."

"Doesn't she?" Queen Lucia agrees from a few seats over. "You were born for that dress, Reva."

I snap out of my haze, tearing my interest away from Tariq's pouty lower lip.

"Thank you, Your Majesty." I sink into my seat far less gracefully than I'd like.

Fin helps push it in before taking his seat beside me. After acknowledging my rigidity, his leg brushes up

FATE DEMANDS SACRIFICE

against mine.

I peer across the table at Tariq, who regards me as he lowers into his seat. He dips his head, suppressing a grin with a quick flare of his nostrils, and I know he already noticed where my attention had been during our stare-down.

This is going to be the longest dinner of my life.

"So, Reva," Eamon says, interrupting yet another standoff between Tariq and me. "How have you been enjoying your time in Saros?"

I silently bless him as I stretch over the table to see beyond his son and wife. Fin leans back into his chair a little more to help, and I rest my hand on his forearm in silent thanks. I ignore Tariq's attention, burning into the side of my head.

"I've been able to visit town a few times," I explain, Fin's breath tickling my neck as his citrus scent wafts over me. "And I'm impressed in so many ways."

"Is it not too busy for you?" Queen Lucia asks, a soft frown pressing her eyebrows together. "I can't imagine it's easy to go from Eldamain to Mariande."

"Mother," Elly mumbles around the lip of her glass.

I wave my hand. "I know what you mean, but you'd be surprised. Main Town in Eldamain is the only real village in the entire country, and people come from far and wide for various… reasons. What was more startling about Saros to me was how alive it was in comparison. Even though Main Town is just as busy, it's much quieter. People are very private there."

"I don't mean to be forward or offensive," Tariq interjects, resting his elbow on the table. He places his chin on the heel of his palm. "But why are Magics so private there? Isn't it essentially a country that belongs to your people?"

The table falls silent, waiting expectantly for my answer.

I tap my front teeth together before saying, "It is, but that community isn't built off the principles you are trying to build in Mariande's Magic communities."

"Do you care to elaborate?" Tariq frowns, contemplative, and I spot his similarities to Queen Lucia despite how much he looks like the king. "Like I said, I don't mean to press, and I know Elly is about two seconds from kicking—" A thump from under the table cuts him off.

I let out a short breath, smirking. "I'll say what I must, then we can stop the political talk for Elly's sake.

"What Eldamain is today was built in reaction to fear; fear of being Magic or anything other." I hold Tariq's stare, hoping he understands the undercurrent of what I mean. "They live in fear of being ratted out, exposed, bullied, taunted. They find it safer to live private lives, and I think those seeking salvation in Eldamain are trying to do that."

Tariq bows his head in a slow nod, reaching for the glass of wine across from him. I swallow, wiping my sweating palms on my dress.

"Reva is correct." Eamon grins, reaching for a piece

FATE DEMANDS SACRIFICE 29

of bread. "We're here to catch up as a family, not as politicians. Without being political, Tariq, how was Riddling?"

"Warmer than here," Tariq chuckles, swirling his wine. "Honestly, it was beautiful. Their architecture makes ours look sloppy. There is so much intricate work and detail put into every building. Don't get me started on Sitora Castle."

"It's something, isn't it?" Eamon awes at what I can only guess is a memory based on the nostalgic twinge to his voice. "Gods, Dary, remember when you, me, and Jed met Seif when he was just a prince?"

"That adventure," King Darius pauses, raising his glass to his lips and avoiding Eamon, "Is a story for another dinner."

"Do you mean King Seif?" Tariq breathes, incredulous. "What could you possibly have done with that man that would require another dinner?"

"Anything that involves Jed usually means a dinner without women present," Queen Lucia scoffs, rolling her eyes as she takes a giant gulp of her wine. Anya giggles across from her, shoving a piece of bread in her mouth to stifle it.

"Was this before or after he was married?" Fin asks, tilting his head to the side.

Eamon waves his free hand at his wife as he finishes his drink.

"This was before he met Bryna," Anya answers for her husband, dabbing her napkin on the side of her lips.

"She tamed him the minute he laid eyes on her."

"Are these friends of yours?" I ask, frowning. "I don't think I've met them."

I thought the only relevant people in this room I hadn't met would've been Pax's parents, despite him not being present. But the fondness and affection they discuss these two people with are drastically different from how Elly has referred to Pax's dad.

The din in the room slowly tampers until the only sounds are plates clinking together as the stewards prepare the main course in the middle of the table. Queen Lucia finishes her wine with a quick tip of her glass before holding it out to a steward passing by with the bottle. Eamon's eyes take on a sad tilt, similar to one I've seen on Fin.

"Jed." King Darius clears his throat, staring at the plate of greens as he fiddles with a ring on his finger. "Jedrek, Eamon, and I grew up side-by-side, similar to Pax, Fin, and Tariq. They have been with me since my young knight training, long before I took to the throne. My right and left-hand men, if you will. Bryna was his wife."

"I haven't met them yet," I say, turning to Elly, whose gaze has softened. "Have I?"

"You won't," Fin mutters under his breath, twisting his wine glass by the stem.

I bounce from him to King Darius, who is still fixated on the greens as if they are speaking to him.

The king's voice is softer than I've ever heard as he says, "They were killed some time back. These kids

FATE DEMANDS SACRIFICE   31

were young—just babies—so they never got to meet them either."

"I'm so sorry," I apologize, my heart breaking for the king.

To know someone since you were young and lose them sooner than you ever thought possible is unimaginable to me.

Another crack breaks off the corner of my heart as Karasi flashes across my mind.

"There was no way you could've known." Eamon shrugs, smiling kindly at me from two seats over. "You were just curious. Besides, it's not like we can't talk about them. They are always alive, if only in our memories."

With that, King Darius raises his glass into the air. We all follow suit in a silent tribute to their friends. I catch Elly out of the corner of my eye, observing me.

***

The night continues in a flurry of drinks, food, and more bottles of wine. If anyone wanted to ever see the Hesper family let loose, all they would have to do is attend one of their private dinners with their friends.

The twinkle in King Darius's eyes is foreign as he listens intently to his children, the boisterous laughter flowing from his lips just as rare.

I've had minimal encounters with the queen up until tonight, and she is as much of a spitfire as her daughter and youngest son. The more she speaks, the more I'm captivated by how agelessly beautiful she appears.

Late into the night, they tell us stories about when they were young. Some events occurred before Eamon, Darius, and their friend married, and some occurred when Anya and Lucia were present to witness true tomfoolery.

Every so often, Anya's eyes linger on me during her stories, a strange look passing over them that I can't decipher. While it doesn't seem Fin divulges information to his father, that may not be the case with his mother.

I take Fin for a momma's boy.

I draw my gaze from Anya to Fin. A broad smile spreads across his face as he listens to the tale, his mouth slightly propped open. He peeks at me from the corner of his eyes and closes his mouth.

His smile drops to a smaller grin, still watching his dad. Under the table, his finger caresses the side of my knee. My stomach flips, and I fight my own grin at the subtle affection.

That's when I glance up.

Tariq studies me intently, even as he sips the dark liquid he switched to halfway through dinner. As he swallows, he swirls the glass with an eyebrow raised.

Clint sits beside Tariq, snickering into his napkin as he looks from Tariq to me. I level the kid with a glare, and he drops his napkin into his lap, struggling to suppress his smile.

Tariq leans to the side and slings his arm over the back

FATE DEMANDS SACRIFICE

of Clint's wheelchair, muttering something into his ear, eyes still latched onto me. Tariq's mouth quirks up at the corner as Clint bursts into a fit of laughter.

I flare my nostrils at them, balling my napkin in my lap. Tariq resumes his casual demeanor as if nothing happened while everyone else at the table swivels their heads between Clint, Tariq, and me.

"Boys," Queen Lucia lectures, but there's a shimmer in her dark blue eyes. "Care to share what has Clint in a fit and Reva looking like steam is about to shoot out of her ears?"

Tariq shrugs, finding the bottom of his now-empty glass far more fascinating than his mother's gaze. "I have no idea what you're referring to."

"You know," King Darius says, rising abruptly from his seat. He lifts his glass like he had at the beginning of dinner, this time directed at me. "I want to propose a toast to our Royal Healer, Reva."

"Oh, Gods," Elly groans.

"You have been working diligently to heal our son, and we are eternally grateful to you," King Darius begins, albeit a little unsteady. Elly's eyes bulge out of her head, her cheeks flushing. On the other hand, Tariq and Clint seem to have a habit of snickering at each other during dinners. "I have full faith we shall see Clint walking again in no time."

"King Darius—" I try to interrupt, but he continues.

"You have already saved both my youngest son and my daughter's lives, and you have molded quite perfectly into this role and this family. I look forward to seeing what else you do in this position and within this kingdom."

The parents at the table echo his sentiment, starting the train of clinking glasses together. Based on how clumsy they are with their glasses and the liquid inside, I'm not shocked they miss the passing glances between their kids and me.

CHAPTER 3

The double wooden doors of the library come into view down the hall at the same time I hear footsteps approaching behind me. I slow my pace, glancing over my shoulder.

Tariq lowers his head and picks up speed to catch up with me. I stop, flaring my nostrils as I reluctantly wait for him.

"Glad I'm not the only one who's late," he says, falling into step beside me.

"And what's your excuse?" I ask, folding my hands underneath my arms.

"I'm the Crown Prince." He throws his shoulders back with a smirk. "What's yours?"

"I'm the Royal Healer," I sneer playfully, side-eyeing him.

Tariq snorts and shoves his hands into his pockets. "Seems like we're just a couple of very important people."

"Next, you'll tell me we're not late, everyone else is just early." I pause, reaching for the door handle at the same time as him. My hand wraps around it first, but then his envelopes over mine.

When I gaze back up, Tariq looks at me with his mouth propped open as if to say something. The heat from his palm over mine radiates up my arm and blooms across my chest.

Tariq clears his throat, removing his hand like our touch burned. "I'd say you're starting to understand me, Reva."

"Tariq," I sigh, shoving the door with my shoulder. "I don't think I'll ever understand you."

"Oh, so now it's just Tariq." He snickers under his breath as I roll my eyes, following close behind me as we walk through the library.

Even if I can't see his face, I can feel the wide-mouthed grin spread across it.

As we emerge from an aisle into our secluded area of tables, Fin, Elly, and Lightning snap their heads to Tariq and me. I stop abruptly at their speculative stares, causing Tariq to bump into my back.

I shoot him a glare over my shoulder.

"What were you two up to?" Elly asks, grinning tightly as her eyes flicker between me and the hulking mass over my shoulder.

I ignore the twitch of Fin's eyebrows, biting my tongue.

"Nothing," Tariq says as he juts around me, rubbing his hands together.

Elly eyes both of us sternly. "Sure it was."

Tariq just winks at her, which has a muscle ticking in Fin's jaw, the first angry emotion I've seen him direct

FATE DEMANDS SACRIFICE 37

at Tariq since he came home. I shove my shoulders back before joining them at the table they're sitting at.

Tariq clears his throat, leaning back in his chair. "Most of you already know my reasons for going to Riddling, but for the new ones..." Tariq's eyes slide from Lightning to me, his lip twitching at the corner when I glare at him. "I primarily went to Riddling to build a relationship with Prince Ruhan and pick his brain about the Abyss and what they know about that history. From what he divulged in the short time I was there, it sounds like they know as much as us."

"They're on their own island across the sea," Lightning sneers, balancing on the chair's back legs. "They don't give a damn about what's happening here so long as it doesn't touch them."

"You may believe that." Tariq folds his hands on the table. "But it's neither here nor there at the moment. I called us to meet today because I think we are all assets to one another in this looming war based on what we know, our positions, and our skills."

"I don't see how myself or Fin have a role to play," Lightning comments, folding her arms over her chest.

I wait for a flicker of irritation on Tariq's face, but it's just a casual mask of indifference.

Which is interesting.

"Correct me if I'm wrong, but you are our contact to the Sirian movement." He shrugs. "You know the Elders and converse with them regularly. Fin knows about Reva, the Sirians, and the Abyss but is also a knight. Until further notice, he is Lieutenant General of the Mariande army."

"Elders?" I ask, wrinkling my forehead. "What are the Elders, and did you say a Sirian *movement*?"

Lightning and Tariq stare at each other over the table. She glowers, her jaw clenched, but Tariq regards her with a slightly arched eyebrow, almost giving the impression that he's *bored*.

I have yet to see Tariq in Crown Prince action, but Gods…

You'd think he was already a king by how calm he is right now.

"Sirians have been collecting themselves together long before the Abyss proved to be growing," Lightning finally explains, tearing her gaze from Tariq. "My mom made it her life's mission to find them so they could train me in the Light. For the last few years, the movement has gathered intel on those wielding the Darkness, trying to find their leader and the person responsible for their rebellion.

"The Elders…" She fixes her attention to a mark on the table. "They're like a council of Sirians responsible for most decisions and order. Training, interrogations, negotiations, keeping the Sirian movement under the radar… Those types of things."

My eyebrows twitch in the middle of my forehead as I glower at Lightning. My irritation bubbles because if they already have multiple Elders leading their Sirian movement, why do they want me to lead?

FATE DEMANDS SACRIFICE   39

And with how much Lightning seems to be communicating with us on their behalf, is she an Elder and hasn't said anything?

"When the Sirians were part of society," Elly jumps in, fiddling with the pendant on her necklace. "There was an elected Council of Elders that ran everything. They ran the official education of Sirians, the Arcane Island—"

"Arcane Island?" I ask again, embarrassment warming my cheeks.

When I think I understand what's going on, the people around me bring something else I've never heard of before to my attention. I wasn't sure how educated Tariq would be on history compared to Elly, but she once said there were no secrets between her and her brother.

In fact, they kept secrets from people.

I wring my fingers in my lap, trying to stifle the simmering anger. Lightning is as vague and secretive as they come, so I'm not shocked she hasn't tried to teach me about my Sirian heritage, but the fact that Elly seems to have known a bit about Sirian lore and yet has communicated nothing to me...

"The Arcane Island was where the Council conducted itself and where Sirians had the option to host their own sabbatical once they turned eighteen to learn healing or combat." Lightning shrugs, reclining her chair on its two back legs again. "Tales refer to it as the Hidden Arcane Island now because no one knows where it is."

"Presumably," Tariq adds with a nod of his head. Again, Lightning levels him with narrowed eyes.

The wheels turn in my head. "Are you saying the Sirian movement is operating out of the Arcane Island?"

"No, that would be foolish." Tariq shakes his head with pursed lips. "From what I've learned, the Arcane Island used to be closer to the Main Continent than it was to Riddling or The Northern Pizi. That would draw too much attention for trade going in and out of here if it's to be believed."

"Is this why we're here?" Lightning snaps, her chair slamming back down with the crack in her voice. "Because if this is just an interrogation on the only living Sirians, mind you, the ones who can save your asses from the Darkness, then I'll just take my leave—"

Tariq cuts her off by casually waving his hand like he's swatting away dust. "There will be no interrogations, Lightning. Your pupil was curious about her people, so I thought it would be wise to inform her."

I glance at him sidelong at the *pupil* comment, but he nods once as if he's done me a great favor.

"We're here to discuss next steps and what's happening right now." Fin finally joins in, glancing warily between Tariq and Lightning. "We all have valuable information that could put us in a better position to prepare for the Sirians wielding the Darkness."

"What sort of information could you possibly have that the Sirian movement doesn't?" Lightning peers at Fin, who shifts uncomfortably in his seat. But I would have to agree because Lightning has made out they know quite a bit more than us about the Abyss and Dark Sirians.

FATE DEMANDS SACRIFICE 41

"Mariande is one of the most powerful kingdoms in the world," Tariq states, not boastful, but as simply as though he were telling time. "We'll always be a target to our enemies. But we've especially put a target on our back since we opened the Magic communities and officially brought one in as the Royal Healer. We try to keep tabs on what they're doing, which means we have insight into the goings on of our presumed allies and enemies."

"A Sirian is your Royal Healer," Lightning snaps, her attention back on Tariq.

"The world doesn't know that yet." His *yet* has bile bubbling in my stomach. "Since we're an obvious target, this Darkness rebel group has started attacking our Magic communities to drive them out. Eventually, they're going to start coming for mortals, including those who reside in the castle. It doesn't help that Etherea continues to bully us any chance they get."

"Wait." I hold up my hand. "What do you mean the Darkness rebel group has *started* attacking the Magics?"

"This is what we meant by the rumblings we mentioned yesterday," Fin answers, but he is looking at Lightning. "Based on the description you'd given us of what the Elders said the Darkness can do, it matches the community reports."

I startle slightly at the fact Lightning has started working with Fin, despite not being his biggest fan, and I had only just now found out about the Magics being attacked.

"Don't be cryptic, Finley," Elly lectures,

straightening in her chair.

"What are they doing to the Magics?" I ask, but it comes out as a whisper. Tariq frowns, but his eyes are soft.

"There are Magics dying from an infection," Lightning explains, still holding Fin's gaze. "They are found with black veins spread across their bodies. When an autopsy is performed, critical organs are black and hardened like tar."

All the times I'd been told the Darkness could infect, I never thought it was literal. I guess it's only fair that if the Light can be used to heal people, then the Darkness could infiltrate like a disease.

"So, Dark Sirians are infecting the Magic community." I nod slowly. "How do we stop them?"

"That's why you're here," Tariq says to Lightning. "Do the Elders have a treatment?"

"Yes, there's a way to treat it." Lightning nibbles on her bottom lip. "There are just a few obstacles we have to overcome to get it to them."

"What are they?" Tariq leans into the table, patiently waiting for Lightning's answer.

Lightning's eyes flash a bright white, followed by a deep, vibrating rumble I swear comes from her body. "I am not your lackey, Prince. I'd be careful how much you command from me."

"That may be so, but you do work for the royal family," Tariq explains without a flinch, rising from his seat to his full height. His tone is level, but underneath

FATE DEMANDS SACRIFICE 43

is a commanding demeanor as he continues, "I don't care what position you hold, whether that be an official assistant to our Royal Librarian or our Sirian Healer's teacher. Involving yourself with our kingdom means you are now loyal to the Mariande Crown and the people within our borders.

"Now, if we are going to resort to intimidation and bullying tactics, we can call this meeting now and go on about our days." Tariq adjusts his tunic. "But know that the longer we wait to figure out this solution without getting the king and any advisors involved, the more Magics will die. I know the Sirian movement has kept a fair distance away from the world's goings on, but do they really want innocent lives on their conscience when we're on the brink of war with Darkness?"

My mouth drops open, and my first instinct is to applaud. Fin and Elly sit in silence, their heads hanging as if they're the ones being scolded.

On the other hand, Lightning simmers like a teapot about to scream. Her lips are pressed together in a tight line as she shoots daggers at Tariq.

"The antidote for the illness has to be made by a Sirian," Lightning explains between clenched teeth, "It needs to be charged before being administered."

"Aren't we lucky our Royal Healer is Sirian?" Tariq grins, lowering himself into the wooden chair. He flourishes his hand over the table, encouraging Lightning to continue.

"That is another obstacle." Her eyes flicker to me

briefly. "Magics can be just as fearful of Sirians as the mortals, and your Healer knows that. Especially if they know they're being attacked by Sirians. Darkness or Light, it's the same to them. If they find out Reva is Sirian, they will not hesitate to sell that bit of information to the highest bidder. You're right that they can't know the Royal Healer is Sirian yet."

I really wish they'd stop using that word…

Yet.

"What about you?" Tariq frowns, tilting his head at Lightning. "From what I understand, you've created a positive, trusting relationship with our communities, particularly the one here in Saros. Wouldn't you be able to create this concoction for them and administer it?"

"In theory," Lightning drawls. "But that brings up the third obstacle. Between my training sessions with Reva every morning and my front during the day as Elly's assistant, I won't be home enough to help them. By the time they realize what's happening to them, they need treatment immediately, and the antidote has to be charged by the Energy before it's taken."

"Recruit one of your other colleagues in the movement." Tariq relaxes into his chair. "Here's the thing, Lightning. These are my citizens we're talking about. I will do what I must to protect them from impending doom. I know for a fact you have other colleagues here in Saros who can do this, but your lot is too worried about revealing themselves to the Magics."

"You've been trailing me?" Lightning's voice goes up

FATE DEMANDS SACRIFICE

45

a notch in volume with each word. She slams her hands on the table, boosting herself out of her chair, which flies to the floor behind her. She points an accusatory finger at the prince. "That was *not* part of this deal. I was to be left alone while I worked for your sister and your Healer."

"Yes." Tariq nods once, solemnly. "But I knew that even if you found out we tagged you, it wouldn't stop you from training Reva. You need her now that you know she has two god-powers."

"The world needs her, Prince." Lightning curls her lip at him. "You're playing a dirty game for someone who doesn't realize the stakes—"

"This isn't a game!" I snap, lurching from my chair. Everyone's attention whips to me, their faces flattened in shock.

Everyone except Tariq, whose lips twitch at either side as he inclines his head.

"People are dying." My voice cracks, and Clint's bright smile flashes in my head. I press my finger to the table, tapping twice. "There are a lot of moving parts right now, but we each carry a piece that will at least help us stay above water."

They're all watching me, which has my stomach backflipping like an acrobat.

I face Lightning first. "The Magics need our help. As the Royal Healer, I can connect you to those I get my supplies from in Saros. Whether it's you or another Sirian from the movement, take your list to them for the antidote. Tell them to put it on the Royal

Healer's bill. Once they find out Sirians are providing an antidote—because they will—maybe hearing the *Magic* Royal Healer is covering the costs will at least start establishing trust with them."

Her face is all tight lines and clenched muscles, but there's a glimpse of understanding there.

The days of the Sirian movement working under the radar are over. Those wielding the Darkness have forced their hands now.

I face Tariq and Fin, both of their eyes twinkling. *Not now.* "Have you increased patrolling in the Magic communities?"

"Both explicitly and undercover," Fin answers, smirking. "Is the Great Reva running the show now?"

I point my finger at him in warning, leveling him with a glare. "I'm going to ignore that. I suggest you debrief with them daily and report anything suspicious to Lightning. This way, her colleagues can keep a lookout, and maybe they can start putting faces to the Darkness infiltrators. Then the Sirian movement can move on that information."

"And where do you think we will—" Lightning air quotes as she says, "*Move on that information?*"

I shrug. "You've mentioned capturing them before. I figured you'd do that again. Exactly what you do with them after that is your business."

"This has all been very astute of you, Reva," Elly grins, her face scrunched. "I'm so proud of you."

"Thanks," I sigh, slumping back into my chair. My

FATE DEMANDS SACRIFICE 47

hands tremble in my lap, so I slip them between my thighs to calm them down.

There's no sign of glowing, but there is a buzzing under my skin as my power boils.

One I've been avoiding.

"I think this is a good move on all fronts for the time being," Tariq remarks. "But we cannot stay separate for much longer. There will come a point when we'll need to join forces, both secretly and publicly. Eventually, the world will start talking about the Darkness, and we don't want the Dark Sirians to be the world's reintroduction. We want them to understand the Light first."

"The Sirians are going to wait as long as we can," Lightning chides. "Some may have forgotten history, but we never did. Part of Korbin's argument for ridding the world of Sirians in the first place was because the mortals would get caught in the crossfire between the Light and Dark. We play your way, and that's exactly how the world will see it."

"So, you're going to let mortals and Magics suffer and die before you get involved?" Fin scowls, anger flashing in those eyes.

Tariq throws his head back and glares at the ceiling.

"War has casualties, Sir Finley," Lightning hisses. "You can't save everyone."

"Alright," Elly snaps, jumping in. "Like Tariq said, we at least have a plan to help the Magics. Any more time in this library together will get someone set on fire or struck down by lightning. Literally."

With a nod of agreement, Tariq is the first to stand from the table, but he heads down the nearest aisle and disappears before any of us can follow after him.

Elly and I meet at the end of the table, and she instantly loops her arm through mine.

"Now that the politics are through," Elly begins, leading us toward the library door, "I have another book from Jorah's collection I want to give you."

"Honestly," I scoff, shoving the library door with my free hand, "I would argue that my powers are starting to become political at this rate."

"Don't be so melodramatic," Elly lectures, poking my side. "Who said it had anything to do with that?"

I deadpan as footsteps rush upon us, followed by Fin calling my name. I turn to see him shutting the library door a few feet behind us.

"Are you off to Clint's room?" he asks, his gaze flickering to Elly. She mouths that she'll talk to me later before continuing on her way.

"Yeah," I say, tightening the grip on my satchel. "What do you need?"

"Do you mind if I walk with you?" He gestures down the hall, those eyes pleading. "I feel like I haven't seen much of you the last two weeks."

"Sure." I swallow the uneasiness in my stomach.

The last conversation Fin and I had alone was when he told me he wasn't afraid of me. Since then, so many things have happened, between Tariq coming home, training every day with Lightning, Fin's new

FATE DEMANDS SACRIFICE 49

responsibilities, and apparently increasing threats to Mariande.

"How has he been?" Fin and I walk side-by-side. "I regret that I haven't been able to visit Clint much."

"Clint has his hands full." I can't help but smile then, thinking about the hard time he's been giving his new guard. "Since Pax was stationed to protect us, Clint has not made it easy for him."

Fin chuckles, eyes crinkling at the corners. "I'm not surprised. I'm sorry, by the way. I tried to get Tariq to put somebody else there who would have been a little more pleasant for you."

"It's only been a few days with him." I shrug, finding myself gravitating to Fin. "Granted, he's not you, but he's tame. He just keeps his mouth shut. I guess he's following that whole 'if you can't say anything nice' motto."

"Not me, huh?" Fin's eyes twinkle, squeezing my heart in a vice. I offer a tightlipped grin. "Well, we can only hope Tariq is right about placing Pax with you guys. I know he has his reasons, but he didn't see how you were treated the last few months."

"I can handle it," I assure, not unkindly, nodding my head. "I know Elly's eluded that there's more to Pax's behavior than just being a jerk, so I want to give him a chance to explain his side of things and show him I mean no harm."

"Your kindness is inspiring, oh, Great Reva." Fin glances down, his hand brushing mine. I try not to jerk away, but my arm noticeably stiffens, effectively snuffing out that twinkle he had in his eyes. "Reva… I wanted to talk about our last conversation before things got crazy."

I know he's talking about when he came to my room after meeting with Jorah, but I also have a flash of Lightning schooling him after he effectively insulted my god-power.

Gods, was that two weeks ago?

Both memories have my chest filling with sharp breaths that sting my lungs. "Which one, Fin?"

"After Jorah's," Fin mumbles. "I thought things ended on a good note, although I can't help but feel like you're avoiding me now."

"I'm not avoiding you." That's only half a lie; we've both been busy with our various responsibilities.

Fin eyes me with a sidelong glare. "Come on, Reva. I know we've been busy, but you shy away from me in public. You're pulling away from me physically, but I'm wondering if it's also emotionally."

"That's not it—" I gasp as he snatches my arm in his grasp, turning me to face him. My palm flattens against his stiff chest, our eyes lock, and I'm transfixed.

Those pools of green are swimming with nearly every emotion as they study me. My stomach swirls at the proximity and familiarity of his touch, my heart straining toward him. He bends in closer, leaving just an inch between the tips of our noses.

"You have to give me something, Reva," Fin whispers, eyes searching mine. "I feel like I can't get a read on you lately."

FATE DEMANDS SACRIFICE

"You shouldn't be reading me," I mutter back, using my hand on his chest to reluctantly push away. My arm slips out of his grasp as I take a few steps back. "Actions speak louder than words, Fin. I know you told me you don't fear me, but I can tell the difference when someone is nervous versus scared."

"I swear, I don't care—"

I wave my hand between us, cutting him off. I keep my voice low as I say, "I know you don't care what I am. That's not the point. You still see my powers as a burden that I have to carry. You admitted as much to Lightning at my first training session with her."

Fin recoils, flinching as though I've struck him, frowning. The fissure in my heart deepens, reverberating through my chest.

"I don't hold it against you," I assure him, resting my hand on his forearm. "Just give me some space. I need to figure out where I fall in all of this, and I think you do, too."

I turn on my heel before I do something stupid. The urge to comfort him burns a hole in my chest, acidic in my throat. I finish the journey to Clint's room on my own without looking back.

CHAPTER 4

The Light illuminates the dimly lit training floor, the force vibrating from my body and the sand trembling beneath me. My arms extend out on either side of me with a slight bend at the elbows. Two perfectly molded balls of Light at my palms are connected by thin vines of gold that climb up my arms under my skin.

"Just a few more seconds," Lightning calls from a few yards away, pitched on one of the pillars.

The sharp air I breathe through my nose stings my airways, and my vision wobbles at the edges. I blink it away rapidly, pressing my brows together.

Lightning sighs heavily, grumbling, "Alright, reel it back in."

It snuffs out like a candle instead of the whip or gradual dimming. I double over at the waist, shoving stray strands of hair away from my face that have escaped my braid, smearing my own sweat through it. I gasp for breath, my shoulders rising and falling rapidly with it.

"Your control has gotten a lot better," Lighting observes, standing in front of me with her hands clasped behind her back and feet shoulder-width apart. "You're

FATE DEMANDS SACRIFICE 53

wielding it at different levels, but you don't have the stamina you should to hold it over long periods of time."

"That was the longest I've held it," I argue, craning my neck to glower. "How much longer should it be?"

"Reva," Lightning deadpans. "You held it for five minutes."

"I don't anticipate holding control over my power for longer than that." I straighten, roll my shoulders, and shake out my stiff hands.

Lightning glares at me. "First of all, war doesn't end in five minutes. You have to be able to wield your power for extended periods of time, especially as small as the balls you held—"

I open my mouth to protest, but she sticks her finger at me, continuing, "And you really think shrinking a mass that has been slowly killing this boy is going to take only five minutes to minimize? You'll be working on it for who knows how long."

I snap my mouth shut, pressing my lips into a thin line and flaring my nostrils.

She's *probably* right.

"How do you propose I go about fixing this stamina?" I ask, folding my arms across my chest.

"Other than us continuously practicing and adding more time each training session…" She shakes her head with a half-shrug. "Some physical activity would do you good."

I nod as I stretch my arms above my head, groaning at the soreness in my shoulders.

Lightning scrutinizes me, her eerie gaze sweeping over my body. "How physically fit would you say you are? Like, how often do you run?"

"I don't," I scoff, my arms falling limp at my sides. "Physical fitness isn't really something I've ever considered a necessity in my life."

"Okay." Lightning rolls her eyes. "What sort of physical activity have you *ever* done?"

"I walked everywhere I went in Eldamain." I shrug, frowning. "I would lift sacks of supplies or pails of water from Orion's Lake. I don't do any of that now, though. Other than lifting Clint on and off his bed to get him into his wheelchair or get him into the bathing tub, that's the extent of my physical activity."

"That's going to need to change," Lightning grumbles, flicking her dark gray dreads over her shoulder. "I'll think of some physical activities to work into our routine. I guess I never considered how much the physical body plays a role in Light stamina. The Elders would be chortling to hear me admit it."

"Is that who trained you?" I ask, folding my hands in front of me. "The Elders? You and Tariq mentioned them during our meeting."

Lightning stares at me, her eyes nearly glowing orange from the flames in a nearby sconce because of their icy color. She takes a deep breath and looks at something over my shoulder, contemplating.

"I want to trust you, Reva," Lightning admits, startling me. "You're a Sirian, but you're too close to the

FATE DEMANDS SACRIFICE

55

Hespers. I don't entirely trust them yet to be giving up the secrets our people have worked decades to try and conceal."

I bite the inside of my cheek. I can't blame her for being hesitant. In fact, I understand more than anyone where the trepidation comes from. It's not easy to share what we are, and maybe I've been too trusting of Fin and Elly when I revealed my secrets after knowing them for two months.

I also know that my gut has never made me uneasy or regretful about the decision to tell them. Now that I look back, it was one of the most freeing moments. It was like removing a veil that's been draped over me my entire life.

"I think you should trust them," I admit, stepping closer to her. "I can at least speak for Elly. I know you have a strange vendetta against Fin because of a bad impression—"

"One he has yet to rectify," she points out, eyebrow raised.

I wave away her comment. "And I truly can't speak for Tariq yet since I've only just started getting to know him. Unfortunately, he and his twin apparently share everything, so my secret was revealed before he got here."

"These are the people you trust with your life?" Lightning folds her arms across her chest, swaying back on her heels.

I suspire, my eye twitching and my shoulders slumping forward. "If you want me to be part of this whole war thing that's going on, I need to know all I can about what you've been working towards. If there is something you don't want the Hespers or anyone else involved in, just say so, and I'll keep my mouth shut."

Lightning flexes her jaw repeatedly, appearing to consider my offer of secrecy and its legitimacy.

After a long moment of heavy silence, she finally relents with a hefty groan, sweeping her hand over the floor. I follow her lead, sitting cross-legged on the sandy ground, crunching beneath our weight.

"Before our people were exiled," Lightning begins, folding her hands between her legs. "The Elders ran any operation involving the Sirians. The Arcane Island was a secluded land where the Sirians could train privately with the Elders. Those with god-powers were actually required to go to this school to learn how to wield them.

"This time around, two of the Elders took on their titles when the Abyss first showed signs of reappearing over 20 years ago."

"Jorah said at first it was a whisper," I say, recalling our last meeting with him.

Lightning nods. "It wasn't much back then, and it has grown year after year, but particularly over the last few years. Decades before the Abyss returned, the two founding Elders were running an operation for Sirians who wanted to live in peace. They created a hidden community from the rest of the world. But since the Abyss worsened from that very first whisper, they officially established themselves as the new Elders and started learning all they could to teach their community

FATE DEMANDS SACRIFICE 57

combat skills. They found old books and had them translated, recruited trustworthy Magics to help them, and gradually grew their movement to what it is now."

"So, you're like this society of Sirians living under the radar, fighting crime?" I ask, wincing. "How many of you are there?"

"I've lost count, to be honest." She shrugs, rubbing her bottom lip. "The last I checked, there were maybe a few dozen of us, give or take any children under eighteen. The Elders have decided not to involve them in the fighting when it comes."

"How kind," I sneer, unable to envision myself as an eighteen-year-old fighting a malevolent Darkness since I can't imagine my twenty-two-year-old self doing so. Lightning scrunches her face at me with a mock grin. "That's still a pretty good amount of people to keep hidden. How have you all stayed in seclusion?"

"I don't think you're ready to learn that bit of information yet," Lightning says, not unkindly but just as a matter of fact.

Again, I hate to admit it, but she's right. If children live in whatever commune they've created, I would protect their location at all costs. No matter who I was talking to.

"So, how did you come to find them?" I ask, resting my forearms on my thighs. "If this community has been around longer than twenty years, were you born there? You can't be much older than me."

"I'll be twenty-three next month," she confirms,

which makes her about four months older than me. "But no. I wasn't born in the community…" She leaves her sentence unfinished, snapping her mouth shut like it's taking all her willpower to conceal her history from me.

"Lightning." I soften. "I know I'm reluctant to wave the Sirian banner and be front and center for your calvary, but that doesn't mean I'm against it. You have to understand where I'm coming from. My upbringing barely prepared me to live anywhere other than Eldamain, let alone lead an army of Sirians. It doesn't make me your enemy."

Lightning averts her gaze, finding her hands in her lap far more fascinating. She shrugs her left shoulder, and for once, she doesn't look like a military general.

"My mom was a Magic," she explains, her face serene. "When she fell pregnant with me, she started having these strange dreams. She said she envisioned the different stages of my life—birth, adolescence, teens—but instead of an actual child, it was a silhouette of light in place of a corporeal form. When she got further along, she started waking up every morning with these headaches in the middle of her head.

"She knew what it meant… She'd been raised learning about the Sirians and what had been done to them where she was from. She'd been taught this was the sign you were going to have a Sirian child."

Lightning pauses, raising her gaze, the silver in her eyes enhanced by the tears gleaming in them.

I want to ask where her mom was from, what Magics

talked about these things, and where her father was in all this, but that feels like a conversation for another day.

Because I fear where this story is going.

"When she fell pregnant with me, she wasn't living amongst those she grew up with," Lightning continues softly. She finally latches her gaze onto me, a tear sliding down her cheek. "The life she was living wasn't conducive for a Sirian, needless to say. I was born in Eldamain instead. My mom managed to make it there before she gave birth."

"How long were you in Eldamain?" I ask, my voice rising slightly.

If we're only a few months apart, we could've been living in Eldamain at the same time.

"I know what you're thinking." Lightning nods, maintaining eye contact. "I was there until I was about sixteen. We lived in the same country, but we had very different upbringings. I know you lived in secret, but you also went into town and had others involved in your childhood. I had no one but my mother. We lived on our own, far from Main Town in Eldamain.

"We were out gathering wood for the winter when they came." Lightning's eyes harden, and I know I'm about to hear the tale of another Sirian orphan. "I'm pretty sure they were Etherean spies. We were ambushed, and I was still inexperienced in my powers. We were outnumbered, six against two, a group of trained Ethereans against a gangly, sixteen-year-old Sirian and her simple Magic mother.

"They murdered her right in front of me."

"Oh, Lightning," I whisper, tears springing to my eyes. I wouldn't say I was lucky, but I'm glad I didn't have to watch either of my parents die. "I'm so sorry."

Lightning sniffs, shrugging again and straightening. "I got my revenge. It also happened to be the day my god-power manifested. The sky was clear, but lightning fell from it at my will. I fried every last one of them from the inside out."

The hair on my arm stands, responding to static in the air. Lightning's eyes glow menacingly, so I let my firepower peek through a crack, warming my hands. I know my eyes must have glowed that orange hue instead of the white-gold of the Light as a devious grin plays at the corners of her lips.

I let my power subside as she finishes her story. "It was maybe a year later when all the effort my mom and I put in to find the Sirian movement came to fruition. One of the Elders found me and brought me to where they'd been hiding. They taught me everything I know. When they said we needed to investigate the Darkness, I volunteered to come to Mariande. I knew I could pass for a Magic with my eyes."

A sliver of a memory crawls into my brain.

When I first met Lightning, I thought she looked familiar. I debated whether it was because she reminded me of Dahlia—which still stands—but now I realize it was her hair and eyes.

I saw her at the pub Fin and I visited when I went to

FATE DEMANDS SACRIFICE

Saros with him.

The same night we kissed for the first time.

"I saw you," I admit aloud, slowly rising from my seat on the ground. "You were at the Magic-owned pub I went to with Fin. You were hanging on some knight's lap."

Lightning purses her lips, blowing out a harsh breath as she rises with me. "I didn't think you'd ever remember that night. Besides, I really didn't want to remember. He wasn't my typical taste, and I could feel his dick poking into me the entire time."

A breathy chuckle falls from my lips, but I squint with a raised eyebrow. "Not your typical taste?"

"I prefer something with a little more—" Lighting strides towards the exit upstairs, tapping the tip of my nose on the way. "Boobs."

★★★

Clint and I try to go about our normal day-to-day routine, but Pax hovering like a fly has not been conducive to our relationship. Clint is one of the few people I can talk openly and honestly with, and vice versa, but we can't carry on our normal discussions like we typically would about the Abyss, Sirians, and god-powers.

Lucky for us, a seamstress has spent most of the day measuring Clint for the Glow Ball in less than a month.

"Do you know why they call it the Glow Ball, Reva?" Clint asks me, peering over his shoulder as he sits at the edge of his bed. The seamstress scribbles notes on a piece of parchment.

I hesitate, muddling herbs in the mortar. "No, Clint, but I have a feeling you're going to tell me anyway."

"No, actually," Clint says, watching the seamstress. "I thought you'd know."

"You had to explain to me what a glowing ball was two weeks ago." I stop muddling to glare at his back. "What makes you possibly believe I'd know why it's called that?"

He shrugs but throws his head back over his shoulder, a mischievous grin plastered on his face. "I don't know. Something in my gut." His eye flickers quickly to my forehead before landing back on my eyes again.

I clench my jaw, grumbling quietly. "*Clint.*"

I glance at Pax out of the corner of my eye, who's staring out the window longingly like he might escape his new, arguably lower position of guarding Clint and me.

Clint dismisses my concern with a push of air through his lips, observing the seamstress as she completes her notes on his measurements. Her eyes briefly peruse them before she nods once, lifts her head to me, and says, "Your turn, Miss Reva."

"Excuse me?" I startle, the pestle clattering against the rim of the stone mortar.

Her face is neutral as she explains, "Princess Eloise

FATE DEMANDS SACRIFICE 63

instructed me to retrieve the measurements for Prince Clint and yourself."

"What about Pax?" I ask, narrowing my eyes. It wouldn't be like Elly not to have Pax measured, despite what is or is not going on with them.

"Knights of Mariande wear their official formal uniform." Pax's voice rumbles through the room like thunder, but there is a tiny twitch at the corner of his lips. "It'd be best if you cooperated. She will report your behavior back to the Princess."

My eyebrows shoot up my forehead.

Did *Pax* just give *me* advice?

Without another word, his shoulders bend toward the window as he redirects his attention.

I survey him momentarily while I stretch my arms out, following the seamstress's instructions. As she wraps the measuring tape around my chest, I turn my gaze back to Clint, whose facial expression mirrors my own. He is frozen halfway into maneuvering himself back against his headboard.

"So," I clear my throat, checking on Pax once more before focusing on the seamstress's moves. "What does this Glow Ball entail?"

"You still need a date?" Clint yells from his bed.

I can't help the smile that curves up my cheeks. "I've got to give it to you, kid. You're persistent."

"I know what I want." He shrugs, pulling the blanket over his legs. "The wheelchair might get in the way, but I think we could manage. Besides, we've got a few more weeks. Maybe we can get me on my feet by then."

"Aim high, huh?" I ask, allowing the seamstress to twist me sideways so I have to face Pax, whose attention quickly snakes back to the window again. "That can be our goal, then. If not, the wheelchair won't be a problem."

"Wait." Even if I can't see Clint, I hear the rising glee in his voice. "Are you saying you'll go with me?"

"You know," I explain, trying to see what Pax finds so interesting out the window. "I've got no one else I'd rather go with, so why not? What does it mean when I have a date to the Glow Ball?"

"Reva," Clint says quietly. He's shouting the next thing out of his mouth. "We're going to have the best time in the world! You won't regret it. I'll be the best date."

I'm glad my back is facing him because he'd be insufferable at the sight of my wide-mouthed grin.

"This means we have to match." Clint's voice picks up speed as he continues to ramble. "We have to stand out at this Glow Ball. It'll be like my coming of age and Reva's grand introduction. Oh, Clary, we *have* to make sure Reva and I match. I want people to be surprised—"

Clint continues his rant about matching and making a grand entrance together, the seamstress—Clary—suppressing her own grin as she measures the length of my legs from my hips to my feet.

When I find Pax observing me, my smile slowly slips from my face. His dark brown eyes study me, the hues lighter than his skin as the sun sneaks through the glass, illuminating them. There's a curiosity and softness to them that is unfamiliar to me.

Chapter 5

I lay in the fresh layer of snow, sliding my arms and legs across its chilled surface. I always enjoyed the cold embrace of the white powder as the woodsy mountain air traveled from the Black Avalanches directly west of us. But a strange, sharp vinegar and metallic undertone mingled with it, and it grew stronger every year.

I rose at the sound of fabric being shaken out, white flakes clinging to my jacket, hair, and cap. The sun reflected off the white expanse, the Mark on my head tingling against the rays.

"What in the Gods," a deep voice interrupted my relaxation.

I startled, jumping up and standing in the middle of the snow covering our plot, a deer caught by its prey. Another being stood before me, something about him reminding me of the bats Karasi found under her roof last autumn.

He approached me cautiously, prowling towards me as one long leg stepped in front of the other. He slowly lowered to the ground, crouching until he was forced to his knees before me. He crawled forward, reaching a long, lean arm out to touch me.

Bright, purple eyes shimmered in the sunlight, framed by heavy eyelashes and straight eyebrows. He tilted his head, his

FATE DEMANDS SACRIFICE

coif of dark brown hair tumbling to the side. His eyebrows twitched into a frown, a corner of his lip down-turning underneath an untamed beard and mustache.

"Who are you, kid?" His voice surrounded me, but my eyes widened at the sharp canine peeking out as he spoke.

I quickly stepped back, stumbling in the snow and falling onto the snowman I'd begun to build—and got bored with. His eyes flared as I fell to my rear with a heavy thunk.

My breathing quickened, praying he wouldn't take me away like Karasi warned.

"I won't harm you," he insisted, lifting a hand again between us. My gaze flickered between it and his face, my attention drawn to those eyes and sharp-angled features from his jawline to his chin.

"I'm a friend of Karasi." He extended his fingers to reveal sharp claws that protruded from his nail beds in a blink.

I gasped, scooting back into the mound of my unfinished friend. I had never seen so many strange features on Karasi. Her eyes were different from mine, but otherwise, she appeared as mortal as I did.

"Is Karasi home?" he asked, but blew out an exasperated breath before continuing, "Who am I kidding… She's not stupid enough to leave a young kid home by herself."

I lowered my chin closer to my chest, wishing I could melt into the snow. I kept my eyes latched onto him through lowered lashes.

The corner of his mustache twitched up with his lip, his purple eyes scanning every part of my face. "Well, you're not hers, that's for sure. Did she just pick you up off the side of the road?"

I don't know what compelled me to answer, but my young brain knew that if he wanted to hurt me, he would've by now. The longer he crouched in the grass with me, the more of a chance Karasi would come out angered.

"I've been here my whole life," I finally replied, my small voice timid.

He blinked rapidly, that frown returning between his brows. He pulled his biceps into his body, resting his forearms against his squatting legs.

"And how old are you?" He continued to watch me, his eyes lingering on my Mark every time he found my forehead.

I sat straighter, tugging my legs in to sit crisscross on the white mound. I held up all five fingers in front of his face. "I'm five!"

"Five," he breathed, barely audible. He leaned back on his heels, peering down at me over the tip of his nose. "Will you give me your name, kid?"

"I'm—"

"Reva," came the answer from nearby.

But that's not how this memory should go.

In the real memory, Karasi yelled at Remy from the porch, demanding what in the Gods' names he was doing here. He would continue to yell at her about leaving for years and taking in a Sirian child while I clung to his leg, my head bobbing between them as they volleyed back and forth at each other.

My stomach drops, and there's a strange flash of light like the flare of a flame.

The sky morphs into a sunrise, the yellows, pinks, and

FATE DEMANDS SACRIFICE

oranges bleeding together. I glance down at my body, which is no longer the size of my younger self but what I expect my sleeping body to look like, complete with the nightgown I wore to bed.

"Reva," the familiar, raspy voice calls again.

Standing next to me in the grass is Karasi, just as I left her.

"Am I dreaming still?" I ask, tears springing to my eyes and my throat burning.

Karasi smiles serenely, bending at the waist to offer me both of her arms. I firmly lock my hands over them, and she lifts me to my feet with ease she hasn't exhibited in a decade.

"I have to be dreaming," I conclude with a hysterical chuckle.

She stares into me, bright, marigold-yellow eyes pinned on my forehead. "We are in a dream state, but the events we are experiencing now are no longer a memory."

"But it's a figment of my imagination," I say, though it tastes like a lie.

She still smiles, then her eyes soften. "If you want it to be."

I can't peel my eyes off her. It's only been about three months since I've seen her, but it feels like a lifetime has passed between us. The void in my chest pulses around the edges, reminding me of its presence. I want to tell her all that I've learned and everything that's happening. I open my mouth—

But nothing comes out. I don't know where to start, and my chest cleaves.

Her hand cups my cheek, and her lavender musk wafts over and around me like a warm blanket. A tear escapes down my cheek and sneaks under her palm.

"I know, aster," she whispers, her thumb tracing my cheekbone. "Oh, do I know."

"I'm sorry," I choke out around a sob. "I've broken all the rules you gave me. So many people know what I am, and I just—"

"Hush, girl." Karasi grips my shoulders in her hands, her nails gently pressing into my skin. "I told you I know. I know why you had to make these decisions. When you left, I instructed you to trust the touch of Fate."

"It doesn't make those choices any less frightening."

Karasi brushes her fingertips against my Mark. Her eyes are still soft, but a thin wrinkle deepens on her forehead. "When the Darkness comes again—" Her eyes flutter briefly to something over my shoulder. "Marks will be revealed."

My heart sinks in my chest, a small crack permeating across it.

"I grow weaker, aster," Karasi sighs, her shoulders hunching. Her hand tickles the side of my face before wrapping under my chin to grip it between her thumb and finger. "You grow stronger."

I wouldn't say stronger, but correcting her was futile, a lesson I'd learned at a young age.

"I have two god-powers," I tell her, searching for any emotion on her face. "Dionne is the fire… Well, I guess the core of the earth. We haven't figured out the other one yet. Do you know what it could be?"

Karasi keeps her eyes trained on whatever she sees over my shoulder. I have the urge to follow her gaze, but something

FATE DEMANDS SACRIFICE 71

inside keeps me rooted to the spot, facing her head-on.

"The Gods mourn their children," she whispers, her eyes frantic, one squinting as the other stares wide.

"The Gods aren't here anymore, Karasi." I try to move my head, but it's impossible between her grip and what feels like a pillow keeping it in place. "You taught me that."

Karasi's face blanches, but it quickly returns to her standard neutrality. She cocks her head to the side as she meets my eyes again. "She watches you."

"Who does?" I ask, my heart hammering against my ribcage. The edges of my vision blur as a bright, white light begins swallowing the memory of my home.

Karasi just smiles, and with that smile, a blinding flash engulfs my vision—

I lurch awake, my breath sweeping in, forcefully refilling my lungs. The dream lingers in my mind, but a weight deep in the pit of my stomach tells me this wasn't just a dream.

I swing my legs over the side of the bed, leaving my robe behind, and rush over to my small wash bucket. I splash water on my face, not bothering to warm it, hoping the cold will relieve this dizziness.

I brace my arms on either side of the vanity, glaring up at my reflection in the mirror. My Mark glows faintly but quickly fades, and my skin is a shade paler than usual, reflecting the swirling in my stomach.

Karasi felt *real*. I could smell and feel her as though she were actually standing before me.

I've never known the full extent of Karasi's powers

and her true capabilities. She has the usual abilities of any Magic: enhanced blood, reflexes, senses, stamina, strength, and snake-like eyes to demonstrate she reigns from the House of Echidna. Her prophecies set her apart from other Magics, a different ability which may hint at her House's long-lost capability, but she's never divulged why she can see things.

But what would this be? Dream hopping? Dream walking? Mind walking? I've never heard of such a thing, though I wouldn't put it past her.

The time I lived with her was but a blip in her existence. She probably has a significant number of abilities I've never been made aware of.

As the sun peeks through my curtains, I remember I'm supposed to meet with Elly in the library today. I quickly throw on a simple outfit to get me through the castle, pushing aside the grumbling in my stomach to get there before I have to report to Clint for the day.

Elly is already at our usual table in the middle of the library, skimming a book with an apple grasped in one hand. My shuffling echoes off the nearby bookcases, and Elly side-eyes me momentarily before reaching down beside her and launching an apple at me.

I catch it just before it smacks me in the face.

"A warning would have been appreciated," I scoff, rubbing the apple on the side of my skirt. I take a chunk out of the side, muttering around it, "What's on the agenda for today?"

"I've just been scouring these books on old lore about

FATE DEMANDS SACRIFICE   73

Danica and her children," Elly explains, relaxing into the chair and meeting my gaze. "Specifically, the children connected to you."

I roll my eyes, slipping into one of the empty chairs on the other side of the table she's camped at. "Nothing better than an early morning lesson on the deep roots of my heritage. It'd be nice if we could pinpoint my parents. Maybe then we could locate my extended family and find out if my hair will start thinning at an early age."

Elly blinks at me with irritation. "Don't be crass, you brat. You never know where this type of stuff could lead."

"Enlighten me," I grumble around another mouthful of the apple.

Elly holds my gaze for a moment longer as she grabs a nearby book, cracking it open to reveal a quill as a bookmark. "Did you ever learn about the Creation story and all the Gods?"

I heave a sigh and shrug, relaxing into the wooden chair. "Eldamain is a melting pot of different religions. Which would you like to hear?"

She snickers, shaking her head. "I was educated in history. I know them; I just want to know how much you know. And not the *beliefs* of the different countries. Just the cold, hard facts about Creation."

Every country knows the Creation story, but each interprets the events and who it worships differently. Most people believe that Kuk and Khonsa—the Deities—wandered the universe in search of a place to create their Beings when they got into an argument and hurtled the Darkness of space and the Light of the stars at one another.

In the crossfire, Aveesh was born.

No matter where you're from, the world believes Kuk was responsible for the Darkness, while Khonsa was responsible for the Light. What that means in the battle of good and evil depends on who you ask.

The Gods are Kuk and Khonsa's children, born to keep the two Deities in check when it came to creating the Beings they wanted to inhabit Aveesh. Khonsa worked with her children to create different creatures that no longer roam our world and Beings that have slowly dwindled into fewer and fewer: the Sirians and the Magics.

Eventually, Kuk and Khonsa caused so many problems with the argument of good, evil, and balance that their children banished them into the stars to fight for the rest of eternity. The Gods took over, occasionally living amongst their creations on Aveesh.

I tell Elly as much, and she nods, not glancing up from her book.

"And the Gods?" she urges, scanning one of the pages intently.

"Dola," I begin, "The Goddess of Destiny and Fate. I have a few choice words for her." Elly doesn't acknowledge my comment. "Then there is Morana, the Goddess of Death and Magic. Rod is the God of Family, Birth, and Humanity, and last is Danica, the Goddess of Nature and Energy of All Things."

FATE DEMANDS SACRIFICE   75

"Jorah said there were nine demi-gods in total," Elly explains, finally looking back up at me. "Only four of them were Danica's, which means they were these all-powerful Sirians."

"I never knew about the demi-gods." I precariously place the apple core on the table, balancing it upright. "I mean, I assumed if the Gods used to walk among us that they had children, but I just didn't consider what that meant for Magics, Sirians, or even mortals."

"I found some lore on all of them, but I figured we'd focus mainly on Danica's since that really affects what we're doing right now." Elly pushes the book across the table, avoiding my apple. "Danica's four children were Phoebe, Asteria, Dionne, and Taranis."

"Taranis is who Lightning gets her powers from," I recall. I find that the page is open to a tale about Phoebe. "We know I have Dionne. So, you've found stories on Phoebe and Asteria?"

She nods, folding her arms over her chest. "I figured if we could find stories that talk about their powers more or how they used them, then maybe you or Lightning would recognize some in you..."

She trails off as my attention focuses on the story of Phoebe in front of me.

Again, it's either a translated version or one that was once told by word of mouth before someone finally decided to write it down.

This tale describes how Phoebe used her gravitational manipulation to save people from death. A child fell from a tree, and its body stopped just inches before crashing to the ground. A carriage was about to roll over an already-injured man when Phoebe used her power to lift the man out of the way to safety. There is even another tale about how she used her powers to propel objects at high speeds, particularly in a story where a man was competing for her hand in marriage.

The story goes that Phoebe had already fallen in love with him before her father, an ancient king of Etherea, called a tournament in her name to win her hand in marriage. She used her abilities to assist him in the competition, allowing him to outrace his opponents, hit the bulls-eye repeatedly, and send men flying off their horses with his jousting stick.

"Phoebe was eventually a *Queen* of Etherea?" I blurt, keeping my finger on the page to mark my spot. "You're telling me not only were Sirians on the thrones but so were demi-gods?"

"The most powerful." Elly shrugs nonchalantly. "We knew Sirians used to sit on the throne. Why is it so startling they'd let demi-gods?"

"Do you think nearly every throne had a demi-god at some point?" I question, tilting my head. "You could be descendants of demi-gods down the line somewhere."

Elly points at me, specifically where my hematite necklace sits. "I was right about your necklace being important. Magics realized the demi-gods and their families could go mad from their power. They found hematite helped ground them, so they created various

FATE DEMANDS SACRIFICE

hematite heirlooms to keep them sane."

"You think you guys would have a hematite item," I finish the thought for her, gripping my necklace in my own hand. "I wonder if Lightning has one. I've yet to see it."

Elly wags her finger at me, eyebrows raised.

I move on to the next story about Asteria. It starts by discussing how her beauty was known throughout the land. It doesn't reveal any specific details about what she looked like, but it says to look upon her was to look upon the heart of the universe.

The world could feel when Asteria was near. It was as if creation and existence bowed at her feet, holding its breath, waiting for her.

Unlike Phoebe, Asteria was not the daughter of a king. She lived in the kingdom of Eldamain before it crumbled beneath the Korbin legacy. It says she worked for the royal family, as their—

"She led Eldamain's military?" I startle, snapping back away from the pages.

"That was my reaction, too." Elly grabs another book beside her. "I even found artistic renderings of her in some of these books. It's not in color, but…"

I cautiously accept the outstretched book. Another quill nestles between the pages, marking where Elly found the drawing.

Asteria's name is labeled underneath the woman, the only indicator distinguishing her from any other demi-god or Goddess rendered in the artwork.

Her hair floats around her, arms outstretched on either side. A faint line is drawn in an arch over her body with smudged marks waving off it. In the middle of her forehead sits the six-pointed Mark, the picture too small for the artist to have drawn any other defining features like her eyes, lips, or nose.

"What is this around her?" I ask Elly, pointing to the faint line.

Elly shrugs. "My best guess is the shield we read about. I'm guessing she was able to manipulate the Light to create it."

I lay my hand flat on the drawing, wishing I could feel a connection between either of these two demi-gods. Karasi flashes in my head.

She watches you.

Did she mean one of my demi-god ancestors?

I've never given much thought to where we go when we die, let alone where a demi-god goes. Can they travel the universe as their godly parents do, or are they bound to the afterlife like mortals?

There's another thought I can't shake, so I vocalize, "Why would Eldamain need a Sirian demi-god to lead their military?"

"There is so much of our history we aren't taught anymore." Elly hangs her head, a stray strand of hair falling into her face. "There is only one person who would know any of this, and we pulled Tariq away from him."

"Ruhan?" I question, "He would know about the

demi-gods?"

"They are very strict about their schooling in Riddling," Elly pauses. "Among many other things. They teach history and lore as though they are one and the same. They believe it helps when we argue what is fair and just in the world. It allows them to consider many possible positions in an argument, court ruling, or war."

"Will they be attending the Glow Ball?" I ask, tilting my head.

"This year will be the first time they've attended, as far as I know." Elly looks over my shoulder. "They responded saying only some of the Riddling royal family will attend: Ruhan, his betrothed, and one of his sisters, Naja."

"Is this the sister Tariq keeps refusing to marry?" I try to suppress the shockingly jealous tone peeking through my calm and collected demeanor, but it doesn't get past Elly.

Per usual.

She raises an eyebrow, pursing her lips to the side. "Yes…" she drawls. "Do you want to talk about *that?*"

I groan, throwing my head back to stare at the ceiling. "Not really. There's nothing to talk about."

Elly folds her arms across her chest. "I'm not blind, Reva. I know my brother better than anyone and arguably know you pretty well. The tension between you two is palpable."

I roll my eyes, my head still tilted back. "You're not so innocent with Pax. Talk about palpable."

"I'll give you that one." She lets out a strained chuckle and continues, "Well, when you're ready to talk, you know I can probably give you the best advice. I've known Fin and Tariq my entire life, and one is my twin."

"Don't remind me." I puff out a heavy breath of air through my lips.

"Just so you know…" Elly's voice is suddenly directly beside me, her hand bracing on my shoulder. "My brother has shown interest in women plenty of times before and acted on that interest, but he's never been so intrigued by someone as he is with you."

She walks away, her skirt fluttering behind her. I twirl in my seat, facing the direction she's left me.

"Is that supposed to make me feel better?" I shout after her.

Her laugh echoes from the aisle she disappeared behind.

CHAPTER 6

Rounding the corner of the training area, I'm bemused to find Tariq inspecting one of the pillars arching towards the ceiling, his nose nearly touching the stone. He peers over his shoulder as I approach, my boots crunching on the sand.

"Where's Lightning?" I ask, folding my arms across my chest.

He twists on his heel with a small grin. "She informed Elly she couldn't train you or come to the library today. She said there was some business she needed to take care of involving the Magics in town."

"Are they okay?" My arms fall to my sides, fists clenching as my heart flutters in my chest. He nods, waving my question away. I frown. "So, I'm assuming there's no practice, but why didn't Elly just come to my room and tell me?"

"You're correct." He tilts his head to the side, a strand of hair falling from his half-bun. "But Lightning said it would be beneficial if you got the chance to practice stamina, and I'm inclined to agree."

I narrow my eyes, and that's when I notice his garb.

And I wish I hadn't.

A tight, black tunic with a black leather vest layered on top strains against his broad chest. The black pants and boots donning his bottom half remind me of the same kind Fin wore the first time he took me down here.

The irony that I've found myself in matching fighting gear with a very attractive man, stories below the castle once again, does not get past me.

"I'm not going to fight you if that's what you're getting at." I shake my head with a breath of laughter. "I could kill you!"

"You're not going to fight me with your Energy, Healer." Tariq rolls his sleeves up his forearms as he takes a few steps toward me. "Like I said, I agree with Lightning. You need to increase your physical endurance. You'd benefit from some mundane training integrated into your regime."

He stands before me now with just a foot between us. I clench my jaw and squeeze out, "Mundane training?"

"Yes. Running, jumping, lunging—all bodyweight exercises." He reaches across the space between us and grabs my braid in his hand. I gasp, startled by his abruptness, yet the swirling in my stomach and tingling in my fingers betray me.

He rolls a hairband off his wrist, twirling the braid into a bun on the back of my head. This close, his muscles flex under his tunic, and his warm scent tickles my nose with every movement.

"There," he says when he's done, taking a few steps

FATE DEMANDS SACRIFICE 83

back. "Trust me, you'll want your hair off your neck."

My hand floats to the back of my head, where my braid is now rolled into a bun. I gawk at him.

He shrugs, clasping his hands behind his back. "*Thank you, Tariq* would suffice." He struts towards the center of the room. "Now, let's get started. How about we run a couple of laps around this room?"

"*Run?*" My voice squeaks, my hand dropping back down to my side. "You're out of your damn mind if you think I'm—"

He silences me with a leveled stare, one eyebrow raised. To my surprise, Tariq jerks his head towards the wall and starts to jog, watching me over his shoulder.

I huff under my breath, but I pick up my feet and follow behind him in more than a couple of circles along the walls, weaving around pillars.

"Did your Magics never teach you how to run properly?" Tariq asks between beats, his gaze flickering to me.

"Why would I need to?" I become extremely aware of how my arms naturally swing. "I didn't plan on running anywhere. I only had to walk."

"You're a Sirian living in Eldamain." Tariq shakes his head, a few strands of hair swinging in his face. "You didn't think at any point you'd need to run for your life?"

"I never once felt unsafe in Eldamain," I explain, a little embarrassed at how winded I am already. "I had Karasi, the boys... Hell, I even had Dahlia and her retractable claws. If I really needed it, I had the Light. I was confident no one knew I was Sirian. As far as anyone was concerned, I was a Magic just like everybody else."

Tariq surveys me from the corner of his eyes, scanning the side of my face. I stare back, breathing heavily.

"What?" I ask, although it comes out as more of a wheeze.

Tariq chuckles to himself, not the least bit winded, as he tears his gaze from me and focuses ahead of us. "You're reckless, aren't you?"

I snort, ready to retort, but Tariq picks up his pace and insists I keep up with him.

Long after my legs have started burning, Tariq orders me to the center of the room for a form of torture he calls *burpees*, which require more maneuvers than one workout should have. He watches intently, but I notice him counting down until he hits sixty before telling me to stop.

I bend at the waist, balancing my hands on my knees, my chest heaving as my heart threatens to burst through my ribcage.

"This is going to be fun, isn't it?" Tariq grins coyly.

I snap my head up, blowing a rogue strand of hair from my face. It doesn't do a whole lot of good since it's plastered to my skin with sweat.

"Oh, don't look at me like I've threatened your life." Tariq folds his arms over his chest. "We've only made it through one of three exercises, and you still have to do the burpees two more times."

FATE DEMANDS SACRIFICE 85

"You can go to—"

"Round 2!" he shouts, clapping in my face.

In a blink, my body wavers, and the image of a ghostly, limp form flies away from me. I straighten instantaneously, throwing up a wall of power that freezes my veins. There's a quick flash of white-blue between Tariq and me, there and gone just as fast as the clap of his hands.

Tariq gawks at me—not in fear—but in general shock, with what could also be irritation.

"Was that the equivalent of copping an attitude with me?" Tariq asks, but his mouth tilts up on one side.

I flare my nostrils, rubbing my filthy, sweaty palms on my pants.

"I'm sorry," I apologize firmly, shaking my head. "I didn't expect that to happen."

"I can't say I did either, yet here we are." Tariq tilts his head to the side. "Your powers have different colors to them."

I startle, frowning.

That's what he has to say?

There was no apprehension, no anger at the sudden outburst of power. In fact, he didn't even flinch.

"They are both mostly bright white," he explains, slowly pacing. "That one had a blue tint to it, though. The other you wield with Lightning always has a gold hue. What's the difference?"

My eyes flutter as I gather myself. "We think that's the one that comes from either Phoebe or Asteria. It burns differently."

"What do you mean by that?" Tariq stops, twirling on his heel to face me again. He starts his agonizing journey back.

"When I conjure firepower, it's what you think," I explain, rubbing my forearm. "It's like I'm burning up from the inside out. When I wield the Light, it's more like a buzzing or tingle. But the deeper power…"

Below the golden glow of the Light sits a blinding blue glow simmering in the pit of my stomach. My entire life, I've always avoided that fine line when wielding the Light, but there have been moments when I have no control and dip into it.

I know that power is also far grander than the Light.

"The deeper power is like injecting liquid ice into my body," I conclude, clenching my fists at my sides.

Tariq stops a few feet in front of me, rocking back and forth from his heels to the balls of his feet. He stares at something just over my head, his face scrunched.

"When we were younger, Nurse Isla used to tell us tales about the universe outside of our world and the stars in the sky," he explains, still not looking at me. "She always said, if you look hard enough, stars have a slight tint of color to them. They're usually red or blue. She said the blue stars are hotter than the sun."

I tilt my head, pursing my lips briefly before saying, "But that power isn't hot."

"Think of a cold lake. The chill is so piercing it feels like it burns your skin. Maybe this starfire is a different

FATE DEMANDS SACRIFICE

87

type of heat or burning we can't comprehend." He shrugs, his gaze latching onto mine. A predatory, playful glint in those burning eyes has my stomach swirling and my heart skipping more than one beat. "Maybe knowing that could help determine whether you're a descendant of Phoebe or Asteria.

"Anyway, you owe me two sets of burpees and another three exercises, Starfire."

"No." I swipe my hand in a line between us. "Absolutely not. There will be no pet names. I've already had this discussion with Finley. I have a name."

"And it's a lovely name, *Reva*." My name on his lips sends the warmth in my head straight through my body. "We can talk about it. Until then, you're not getting out of these exercises."

I flare my nostrils, my arms stiff at my sides.

He groans, glaring up at the ceiling. "Would it make you feel better if I did them with you?"

A slow, sinister smile spreads across my cheeks, and I follow his lead.

Tariq leads us in two more rounds of burpees. He guides me through the next two exercises—lunges and jump squats—and has us do three rounds each before calling it for the morning.

"Eventually, I think you would benefit from learning how to combine your Light with swordplay," he explains, wiping sweat off his forehead with the back of his arm. "From what I heard, you lifted a knight's sword and were able to—"

"No sword," I snap, twisting away and stalking off. "I won't touch it."

His feet shuffle against the sand, and he snatches my arm, twirling me around. He gently pulls me close to him, minimizing the amount of space we should keep between us. His brows are furrowed in concern, and his eyes search mine.

"I'm not saying we do it tomorrow," he says cautiously, his face softening. "I just mean, think about it. Is there a reason you're against it?"

I swallow loud enough for Tariq to tilt his head back. I avert my gaze, watching the glow from the sconces dance across the tan surface.

Tariq's finger and thumb gently grip my chin. He turns my head just enough to shift my gaze back to him, my wrist still secured in his other hand.

Outside of the different training exercises, I can't avoid the number of times he's grabbed or caressed me today unprovoked.

"Your tantrum earlier with your power... It was in response to the clap, wasn't it?" He must find what he's looking for on my face because he nods once. "If you ever want to talk about it, I'm more than happy to listen. I may be able to lend a little advice, should you want it."

His hands are still on me, and his invitation settles in my chest like warm, mulled wine on a chilly winter night.

I open my mouth to thank him or tell him maybe I will take him up on that offer, but instead, I say, "You keep touching me."

FATE DEMANDS SACRIFICE   89

Tariq's eyebrows fly up his forehead, an expression I'm not quite used to seeing on the Crown Prince. He looks at his hands on me with a frown as if he didn't notice, hesitating before he shoves them into his pockets and takes two steps back. "Do you not wish to be touched?"

The question stumps me. Again, I open my mouth to speak but snap it shut and purse my lips.

Flustered, I stumble over a few answers. "Well, it's not that. I mean, I don't mind being touched—not like that. Not like that by you—not that I don't like you touching me…" I trail off as those supple lips of his morph into a self-satisfying smirk. I glare, pointing at him. "*You* never seem to want to touch *me*. You always have your hands in your damn pockets!"

His smile softens and his eyebrows arch, but this time in intrigue. He retraces the two steps, removing his hands from his pockets at a painstakingly slow pace. He brushes a stray hair from my face and tucks it behind my ear.

I hold my breath as that finger trails down my jaw, neck, and across my shoulder. Chills follow his path down the side of my arm until he reaches my hand, gripping my fingers in his own.

He lifts my hand to his mouth, his lips brushing against the knuckles, and says, "You've misread me, Starfire."

I want to glare at him for the nickname, but those soft lips press against my skin, lingering before he releases it back to my side.

He looks me dead in the eye, pinning me to the spot. "I kept my hands in my pockets because I knew once I touched you, I wouldn't be able to keep my hands off you."

I stand in stunned silence, willing my lungs to breathe as Tariq saunters to the archway leading back up the stairs. He glances over his shoulder, adding, "And we wouldn't want to cause a scene in front of our friends, now would we?"

CHAPTER 7

As I walk down the hallway with a tray of lunch for Clint, I'm startled to find Pax running towards me, leaving Clint's door ajar.

My whole body stiffens. "What's wrong?"

"Clint," Pax begins, his thumb pointing towards the room. "He started vomiting, and he's not lucid."

I forget about lunch, the tray clattering to the floor and echoing off the walls as food splatters across the carpet. Pax skids to a halt halfway to me, then turns on his heel to race back to Clint's room. I hold my skirts in my hand, lifting them as I run. My legs scream at me from the last two workouts with Tariq, but I shove the pain down with my powers buzzing in my head.

I peel around the open door, throwing myself into Clint's room and slamming it shut behind me to allow us privacy for whatever I may need to do.

My heart plummets, and a corner of it cracks off.

The front of Clint's white shirt is covered in the black-green, sludge-like vomit he's experienced before. It drips off his chin, down his neck, and into the pool in his lap. His skin glistens in sweat, shades paler than I've become used to.

"Throw the window open," I demand, waving my arm towards it. I don't wait to see if Pax obeys. I lunge into action, working quickly.

I press the back of my hand to Clint's head, damp and radiating heat like a fire. I peel back both eyelids to check his consciousness, but they're rolled so far back I only glimpse the bottom curve of his amber irises. I curse under my breath, pressing my two fingers to his pulse, which is fluttering like the wings of a bird.

"He's going to start convulsing," I warn Pax as I fling myself towards my work table.

He stands on the opposite side of Clint's bed, a gentle breeze now wafting into the room, the stench of the vomit sharp as it travels toward me.

"If he does," I explain as I grab various vials, "You need to move him onto his side so he doesn't choke on spit or more vomit, understand?"

"Yes, ma'am." Pax answers in a deep, knightly tone.

I ignore it, focused on the level of valerian and lemon balm I combine, hoping these both will sedate him enough and combat the inevitable seizure. I grind the root and leafy plant into a powder in the mortar to mix with water and ensure Clint swallows it without drowning himself or choking on it.

"He's making sounds, Reva," Pax calls from the side of his bed. "Do I need to turn him?"

I leap across the short distance between my work table and Clint's bedside, sweeping my gaze over his body. I curl over him with the glass of water, pressing it against his lips as soft whimpers tremble from them. Tears sting the corners of my eyes as I shake my head.

I can't mask the sob that hiccups as I explain, "He's in pain. Help me administer this. I need you to gently and carefully lift his head off the pillow." Pax does so without pause, so I instruct him further, "Now, crane his neck at a slight angle."

Once Clint's mouth is propped open, I grasp his chin and use my thumb and finger to press his jaw open further. I tip the liquid back with a quick flick of my wrist, hushing Clint as he sputters, but he swallows it.

I sigh, the breath dragging down my throat into my chest and flowing through all my limbs. I slump onto the side of the bed, the glass hanging limp in my hand as I hunch forward. I shut my eyes against the tears threatening to escape, trying to control my trembling.

Clint has never convulsed before, but there's no doubt I fought the clock with the remedy to stop it from happening.

I'm not sure what a seizure would do to his body or how bad it would be. He's still malnourished and weak, and a serious seizure could send him into a deep, never-ending sleep, one step away from death.

Pax steadily lowers Clint's head back down to the pillow, slipping his hands out from underneath him. His dark brow furrows in concern and confusion, blinking rapidly as he presses his lips together.

"Can you help me change him out of this?" I ask

quietly.

Pax's gaze snaps to me, but he nods once.

After we've slipped a new shirt and bottoms onto Clint and changed out his top two blankets, I take my notebook to a chair in the corner of the room to write down this incident.

As I scribble the formula for a new daily tincture to prevent this from happening, Pax blurts, "Why do you bother?"

My quill stops mid-sweep, the markings I've made blurring. I sluggishly lift my head, meeting his deep, dark eyes.

He's back at the window, resting his shoulder against the wall with one boot crossed over the other. His arms are folded across his chest, gaze penetrating through my soul.

"What do you mean by that?" I mumble around the thickness in my mouth.

He quietly drags his attention back out the window. I wait for him to elaborate, but my patience grows thin the longer we sit in silence, Clint's heavy breathing and chatter from knights on their watch outside the only sounds.

"It's clear he's dying," Pax says not unkindly and to my surprise, without a hint of accusation. As if reading my thoughts, he continues, "I thought he was getting better when you first arrived, but now he seems only to get worse. I would insist you're poisoning him, but..."

He trails off, my heart picking up its pace and my

FATE DEMANDS SACRIFICE

95

chest clenching. I pry, "But?"

He heaves himself off the wall, strutting across the room on light feet to collapse into the chair against the wall to my left. He yanks on a chain underneath his knight uniform, gripping the pendant hanging from it. "While you handled that well, I could feel your panic. If you were trying to kill him, I would have caught some level of satisfaction from you. But I caught pain.

"Finley told me you spend day and night studying old Magic books to find a cure for Clint. Why?" He bends at the waist, resting his elbows on his thighs and letting the black pendant swing. He twists his head to me, his eyes soft and sad. "Why do you do that? You're convinced you're going to find something in time?"

"Because I love him," I admit for the first time, turning my attention to the limp child on the bed. "From the moment I met Clint, I vowed to myself I was going to heal him. Spending so much time with him, I've come to love him as though he were my own family."

"Is that why you agreed to be his date to the Glow Ball?" Pax can't hide the mirth in his voice.

I side-eye him, catching the slight lift at the corners of his lips. While it's hardly noticeable, it brightens his face, reminding me how handsome he is with his strong jaw and big, brown eyes.

"He's been pining for me to go with him since before Tariq got home," I smirk, letting out a breathy chuckle. "I couldn't deny him anymore."

There's a moment of comfortable silence between us

until he says, "Do you think he'll make it that long?"

I can't meet Pax's eyes. He's incredibly skilled at reading people, that much I've gathered even from the rare encounters we had before he became our guard. If I want to share what I know, I have to be selective.

"I haven't left this castle since things started turning south," I explain, grasping my own necklace between my fingers. "I can't leave him, and I need to be accessible until we perfect his cure."

"So, you have a cure? How sure are you?"

"We're working on something, and I'm nearly convinced it's going to be the solution." I pause, finally meeting his gaze. He's studying my face, reading me. "It's very tricky, and one wrong move could kill him."

"Do Elly and Tariq know?" Pax's voice changes, rising a level but still deep and reverberating.

It's the way he used Elly's name that startles me most.

I've never paid much attention to how much someone's voice or how they talk can change their appearance. I've always perceived Pax as hard lines and stiff movements, but suddenly, it's like a veil has lifted off his body.

Those hard lines curve instead of cut, and his broad, muscular shoulders tilt inward as he slouches in the chair. His hands hang limp between his legs as he waits for me to answer.

I clear my throat. "Elly, Tariq, and Fin are all part of it. Elly was the one who helped me and one of her assistants find the cure. They're all aware of the risk."

FATE DEMANDS SACRIFICE   97

"And King Darius?" Pax presses, a thick eyebrow arching.

"He's instructed me to do whatever I need to." I shrug, a bird flying across the window, drawing my attention toward it. "From the moment we met, he put all his faith in my capabilities."

"Without knowing anything about you." Pax shakes his head back and forth, still pinning his eyes on me. "I don't know if I can ever understand how they all so freely gave their trust to you. Tariq has been home for two weeks, and he forced me to become your daily guard because he's so convinced."

I swallow against the lump in my throat, knowing that Pax has every reason not to trust me. He thinks I'm a Magic when, in fact, I am arguably more dangerous than that.

I shrug, peering at Clint again. "King Darius knew Karasi from Clint's birth, but he made it seem like they have a deeper history than that. Regardless if that's true, he trusted Karasi, so he must also trust those she endorses. As for your friends I've unintentionally taken from you—"

I turn in the chair, facing Pax head-on. There's a flare of anger in his eyes, but it settles when I level him with pointed look. "I never meant to turn them on you. They cared so deeply about Clint that they were ready to open their minds to alternative options."

"You didn't take them from me, Reva." Pax inches off the chair to tower before me, averting his gaze. "Losing my friends was my own fault."

***

I curl up in one of the large plush chairs by my fireplace, my legs tucked into my chest. With my arms wrapped around my shins and chin resting on my kneecaps, I gaze into the flames with a journal and various vials spread across the coffee table before me.

In the three months I've been here, Clint covered in black vomit about to convulse had to be one of the most terrifying moments since the attack on the castle. The severity of his illness sits on my chest, making it difficult to take a deep breath. It was nearly impossible to leave him for the evening in the care of another Magic, even if I demanded they get me if anything happened, regardless of the time.

I bite back the tears that have threatened to spill all day, grinding my teeth together. Crying won't change the facts.

I'm not moving fast enough, and Pax was right.

Clint is dying.

I swallow around a sob, pressing the tips of my fingers against my lips. I close my eyes, shivering at the sorrow that threatens to pull me under and consume me.

Night came a while ago. I've been secluded in my room since shortly before dinner to finish taking my notes so I could focus without being constantly pulled to

FATE DEMANDS SACRIFICE

Clint's body lying still on his bed.

I've worked out a new tincture to treat the convulsions, but I'm concerned about its interactions with the kava I've been giving him to treat his stomach. If I add any more herbs to his list of daily potions, I run the risk of damaging other vital organs like his liver. I've been trying to rearrange some doses and decide what he desperately needs versus what he can—for lack of a better term—live without until I've mastered the Energy.

I gasp, startled by the knock resounding through my room. I take a shallow, steady breath to relax my racing heart before walking to the door.

I cautiously swing it open, running a hand through wild curls that have fallen out of their braid and suffered my constant tugging since Clint's incident.

Fin's eyes widen briefly before his face scrunches in concern. Without a word, he grabs both of my shoulders and shoves me back inside my room, using his boot to kick the door shut behind him.

"Gods, Reva." Fin rubs my shoulders, leaning closer. "You look manic. Is everything alright? I just got back from town, and Elly said you didn't come to dinner…"

Gods. I was supposed to have dinner with Elly and her mother to support her as they discussed specifics for Glow Ball planning. I toss my head back, folding into myself and crossing my arms over my stomach as I let out an exasperated sigh.

"Reva," Fin says again, softer. "Are you okay?"

His voice wraps around me, calling me into him. My

head falls back down, my forehead slamming into his chest. His grip slips from my shoulders as he stands rigid, so unlike him.

And I fall apart.

A silent sob cleaves my heart, my hands tightening around Fin's knight uniform wherever I can grasp it. Hot, burning tears pour from my eyes as I suck in a harsh breath, followed by a sob that's ripped from my chest.

Fin swears, shifting beside me. He moves down my body, and as his arm twists under my knees, I'm lifted against him, cradled in his arms. I wrap my arms around his neck, my hands locking onto my elbows, and bury my tear-streaked face into his neck. On my next heaving sob, Fin's scent overcomes me, and the ache in my chest deepens.

He walks us close to the fire, the light shining through my closed eyelids as I try to regain control over my breathing. Failing to do so as my sobs morph into hyperventilation, Fin's body lowers into one of the chairs. He holds me against his chest, humming my name repeatedly as one of his hands flattens against my back, the other stroking down my hair.

Maybe it's because he's noticed the vials and notes strewn across the coffee table, but Fin asks, "Is it Clint?"

All I can do is nod against his neck, trying to count between my breaths.

His hand stops moving against my hair. "Bad?"

Just when I think I've got control, the scolding tears spring up again, burning behind my eyelids. My mouth

FATE DEMANDS SACRIFICE 101

quivers as I hold my breath. Fin pushes against my shoulders, peeling me off his neck. He slides his hands up to cup my face in them, tilting my head to look at him.

My eyes are raw, squinting against the fire as the tears slide down my cheeks.

His eyebrows are downturned as he scans my face. There's a slight pout to his bottom lip as he wipes my tears with his thumbs, trying to catch any new ones before they fall down.

"As worried as I am based on your reaction," Fin begins, lowering his voice. "I won't ask if you don't want to talk about it."

I inhale through my nose, my lungs expanding until they burn, and then I release the air through my mouth, nodding slowly.

"I'm okay now," I whisper, my voice hoarse, "I thought he was going to die today, Fin. I can't keep up with this, and I'm not learning fast enough."

He unclasps my face from between his hands but moves them down my arms before gripping my waist. His thumb traces a soothing pattern. "Why won't Lightning do this? Why is she making you?"

I shake my head, frowning. "I don't know. She wants this to be a learning opportunity, but I don't understand why she can't get started on things. I don't know if she doesn't want to mess up either and be held responsible if she screws it up… She's got some reason, but I don't know the full story."

"I don't want this to come off as pushy—" Fin pauses,

biting the inside of his cheek before adding, "Do you think you're close to being able to shrink it?"

I consider the daily progress, and I nod. "I know I am. It's a lot of effort to do it, but I think I'll be able to start soon. I might not be able to get rid of all of it at once, but I can hopefully shrink it enough to start chipping away at it."

"And it looks like maybe you've figured out a way to reverse or treat what happened today?" Fin waves his hand over my shoulder at the table behind me.

I twist enough in his lap to eyeball some of the papers precariously dangling off the edge. "I suppose."

Fin chuckles, his chest rumbling with it. He tucks his finger under my chin, turning my head back to him as he says, "Take the wins, oh, Great Reva. You have to remind yourself you are doing the best you can."

I glare at him with stinging eyes, pursing my lips.

He chuckles again, pressing his thumb on my chin just below my lip, whispering, "There's my girl."

The tip of his thumb just grazes the bottom of my lower lip, the touch drawing his attention to it. His throat bobs as he swallows, his eyes drawn back to mine.

The subtle tension between us flares to life. Shadows cast across his face, those glowing eyes like a field of pure, green grass on a summer's day.

His thumb twitches, slowly inching up my lip and pressing down on the supple skin. He gravitates closer, and I allow him to until the tip of his nose brushes mine. My eyes flutter shut.

FATE DEMANDS SACRIFICE 103

Fin skims his lips against mine like a whisper, a question.

Gods, I'm going to hell.

I crash my lips into his, moaning at the familiarity and comfort in them. I snake my hands around his neck, intertwining my fingers in his hair and tugging gently. He answers, moving his mouth against mine as his hands slide down and around my waist.

With my lips still sealed against his, I swing my left leg over his lap, straddling him in the chair. His hands move down, down until he palms my ass in his hands over my dress, groaning against my mouth.

I plunge my tongue into his mouth, rolling my hips forward and silently pleading for him to press me against him, to rip my dress off, to touch me more—

I wouldn't be able to keep my hands off you...

I shrink back at the memory of Tariq's voice in my head, pulling away from Fin to see his face. His lips are swollen from my assault, his eyes wide with shock from...

Well, probably everything.

I pull a hand into my chest, gripping my hematite necklace as the other flies to my lips. I mumble around it, "Oh, Gods. I'm sorry."

Fin grabs my waist again, holding me firm and frowning. "Why are you apologizing, Reva?"

"I can't," I whisper, shaking my head as I peel myself off his lap and start pacing in front of the fire. "I told you I needed space, and I just took advantage of a vulnerable moment."

Frustration flashes across his face as he tilts his head. "I would argue it was more like me taking advantage of *your* vulnerability."

I wave my hand but pause, considering. "Did you?"

"For fuck's sake, Reva," he snaps, staring at me like I'm a stranger before lurching from the chair and adjusting his pants. "After everything we've talked about—after everything we've been through—and you think I would do something like that? You think I'd stoop that low just to… What? Have sex with you? I would think you know me *way* better than that by now."

I fold my arms around my body, staring at the fire and averting my gaze. His boots clicking against the stone floor mixes with the crackling embers until his presence hovers behind me.

"Maybe you were right." I close my eyes against the sorrow in his voice, fresh, new tears itching my throat. "Maybe we need to continue to give each other a little space. Once Clint is better, we can approach whatever it is you want again."

"Fin," I say, twirling on my heel, but his hand is already pulling on the doorknob.

"I brought you dinner, by the way." He gestures to the coffee table where a brown paper bag sits, completely unnoticed by me until now.

My heart sinks, and the crack from earlier deepens when the door slams shut. I stare at the fire longingly, a part of me wanting to run after him.

But I can't shake the feel of Tariq's lips against my

FATE DEMANDS SACRIFICE 105

knuckles.

I yell in frustration, aiming my hand at the decorative vase on the mantle. When the Light collides with it, I wince as it shatters into dust.

CHAPTER 8

Tariq, Fin, and Elly all sit against a far wall of the training area, spectators to my training with Lightning today. She insisted they attend this practice to see the progress I've made in action.

Fin averts his gaze, whether it's from what happened a few days ago or because the true control of my powers is still yet to be seen. Elly hunches where she sits on the ground, her eyes wide in awe, a smile cracking occasionally. Tariq props himself against the wall, standing with one leg crossed over the other and his arms folded over his chest.

That stupid smirk sticks to his lips.

"Next, I want you to create a ball of Light," Lightning instructs, pacing in front of me and demonstrating the size she wants with her own hands. "The size of a handball should do. I want you to gradually increase its size until it's this wide." Again, she holds her arms in front of her, roughly 3 feet wide.

I nod once, smearing the sweat from my forehead into the braid. I stand with my feet shoulder-width apart, mimicking the initial width Lightning requested.

FATE DEMANDS SACRIFICE 107

The Light comes to me so effortlessly now, the ball growing from the size of a coin to the size of a handball instantaneously.

It's a perfect circle with wisps of smokey, white-gold light, reminding me of the moon on a cloudy night, its glow reflecting a translucent haze. The veins running up my hands and arms mirror the same color as the Light, pulsing in time with my heart. I'd guess my eyes have the same golden glow.

After holding the Light momentarily, I let my arms float outward, the ball growing with every inch my arms extend. I concentrate, my heart rate spiking as my arms quiver the wider they go.

"Steady," Lightning warns, her boots crunching in the sand. "Maintain that pace."

"She's gotten really good," I hear Elly's voice softly bounce off the wall. For all I know, she could be whispering, but the acoustics down here are obnoxious.

"I come and watch her most days." Tariq's voice almost makes me waver in my concentration when he says, "I don't think she knows I sneak down here every day."

"Every day, huh?" I grumble through clenched teeth, finally reaching the width Lightning requested. I may not be able to see him, but I can *feel* that smug look from across the room.

"That was great, Reva." Lightning's clap sounds like a chorus.

I release the power, which has become just as

effortless as calling it to me. I no longer worry about it rolling or snapping back into my body like a bandalore. Hope blossoms in my chest as I consider using this power to help Clint.

Elly interjects as if reading my mind, "Reva, you are stunning, as always. Does this mean you can start using it on Clint?"

I turn to Lightning with a raised eyebrow. "What do you think, Teacher?"

"First of all—" Lightning holds up a finger. "I refuse to be called Teacher. Now, Master is something I could get on board with." I snort, rolling my eyes. "Second of all, you've been suppressing both of your god-powers. Now, if you only had one, I would maybe be comfortable with it—"

"That's shit," Fin blurts, springing up from the ground. He marches across the floor to Lightning until there's just a foot between them, sticking his finger in her face. "You keep coming up with a lot of excuses not to help this kid. If I knew any better, I'd think you want him to die."

"Excuse me," Lightning screeches. At the same time, Tariq, Elly, and I shout variations of Fin's name.

What in the Gods...

"You won't step in to help and use these powers you claim to have mastered," Fin sneers, curling his lip. "And now you have an excuse why Reva can't get to work trying to help him?"

"We don't know how that mass will react to her

FATE DEMANDS SACRIFICE 109

messing with it!" Lightning slaps his finger out of her face, standing chest-to-chest with Fin, glaring up at him. "What if she has Phoebe's powers? Did you know Phoebe can cause things to accelerate in speed? What if she accidentally accelerates the mass's growth?

"And if she's Asteria? Gods know what the hell could happen then." Lightning throws up her arms. "Asteria was arguably the most powerful Sirian to have ever lived, so those who descend from her inherit that badge of honor. If she were to accidentally clone that mass, I guarantee your young prince wouldn't survive another mass in his stomach when just one is killing him."

The room falls into a penetrating silence that spears through my gut.

Or maybe it's all the things Lightning has pointed out. While I think I've finally got control over my Sirian powers, I haven't scratched the surface of Dionne or my other one.

Lightning takes two steps back from Fin, putting space between them. "I have a theory I want to test, though, so I'm glad you brought this up. This is actually the real reason I requested you all here today. It should take us in the right direction."

I frown, my head snapping toward her. "What do you mean?"

"Tariq told me about the incident at your first training session with him," Lightning begins, pointing at Tariq and then bending her finger to beckon him over.

Fin's head swivels on his neck, first to Tariq and then

to me, confusion evident in the frown between his brows, narrowed eyes, and parted lips.

Lightning saves me from needing to elaborate as she continues, "He mentioned something to me about the color of your powers and a theory on why the one you only let us have glimpses of is tinted blue instead of gold."

Tariq stands side-by-side with Fin in front of Lightning, arms still folded over his broad chest. He swings his gaze around Fin to look at me, winking.

But my blood boils.

Another person kept something from me. He could've said something when we talked about it together that day, but he chose to speak half his mind.

I'm simmering when Lightning backs away, giving herself a few more feet between the boys. She leisurely twists her head towards me, lifting her hand in front of her face. A small ball of Light swirls there menacingly, illuminating the sly grin spreading across her cheeks. Her eyes glow the white-gold I'm used to seeing in my reflection instead of her normal silvery blue.

"You care about your boys," she chuckles, turning her attention to Tariq and Fin. "And I, for one, have wanted to do this since the library."

"Lightning!" Elly yells, shooting up from the ground.

I hold my hand out to Elly in warning, my other palm facing Lightning, Tariq, and Fin.

Fin takes one step back, but Lighting clicks her tongue against the back of her teeth, shaking her head. "You're a participant today, Sir Finley." She weaves her

FATE DEMANDS SACRIFICE 111

head back to me. "Now, Reva. As if I were wielding the Darkness... Save them."

She moves slowly, but not slow enough. I'm struck dumbfounded as she swings sideways, pulling her arm back as it glows brighter, and I swear there are mini streaks of lightning flickering off her hand.

My mind races, my heart rattling in my ribcage. As always, I'm racing against time, trying to come up with a solution to protect the people I care about.

I could replicate what I did in our first training session together when I snatched the ball of hurtling Light from the air and sucked it back into my body, but that would mean I need to know who Lightning plans on attacking, and she's only got one hand raised. She could also plan to send a stream of Light at both of them, in which case that absorption trick won't work anyway.

If I could just create a barrier...

Bells ring in my head, and I've never felt dumber. When I was young, the rain fell around me when Karasi looked on from the porch, not a drop landing on me or my clothes.

When the knight attacked me in Clint's room, I held his hand mid-air between us with a strange reflection of Light.

When Tariq clapped at me the other day, I projected a wall of blue and white light between us.

Just as the Light leaves Lightning's fingers, I open that never-ending depth of blue-tinged light within me, and it melds in with the white-gold of the Sirian powers.

A straight line shoots out from my hand, hovering just inches from my palm and across the space in front of Tariq and Fin.

Fin flinches, throwing a hand up to veil his face, but Tariq stares in wonder as the blue wobbles on impact. When the Light bounces off the wall in front of them, it feels like the Light is bouncing off my body, as if someone jabbed me in the stomach.

Despite that, the wall stays in place, a burning cold spreading up my arms as it settles into my veins longer than it has ever been allowed to.

"Hold it as long as you can," Lightning quietly whispers, dumbfounded.

I fight the biting at the base of my neck as the burning spreads. My hair lifts at the ends, flowing around me like I'm underwater. Aside from the low hum reverberating from the wall of Light, the room is eerily silent, as if the creatures that live in the crevices have ceased movement.

A searing, cold blaze casts up my arm like a blade of ice slicing me, breaking my control. I cry out in pain and shock, falling hard to my knees in the sand. Someone shouts my name, but I can't hear past the ringing in my ears.

I press my forehead to the ground, breathing as I will my heart back to a normal rhythm. Two legs crouch in front of me, and a hand presses underneath my chin, raising my head. I meet Tariq's glittering, amber eyes.

"You alright there, Starfire?" he breathes, chuckling in disbelief.

FATE DEMANDS SACRIFICE 113

His warm finger is like a brand on my skin, all senses fixated on the featherlight touch. My mind swims as the blue Light settles beneath the line again, just like the burnished gold of his gaze swirls as he waits for my response.

Kneeling before the Crown Prince brings a new warmth to my stomach.

"I bet you love..." I can't help the smile cracking my exterior, managing through my pants, "To see your Healer on all fours in front of you."

"Oh Gods, Reva," he laughs, rolling his eyes, but he unabashedly grips both my arms to hoist me onto my feet. "All that power went straight to your head, didn't it?"

"Shielding." Lightning gawks, her face void of any emotion. "You have Energy shielding."

"What does that mean?" Fin shouts, stirring himself out of the strange trance he was in. "What was that?"

"I just told you, dumbass," Lightning grumbles, leaving Fin rooted to his spot as she strolls over to meet Tariq and me. "Energy shielding is exactly as it sounds. You create a shield using the extra god-power. From what I read in Jorah's books, she could use the shield to absorb Energy, negate it, redirect it, or redouble it and send it back to the dealer."

"Who did?" I ask, still struggling to catch my breath. I lift both arms above my head like Tariq taught me, interlocking my fingers on top of my braid.

"Asteria," Elly answers from the other side of the room.

I blanch, my stomach dropping. "The so-called most powerful Sirian to ever live?"

"The one and only." Lightning clasps my shoulder, and I wince. "Even before the Korbins wiped us all out, tracking Asteria's descendant line was difficult, so they say she only ever had one line. I suppose she knew what she was capable of and didn't want to share."

"I highly doubt that was her thought process," Tariq chastises, his hand resting gingerly on my shoulder blade.

"How did you guess this?" I flick my gaze from Lightning to Tariq, and even Elly by the wall.

"After we talked about the difference in stars, I asked Elly about the difference between Asteria and Phoebe." Tariq walks in front of me, gently peeling one of my arms down from my head. After I lower it, he slips his hands into his pockets, and I simper. "When she said Asteria pulled from the galaxy and stars versus Phoebe from the moon, I knew I had to talk to Lightning."

I can't help thinking maybe he should've talked to me, and I stop trembling from the cold as my veins turn molten.

"If you had Phoebe's god-power, your other glow would be more like a pure white or white and silver glow," Lightning interjects. "I've watched you shove it down multiple times, so I figured you would need incentive to try it out."

My jaw flexes as I clench my hands into fists on either side of me. "Next time you two want to run an experiment on me, consult me first."

FATE DEMANDS SACRIFICE 115

"You weren't the one about to be shot at with Light," Fin grumbles from his spot in the middle of the room.

I level him with a glare before returning my attention to the schemers before me. "I don't use that power because the first time I ever did, Karasi looked *worried*."

"It's probably because she realized you had two god-powers." Lightning purses her lips at me.

"That's not the only reason," I snap. Tariq's eyebrows raise, scrutinizing my tantrum. "For one, it burns. I told Tariq how it feels to wield this power. It's like ice in my veins. Second of all, I've just gotten used to wielding the Light. This other power is endless."

"What do you mean endless?" Lightning asks, but she unfolds her arms from across her chest.

"I can feel where the reservoir ends for the Energy," I explain, holding one of my hands in a straight line with my arm. I wave my other hand underneath. "The god-power is below it, and it has no bottom."

"If Asteria pulled from the galaxy and the stars," Tariq mulls, scratching his beard and turning to Lightning with a shrug. "As far as we know, the universe is endless. It would make sense if that power well is, too. Or at least so deep she's never seen the bottom."

"She's standing right here." I stomp my foot for emphasis, but Tariq's eyes flicker down to my foot and back up to my face with an eyebrow raised as if to say *really?*

I curl my lip in a snarl.

"There's a lot I am going to need to discuss with the

Elders," Lighting sighs, her fingers pressing against her temple. "I really think you need to meet them, Reva. Now that we know your other god-power, it's time."

"I can't leave this castle until I know Clint is stable." I shake my head fiercely, my braid whipping across my neck. "Until then, it's going to have to wait."

"Before we try anything on Clint," she says, walking towards the exit. "We need to make sure you have control over the line between Asteria's god-power and the Energy so you don't do something... stupid."

"Thanks for the vote of confidence." I scrunch my lips in a faux, tight-lipped grin.

"I'm here for the honesty," she calls over her shoulder, her gray dreads swinging across her back. She skirts around the doorway, disappearing within the corridor.

The rest of us are not far behind. Elly meets us directly under the archway to lead Tariq and me up the stairs while Fin drags behind us, keeping a fair distance.

"Did you know about this?" I grill Elly, casting her a sidelong glance.

"Despite him coming to me about Asteria and Phoebe..." She frowns, but it's directed at her twin. "No, I didn't. You're keeping things from me, brother?"

"Don't *brother* me," Tariq chuckles darkly, strands of dark blond falling into his face as he shakes his head. "I would have discussed this theory with you if you'd been in the library when I sought out Lightning. I thought it'd be easier to explain to everyone else by demonstration."

Elly doesn't seem to buy it, her frown transforming

FATE DEMANDS SACRIFICE 117

into a scowl. She even huffs as she snaps her head forward, focusing on the steps.

"Well, I would've liked it if you discussed *my* powers with *me*," I add, glaring at him. "If you had this theory when we were training, why didn't you discuss it further?"

"We were training." Tariq shrugs, but he fights the grin tugging at the corner of his lips. "We were also discussing other topics that seemed more... important."

He turns his head entirely toward me, danger dancing in those eyes. I clench my jaw to avoid saying anything stupid, like calling the Crown Prince of Mariande a brute.

"You're not going to win this one," Fin interjects from behind us, gaining a few steps closer. "Elly and Reva have become thick as thieves, and when you've got them on the same side, nothing you say will move them."

Tariq throws his head over his shoulder, rolling his eyes at Fin, which earns a breath of laughter and a quirk of Fin's lips.

Reaching the top steps, Elly sticks her head out to make sure the coast is clear before we all file out of the concealed doorway. Fin mumbles something about needing to get to his shift before stalking down the hallway.

Elly points her finger at Tariq. "We'll talk tonight—" She reels on me, her face softer. "I'll catch up with you later, Reva. If Clint's okay, come to the library after dinner. And don't bail on me!"

I wait for her to round the corner before twisting

on my heels to face Tariq fully. I glare at him with my nails digging into my palms, and my irritation flares at the smug smirk glued to his face.

"You're going to yell at me, aren't you?" he says from the corner of his mouth.

I flare my nostrils, trying to control the contradicting emotions. Anger and frustration from something being kept from me *yet again*, and anxiety at the proximity between us around Fin, especially after my incidents with them both.

Instead, I march towards my room, if only because I know Tariq will follow me.

"Reva," he calls, his quick footsteps catching up to me. "Why is this so serious for you? We figured out your other god-power. You'd think you'd be excited—"

"I'm not," I snap, briefly glancing at him and regretting it. His eyes are wide in shock, confusion contorting his face. "You really don't know much about me, Tariq."

"Then let me in, Reva," Tariq blurts, and my heart clenches in my chest.

I shy away, the warmth rising from my chest to my face. Under a hushed breath, I say, "I can't discuss this with you here."

Tariq stares at me, his Crown Prince mask slipped over so I can't read any of his emotions. He peers down the hallway on both sides of us before snatching my wrist in his and yanking me through the nearest door.

It's nothing more than a washroom equipped with a

FATE DEMANDS SACRIFICE

119

bucket, spout, mop, and broom. When I turn to where he stands guard in front of the door, arms crossed over his chest, I count maybe four feet between us.

He waves his hand. "Well, have at it then."

I squint, inhaling. "First of all, how dare you?" Tariq's eyes flicker with amusement, a smile tugging at his lips.

"Second of all, you don't understand a thing about me. Gods, some days I don't. Who I am has been kept from me my entire life, and I am learning so many things I never knew. Karasi spoke in riddles and lessons instead of just outright telling me things. I constantly feel like I don't have any real control over my own Fate and that it's all just a giant game.

"And lastly, just because we figured out my power doesn't make me happy. In fact, it scares me. I have a bottomless pit of it that pulls from the stars that I can't even control. For fun, let's add fire into the mix." My voice rises by the end of my rant, my breath coming out as huffs. "What am I supposed to do with all of this?"

I've taken steps closer to him, so only a foot is now between us. He raises an eyebrow, giving me a moment to collect myself. I take a few deep breaths in and out, calming my racing heart.

After I feel a little less chaotic, his voice permeates the silence, "Better?"

I tilt my head to the side and peer up at him. "You're arrogant."

He tilts his head back, a laugh bursting from his lips. I can't help the slow grin that climbs up my cheeks, the weightlessness in my chest making my heart flutter.

His laugh subsides, but the smile is still on his face when he reaches between us, grabbing my shoulders in his hands. He hunches forward so we're level, explaining, "Any time you want to vent, Starfire, let me know. I'll shove you into the nearest room, and we can have at it."

The image that the last statement conjures into my head only furthers the conflicting feelings of wanting to be angry with him and wanting to know the taste of those full lips.

"It doesn't count when you're the one who caused me to vent in the first place," I grumble, trying to ignore the rising heat in my stomach.

He shrugs, still holding onto my shoulders as he leans in further. "It got you to open up a little bit, both downstairs with your powers and your anxieties with me. Now, in the future, I know you prefer I discuss things with you in great detail rather than assume how you'll react."

The urge to snarl at him is overwhelming.

Instead, I muster a neutral face that I've seen him conjure repeatedly, braving a stare down.

Instead of getting him riled up, he scans my face from where my Mark is hidden behind my salve to my eyes, then lingers on my lips. My own attention is drawn back to his naturally pouty lower lip calling my name.

One of his hands moves from my shoulder, sliding up to cup the side of my neck, and that warmth in my stomach spreads lower. His thumb tucks underneath my

FATE DEMANDS SACRIFICE

chin, pressing and tilting my head. He uncurls from his hunch, which only moves my body closer to him.

A low hum rumbles in his chest, the vibrations rattling my bones. "I told you I wouldn't be able to help myself."

My mouth goes dry, and I swallow, keeping my body as still as possible. My voice comes out gravelly when I say, "Help yourself?"

Why does this man put me at a loss for words?

His face bends toward mine, his beard tickling my cheek as he lowers his lips to my ear. My back presses into the wall beside the door, trapping my body between it and Tariq's broad chest, my hands stuck at my sides.

Anticipation tingles at my fingertips.

"I felt your power emanating from you downstairs," he whispers into my ear, his breath caressing it. "When I helped you up, all I could think about was what that power would taste like."

I hold my breath as he gently brushes his teeth along my earlobe, my knees quivering as I clench my legs together.

"And yes, Reva," he whispers again, pulling back to lock his blazing gaze onto mine. "Seeing my Healer on all fours definitely did *something*."

Gods, save me.

His hands trail down my body, my skin prickling. He stops their journey at my waist, gripping tightly as he hauls my body into his.

I gasp, my hands splaying across his chest, finding

nothing but honed muscle underneath his tunic. Every part of our bodies touches now, from my breasts down to my thighs.

His voice is low and sultry when he says, "I deserve an award for how much restraint I've shown."

I want to tell him to take his reward—to take me—but instead, I repeat myself. "You're arrogant."

"That mouth," he growls, pressing his hips into mine, drawing my attention to the firm length between us. "You're going to send me to my knees."

Shockingly, he gently pushes us apart, his forearms flexing at the effort it seems to require. He reaches for the door handle and says, "But it would be an honor to kneel before you."

My mind empties, and my mouth drops open as he leaves me standing alone in the washroom, the door slightly ajar.

"Gods," I breathe, all the tension leaving my body with that puff of air.

CHAPTER 9

I stare at Elly behind her desk, frozen in front of the library door. She's hunched over a pile of books, as usual, both eyebrows raising at the sight of me.

"You want to talk about it now?" Elly asks with a devilish grin.

"I don't know how I got myself into this position," I say through clenched teeth, dragging my feet to her desk. I throw myself into the chair across from her and ask, "How did I get myself into this position?"

Elly chuckles darkly, slowly lowering into the chair behind her with eyes pinned on me. "And what position, pray tell, is that?"

I deadpan, "This stupid triangle between Fin and Tariq."

She presses her lips together and angles her head, humming. "I thought you weren't focusing on men."

"I'm not—" She levels me with a glare, so I correct, "I wasn't. I told Fin that weeks ago, and I've reiterated it to him. Especially regarding his feelings towards my powers. I think earlier made it even more evident that he doesn't know what to do with the fact I'm some all-powerful being."

Elly rolls her eyes but shrugs her shoulders. "And what about my brother?"

"When I'm about to vent to you and ask for advice on men, it'd help if you didn't refer to him as your brother."

She laughs, tipping her head back before she manages around a mischievous giggle, "But he is my brother, Reva. Not just my brother but my *twin*."

"Is that a problem?" I question, raising an eyebrow.

She blows her lips out, waving me away. "I don't care. I am not his keeper. He can do whatever he wants."

"Okay, then," I sigh, slouching into the chair. "Anyways, like I said, I did tell Fin I can't be focusing on whatever's been happening..." She waits, an eyebrow raised. "But Tariq is complicating that because *he* keeps focusing on *me*."

"I told you I've never seen him this intrigued by someone before." She shakes her head, that playful glee lighting up her eyes, identical to said twin brother. "You know you have all the power to tell him to leave you alone if it bothers you, but by the sheepish look you're giving me, I'm going to guess it doesn't bother you."

"Not in the 'I want you to stop' way," I finally admit aloud.

I can't deny my attraction to Tariq—I mean, he's *immaculate*—but this is something I've never experienced before. It's magnetic, and I find myself unintentionally gravitating toward him when we're in the same room. There are moments I want to slap him, and then there

FATE DEMANDS SACRIFICE 125

are other moments when he brings an inner peace I don't even realize is there until he's walking away from me.

Not to mention the things he does to make me imagine his hands everywhere, my hands everywhere…

Elly clears her throat. A slack, bored look on her face reveals she knows where my thoughts have gone.

"I didn't think much of Tariq until the day he trained me on Lightning's behalf," I explain to her, keeping my gaze latched onto my hands, twisting in my lap. "The tension is clearly there, and we tease each other, but I thought that was it. But this is more… It's been like a moth to a flame.

"Then, to complicate it more, Fin came to check on me when I missed dinner…" I slam my head into my hands, groaning. Elly's breathy chuckles echo as I yank my hands through the strands of my hair. "Something happened that I know is my fault and shouldn't have. I stopped it before we were reckless, and Fin got mad for the first time. He's been giving me the cold shoulder since, and I don't blame him."

"You can't keep leaving yourself alone with him," Elly offers, frowning. "I don't blame Fin for getting upset. You're giving him even more mixed signals than you were over a month ago."

"You think I don't know that?" I point my finger at her. "I'm well aware I've screwed up there. But I agree. His shifts have allowed us time apart, giving me time to think."

"And what do you need to think about Reva?" Elly

snorts. "My brother?"

I grind my teeth together, lips thinned and eyes wide. I nearly growl at her, and it's because she's right.

"I can't be left alone with him either," I whisper. "We get closer and closer to crossing a dangerous line every time we're left alone."

"How dangerous?" Elly teases, the corner of her mouth quirking up, alarmingly similar to Tariq.

"Do you really want to know the specific details of what your brother said to me in a washroom?" Her wince is answering enough, but I explain, "We haven't kissed, but we've been close. And the fact we haven't even kissed is also baffling because somehow the things we've said to each other are—"

"I think I get the picture," she grumbles, adjusting her wavy, golden blonde locks. "I don't understand what's dangerous about a fling?"

I roll my bottom lip between my teeth, considering. "He's the Crown Prince of Mariande, and I'm your Royal Healer. You can't tell me that's not a problem."

"No one's asking you to marry him, Reva," Elly giggles, reaching for a book nearby. "You can have *fun*, you know. Maybe it'd relieve some pent-up stress."

"My reasoning for Fin would also stand with Tariq." I lean forward. "I don't want things to get complicated. I have too much on my plate with Clint, especially now. And with this looming responsibility to master my powers, meet the Elders, and lead an army I've never met? I can't fathom it."

"I know, Reva. I'm sorry you're so overwhelmed with responsibility right now that you can't find room for..." Elly takes a deep breath, stretching the book out between us. "I think you just have so much swirling in your head that you're trying to chase. Regardless, you know I'm here for you and, in his weird ways, so is Tariq."

I roll my eyes, hesitantly accepting the book from her. "And this is your way of sympathizing with me? Giving me more research?"

"I've spent all day digging through the books I've found on Gods and demi-gods," Elly says, averting my question. "There's nothing new on Asteria and Dionne besides the myths I showed you."

"You mean Asteria being a military general for Eldamain?" I carefully flip through the pages of the book, the one with the sketches of Gods and demi-gods where I saw Asteria's shield.

Elly wags her finger at me, searching through the mountain of books on her desk. "I couldn't get that out of my head, and I've been researching since we last spoke about it. I can't find anything in our collection about why an extremely powerful demi-god would be a general. I think we'll have to lean on Ruhan for that at some point."

"While he's here for the Glow Ball?" I ask, pausing to glance up at Elly.

She gnaws on the inside of her cheek. "I don't know if there's a conspicuous way to ask Ruhan about a Sirian demi-god without raising questions. He and Tariq are a match when it comes to wit and observation. He will go digging."

"So, we have to wait until…" I trail off, propping my elbow on the desk and holding my hand. "What? He knows that Sirians are in the world, both Dark and Light trying to battle?"

Elly glares at me before resuming her hunt through her books. "That's one way to put it. Unless Tariq can figure out a way to out-wit him, I don't have a clue how to navigate it."

"Princess Eloise Hesper," I huff, feigning shock. "Did you just admit to not knowing something?"

"Honestly, Reva," Elly laughs, throwing her head up to the sky in silent prayer. "You're something else today."

I shrug, focusing back on my art studies. "Okay, what else have you been questioning that you needed to hand me this book? I've already looked at the pictures."

She slams a heavy tome on the desk in front of me, an empty china glass rattling somewhere. I startle, frowning at her.

That sly little grin she gets is plastered on her face, her eyes twinkling in the dimly lit evening light. "My philosophy in life is to always ask questions, no matter how stupid they sound."

She runs her hand over the leather cover of the tome, caressing it like a long-lost lover. She's beaming as she says, "So many of these demi-gods ruled kingdoms. Enki was the son of Rod and a human woman, and we know him as the First King. Phoebe was eventually Queen of Etherea, Dionne was King of Riddling, and Taranis was

FATE DEMANDS SACRIFICE 129

also King of the Northern Pizi. But for how long?"

"I would assume until their death or until they wanted their kids to take over," I guess, but that sits wrong on my tongue.

"If Magics can live hundreds of years like Jorah and Karasi, how long does a demi-god live?" Elly asks, her gaze meeting mine. "How long do their descendants?"

My heart stops in my chest, my blood running cold.

I never considered my lifespan would be any different from that of a mortal. Sirians' lives are usually a typical mortal life span; at least any books Karasi could provide for me growing up alluded to that.

It never crossed my mind I could live past one hundred, let alone as long as Jorah or Karasi. I could significantly outlive all my friends.

Those inner demons Willem, Remy, and Dahlia constantly battled giggle in the back of my conscious.

I shake them away, focusing back on Elly and her research. "I would assume they are almost immortal."

"That's what I thought, too." Elly tucks a stray golden strand behind her ear. "I never thought the demi-gods involved themselves in the lives of mortals that directly, not enough to have led at least three separate countries. Myths and religions are very vehement that the Gods coveted their children, so how involved did the Gods get in the mortal world, and for how long? Did they stop when their children passed on, whatever that means? Or did they stick around for a few generations?"

"And when did the Gods and demi-gods start

disappearing?" I finish for her. "Well, at least, start having less involvement. I've always wondered where they go when they die."

"Another beautiful question." Elly claps her hands together. "I'm such a good influence."

I roll my eyes so far back it hurts. "Alright, Professor. So, were you able to find anything? I have a hard time believing that if you don't have anything on a general in Eldamain, you're not going to have much on how long Gods live."

"Yeah," Elly suspires, tapping the book. "I had to collect different accounts and work with an assistant to date them." My eyes widen, but she waves me away. "Since I was looking for all of them, it was easy to play it off as a bigger project."

She reaches underneath the desk, pulling out a few pages of loose parchment with scribbles in different handwriting. I snatch them from her hands, the anxiety still fluttering in my chest from involving more people in our business.

The Gods' and demi-gods' names are listed on the pages, first the Gods and then their children underneath them. Beside their names are two wobbly columns labeled *First Appearance* and *Last Appearance*, respectively. Each column beside the names has a date or question mark and three words.

The first is Morana, the Goddess of Death and Magic. Elly and her assistant were only able to find one mention of her in their digging, placing her well over three thousand years ago in Eldamain. The words beside the date are *child*, *gift*, and *Avalanches*.

Underneath her is the only child she had, the demi-god Sybil, who is responsible for creating the House of Echidna. Her first mention is the same date as Morana's, and her three words are the same.

I'm guessing this refers to the story of Sybil's birth.

The last mention of Sybil dates back nearly one thousand years ago, shortly before the Korbins essentially decimated the Sirians and sent Magics scattering. The words associated with her are *Magics, Korbin,* and *vanished*.

I could spend an entire day asking Elly questions about all the Gods and demi-gods listed here, but I'm more interested in the ones I descend from. I want to know when they last walked this plane because maybe it can lead me to my heritage or help us find answers to questions we're not even asking yet.

Like how long I'll live.

I'm almost surprised to see that Danica was last seen at the same time as Sybil with nearly the same words, except *Magics* is switched out for *Sirians*.

"I never thought the Gods *actually* vanished when the Korbins went wild," I explain, lifting my head. "You're telling me you found a story around that time?"

"Well, not exactly." Elly grins sheepishly. "You said yourself that Magics believe the Gods left when the Korbins were killing Sirians and Magics. That's a myth, so there has to be something to it. Whether Magics have passed down tales or somehow watched the Gods leave us, then we have to count that as the last time anyone heard from them."

I stare at the page, disappointed she hasn't found anything new.

The dates for all of Danica's children predate the Korbins. The gap between Asteria's first mention to her last mention makes her almost a thousand years old, and the last time she was mentioned was roughly three thousand years ago. The other demi-gods look to have been in the hundreds as well.

"So demi-gods can live hundreds of years." I hand the stack of papers back to her. She eyes me suspiciously. "How long did their kids live? Their grandkids?"

"How long will you live is what you're asking me?" she whispers, her face downturned. She shakes her head slowly, her eyes soft. "I would say not to worry about it, but you have two demi-gods power in your veins. Maybe Jorah can help."

"Because Karasi isn't much of a big help." I remember the dream I had with her in it the other night. Her phantom touch sends shivers down my spine, but none more than what Elly says next.

"I found something about Karasi."

My head lurches back. I open my mouth to ask what she means, but nothing comes out, my throat clogged with emotion.

She averts her gaze, looking toward the door. "We were only making a list of the Gods and demi-gods, so I didn't want to write any other descendants down if I

FATE DEMANDS SACRIFICE   133

thought it'd lead to a dead end. I can't go around making family trees—"

"Elly," I snap, my heart now working overtime as my vision gradually tunnels in on where she bites her lip. I soften. "Please."

She presses her lips together, folds her hands, and fiddles with her fingers. "Sybil's powers as a Magic and demi-god made her an exceptional healer. She could cure disease, and there were myths she could raise people from the dead, being Morana's daughter and all. It also said she had prophetic powers."

If time could stop, I would argue Elly has the power to do it.

My pulse thrums in my head, and my stomach churns, the bile burning up my esophagus.

"There was another tale that talked about Sybil having only one child, because being Death's daughter made it near impossible to conceive children. She had prophecy powers like Sybil, and King Korbin even called on her when she was young." Elly pauses, letting me absorb. My mind is empty, just like my body is empty of all emotion. "They called her the Great Child."

I soar from my seat, the chair clattering to the ground, deafening in this silent library. Elly doesn't flinch, but her eyes glisten with tears.

Something wet and warm falls down my cheek.

"Reva, I'm so sorry," Elly pleads, carefully rising from her seat. "I debated telling you but I know you don't like things kept from you, and I promise I just discovered this after we all met this morning. I didn't want to add more to your never-ending plate of responsibility and unearthed secrets—"

"I'm not upset with you," I manage through the anger bubbling in my chest like molten fire. I swallow the smokey burn in the back of my throat. "I'm grateful for you. I'm just angry that Karasi was a descendant of a demi-god, something she had to have known *damn* well I was, and if anyone could understand this feeling of 'other', it would have been her. And she didn't share it with me."

Elly reaches across the desk, her hand landing where mine would have been if I'd stayed in my seat. "You said so yourself that Karasi would keep things from you because of her prophecies and what that would do to the outcome. You know she had a reason to do what she did."

"It doesn't make it hurt any less," I yell, throwing my hands out wide. The throbbing in my head shoots through me, snaking through my veins. The hot, scalding burn reminds me of the power I've been suppressing for too long.

"I really am sorry, Reva," Elly whispers, sitting back in the chair.

"I just want to know where I come from." My throat closes up as I grab my bag from off the floor, so I'm quieter as I continue, "Who I am, who my parents were, what that means for me, what my future is... I feel like I don't know the first thing about myself."

Despite sharing this information about Karasi and

comforting me, Elly sits back in her seat, her lips pressed together as if hesitant.

It's unsettling, and I'm unsure what to think. Based on the burning in my veins, I'm hoping my power hasn't been flashing in and out.

She's threatened me about using my firepower in the library before.

"We'll figure it out," she whispers, wrapping her arms over her stomach.

Before she can say anything more, I nod once before leaving the library, worried that if I stay in there any longer, I'll set the place ablaze.

Chapter 10

"You have a small fever." I squint at the thermometer, shaking it out before placing it on his nightstand. I peek at him from the corner of my eye, eyebrow raised. "Does anything feel wrong outside what we've been dealing with?"

Clint closes his eyes, slowly ticking his head back and forth, hunched forward with his hands in his lap. The deep purple around his eyes hits me square in the chest as he flickers them toward me. "Can I go back to sleep now?"

I press my lips together into a half-hearted grin, nodding once as I motion Pax over. He quickly moves but is gentle when he carefully slips his arms under Clint's back and knees, adjusting him to lie down. Clint winces, hissing through clenched teeth. Once we've got him on his back, it's not long before he closes his eyes and his breathing slows.

Ever since his last episode, Clint has gradually declined. He sleeps most days, conscious enough to let me know how he's feeling and give me a smile or two to convince me his spirit lives. My hands tremble every time

FATE DEMANDS SACRIFICE 137

I administer another dose of medicine, and my vision blurs around the edges. I can't be sure my heart even beats at a healthy rhythm as I watch him sleep, his chest rising and falling.

After I came in from my morning training with both Lightning and Tariq, he had woken up to receive some broth and medicine, but he's been even quieter than normal.

Pax takes up his usual spot by the window now, but he's slumped forward in the chair, twirling his sword between his legs.

He never takes his gaze off Clint unless I ask for assistance moving or changing him. The corners of his eyes are tinged red, and his face is slack, which contradicts his usual demeanor. Even his uniform is disheveled, his jacket completely unbuttoned to reveal the white tunic layered underneath and his dangling necklace.

"Have you been sleeping?" I ask Pax quietly, adjusting Clint's blanket. The young prince whimpers in his sleep, his face scrunching in discomfort.

"I spend all my time here," Pax admits, the chair creaking underneath him as he readjusts his position. "Ever since his episode… I can't leave him alone."

"You shouldn't have to do that." I peer over my shoulder, pressing my brows together. "The other Magics come in to watch him through the night. They will come get me if something happens."

"They do a good job," he grumbles, avoiding my gaze. "I just feel like I need to do this. It should be me or someone he knows if…"

Burning tickles the back of my throat, stealing my breath away. I swallow against the threatening tears.

I will admit I've come to appreciate Pax's honesty, but Gods, does it sting.

A few rapid knocks on the door are the only warning we get before two chortling men burst through the door. Tariq stands directly behind Fin, his hand clasped on his shoulder, with Elly trailing behind them, who looks less than pleased to be accompanying them. Pax and I exchange a brief glance at each other before checking Clint, whose restless sleep makes his face scrunch up again.

"Would you two hush?" Pax hisses through clenched teeth, gripping the handle of his sword between both hands.

The two men pause mid-stroll as Elly quietly shuts the door behind them. Tariq and Fin finally notice Clint's sleeping, limp body on the bed, flinching at the sight of him.

I look down at the poor kid again, studying the grayish hue of his skin and the bruised circles around his eyes. He's stopped shivering, but his breathing is shallower. A lead weight settles into the pit of my stomach.

"Sorry," Tariq whispers, walking over to clap Pax quietly on the back. "You two seem to be cordial."

Pax and I ignore him. Elly steps beside me, curling her arm around my back and resting her head on my shoulder as she watches her brother sleep.

"What brings you guys here?" I ask her, but Tariq answers instead.

"We thought maybe our little brother could use a visit from his favorite people," he explains quietly. I peer at him from the corner of my eye as he walks up to the other side of Clint's bed. "Maybe having everyone here at once could lift his spirits."

"He's not been awake much these last few days," I mutter quietly, sliding my gaze back to Clint. "Only for a few hours of the day. He just went back to sleep."

"Does he say anything?" Fin asks, his tone incredulous.

"Occasionally," Pax answers. "He'll talk about the Glow Ball, him and Reva—"

"Him and Reva?" Fin and Tariq exclaim at the same time. Pax shushes them as Elly pokes her free hand into my side, and I tap her shin with the heel of my shoe.

"Clint is taking Reva to the Glow Ball," Elly interjects, tilting forward to converse around me. "They're going to be wearing matching colors."

"Reva," Fin whispers, but I refuse to acknowledge the awe in his voice. I keep my eyes glued on Clint, frowning as he exhales and pauses far longer than normal. After he inhales again, the next breath is quick.

I calmly slip from Elly's grasp, moving aimlessly so I don't alert the others of my impromptu examination. I sit beside Clint on the bed, brushing his hair back from his cold head. They continue to chatter about the Glow Ball and who's coming, but I'm more concerned about Clint's irregular breathing. I inconspicuously slide my fingers to his pulse, my heart rate spiking in contrast to his slow beats.

I can't contain my trembling hands as I peel back the covers, feeling the pulse at his wrist to make sure I'm not hallucinating. At the pulse slowing there, too, I reach for his bed shirt.

"Reva?" Tariq questions, concern laced in his voice.

The room silences as I lift Clint's shirt, my heart and stomach dropping to the floor as my hand flies to my lips.

The pale skin of his stomach and chest are blotchy and mottled like the blood is struggling to circulate. Bile burns in my chest, and I have to swallow it as I lunge for the side table, sifting through my vials.

"Reva, what's happening?" Elly asks, panicked, as she nears me.

I shake my head, unable to keep the tears at bay as they slide down my face. My hands quiver as I scan the vials, tossing any that might not work to the floor.

Hell, I don't know what to look for right now.

My voice quivers as I explain, "His breathing is shallow and irregular, and he's losing circulation in his abdomen. I'm trying to—I don't know what…"

The scream that rips from my throat scratches it raw as I launch the crate of vials across the room, glass shattering and ricocheting in different directions.

"Reva!" Pax yells, the clatter of his chair echoing as he shuffles towards me. He grips my arms hard enough to

FATE DEMANDS SACRIFICE

141

bruise, twirling me around.

One look at his face and the stark clarity has me burying my head in my hands. He releases me, shoving me back with little passion as he takes a few steps back, his hands still hovering between us.

"Reva..." Elly's voice quivers, and her timidness tells me she already knows.

"I think the mass is cutting off the blood supply of a major artery in his stomach." I choke out around a sob, "He's dying. Right now."

"Do something!" Elly screams, lunging for the bed. She cups Clint's face in her hands. "Oh, Clint, please. Don't do this now. You can fight this."

"He can't fight something like this," I whisper, barely audible.

I'm frozen in place, unable to act. My vision blackens around the edges like I'm looking through a hole in a door. Every limb of my body trembles, my stomach swirling as I fight the urge to vomit on the floor.

I don't even register Tariq standing in front of me until he grabs my head between his hands and tilts it until we lock eyes.

"Clint is dying," Tariq says, yanking me back into my body. Time stands still as he nods once, adding, "He'll die if you don't try something, so it's time to take that risk."

My internal clock starts ticking again, slowly at first, before rushing to catch up with reality. I'm thrown back into my body, my arms falling limp at my sides. My gaze flickers to Pax, who stands watching Tariq and me with nothing but horrified curiosity.

I quickly walk over to the side of Clint's bed with Tariq, who gently grabs Elly's shoulders to peel her off Clint. She snarls, shoving him away. As she tries to ward off her twin, Pax moves quickly, wrapping both of his arms around her middle and restraining her against his chest.

I focus on Clint as Elly's screams in protest fade out of existence. I lay both hands on Clint's stomach and shut my eyes, imagining the mass as a cluster of Energy, trying to discern its vibrations.

It doesn't take me long to find.

It's massive compared to a month ago, nearly the size of his entire stomach and extending into the lower half of his esophagus. It pulses with Energy like a fresh wound that throbs with the beat of his heart, struggling to pump blood through his body and his lungs warring against the lack of fuel to keep them going. I swallow the lump in my throat as I push the noise, distractions, and time from my senses.

I follow my instincts, and maybe it's fate guiding me again.

I open up my body, cracking it down the middle to make space for the Energy this mass is made up of. Instead, a rush of blazing ice bursts through my chest, temporarily knocking the wind out of me, even as it spreads to every limb.

I push my palms further into Clint's stomach, his distant whimper muted by the thrumming in my ears, a

FATE DEMANDS SACRIFICE

143

steady drum beating.

You are mine to command, I call to the mass, projecting some of my own Energy like a beacon. *You will come to me.*

It resists me, flaring a bright white-gold in my mind, ready to battle. I grit my teeth, barely registering my head tilt to the side.

You cannot defy me, a strange, foreign voice shouts back at the mass, a mix of my own with something chillingly unfamiliar. *I am made of the Universe and the Stars... and I command you.*

It flares white-gold once more, dimming as if it's trying to hide from me.

I reach beyond the line within me, gathering the white-blue-tinged Light into my mind. The coldness coursing through my veins turns frigid, and I tremble at the rigidity.

I surround the mass of Energy within a shield of this strange power, and it stops pulsing and glowing altogether, the connection to Clint —its lifeforce—cut off.

The memory of lightning striking the trees of the Overgrowns flashes into my mind, and I try to replicate that. With it trapped, I attack.

Like storm clouds in the sky, I send a single strike of white-blue lightning into the mass from the shield, and I swear I hear it cry out in a high-pitched ring. I wait a few seconds before I strike again, eliciting the same response.

I repeat this cycle over and over again, and after about two dozen strikes I notice the size of the mass has reduced.

Not as much as one would think, but enough so there are a few centimeters of space freed on one side of the shield.

I don't know how long I continue to strike the mass with the power of Asteria, but when Clint gasps, the deafening sound crashes through my concentration. My eyes snap open, and the first thing I notice is Clint's wide, frantic eyes as his breath comes in sweeping pants. He stares at me in awe as some of the mottled skin fades to its normal hue.

I yank my hands off his stomach but keep them hovered above just in case I need to go back in. A drop of sweat runs down the side of my face, fully restoring my senses in a wave of fatigue. My body trembles from the cold power, and I sway slightly, but a hand steadies against my shoulder. I swallow, the saliva dragging against my dry throat.

"How are you feeling, Clint?" Fin interjects, his voice barely audible.

"Like I'm not going to die," Clint replies hoarsely, glancing down at his body. "I feel different."

"I would expect so," Elly giggles around tears, choking on a sob. I'm finally able to feel all my limbs again, my extremities tingling.

"Do you need help?" Tariq's voice asks in my ear, and all I can do is nod.

His arms cup under my elbows, his grip firm as I straighten my legs, and I'm lifted off the side of Clint's bed. My knees wobble as I try to steady myself, so Tariq tightens his hold.

FATE DEMANDS SACRIFICE   145

Elly rushes in front of me, her hands running over Clint's face, torso, and arms as she frantically examines him. Once satisfied, she grips his cheeks in her hands and kisses his forehead in rapid succession. He has the gall to swat her away, grimacing.

And she lets him because she's suddenly facing me, gently tearing my arms from Tariq's grip to transfer my weight into her.

"You did it," she breathes, her face a mess of dried tears and strands of golden hair clinging to the sides of her face. "You saved him."

"For now," is all I can manage through my exhaustion. I don't think my heart has slowed a beat since the moment I realized Clint was dying.

"But we know you can do it," Elly laughs, fresh tears springing to her eyes. "You can really save him."

My lower lip trembles as the fatigue takes over and the adrenaline continues to wear off. My entire body starts trembling again, and Elly takes notice. Her arms wrap around me, squeezing me against her in an embrace that also works expertly at holding me up. At first, I'm still too stunned to move, my arms stiff on either side of her.

Clint nearly died. The realization settles into my bones, and I'm faced with how close I had been to losing him, the quivering in my body intensifying. When she buries her face into my neck, I return her embrace, tears and sobs flowing out of me from fear and relief.

I dig my chin into her shoulder, trying to calm down, but I can't catch my breath, which is coming in heavy hiccups that send my pulse into my head again, throbbing with pressure.

Elly doesn't relent, stroking the hair hanging down my back and pressing her cheek against my head. Tilting my head, my cheek lays against her shoulder, but I'm also able to lock eyes with Clint.

He lays against his pillow, his amber eyes glistening in wonderment. There's a ghost of a smile on his face, slack yet serene.

Whether or not everyone else had been able to see what I'd done, something tells me he watched every moment of me battling the mass that tried to take his life.

"What," Pax bursts out, forcing Elly and I apart. I stagger, but Tariq is there to catch me against him, his hands clinging to my waist. "The *fuck*."

***

I send Fin on an errand to my room to grab more salve for my Mark and some new, unbroken ingredients for Clint. I also instruct him on where to find something that'll ease my own anxiety, which hasn't simmered from the rapid sequence of events.

Or maybe it's because Pax won't stop staring at my fully-exposed Mark. His face is a blank slate, which is more unnerving than his usual scowl.

"Are you sure you don't want something more wholesome to eat?" Elly whispers beside me, her hand

FATE DEMANDS SACRIFICE 147

gripping mine as if I'm her anchor.

Which is ironic, considering I can barely keep myself grounded right now.

"This bread is fine," I assure her, waving the small slice with a single nibble out of it. I try to muster the courage to eat more, but every time I bring it to my mouth, my stomach lurches like a punch to the gut.

We fall into silence again, and my gaze snags on Tariq, who's taken up Pax's usual post by the window. Instead of staring out into the distance, he keeps a keen eye on me, those amber eyes peering down and spearing through me.

"Are we going to talk about this?" Pax scoffs, folding his arms over his chest and leaning back in the chair. "Or are we going to continue pretending she isn't Sirian?"

"Pax," Elly snaps through clenched teeth.

He raises his hands before him in surrender, eyebrows shooting up his head. "I just think I'm owed an explanation."

"Why do you feel like you're owed anything?" Tariq frowns, not unkindly but speculative. "What do you think gives you that liberty? You may be Lieutenant General, but you aren't a member of the Royal Court responsible for employing her in the first place."

"From the moment she stepped through these doors, I said something wasn't right," Pax explains, his finger pointed at me, condemning. "You all said she was to be trusted. Here she is, a *Sirian* posing to be a Magic—"

"Are you kidding me?" I shout, slowly rising from my

chair and, embarrassingly enough, using Elly's offered arm to keep balance as my vision tilts. "After everything we've been through over the last couple of weeks, and after you just saw me expend myself to save the prince, you still don't trust me?"

"I don't like you lied about who you are." Pax rises from his chair, provoking Tariq to stand at attention now. "You have to give me a little more credit here."

"*You* have to give *me* more credit." My voice cracks, and I clench my free hand into a fist at my side. "Would you expect me to reveal what I really am versus pretending to be a Magic? I've spent my entire life protecting myself because of this." I gesture to the Mark on my forehead.

Pax rubs a hand up and down the side of his face, drawing on his chin as he scratches his beard. He slowly shakes his head side-to-side without breaking eye contact. "I'm just at a loss, Reva. I didn't even think your kind existed anymore. I just thought... This was the last thing I expected."

"It's a lot to take in," I agree, nodding. I lower back to the chair, my knees wobbling. "I don't expect you to like me. Gods, I even expect you and me to start at square one again. But I want you to know that everything you've learned about me is still the same. Everything I've done since I got here has been to help Clint, first and foremost."

Pax's gaze bounces from me to Elly, holding hers momentarily before he twists to Tariq. "How much did you know?"

FATE DEMANDS SACRIFICE 149

"Everything," Tariq answers, his tone even.

"And for how long?" Pax crosses his arms in front of his chest.

Tariq considers this, tilting his head to the side. "Elly coded it in a message to me while I was in Riddling, shortly after she found out."

Pax whirls back to Elly, who flinches beside me. The hurt and betrayal that flares in his eyes clenches my heart. "And how long did you know?"

"Since the knights attacked the castle," Elly whispers, eyes falling to the floor as her voice quivers. "You have to understand that I wanted to tell you. But you were so angry about Magics, I wasn't sure what would happen if you found out she was a Sirian."

Pax presses his lips together, his face hard, but I witness the inner battle happening within him. The anger he's warring with doesn't seem to be directed at Tariq or Elly.

"I knew you were lying about what happened in this room that day," Pax mumbles, his attention still latched on Elly. "I know your tells."

Elly swallows loudly beside me, slouching into herself.

"There's a lot we need to fill you in on if you're on our side again," Tariq explains, stepping up beside Pax and clasping him on the shoulder.

The door creaks open behind us, inciting a gasp from Elly. We all pitch toward it to find Fin sneaking in through a crack that's barely bigger than him. He carries various bottles in his hand and the tin of salve.

Pax waits until the door is shut behind Fin. He avoids my gaze, his shoulders slumped when he says, "For what it's worth, Reva, I don't plan on revealing your secret."

I wordlessly accept the tin from Fin's outstretched hand with a tight-lipped grin. Tariq studies me from across the space, his lip ticking up at the corner, but he dips his head at me.

CHAPTER 11

"Why the hell aren't you in your training gear?" Lightning calls from across the room, flashes of silver sparks dancing off her fingertips. She pushes off the wall, strutting across the floor to meet me, Tariq, and Elly in the middle of the room. "Gods, Reva, you look terrible."

"Thanks," I hiss, running a hand through my semi-tamed hair.

A quick glance in the mirror earlier nearly took my breath away from how ghastly I looked. You'd think I'd caught something; dark circles peek out from underneath my skin, which even looks a shade or two lighter than usual.

"And to what do I owe the pleasure of another visit from the Crown Prince and Princess of Mariande?" Lightning grins, dragging her gaze from me to Elly before latching onto Tariq.

"We wanted to talk about something that happened yesterday with Reva and Clint," Tariq begins, slipping his hands into his pockets.

Lightning blanches, the typical glint in her ice-blue

eyes dimming. "The mass…"

"He was dying," I croak, fighting the tears that sting the corners of my eyes. Even if I know Clint is upstairs breathing, alert, and lively as ever, my heart speeds up like I'm back in that room again when I think of how close we'd been… "I had to do something."

"Gods, Reva." Lightning shakes her head and rests her hands on the back of her head. "You could've killed him—"

"He was going to die anyway," Elly shouts, wrapping her arms around herself. I chance a peek at Tariq, whose eyes are already pinned on me.

That's exactly what he said to give me the extra push yesterday.

"So, what happened?" Lightning crosses her arms over her chest, tapping her foot. "I want a play-by-play of what you did to him."

I recall the story for all of them from the moment I placed my hands on Clint's stomach until I was pulled out of the strange trance I'd been in. At first, I'm hesitant to tell Tariq and Elly that it felt like the mass was communicating with me, refusing to leave, especially since I think I spoke back.

Or did *something* back.

But I relent.

"You think?" Lightning asks, unable to hide the hesitation in her voice as her head tilts back.

I rub my hand along my arm with a shrug. "It felt like my voice, but it really wasn't. It felt like someone else's

FATE DEMANDS SACRIFICE

153

or multiple someones."

"And that's when you had to use Asteria's god-power?" Lightning squints, and I can almost see the wheels in her head turning.

I nod. "I was already using it. I think I might've created a shield around the mass before I started... zapping it."

"You zapped it," Lightning repeats, her eye twitching. "Like what? Like lightning?"

"Well, kind of," I scoff, throwing my arms up. "I followed my gut, Lightning. I don't know why I chose to do what I did to minimize the mass."

"You looked different," Tariq cuts in, peering at me with narrowed eyes. "Right after you put your hands on Clint, it was all so different from when you normally use the Light."

"Explain," Lightning demands, wheeling on him. Based on how tightly her face is drawn, I know she's losing patience with us.

Tariq raises an eyebrow at her in challenge before gazing back at me to explain. "When you used the shield the other day, your hair started to float around you. The same thing happened when you were helping Clint. Your veins were also glowing with that blue-tinted light, and it was almost like they were going *into* Clint from your hands."

Lightning's arms lower slowly, no longer watching Tariq. Out of the corner of my eye, her gaze pierces into me as Tariq continues, "The atmosphere in the room changed, or at least it felt like it did."

"Everything was quiet," Elly jumps in, taking a few steps closer to me. She tilts her head. "Well, it wasn't quiet, per se. It was like clamping your hands over your ears." She holds her hands beside her head to demonstrate. "Everything was buzzing, but not the sound. It was like a rumble, almost like everything that carried Energy in that room was responding to what you were doing."

"And the air around you was waving—"

"Like heat from a fire," Lightning interrupts Tariq, finishing the thought for him.

Lightning had explained a similar phenomenon nearly a month ago when we first trained, all but confirming Jorah's hypothesis that I had two god-powers.

My gaze frantically jumps between the three, unsure what to make of all this. I know how the events unfolded from my point of view, but their version of the story sends chills up and down my spine.

From the beginning, Jorah and Lightning both hinted that having two god-powers was a big deal, long before we knew the other was Asteria. While we discussed Asteria being the most powerful Sirian, I didn't believe that meant I was *actually* the most powerful Sirian right now. Not only that, but now there's a potential I could outlive everyone around me.

I honestly believed it all to be some joke, just as I convinced myself the jabs from Lighting about war and leading an army to mean nothing. I never considered what would come next when I started actually healing

FATE DEMANDS SACRIFICE 155

Clint. I pretended that if it wasn't happening, then it wouldn't.

For so long the clock I was fighting was Clint's illness, but a new ticking echoes in my head as I realize the next step in my journey could be leading a Sirian army.

Tariq, Elly, and Lightning start another conversation, but my mind spirals down the line of everything I'm learning, my vision tunneling. My body locks up, every muscle tensing from my shoulders down to my knees, and my heart races in time with the thoughts shouting in my head.

My brain fogs as my breathing quickens, expelling faster and faster. I attempt to gain control, but easing my breath feels like trying to grasp at a rope that keeps swaying out of reach. I think I hear my name called, maybe once or twice, but my vision narrows further. I see what's before me, but everything feels out of focus.

My tingling fingers register rough, calloused hands scratching them and gliding up my arms until they grip my shoulders. My eyes find focus, latching onto the soft amber ones blocking my line of sight.

"Does touch help?" Tariq's voice cuts through the blood rushing in my ears, caressing. My head is light, dizziness sweeping over me as my eyes flutter. "I need you to *breathe,* Reva. Can you breathe with me?"

His hands firmly grip my head between them, those same callouses now pressing against my cheeks as his forehead touches mine. "Just take a deep breath in—" He breathes in through his nose.

When I don't follow, and my breath quivers in short pants, he pulls back with a smirk playing on his lips. "So stubborn, Starfire, but I promise you'll thank me later. Now, breathe in."

That stupid smirk and nickname rattle in my head, breaking through my thoughts so I can follow a deep breath in that strains against my panicking lungs. I keep filling them until Tariq stops, nodding once before we both exhale from our lips, our breath tangling in the free air between us.

"Perfect," Tariq whispers, his thumb stroking my cheek. "Again, with me."

We do this a few times before I find my peripheral vision expanding. Lightning and Elly stand a few feet from us, closer than they had been during our previous discussion. Lightning watches us like a hawk, her eyes tight with apprehension.

When is Lightning *not* guarded or suspicious?

On the other hand, Elly has a strange glint in her eye, her lips pursed.

"I think it's time you meet the Elders," Lightning says, shaking her head as she scans my face. "It may help relieve some of this... stress you're putting on yourself. You can talk to them, hear things from their perspective."

Tariq's hands gradually—and almost reluctantly—fall from my face as he nods once.

Lighting continues, "You know how to help Clint now, and you know you can do it. You'll be able to leave him without worrying he'll kick the bucket."

FATE DEMANDS SACRIFICE

"Gods, Lightning," Elly grumbles beside her, rubbing her fingers across her forehead.

"Give me a day to try and minimize the mass more. At least so the kid can start keeping food down," I sigh, straightening the vest over my shirt.

"Jorah can set something up for us," Elly offers, hand poised in the air. "He'll be able to organize a safe, neutral territory where you could avoid any suspicious onlookers. He's got that room in his shop."

"Good idea." Lightning nods but wags her finger at Elly. "Except there is no *us*. The Elders will only meet Reva right now—"

"That's not an option," Tariq interrupts, his voice even and confident. "I mean no offense, Reva, but I will not send a Royal Healer to talk alliance terms."

"No offense taken," I whisper.

At the same time, Lightning snaps, "This isn't a meeting about an alliance, Prince." Her hands latch onto her hips. "This is about the Elders speaking with Reva about the position we're in and the position she's in. We don't need you."

"Pray tell." Tariq calmly clasps his hands together in front of his chest as if he's actually about to pray. "How is it *not* an alliance meeting if you are speaking with the Royal Healer of *Mariande* on her *leading* the Sirian army you've built?"

Lightning smirks, clasping her hands behind her back as she leans on one leg. "You don't own her, Prince. She can easily quit this ridiculous role and come be with her people."

"You know," I laugh, throwing my head up to beg the Gods to spare me. "I'm getting real sick and tired of people speaking for me when I'm standing right here!"

Lightning startles, blinking rapidly at me, while Tariq shoves his hands into his pockets with that neutral princely mask.

"First of all," I begin, pointing my finger at Tariq. "No offense taken, honestly. I wouldn't know the first thing about negotiating an alliance. But unfortunately, I am Sirian, and she's right. You don't own me."

I wheel on Lightning, my jaw ticking. "Second of all, I will not be leading an army of Sirians if they're insistent on keeping themselves separated from the rest of the world. That is not going to fix this world. We are in this position—getting ready to fight an unknown, ancient Darkness—because someone thought they were better than others."

She suppresses a tantrum as her lightning power flashes in her eyes, a storm muted by heavy rain clouds. I level her with a glare for good measure, extending my pointer finger between us in a challenge.

She relents with her palms up.

"I agree with Tariq on not letting you go alone," Elly interjects softly. "It doesn't feel safe or responsible."

"I'm a grown adult." I nod, more so to encourage myself. "And apparently the most powerful Sirian to exist in Gods know how long."

"Whether or not Jorah organizes this," Tariq says,

FATE DEMANDS SACRIFICE   159

taking a few steps toward Elly. "We're going to draw attention if the Royal Healer is caught with people she's yet to be seen with. There have to be Dark Sirians hiding out in the Magic community, and they'll take that as an opportunity. With five Sirians in a room, two of which have god-powers—"

"Three of us," Lightning quietly adds.

Tariq tilts his head to the side, shrugs, and continues, "The *three* of you with god-powers and the other two Sirians may be more than enough to handle a surprise ambush, but I want your meeting organized around an evening Fin is patrolling in the Magic community. He's become intimate with them, and they trust him. His presence won't appear out of place."

"That's a good idea," Elly smiles, her shoulders loosening. "Fin won't partake in the meeting, but he'll be ready if anything happens."

Lightning pauses, an awkward silence snaking its way between us, my muscles tensing again.

It feels like several minutes pass before she finally stops her stare-down with Tariq, her hands falling limp at her side.

"Alright," Lightning says, but her body is turned away from Tariq and me. "I can contact Jorah about the meeting. I'm hoping the Elders arrive today, so I'd like us to rendezvous in a day or two so word doesn't spread that they're here. The last thing we need is the Darkness tagging them and endangering the Sirians."

"Thank you," I breathe, the tightness releasing from

my shoulders.

It doesn't hit me until we're halfway up the stairs that I realize what I've agreed to. The idea of leading an army of Sirians has the panic creeping up on me again, but I take easy breaths in and out, counting. Tariq must catch me, glancing my way.

As the responsibility of leading presses in, I think I might understand why Elly relinquished the throne to her brother so easily.

***

Old habits die hard, and I find I focus a lot better when I'm in the study. The warmth in this room, from the maroon accents to the mahogany wood, helps me relax into the chairs with my notes, reconfiguring Clint's medication. Now that I've found the cure for his mass, all I have to focus on is anti-inflammatory and nourishing remedies.

After we met with Lightning, I was ready to take some of my concern and anxiety out on that still-large mass in Clint. I could only shrink the same amount of damage as I did yesterday before I felt sapped and strangely cold.

Pax, whose mother hen side is showing now, sent me off to my room after I started trembling. He said he'd tell the other Magic nurses that I was coming down with something and to send me soup. I'm pretty sure my eyes were closed before I hit the bed.

FATE DEMANDS SACRIFICE 161

"I wouldn't take you for a castle study type of researcher," a rumbling voice calls from the doorway.

I incline my head over my shoulder and the back of the chair to find Tariq leaning against the doorframe with his hands crossed over his chest.

"Fire," is all I say, gesturing toward it with the quill in my hand.

He exhales a chuckle through his nose, and I return my focus to my notes, but I'm not shocked when the chair beside me groans in protest. I glower over the top of my knees laying on the arm, my feet inches from where his hand rests.

"You've got a fireplace in your room, don't you?" he questions, pouting.

I shrug, trying to keep my eyes trained on the parchment. "I've been secluding myself in my room for the last few weeks because I know I tend to be interrupted when I'm in this study. I thought it'd be healthy to reintegrate my presence now with Clint on the mend."

"On the mend," Tariq repeats slowly like he's tasting the words on his tongue. "I suppose you can call it that. I would say you cured him."

I scoff, scratching out the formula I've messed up. "The mass is still there."

"But it'll be gone eventually," Tariq laughs, the ends of his dirty blond hair brushing the top of his shoulders.

For once, he's not donning his usual bun. Instead, it hangs straight, parted just off-centered from the middle.

His eyebrows raise in amusement, and a blush warms

my cheeks. No use denying I was gawking at him, especially as he says, "Like what you see?"

"That ego," I mumble, tearing my gaze away. "Your hair. It's not pulled back today."

"Neither is yours," Tariq observes, grabbing my foot and digging his thumb into the arch. "You don't see me undressing you with my eyes."

"I was not—" I kick my foot from his grasp before he realizes it's ticklish. I shoot him a glare. "You're always undressing me with your eyes."

Tariq throws his head back, a boisterous laugh cracking his usual facade. His eyes squint and his smile broadens, which has me fighting my own grin with wavering lips. I raise my hand and pinch them between my fingers to help me out.

"I'll give it to you, Starfire," he says through the remnants of his laughter, that smile still on his face. "I have never met someone who keeps me on my toes, puts my wit to shame, and rolls their eyes at the fact that I'm a Crown Prince."

I chuckle darkly, placing my quill between the pages of my book since it appears I won't be getting any more work done. "You give yourself too much credit. Besides, you forget I wasn't raised in a kingdom with royalty, so I don't know what the proper decorum is supposed to be. Do you expect me to bow whenever you come into a room?"

"Most would." He wags his finger at me. "That's not what I mean, though. Even those I'd consider friends are

FATE DEMANDS SACRIFICE   163

afraid to challenge me or speak against me. I feel like I have to bully Fin to get him not to agree with everything I say."

I suppress my wince at the mention of Fin, if only because I'm blatantly reminded they've been best friends since childhood. I try to play around that. "Did that happen after you all came into your positions?"

"For the most part." Tariq shrugs, settling further into his chair. "When we're not in 'Knight and Crown Prince of Mariande' mode, Fin will speak up if he thinks I'm being an ass. But I want him to speak up more than just then."

"I learned he has a problem with—" I pause, considering my words. "Challenging authority."

Tariq nods, pressing his lips together. "Elly mentioned there were a few instances between Fin and Pax when it came to standing up for you. As the Crown Prince, I will apologize for that. I wish you didn't face the prejudice you did."

I wave away his apology, rolling my eyes. "It's really not needed. Fin and your dad apologized. So much has happened since then."

Tariq smiles softly, leaning his head back to rest on the back of the chair. The crackling of the fire is the only sound in the library besides his calm breathing. While the silence is comfortable and light, I fidget at the question that's been bugging me since we parted earlier.

Tariq's eye closest to me cracks open as he peers toward me. "Yes, Starfire?"

I glare at him but set my notes on the coffee table in front of us. I curl my legs underneath me, fold my hands in my lap, and intertwine my fingers. "How did you know what to do earlier? With my panic attack?"

Tariq grunts as he readjusts in the chair so that he's twisted toward me, his ankle resting on his knee.

"I took a guess on whether you'd respond positively to physical touch." He shoots me a knowing look with a devilish tilt to his lips. "That's why I didn't grab your face right away. Some people don't like it when you grab them during an attack, but when I saw my touch on your hands and arms pulling you out, I knew grabbing your face would help you focus.

"The breathing technique I've learned for my own benefit." He pauses, staring away from me. "Contrary to my charming personality and good looks, I didn't know I'd be the heir to the throne well into my childhood. That may not seem like a lot, but other royals know they're getting the throne from the moment they can comprehend what that means. They're prepared for that responsibility. I, however, was not."

"You have panic attacks?" I question, tilting my head to the side. Staring at the broad-shouldered prince, the expert mask he wears, and the way he handles conflict, I would never have thought he suffered from anxiety.

"They were a hell of a lot worse when I was younger." He pats his knee, shrugging. "I didn't get a good handle on them until I was eighteen. They are very rare now, and I will say it takes a lot to get one from me, but it's

FATE DEMANDS SACRIFICE 165

because I've practiced."

"So, the Prince mask, the placidity in conflict, the control over your mannerisms and voice…"

"I mean, that's all learned," he explains, unfolding his legs to lean closer. "It really comes down to a good breathing pattern and one that goes unnoticed. You'll be shocked at the difference you'll see when you just remind yourself to breathe."

I imperceptibly shake my head, a little awed by the man in front of me.

When it comes to men, I know most of my experience stems from physical aspects of them, but I like to think between a couple of The Red Raven regulars, Willem, Remy, and even Rol, I have a good grip on how they act. I don't know what I expected meeting Tariq, but I never thought the Crown Prince of a kingdom would openly admit to having anxiety, let alone dive into why.

My heart swells in my chest, and I remind myself to breathe like he said. I clear my throat. "Well, thank you. It's reassuring to have someone who understands what I'm feeling and how to pull me out of it. Not that it's your responsibility to pull me out of something like that."

Since he leaned closer, I've been gradually inching toward him like a magnet. His hand reaches across the space between us, tucking a loose strand of hair behind my ear, holding that piece between his thumb and finger.

"If that's what you need from me," he whispers, his gaze trained on the strand in his hand as he stands, towering over me. "Use me as you wish."

My heart twists in my chest, pressing against my ribcage as if it could reach out and follow the Crown Prince of Mariande as he leaves me in the study with a stiff salute. I swallow the swelling emotion in my throat, pretending this tension between Tariq and me isn't sharpening and digging its claws into me.

CHAPTER 12

Saros is alive with people by the time I arrive to meet Lightning. While there is plenty to distract everyone, from the carts posted on street corners with knick-knacks and trinkets to the children skipping alongside their parents, heavy gazes follow me down every turn. I catch a few women whispering to their companions, who all exchange fleeting glances with one another.

I keep my head down, still aware of my surroundings, as I increase the pace of my leisure stroll. At this point, I'm confident enough in the village layout to navigate my own way to Jorah's storefront.

I'm not sure if I'm meant to wait out front for Lightning, but I consider what sort of attention that will draw, particularly with any Dark Sirian spies that are lurking in the community, and decide to enter. The bells chime, alerting anyone within the store of my arrival.

"The Great Reva," Jorah hums, his head popping out from an aisle with those swirling ocean eyes. His body follows, slinking out with multiple raw gemstones clutched in his hands. "I'm always pleased when I'm right.

Then again, I'm rarely wrong."

"You mean you being right about the second god-power?" I follow him to the back of his shop.

The gemstones tumble out of his hands onto his worktable, echoing through the quiet store. He wipes his hands on his shirt, peering over his shoulder. "I told you there was more than one demi-god's power in your veins. I'm pleased to hear you've started mastering the Light and Asteria's gift."

"I would argue I've still not mastered either by any means," I chuckle, rubbing the back of my neck. "I understand the powers better if that's what you mean."

"You understand the Light." He bends his finger to follow him to his secret room, his manicured nail glinting silver. "Maybe one day you'll stop fearing Dionne's power to understand it. I don't think you or your allies can begin to fathom Asteria's gift."

I roll my eyes as he tugs open the hidden door. "As always, Jorah, your words of wisdom are inspiring."

I start to dip into the back room, but Jorah's hand snatches my wrist, his thumb pressing against my pulse. I snap my head toward him, watching his face contort.

The longer he holds my arm, the faster the deep blue in his eyes swirls with strange strips of silver, churning like frothy waves. His lips quirk briefly at the corners, the iridescent scaled skin twitching at the base of his neck.

"So many new things flowing in your blood," Jorah mutters, tilting his head to the side. A silver-streaked strand of dark hair falls on his forehead. "Your blood sings

FATE DEMANDS SACRIFICE

169

your heritage, now. I don't know how I never saw it before."

"What do you mean?" I startle, reeling back. "My heritage, like my god-power?"

"Your parents," he whispers, his eyes now scanning my face frantically. "I was so startled by a Sirian trailing after the Princess of Mariande, let alone one of your caliber; I missed the familiar taste."

I shiver at the idea that somehow Jorah's attachment to water allows him to *taste* me, but the hollowness in my chest drops to my stomach. "You knew my parents? Who were they?"

"I never knew her name," he explains, dropping my hand from his grasp. "She came with a friend... They had suspicions you'd be Sirian and came to me to confirm."

"My mother," I gasp, my hand instinctively flying to the necklace around my neck. "What... What was she like?"

Jorah stares for a heartbeat longer before waving his hand between us like he can brush away the whole encounter. "It was a brief exchange, but she looked just like you. Except for the eyes... She had different eyes."

A small shiver runs through me, even as I step into the room with a gentle pat on my shoulder from Jorah. I shoot him a glare in time for the door to click shut.

And now I'm meant to meet the Elders of the Sirian movement...

"Reva," Lightning's voice interjects, jolting me out of my trance. I whirl back to face the room, my eyes landing on the three figures sitting at the table with Lightning lounging against the back wall of bookshelves.

"Sorry," I mumble, my face heating as I furl my hand behind me at the door. "Jorah did a… Jorah thing."

"You can always rely on Jorah to completely rock your world any time you see him," one of the men at the table says, officially pulling my attention to them.

"This is Reva," Lightning introduces, extending her hand toward me. "Reva, these are the Elders: Megara, Osiris, and Aithan."

My eyes trail over them in that order, trying to commit them to memory. I don't know what I expected the Elders to look like, and maybe living with Magics all my life has tainted my views on what other beings should look like, but I didn't expect them to look so mortal.

Megara and Osiris have either suffered a lot of stress in their life or are both in their late to middle ages. Megara has subtle creases on her forehead around her exposed Sirian Mark and mouth, but her chestnut, shoulder-length hair shows no signs of graying. Despite the wrinkles, her face is soft and nurturing, exuding warmth.

Osiris's wrinkles are much deeper around his Mark and eyes, sunken lines extending from the corners of his hooked nose to the sides of his mouth. Despite the receding hairline and pale, almost white-blond hair, the piercing blue of his eyes convinces me he may have been handsome a long time ago.

Aithan, on the other hand, can't be that much older

FATE DEMANDS SACRIFICE

171

than Lightning and me. His olive-toned skin is about a shade or two darker than mine, contrasting with the rich, red-brown tone of his eyes, which churn like flames the longer they linger. I squirm under his scrutiny as his eyes trail from my face, down my neck, and back up again. His brows are uneven as his mouth props open slightly, his close-cropped stubble twitching at the corner of his mouth.

"Gods, Aithan," Lightning groans, reaching over to slap him in the back of the head. "Keep it in your pants for maybe ten minutes. That's all I ask."

He runs both hands through the golden brown hair flowing to the nape of his neck, his biceps flexing.

"You can't keep smacking him, Lightning," Megara chastises, rubbing her fingers against her temples. "He's an Elder."

"Barely," she sneers, leaning back against the wall again.

"Excuse the children, Reva," Osiris interrupts, shooting Aithan and Lightning a tight glare. "Aithan has only been made an Elder in the last few years after mastering his god-power. As one of the few in our community and oldest with a god-power, we felt it necessary to grant him that title."

"What god-power do you have?" I ask, stepping towards the table with shaky knees. For some reason, my heart is hammering in my throat, and my nerves are on edge. Maybe it's the fact they're all watching me intently, especially Aithan.

Or maybe I'm steadily realizing I'm in a room with four other Sirians after spending nearly twenty-three years alone.

"Since I know both of yours, I suppose it's only fair if I share," he answers with an unfamiliar accent that has a harshness to it, a slight bite to certain words compared to Etherean. "I also have Dionne's firepower."

"And you've mastered it?" I laugh, impressed. "I will need to pick your brain at some point."

"We hope when the time comes, you allow him to help train you in it." Osiris leans back in his chair, crossing his leg over the other and folding his hands on his knee.

"When the time comes," I repeat, remembering the real reason we're all here. I lower myself into the seat across from Megara, keeping my eyes on her. "I guess there is a greater purpose we've all gathered for."

"Indeed," Megara agrees, extending her head back an inch and tilting it to the side. "I'm sure you're used to being badgered with questions, Reva, so we want to open up the floor and allow you to ask anything you want to know. We'll try our best to answer."

I bite the inside of my cheek, crossing my arms over my chest. It's nice to ask questions with at least promised transparency for once.

"How did you all come up with this idea of a Sirian community, and how long have you been—" I pause, unable to devise a better word choice. "Collecting Sirians."

Aithan chuckles under his breath, fighting a smirk.

FATE DEMANDS SACRIFICE   173

Megara rolls her eyes at him, so Osiris steps in to answer. "I think I'm best equipped since I'm the oldest among us."

"I was born to two very normal mortals in a small village on the outskirts of Saros, believe it or not," he begins, his face growing distant. "Your King's grandfather was on the throne and he was ruthless. The Mariande you know today is startling compared to what it used to be.

"Because of that, we had no Magics that we could go to other than those in Eldamain to find a solution to hide my powers. Rumor had it there was a Magic who resided there who could help us with our needs, no questions asked."

My jaw slacks because there is only one Magic in Eldamain who would ever help outsiders with discretion. "You knew Karasi?"

"I have to admit I met her when I was a young boy," Osiris shakes his head. "After she gave us this salve, she warned my parents it was best if I learned to hone my skills and educate myself on the Light rather than live in fear of it. She gave us Jorah's contact and said he had an extensive collection of books that would help teach me."

Sharp chills roll up my arms, gooseflesh rising. So many questions stir with each web of Fate connecting us all. Karasi knew Jorah had his collection and told Osiris, and hauntingly told me my answers would be in Mariande. I always thought she meant the castle library…

Maybe she meant both.

174   K.M. DAVIDSON

I run a hand down my face, trying to calm my rising blood pressure at yet *another* bit of information Karasi chose to keep or had to keep or whatever the Gods required of her because of her stupid prophetic gifts.

"Makes you question whether the Gods really, truly left us a thousand years ago," Aithan cuts in, pulling me out of the spiral of connections I was about to fall down.

"As I got older and continued to master my powers, I knew there had to be others out there like me who were either living in fear or searching for somewhere to belong," Osiris continues, angling his head towards Megara. "I was starting to configure my plans for a Sirian community when I met Megara. I was in Eldamain, visiting a Magic acquaintance of Karasi's who sold one of the key ingredients for the salve when we ran into each other at The Red Raven. The acquaintance assured us we were one and the same."

"That Gods-damned pub," I swear under my breath.

"After we figured out a safe place to establish our community, we came up with a way to let Sirians know how to find us," Megara takes over, a ghost of a grin tugging at her smile lines. "We took a little advice from Karasi and came up with a code to usher Sirians to us using the Magic community. After it brought Osiris and I together, we knew there had to be more overlap when we realized we knew Karasi and Jorah."

Those two…

With Jorah's ability to sense what runs in the blood of others, Karasi would have jumped on the opportunity

FATE DEMANDS SACRIFICE

to ally. She's always collected the special Magics and kept them in her close circle, but I thought maybe it was for purer reasons like not wanting to be alone, what with her prophesying and all. I just never thought it would be to assist Sirians decades before she would take one in herself.

Considering at least three of us have known Karasi and Jorah on various levels can no longer mean it's just a coincidence.

Karasi has always been protecting Sirians.

"And where do you come into all this?" I ask Aithan, twisting toward him before resting my head in my hand.

He perches both elbows on the table, folds his hands in front of his mouth, and talks around them. "My parents were Sirian. They were among the first to join Osiris and Megara's community after fleeing Riddling. I was a young kid when we finally got to them."

"One of the first five children we had in the community." Megara looks at Aithan fondly, her eyes glowing. "His parents are still a huge part of our community, as well. They help get us the supplies we need to build homes, farm, make clothes—the necessities."

"How long have you had this community, then?" I fold my hands on top of one another on the worn, wooden table. "Lightning said you started to establish this idea of the Elders over two decades ago."

"That is correct," Osiris nods, scratching his chin. He peers at Megara. "Your memory is better than mine."

"Well, I was only sixteen when we met," Megara

recalls, looking up at the ceiling. "It took us two years to officially plant the flag, so it's been almost forty years."

"*Four* decades?" I shout, my voice tapering at the end. "And in that time, how many Sirians would you say live in your community now?"

"Including ourselves..." Megara's eyes flicker over to Aithan.

"We're nearing fifty of us," Aithan answers. "If you're asking army numbers, it's a little less than that."

Aithan continues to explain the number of children under eighteen who live there and the number of fighting adults, diminishing the "army" to forty. He also reveals they have four Sirians with god-powers, including him and Lightning. There is a descendant of Phoebe and another Taranis descendant in their mix.

Making me the only one with Asteria's power that we know of and, as everyone continues to remind me, the only Sirian with two god-powers.

I click my nail against my top teeth, these facts seeping into my skin. A bitter burning crawls up my throat and settles in the back of it as my gaze latches onto Lightning's.

"So, you guys are really about this war and fighting, too," I finally say, meeting each of their stares. "Do you know how many Dark Sirians there are in comparison?"

"The intel we have is a little outdated," Osiris says, rubbing the back of his neck. "The last we heard, they were higher than fifty, but we do not believe any Dark Sirian has a god-power."

FATE DEMANDS SACRIFICE 177

"So you think five Sirians with god-powers, including me, somehow even the field?" My heart pounds in my chest because these are not promising numbers or statements.

I truly thought a community of this size, with the resources they make it seem they have, would have more than fifty people.

Megara and Osiris exchange a brief, fleeting glance, silently communicating something to one another. Megara is the one to lean across the table, grabbing my hand in hers. "Lightning has brought us up to speed on a lot of things about you, and I'm sorry you couldn't have told us yourself, but we constantly fear time is not on our side. With your Magic community being attacked here, you can't ignore the Dark wielders are on the move."

"And you really believe it's going to lead to war?" I question, scowling. "These people can't be reasoned with?"

"Being Sirian, I get they're angry and want retribution," Megara admits, reclining in the chair. "I don't agree with the way they're going about it, but the time for reasoning passed long ago when the kingdoms continued to execute us and refused to acknowledge our existence was valid."

"Even now, you work for a kingdom that may be validating the Magics." I don't miss the disgust dripping from Aithan. "But their royal children know of your true heritage and have yet to plead the Sirians' case to their father."

"Living amongst mortals and Magics my entire life, I can also understand their side," I snap.

"Let's not get ahead of ourselves," Megara interrupts, glaring at Aithan before turning her softened gaze on me. "Lightning told us you've figured out how to save the young prince. Now that you can heal him, where do you stand?"

I clench my jaw, slowly lowering my fists to my lap. "What do you mean by that?"

"While Aithan's delivery was harsh," Osiris adds, lifting his head to look down his crooked nose. "He posed a valid argument. Lightning has told us that, during discussions with the Crown Prince and Princess Eloise, you frequently favor their side."

"Their *side*?" I repeat incredulously, curling my lip. "In my eyes, if this Dark presence is coming for us, there are only two sides: the Dark and the Light."

"Naive," Aithan mumbles, but I level him with my jaw set.

"We wish things were that simple, child," Osiris sighs, shaking his head in evident disappointment. "As Aithan said, Mariande has yet to acknowledge Sirians within their castle. I doubt they will lend their army to fight alongside our people."

"You don't know that," I start, slowly rising from the seat as my hands tingle. I breathe, wrangling in the power simmering underneath my skin—all variants of my power.

I conjure my inner Tariq, contemplating how he

FATE DEMANDS SACRIFICE 179

would handle this situation.

He would wear that mask, shove his hands in his pockets, and calmly explain the reality of the situation.

But what is the reality of the situation? The Abyss reappeared roughly twenty or so years ago, but I lived in Eldamain my entire life, and those mountains have gotten even worse in the last few years.

As though the Abyss were getting stronger.

"Tell me, *Elders.* In forty years, you have only been able to gather a few dozen Sirians outside those who weren't born in your community, which I venture is quite a few. While you saved many Sirians, how many were not so lucky?" I wave my hand up and down my body. "You plotted your community of Sirians, and did you not think maybe someone else was plotting the same thing except for nefarious purposes?"

Osiris and Megara exchange a look, something akin to doubt flickering in Megara's grayish eyes.

I continue, "You need the non-Sirian and the non-Magic folk just as much as they need us. Dark Sirians are already attacking Mariande, hoping to scare Magics away, which means they know Magics would be an asset. If you approach a battlefield of sorts with the Mariande army behind you and Magics, they won't stand a chance with all those numbers."

"Are you ready to expose yourself to your precious King to let him lend you his army?" Aithan chortles, slamming his hands on the table and directing his attention to his co-Elders. "She has been around the

Magics and mortals for too long. She barely knows her own powers—"

"I wouldn't need the King's approval." If I learned anything about the military from Fin and King Darius… "The military is the Crown Prince's to command."

I catch Lightning out of the corner of my eye, her mouth twitching ever so slightly. I keep my gaze fastened onto Aithan as he lowers himself back into his seat.

"And what makes you think the Crown Prince would potentially go against his father to help *you*?" Osiris questions, not unkindly, but rather pointedly. "I know he's aware you're Sirian—"

Aithan's low laughter fills the room as he tips his chair back on two legs. Devilish glee dances in his eyes as he says, "Because maybe Reva and the Crown Prince—"

"Are allies," I cut him off before he ruins my credibility with the two older Sirians, keeping my face neutral. "If you want me to be part of your efforts, you have to ally with Mariande or at least the Hesper twins. They are fiercely protective of their people, Magics and mortals alike. It was Tariq who insisted you help the Magics fight the illness the Dark Sirians are attacking them with."

"So, you're on a first-name basis with the Crown Prince of Mariande?" The look on Megara's face is full of pity and disappointment, two emotions I never thought would make me feel so small.

Fuck. I didn't need Aithan to ruin my credibility because I just did.

FATE DEMANDS SACRIFICE   181

"Reva," Lightning whispers, her head falling into her hand, shoulders slumping.

The door to the hidden room suddenly flies open, revealing a frazzled Jorah, his hair disheveled, sleeves rolled up, and eyes glowing.

"Your presence is *highly* requested at the moment," Jorah breathes heavily, swallowing giant gulps of air. He meets the eyes of every single Sirian in the room before revealing, "The Dark wielders are here. They're attacking the community."

CHAPTER 13

We run through Jorah's store in a single-file line, the blood rushing in my head and breath echoing in my ears as I force it in and out of my nostrils.

Osiris and Megara lead us, following Jorah down an alleyway where the sounds of shouting, screaming, and crying filter through buildings. Their hands are already glowing with white-gold Light when we round the corner into a cobblestone street. I skid to a halt, Lightning slamming into me with a curse.

There are already two Light Sirians I've yet to meet battling head-to-head with two Dark ones, attempting to divert their attention away from the Magics filing into store alleyways.

The Darkness taints the air, pressing in like humidity, the same way the Abyss has been described in the Black Avalanches. I'm transfixed as one of the Dark wielders manically stretches his hands out in front of him, an inky, oily substance writhing through the air toward one of the Sirians, a strange tug tightening my chest.

A ball of fire dances across the stream of Darkness, cutting the power in half. The flame burns down the black tendrils like a cigar before it sparks off the fingertips of the Dark Sirian wielding it. My eyes snap to Aithan as flames erupt in his hands on either side of him, charging towards the Dark wielder and fellow Sirian. My heartbeat flutters at the sight of the flames taunting the Dark wielder, licking her feet.

"Look alive, Reva," Lightning shouts over the screams from Magics trying to scatter from the fight.

Actual lightning crackles along her arms, radiating off her like a flashing aura. I ogle as she effortlessly swipes her hand down at an angle in front of her, a bolt of lightning shooting from the clear evening sky and spearing through one of the Dark wielders.

He falls into a limp, lifeless heap on the ground.

A dark blur runs past me in my peripheral, pointed black tendrils shooting toward Lightning. Without blinking, I stretch out my palm, yanking on that glowing blue power and shielding her from the attack. The Darkness bounces off the shimmering wall of blue and white light, the impact sharper than Lightning's power had been and a strange something coats the back of my throat like I've inhaled pepper.

The Dark Sirian wheels on me, their face contorted in rage and annoyance. When they call to their power, their pupils consume the whites of their eyes, black lines stretching from the Mark on their forehead—

Something pierces the skin of my ankle like a rope made of thorns, digging into my flesh. I cry out as the pressure deepens, the world around me blurring in a mix of black, browns, and deep blues before my back slams onto the stone street, the wind rushing out of me.

I forget the throbbing around my ankle as the sky starts rushing overhead, my back dragging against the ground. I clench my jaw past bites of rock that scrape my skin and use the adrenaline pumping my heart to call the Light into me.

I envision that blue light mimicking the sparks of power that danced along Lightning's arms. The corners of my vision illuminate the same color as the Asteria god-power, that same chill sneaking into my veins. The Dark wielder releases the grip on my leg, and my body stops sliding across the street.

I scramble to my feet, echoing the defensive stance Lightning and I practiced, two floating orbs of Light glowing in my hands.

The Dark wielder hisses, seething at her palms. Her gaze snaps to mine, those eyes like gazing into the soulless depths of night. "What kind of power—"

She's cut off in a garble as blood bursts from her lips. We both look down at the sword protruding from the middle of her chest, the tip slick with blood glistening in the street lamps. When the sword vanishes back out of her body, I hurl a ball of Light at the same spot on her chest. It throws her backward into another Dark wielder who had been gaining on Megara.

"You alright?" A familiar voice pants before two emerald green eyes pop into my view, breaking my attention from where the Dark Sirian lays lifeless on the

FATE DEMANDS SACRIFICE   185

ground. "I saw her dragging you across the ground. Are you hurt?"

"I don't know," I whisper, barely audible. Fin grips my shoulders, turning me around to check out my back.

He lifts the hem of my shirt but pauses before examining my back. "Reva, look out!" He swirls around my flank, using his body as a shield.

"Fin, no—"

He flails his arms backward, preventing me from lifting my own and blocking my view. He cries out as he's either thrown or falls to my right.

I groan through clenched teeth as I throw a wave of white, gold, and blue light at the Dark wielder before me, a burst of cold power rattling my bones. Instead of flying back, the assailant's body stiffens before their eyes roll to the back of their head, and they collapse with a crunch to the ground.

I throw myself towards Fin groaning on the ground, his sword discarded and his hands clenched in fists beside him.

"Let me see," I plead, my heart pounding in my chest as I examine his body. I suck in a harsh breath of air through my nose as all sound ceases around me.

While his uniform is still fairly intact, there is a single hole in his shoulder below his collarbone. Blood seeps from the wound, mixing with the oily black as though someone dumped a jar of ink into him.

"Gods, Fin," I swear as I press my hands to his wound. He hisses, rolling his eyes back into his head. "Why did you do that? That was so incredibly stupid."

He clenches his jaw, his eyes frantic as he manages to bite out, "It *burns*, Reva. It feels like I'm on fire."

Footsteps rushing toward us have me calling to the Light, holding out my glowing, blood-coated hand above Fin in warning.

Lighting falls to her knees next to me, hands up in surrender. "Just me, girl," Lightning breathes heavily, her chest expanding with each inhale. She tries to usher me away, bending over Fin. "Let me see it."

I give her room to scan him, her fingers hovering momentarily over the wound as if she wants to touch it.

"The potion we use for the Dark illness should work," she mumbles. She unfolds from her crouch, her head searching the quiet street around us before narrowing on her target. She waves her hands above her head. "Jorah!"

Numb, I steadily rise to my feet, standing over Lightning and Jorah as he yanks out a vial from a sack slung over his shoulder. He shoves it into Lightning's hands, but my eyes stay trained on Fin and his breathing, even as he cries out when Lightning pours a thick, glowing white-gold liquid directly into his wound, the sound piercing my chest. When a mix of a whimper and growl trembles from Fin's lips, I finally turn my head away, surveying the wreckage.

Surprisingly, the buildings on the strip are not damaged much, save for a few loose bricks on the side of one storefront and broken front glass on another. Other than distant moans and hushed cries from alleys and

FATE DEMANDS SACRIFICE 187

apartments above the stores, the street silences as night descends.

Megara walks up beside me, wincing, her hands perched on the back of her head. She watches Lightning work for a moment while Fin's whimpering quiets. "Is he someone you know?"

"He knows about Sirians, if that's what you're asking." I peek at him from the corner of my eyes, relieved that while his eyes are shut, his breathing is even. "But yes. He's a friend."

"Your prince had him patrolling alone tonight," she observes, searching. "We're lucky he's the only knight who answered the Magics' call."

I exhale in disbelief. I flare my nostrils and fight a cynical laugh. "Lucky?"

"This was not a planned attack," Osiris blurts, joining us with Aithan. "They must have caught wind of our gathering and decided to act on their own accord. We met up too quickly for them to report back to their base and get orders to attack."

"You have an idea where their base is?" I question, frowning.

Aithan nods, wiping what looks like black soot from his forehead with the collar of his shirt. "Somewhere between Etherea and Teslin."

My brow furrows, but I file that piece of information in my brain for later. If anyone could draw conclusions, it would be Tariq and Elly, and if Fin weren't lying on the ground unconscious, I'd relish that I might know something the twins don't.

"Whether it was staged or not," Megara pauses, her eyes scanning the apartments' windows. "We are running out of time. If you think the prince is an ally, then we will eventually need to meet."

My gaze follows hers to where Magics watch the streets from above, hesitant and fearful even from this distance.

***

After spending a few minutes trying to flag down some of the other Mariande knights on patrol outside the Magic sector, I snag a carriage ride back with a very heavy, limp Fin, his head resting in my lap in the middle of the floor. One of the other knights rides off on a horse ahead of the carriage to prepare the castle for our arrival and alert them about what happened.

Well, at least our twisted version of what happened: a bar fight gone wrong.

The Elders and Lightning worked on clearing the Dark wielders' bodies out of sight while Jorah helped me drag Fin down a block or two to the bar district so it was a little more realistic. After he helped get him into the carriage with two other knights, he assured me he'd take care of the Magics who saw the short battle.

Apparently, like Magics in Eldamain, there's nothing a little coin can't solve.

FATE DEMANDS SACRIFICE

I spend the entire carriage ride back to the Castle of Andromeda praying to the Gods that Jorah has enough influence to convince Magics to keep their lips sealed. The last thing I need right now is to be outed for being Sirian before convincing Mariande not *all* Sirians are to be feared.

We lurch to a sudden stop, and it doesn't take long for the carriage door to swing open before me, two figures shadowed in the doorway.

"Gods, Reva," Pax grumbles, jumping in and sidestepping Fin's body so he can grip underneath his shoulders. He leans into me as he bends, whispering, "This wasn't a bar fight, was it?"

I silently pull my legs from underneath Fin's head, pressing into a seat as Pax replaces me. The other figure outside grabs Fin's legs and starts tugging him out of the carriage.

"Does he need medical attention, Healer?" Tariq's voice calls from outside, his head peeking in as he holds the bottom half of Fin.

"Eventually," I croak, clearing my throat. "I treated him for now, so I'll need to check on him shortly to bandage him. Just take him to his room, and I'll meet you there."

"You know where his room is?" Tariq inquires, an eyebrow raised.

I glower with a curled lip. "No, but I'm sure I can figure it out."

Tariq nods once, but he eyes me cautiously with

burning flames of amber. As he marches toward one of the doors, another figure pops into the doorway, their hands reaching into the carriage and wrapping around my legs. I immediately cry out from the sharp sting that shoots up my right leg, then tapers into a dull ache.

"Hey," Elly coos, her thumb caressing the shin of my uninjured leg. "Are you hurt?"

I nod, accepting her outstretched hand as I duck out of the carriage. Stepping onto the gray stone, the throbbing intensifies as the blood rushes down my leg. I steady myself with a hand on Elly's shoulder.

"Let's get to your room and get you treated before we meet the boys in Fin's room," she whispers, firmly gripping my hand.

I have Elly pick out any remaining rocks in my back and apply a wound care salve before changing my clothes. After I rub some burn cream onto the red-hot wound around my ankle and wrap it in a bandage, Elly and I travel down an unfamiliar corridor and up a few flights of stairs to Fin's room with vials of medication clanking in the bag on Elly's shoulder.

She raps twice on the door before turning the handle and shoving it open. She presses her face in the crack between the door and the frame, announcing, "It's just me and Reva."

One of the boys says something incoherently, but it must have meant we were good to come in.

Fin's room is roughly the same size as mine and equipped with all the same amenities. Where I have a

FATE DEMANDS SACRIFICE 191

kitchenette for my supplies, he has a desk cluttered with various daggers and books. He lays peacefully on the bed, his shirt having been removed and his wound leaking on his chest.

Inconveniently, it dawns on me I've never seen Fin shirtless. I knew he was muscular underneath his clothes, but I never realized how cut and lean he was.

A defined abdomen creates subtle shadows on his torso; even as he lays completely still on the bed, his breath lifts the stiff muscles of his chest. His arms are just as noticeable, biceps sculpted by the hands of the Gods themselves, the veins of his forearms—

"Fin is going to be so pleased to know you were gawking at his half-naked body when I tell him," Pax teases, offering Elly the chair he was sitting in.

She pauses before accepting it with a bob of her head, lowering beside her brother.

"You will do no such thing," I hiss, walking over to Fin's bedside with the bag we brought.

I lay out the vials on his nightstand in the deafening silence, fighting the impulse to sweep the strand of hair lying on his forehead. As I grab one of the extra pillows beside Fin's head, Tariq speaks up.

"What happened out there, Reva?" he asks softly.

With a deep breath, I recount everything that happened as I apply more tinctures to Fin's wound and bandage it up. I start from when Jorah busted into his hidden room and end with the carriage journey back alone.

By the end of it, my hands tremble from the memories of those eerie black eyes flashing just before Fin's sword burst through her chest.

Elly senses my exhaustion at the same time Fin stirs. "It's getting late. Let's leave so Reva can get Fin comfortable for the night."

Tariq's eyes switch from me to Fin, nodding in agreement. "We can talk more tomorrow. I'm sure there's a lot more that happened."

"Yeah, the damn meeting," I sigh, rubbing my forehead.

Pax offers a sympathetic, tight-lipped grin before opening the door for Elly and Tariq. Tariq pauses in the doorway, twisting back towards me and bracing his hand on the frame. He opens his mouth like he may say something but snaps it shut and tilts his head to the side. He presses his lips together before following after Pax and Elly.

"Am I dreaming?" Fin grumbles, his voice rough and gravelly.

I let out a breath of laughter, sitting on the edge of his bed. I gently placed my hand on his injured arm, now elevated on the pillow, curling my fingers over his forearm.

"We're back at the castle," I assure him, my thumb lightly tracing a vein in his arm. "I've got a few medicines for you, but I wanted to talk to you before heading to bed."

"Yes, Royal Healer," he smiles softly, his eyes

squinting. Despite his position and a decent wound, those green eyes twinkle up at me, warming my heart.

But the feeling is short-lived when the image of him jumping between the Dark wielder and I pops into my head.

I bite the inside of my lip before blinking once. "What in the world were you thinking? Why did you jump out in front of me like that? You kept me from conjuring a shield for us."

"It was an instinct, Reva," he groans, rolling his head on the pillow to avert his gaze. "It just felt like the right thing to do."

"I'm Sirian, Fin," I whisper, tightening my grip. "If anyone can fight the Darkness, it's me."

"I wasn't sure…" He trails off, shaking his head against the pillow, still not looking at me. "You hesitated and—"

"Hesitated…" A lead weight drops to the pit of my stomach. "You didn't think I could handle it, did you?"

Fin blinks once, slowly. "You aren't really in control of your powers, Reva. You said you got distracted during the attack on the castle, and you hesitated when Lightning tried to attack Tariq and me. I saw you freeze with that other one and didn't want you to get yourself killed because you were going to freeze again.… I just wasn't sure if I could…"

He trails off, but I know what he will say, so I finish his thought. "You weren't sure if you could trust my control."

"Reva—"

"Gods, Fin!" I shout, lurching up from the bed. I throw my arms out wide. "I'm so sick of you acting like I'm going to detonate any time I use my powers!"

"You know that's not what I think, Reva," Fin pleads, finally meeting my gaze, his eyes ablaze.

I snap, leveling my finger at him, "No matter what, you don't trust me with my power. You don't accept who I really am."

Fin presses his lips together, the breath he takes through his nose audible. My heart slams in my chest, said power tingling.

"Do you really want to lead an army?" Fin asks quietly and carefully. "I thought with Clint being cured, you'd want to step away from responsibility—"

"For you?" Fin flinches and the fissure in my heart elongates. "What if I don't want to step away? You were in that alley, Fin. You finally saw what the Dark wielders can do. They're just openly attacking innocent Magics… The more I get to know my power, the more I really wonder what my purpose is here. Even if I don't know if I can lead, I have to do something."

"So where does that leave us?" Fin whispers, searching my face.

And Gods, if I still don't know.

I didn't hesitate to kill someone for him, but I did the same thing for Elly and Clint a few months ago. Does that make us friends, or still something more?

Tears burn the corners of my eyes as I swallow the

FATE DEMANDS SACRIFICE

pain of my reality down. "I don't know who I'll be by the end of this. But you're so focused on the old version of who I was—a Magic Healer—that you found in a shack in Eldamain."

"Reva, please." Fin's voice cracks, the tears welling in those bright emerald depths. He moves his bad arm toward his face, his face scrunching as he lowers it back down on the pillow. I swallow a sob, holding up a hand.

"You need to change the dressing at least twice a day and apply the wound salve I left there," I whisper quietly, inching towards the door. "No physical exertion for the next few weeks. The salve will speed up your healing faster than by itself, so you'll only be down for four or five weeks."

Without another word, even as he calls out to me, I storm out of his room with tears streaking down my face.

Because we both needed to face reality.

I'm not who we thought I was.

CHAPTER 14

"*I*'m not really dreaming, am I?" I ask Karasi.

We're in our home, but there's something off about it. Other than the fact I know we're not actually there, the wood paneling on the floors and walls is richer, and it gives off a pine aroma similar to the Overgrowns.

Karasi stands in the middle of the room, her hands clasped in front of her. The same serene smile sits on her lips like the first dream she came into, her marigold eyes glowing.

"It is a dream." Karasi's head tilts. "Your dream and my memory. Last time, it was your dream and our memory."

"What memory is this?" I frown, raking my gaze across the hut again.

I crane my head towards the hallway where my bedroom door stands ajar, except none of my things are there. It's actually bare besides a freshly made bed that's nowhere near as rickety as mine.

"Long before you showed up on my doorstep," Karasi chuckles, waving her hand to the table between the kitchen and the living space.

It's an entirely different table with just two chairs instead of

FATE DEMANDS SACRIFICE   197

the four we have. I lower myself into the chair nearest me. Even though we're in a memory of hers that predates my existence by Gods-know how long, she's the same as I left her, pudgy body and gray locks piled on top of her head.

Speaking of before me…

"There's something I want to ask," I whisper, twisting my fingers in my lap.

"I know, aster.*" She bobs her head slowly. "I feel your turmoil. There are many emotions swirling inside of you right now. Some rather intriguing—" She levels me with a raised eyebrow. "But most concerning."*

I rest my hands on the table between us, my shoulders slumping. "I know who you are."

Her eyes are distant as she twists her head towards the window. "I suspected your research into your god-powers would lead to me."

"So, you are the Great Child," I conclude, my heart sinking. I hoped maybe we were wrong and it was all a strange coincidence, that this hadn't been another thing Karasi kept from me. I need to stop believing those exist. "You're Sybil's daughter."

"Me being the child of a demi-god is what you're really upset about," she guesses, slouching into the chair with a deep sigh. "Yes, Reva."

"So that makes you…" I pause, unable to vocalize what I saw on that parchment from the notes Elly gathered.

"I was born before the Sirians vanished from the world," she explains, her face a neutral mask as though she weren't admitting to being over a thousand years old. "I was born

shortly after King Alrik was officially crowned king."

"I don't think I will ever understand why you never told me that," I admit, my voice cracking. "You knew I had both Dionne and Asteria's god-powers. I would've felt less alone, especially knowing my own guardian understood—"

"You were never alone, child." Karasi's eyes darken, those vertical pupils pulsing. "My age never mattered, and even for the reasons you believe it would've, all I could do was raise you the way I had. You needed to go through life the way you did and the way you will to fight the Darkness."

I rest my forehead in my palm, my fingers tangling into my hair. I bite back the very real burning of tears. "Why?"

"Fate demands sacrifice," she says softly, her fingers grazing my elbow resting on the table. The hairs on the back of my neck prickle. "That was established long before you and I ever existed. The sacrifice it will take for you to come to your power would never have transpired if your life did not play out as it has. You would have gone down an entirely different path than the one you are on."

"Sacrifice?" I breathe, my mouth dry as I try to understand what she said. "I will never get to know my parents, and I had to leave the only family I've ever known…Haven't I sacrificed enough? "

"Not according to Fate." Her eyes downturn, a slight pout to her lower lip. "I wish you didn't have to know any pain, aster. Not like this."

"So another thing you can't or won't tell me?" I snap, clenching my fist.

"I wish I had more time to explain to you the limitations

FATE DEMANDS SACRIFICE

of my gifts." Karasi stiffens as if she is physically restraining herself. "My Magic has been a burden my entire life because it created walls between myself and the people I loved. Just because I knew something didn't mean I got to speak its entirety. There are so many things I wish I could tell you that I know, aster."

It's my turn to stare out the window now, Orion's Lake sparkling in the sunlight just beyond the fertile lawn that stretches between us. A warm tear burns a path down my cheek. Karasi's thumb tucks underneath my jaw, swiping it before it falls to the table.

"If you're the descendant of a demi-god and have lived to be over a thousand years old," I begin quietly, my voice hushed and gravelly. "What does that mean for me? Will I live long after all my friends are gone?"

Her eyes flash quickly, more gold than yellow, as her head snaps back like someone slapped her. "The Sirians always lived mortal lifespans, and it was never any different for those who descended from the demi-gods. I cannot speak for two god-powers, however. As for your friends—"

There is a low bellow like a groaning beast as the house starts shaking, the table quivering underneath us. I lurch from the table, my chair clattering to the ground, but Karasi stays planted.

"Is this part of your memory?" I ask, frantically searching for the source.

"She is losing patience with me," Karasi smirks, watching me intently. "She doesn't want me answering any more of your questions."

"You mentioned a 'she' last time, too," I yell over the near-deafening grumble surrounding us. *"Who are you talking about?"*

Again, like the last dream, Karasi just smiles softly as she says, "There was always a reason I called you aster—"

Rousing from this dream is slower as my eyes snap open, staring at the ceiling above my bed. It takes a minute for my eyes to focus and my body to register all the many functions of itself. My fingers and toes twitch first, pins and needles poking at the tips of them. The sensation creeps into my limbs, up my torso and sore back, and straight to the Mark on my forehead.

I lay on my back for a few minutes longer before I urge myself to get ready for the day ahead. As I sit in front of my vanity and rub a healing salve on my back, I can't shake the unease from my conversation with Karasi and the statements she made, not only about Fate and Sirians but also about this ominous *she.*

***

I spend most days trying to minimize Clint's mass, but not to the point of weakening me like I had the first two times. Collapsing in a useless heap was going to do no one any favors, especially when discussions needed to be had about what the Elders told me and where their feelings really stand with Mariande.

And the fact the Dark ones attacked us in front of

Magics.

Not to mention the *she* Karasi insinuated is interfering with my fate.

Pax and I are working with Clint on strengthening his leg muscles with resistance exercises when Tariq strolls through the door, using his backside to shut it behind him.

"Sorry I'm late." He smirks, pushing off the wood with his hips. "Lots of exciting meetings with my father and Eamon about the attacks on the Magic community."

"I didn't know we were expecting you," I say at the same time Pax asks, "Were you able to divert their questions?"

"If by divert you mean strategically pose a believable scenario," Tariq walks around to the opposite side of the bed, plopping beside Clint and extending his feet out. "Then, yes."

The wide grin spreading across Clint's face is enough to melt my heart.

Ever since his near-death experience, and as the mass minimizes at a painstaking pace, much of the boy I first encountered has returned, including the normal fair color of his skin and the glowing of those identical amber eyes.

"So, what's the cover story?" I ask, snapping my fingers in front of Clint, pulling him away from admiring his older brother. I gesture my hand to where his foot is flat against my palm. He narrows his eyes and grits his teeth as he pushes lightly against it.

"With the new remedy you've found for Clint, Elly

advised a change of scenery and some fresh air for you," Tariq begins, his hands out in front of him. "You went out for an evening with a fellow Magic you've befriended when you happened to stumble across Fin after he was stabbed by an assailant who unfortunately managed to get away."

"Smooth." I roll my eyes and shake my head. "What about the damage done to the buildings?"

"Well, of course, the drunken assailant got away by horse-drawn carriage," Tariq smirks at me, wiggling his head. "Him being drunk, he was rather reckless."

Clint snickers under his breath, his foot flopping to the bed as I release it.

"And what of these Elders?" Pax's gaze jumps from me to Tariq. "Reva said they took care of the bodies?"

"I spoke with Elly this morning after Lightning came in for her shift." Tariq speaks to me, "The Elder, with your firepower, burned the bodies down to nothing, apparently."

"It's not *my* firepower," I correct, fixing my hands on my hips. "But good. Have they left?"

"Lightning said they headed out on the first ship this morning." Tariq rests the back of his head on the headboard. "Per usual, she didn't elaborate beyond that and said you two will need to speak at some point. She has assumed you'll spend most of your Sirian Energy with Clint until he's healed."

I turn away from the boys toward the worktable against the wall. I rest my hands on it, replaying the encounter with the Elders in my head, particularly before Jorah interrupted when I'd thrown my credibility out the window with my slip-up on Tariq's name.

"What were the Elders like?" Clint interjects, his voice full of wonderment. "Did they look like Magics, or did they look like you, Reva? Were they really old?"

"Two were older than the King," I grumble. "The other couldn't be older than thirty."

There's a moment of silence before Tariq says, "You don't have to share the entire conversation you had with them, Reva. I understand you may feel a level of security with them that none of us could ever comprehend. But if there's anything you think is vital for us to know, we're open to it."

On the carriage ride back from Saros, I thought a lot about the conversation with Megara, Osiris, and Aithan and the brief altercation with the Dark Sirians. So many things happened in such a short evening, leaving a strange chill in my bones I still haven't been able to shake.

I twist around, resting my lower back against the work table. Clint's eyes dance excitedly over being part of the conversation and hearing things he's been waiting to learn about. I take a deep, steady inhale through my nose before diving into the parts of the conversation I feel obliged to share with Tariq.

He and Pax watch intently from where they're sitting, Tariq still beside Clint in his bed and Pax in the chair by the closed window. I explain how the Sirian movement came about, especially how Karasi and Jorah seem to be part of some underground Sirian assistance link. I don't tell them about the full number of Sirians that live in their community, but I do reveal the amount they consider able-bodied to battle if it comes to that.

"They're just as convinced as we are that it will come to war with the Dark wielders," I sigh, moving to sit on the edge of the bed beside Clint's legs. "They asked me where I stand."

Pax frowns, his dark skin shadowed. "What do you mean where you stand?"

"I said the same thing," I explain, shaking my head. I direct my attention to Tariq. "Based on how some of our chats with Lightning have gone, we shouldn't be shocked they don't trust you or Elly, even if you've shown acceptance towards me. They insisted we would need to win your dad over to really prove to them Mariande is on the same side as them."

"I'm not involving the King until necessary," Tariq asserts, his back straightening.

"Considering there are now more people in Mariande who know I'm a Sirian than back in Eldamain, I have no problems with that. I might have told them we wouldn't need your father's approval and you command your military."

Pax bursts into a fit of laughter, slamming his head into both of his hands. His shoulders bounce as his muffled giggles sneak out from between his fingers. Tariq studies me with raised eyebrows, tucking his lower lip between his teeth.

FATE DEMANDS SACRIFICE

205

"Oh, Gods," I groan, rubbing my face. "Was I wrong?"

Clint chuckles, his gaze bouncing between the three of us. "I feel like I need to take the opportunity here and gloat that I'm smarter than Reva for once."

"Clint!" I squeal, swatting his leg.

"What he means is technically, yes, you were wrong," Tariq jumps in, glaring at his brother. "If it came to an all-out war, the army is my father's to command, but I have a much better relationship with all of them, considering the Generals underneath me or beside me were hand-picked by me."

"So…" I wince with one eye closed. "You could command them?"

"If you wanted anarchy." Pax grins, dramatically wiping a fake tear away. "You still need Darius's permission."

"Regardless, I told them the Crown Prince and I were allies." I scan Tariq's face, even though I know I won't be able to gauge his reaction unless he really wants me to see it. I sidestep the slip-up I had using his first name. "Before Jorah interrupted, I told them if they wanted me to be part of their efforts, then they needed to ally with Mariande or at least you and Elly."

Pax and Tariq exchange a grave glance, the former shrugging with a cringe. My shoulders slump heavily, not ready to face yet another mistake I made in that conversation.

"You didn't have to do that," Tariq explains, his hand

resting on Clint's shin as he tries to reach for me. "They're *your* people, Reva. We would've understood if you felt a loyalty to them over us. You didn't have to give them an ultimatum on our behalf."

"It's not on your behalf." I rise from the bed. "It's on behalf of the world. Sirians need all the help we can get, even if we march onto a field with thirty Sirians and a royal army of hundreds to battle a small group of Dark wielders. If we want a place in this world, we need to stop hiding ourselves."

Tariq and Pax look at each other again, a silent conversation I'm clearly not privy to. My heart aches at the familiarity in their expressions, Karasi and the others in Eldamain on my mind.

"Any other notable tidbits?" Tariq asks, swinging his legs over the edge of the bed.

Clint reaches for one of his books on his nightstand, opening it to where his bookmark rests. One of the last things the Elders said to me flashes like a beacon in my mind.

"Yes!" I point my finger at Tariq. He holds his hands up in surrender, but I sneer at him before elaborating. "An Elder said the attack wasn't planned. He came to that conclusion because they've roughly pinpointed where the Dark Sirian base might be."

Tariq's eyes flicker to Pax as he slowly rises from his chair by the window. "Where?"

"He said somewhere between Etherea and Teslin," I answer, watching again as they snap their heads toward

FATE DEMANDS SACRIFICE 207

each other. "Why?"

"Do you think—" Pax stops himself, squinting his eyes. "There's no way either of them would…"

"We'll discuss it further with Fin," Tariq concludes, straightening his tunic before directing his attention toward the door. "May I escort you back to your rooms for the evening, Reva?"

I hesitate, debating whether I should demand they tell me what they're talking about, but a glance at the clock indicates it's time for me to head back to my room before dinner anyway.

"That would be great, actually," I agree with a nod, gathering my things and following him out of the door.

As we silently traverse the halls, I replay the interaction with Jorah in my head and what Karasi said about the unknown woman who watches me. I can't help but wonder if it's my mother who watches me in the afterlife, wherever our souls go when we die. We've always been taught when someone passes, they're always watching, but how can they?

"You're alarmingly quiet," Tariq finally interrupts as we approach my door. I fumble with my key as I unlock it. "Did something happen at the meeting? Did they upset you?"

I finally slide it into the lock and turn, contemplating. "It was before the meeting."

"Do you want to talk about it?" he asks, his shoulder leaning on the wall.

I glance behind us down both ends of the hallway

before motioning for him to follow me into my room. As the door shuts behind him and plunges us into complete darkness, I shoot a stream of fire into the fireplace, and it roars to life.

Tariq's eyes blaze as he gazes at it in awe. "I don't think I've seen you do that yet."

"It's a party trick." I splay my hand out towards the chairs in front of the fire. We sit comfortably in the plush chairs as I explain, "Jorah said something to me before the meeting that has really just jumbled my mind."

Tariq waits patiently, propping his forearms on his thighs as he offers his unyielding attention. The orange and yellows in his eyes illuminate with the fire, mimicking the color of the flames.

"I'm assuming Elly has explained to you how Jorah's power works from his House," I start, and Tariq nods. "He read my blood again and said he recognized it. He said he met my mother when she was pregnant with me, that she came to him for help to confirm I was Sirian."

Tariq's eyes widen, his head twitching to the side. "Did he tell you her name?"

I shake my head, fighting the tears burning the corners of my eyes. "He didn't catch her name. He said she came with a friend of hers…"

"Do you think she was from Mariande?" He reclines back in the chair, resting his elbow on the arm as he cradles his chin in his hand.

I shrug, rubbing my head in my hands. "I don't know. Look how information travels through the Magic

FATE DEMANDS SACRIFICE 209

communities here. Mortals are willing to travel from all over the Main Continent to Eldamain to seek Karasi's help. Who's to say there aren't rumblings about Jorah being able to read something like that?"

"Do you think your mother was a Magic, then?" Tariq asks, and I can tell he's trying to help me piece my thoughts together.

What he doesn't know is that I've asked myself these very same questions repeatedly in my head. Like everything else in my life, I don't *know*. Most days, I walk away with more questions than answers.

"Hey," Tariq whispers, lunging from his chair. He skirts around the coffee table, grabbing my hands as he raises me from my seat to stand with him.

I don't realize I'm crying until his hands grip my face and his thumbs swipe across my cheeks, smearing tears across them.

"I have a lot of resources I can use to help you figure out who your family is and what happened to them," he assures me, tilting my head up to look at him. "I can learn more from Jorah about what she and her friend looked like. Unless you asked?"

"I mean, I asked, and he said she looked like me, but that was it." I press my lips together, shrugging. "I'm so sick and tired of everything being a mystery. My life is just one big question mark. I just want control over things for once. I want to ask a question and not get half of an answer that produces ten more questions. Hell, I'm still learning how to ask questions. My entire life, Karasi wouldn't give me straight answers, so it's hard to ask others when I'm not even sure if I'll get a real answer."

Tariq gently pulls my head into his chest. I rest my forehead against the firm muscle underneath his shirt, inhaling deeply as my hands splay against the sides of his ribcage. His arms wrap around the back of my head and shoulder, blocking out the world, and I'm engulfed in him.

His scent invades me, woodsy and sharp but with a sweet, velvety twist. I swallow against it, unable to hide the gulp that comes from my throat.

Tariq slowly peels me away from him, something predatory underneath his burning gaze. My tongue grazes my upper lip, and he latches onto that movement. Mindlessly, my legs move underneath me, stepping backward toward the chair. The back of my thighs bump against the arm of it, but Tariq doesn't stop his advance, his leg settling between mine. He catches my waist in his grip, pulling me closer into him as his thigh presses into my pelvis. I angle my head to look up at him as he slants his down.

"Tariq," I breathe. "We can't…"

"Can't what?" he mumbles, his breath whisking across my cheek. He rolls his lips together, drawing my attention to them.

"Us." I swallow, my mouth dry, and I wonder how much kissing him would quench my thirst. "You're the Crown Prince—"

"I'm well aware of my station." He cocks his head to

FATE DEMANDS SACRIFICE
211

the side, and it doesn't get past me how much this angle perfectly aligns our lips. "I'm also a grown-ass adult who can make his own decisions."

Where have I heard that before...

"Tariq," I gasp again as he moves his head closer to mine, but he snakes around my cheek, kissing the skin just below my ear.

My knees shake from the position I'm in and the sensitive spot he caresses with his lips, and I hope he can't feel how warm I am against his leg. He kisses lower, closer to my collarbone, and I breathe again, "Tariq."

"Say my name like that again," he mumbles against my throat. "And I'll make you say it for the rest of the night."

Sweet Gods.

"I'm the Royal Healer," I remind him, my voice weaker than I'd care for it to be. He nips at my throat along my jugular, and my eyes flutter, gooseflesh rising on my arm and my nipples peaking underneath my shirt. "We just can't..."

Tariq shifts back enough so I can stand straight. He grips my chin between his thumb and finger, forcing my eyes to lock onto his fiery ones.

"While your argument is *compelling*," he drawls, rolling his eyes. I clench my jaw, and he smirks. "I disagree."

He takes a few steps back, putting a healthier distance between us. The absence of his body heat creates a chill that runs over my skin, but especially startling where the warmth had been gathering against his leg.

He casually straightens his tunic and brushes off his sleeves, his face a mask of neutrality. He reaches for the door, but before he opens it, he reels his head on me.

"I would never kiss you without your permission," he admits, pushing out that bottom lip. "But I want you to know, I will be asking next time… So, think about what your answer will be." He opens the door and stops on the threshold to add without malice, "And maybe a little more confidence behind that answer would help, too."

He gently shuts the door behind him, the click of the latch snapping me out of my trance. I slide into the chair, sinking as deep as possible with my knees pulled up.

Because I don't know how much longer I can stop myself from saying yes.

CHAPTER 15

Walking into Clint's room the next morning, I'm shocked to find Elly, Tariq, and Fin with Clint and Pax. I stop just within the doorway, frowning.

"What's going on, guys?" I place my crate of elixirs and ingredients on the ground because they're all more than suspect.

Fin stands with his good arm in one pocket and the other in a sling, rocking back and forth from the balls of his feet to his heels with a massive smile spread across his face. Tariq is a mask of indifference as usual, but there is something glistening below the surface. Elly presses her lips together, her hands clasped in front of her chest.

"We have a surprise for you," Tariq says, cocking his head towards Clint. "Well, he does."

I turn my attention to Clint and Pax, the latter standing next to the young prince's bedside.

"Pax and I wanted to try something last night after you left," Clint explains, looking up at Pax with wide eyes. "But I wanted to show you before the Glow Ball in a few days."

The crease between my eyebrows deepens as he

shifts, throwing the blanket off his legs and swinging them over the edge of the bed. He fixes his eyes on the floor in concentration and grips Pax's extended arm. Hands flexing, he uses Pax as leverage to slide his feet to the ground.

"Clint," I gasp, barely above a whisper, my hand flying to cover my mouth with wide eyes.

His gaze stays on the floor, and I hold my breath, my heart hammering against my ribcage when he braces himself on Pax's arm to hoist himself upright with a slight bend to his waist.

I don't breathe as Clint pauses, testing his balance before straightening out to full height. Every part of me swells with pride, tears springing to my eyes as a small smile climbs up my cheeks.

"You can stand—" I'm cut off as another gasp is ripped from my lungs because Clint and Pax take a step towards me.

And another.

And another.

One step after the next, careful and cautious, until Clint stands directly before me.

His eyes have been locked onto the floor and his own two feet the entire time, brows furrowed in concentration. One of the tears hiding in the corners of my eyes manages to escape down my cheek in a rush.

"I'm good," Clint utters under his breath. With a nod, Pax takes two steps back, staying within arm's reach. Clint raises his head to me, those bright eyes, identical to

FATE DEMANDS SACRIFICE   215

his brother and sister's, finding my own. "I'm just a head shorter than you, and I'm only thirteen. If I keep eating and taking those nourishments, could I grow to be taller than Tariq?"

As the image of an adult Clint flashes in my mind, happy and *alive*, something between a sob and a laugh escapes my lips. I carefully grab his face between my hands, and his hands slide up to grip the back of my arms for stability. I open my mouth but am too stunned to form a single word.

The young, sick prince I was hired to heal *stands* before me.

He just *walked* to me from across the room.

"Gods, Clint." I fall before him, my knees hitting the ground with a soft thunk, and look up at him for once. My arms clasp onto his elbows, pinning them to his sides. "You and your surprises."

"I thought it would be nice to have a good surprise for once," he whispers, his eyes rimmed with silver. "You deserve good things, Reva."

A sob rattles my chest as I gently press my forehead against his sternum. He slips his arms out of my grasp to wrap them around my head. I let my hands fall to the side of his knees, where the muscles quiver from strain.

But I want him to have this moment.

Selfishly, I want to have this moment with him.

This win in a world determined to let me sacrifice the things I care for.

I sniffle, pulling away from Clint. Pax is already

beside him, ready to guide him back to his bed. There is some foreign emotion I'm not used to seeing on Pax's face as he towers over me. It softens his eyes and features, making him appear younger.

I stay on the floor, watching him guide Clint back to his bed. If I look away, I'm worried it will all evaporate into a dream.

My view is suddenly blocked by two legs before the body bends down in front of me. Tariq kneels on the floor with me, our knees touching. There's a serene smile on his face as he grabs both my hands.

It would be an honor to kneel before you.

"You've really done it." Tariq's eyes frantically scan my face, lingering on the tears silently falling. "You saved my brother."

I stare at him, my heart squeezing in my chest from Clint's surprise and the Crown Prince on his knees before me.

"Don't think the kingdom of Mariande will forget this." One of his hands leaves mine to cup my cheek. His thumb lightly brushes a tear away. Quieter, he whispers, "Don't think I will ever forget this."

I swallow the lump in my throat. "I was just doing my job."

Tariq presses his lips together, his gaze flickering to my mouth and back to my eyes. With a slight shake of his head, he pulls me into him as I fling my arms around his neck.

I press my face into the crook of his neck, scorching

FATE DEMANDS SACRIFICE

217

tears running rapidly down my cheeks, no doubt soaking his shirt. The hand that was on my cheek now grips the back of my head, holding me there with a fistful of my hair, his arms fastened around me like falling into a bed after a long day's work.

"Quit hogging her," Elly's tearful voice shouts. Tariq uncurls from me, allowing Elly to take my hands and help me back to my feet.

She nearly knocks me to the floor as she throws her arms around me, squeezing tight enough to force a breath of air from my lungs. Over her shoulder, Clint is back on his bed, Pax and Fin helping him get comfortable again.

"Maybe if we get me a cane, I can have at least one dance with you before the Glow Ball ends," Clint calls from the bed. Elly and I pull apart, giggling. "I can't let my date dance by herself."

Tariq and Fin chuckle, but I level Clint with a stare. "We'll see how you're feeling by then. If you're up to it, I would prefer you go in your wheelchair so you don't pull something from standing the whole time."

"I don't mind that," Clint sighs, rubbing his fists along his thighs. "I was already sore just from practicing with Pax last night. I can't imagine not having the wheelchair for the Glow Ball."

I laugh again, amazed.

"This calls for celebration!" Elly squeals, clapping. "It's a beautiful day out! We should all go to the beach this evening for a little picnic and wine."

"I'm going to pass out before dinner." The fatigue

is evident in Clint's soft features. "It wouldn't be fun anyway if you're all going to get drunk. I don't want anyone trying to steer a wheelchair and horse around that beach."

"You sure, Clint?" Fin asks, ruffling the boy's blond hair. "We could always have the picnic in the garden instead."

He swats away Fin's hand, smacking his forearm a few times in the process. "I really don't mind. Maybe Dad can come and hang out with me? I can at least show him I'm standing, right?"

"If you're up to it," Pax shrugs, smirking at Clint in challenge. Clint nods sternly, looking towards the door as if the king was already there.

"I'll go get him for you," Tariq grins before extending his head to Elly. "Why don't you work with Chef B on gathering supplies for the picnic? We'll all meet by the stables to snag a few horses to ride down there."

Elly claps again, hugging me from the side as she plants a kiss on my cheek. Pax smiles, shaking his head at the both of us as Tariq takes his leave with her. Fin settles beside Clint, wincing as the kid actually jabs him in his bad shoulder before bursting into a fit of laughter.

A warm, fuzzy sensation crawls through my veins and into my heart, settling into one of the many hollow holes created by the loss of those I never knew.

***

FATE DEMANDS SACRIFICE 219

Pax, Fin, and Tariq stand at the side of the fire with their glasses of wine, chattering about something important. I chuckle as Fin tries to explain whatever he's getting at with one hand, cringing every time his hand reflexively tries to mimic the other.

Elly and I pass the second bottle of wine between one another, huddled by the fire I ignited with a blanket draped over our shoulders. The sun sets behind us as we watch the boys and the ocean extending beyond the horizon, the spring warmth quickly fading.

"What do you think they're talking about?" Elly whispers into my ear.

I shrug, repeating my previous thoughts aloud. "Something important. Probably military things."

"I guarantee you—" Elly pauses, gulping another swig. She points the neck towards them. "They are talking about a stupid game they play in knight training."

I whirl my gaze on her, finding a sly smile glowing in the fire's light. I shake my head, a breath of laughter escaping from my nose.

She twists her head towards me, shutting her eyes as she shrugs sheepishly. I laugh loudly then, throwing my head back as I reach for the wine. She extends her arm behind her before she presses the rim to her lips, throws her head back, and starts chugging.

"Elly!" I squeal, reaching across her to try and snag it from her. She jerks away, a drop falling down her cheek. "Don't be sloppy!"

She nearly spits out the wine from giggling, shoving

the now-empty bottle into my hands. I try to fight the smile on my lips as she jumps to her feet, wobbling on the uneven rocks before gathering her skirts in her hand.

"I'm going to dip my feet in the water before we head back to the castle," she hiccups, covering her mouth.

I giggle again, the boys frowning as they watch Elly march through the pebbled beach to stand in the water that laps up onto the rocky shore.

Pax leans into Fin and Tariq, whispering something before strolling toward the fire and me, rubbing his hands together briskly. He sits beside me with a soft grunt, staring off into the distance, and pulls his knees up to rest his forearms on them.

We sit there in a short silence, both of us watching Elly stand unfazed in the cold water up to her ankles, the bottom of her skirt darkened in color. Out of the corner of my eye, Fin and Tariq are still chatting about something with less enthusiasm than before.

"You've seemed to change your mind about me rather quickly," I suddenly blurt, the wine giving me the courage I normally have when dancing on tables and enticing foreigners at The Red Raven.

I swallow against the spear of nostalgia that pierces my chest.

Pax chuckles darkly. "I have seen things I can't explain working alongside you with Clint."

I wait patiently now, biting my tongue to keep from snapping with a snarky remark or saying something that will break this fragile thread between us.

FATE DEMANDS SACRIFICE 221

"As you get older, I think you start to see things differently," he muses, tilting his head. "For so long, I blindly believed my father and his version of things because I didn't have another. I still don't, even after all these years. But something tells me his story isn't correct."

"What story?" I ask, studying the frown on his face.

"About everything," he huffs, pausing for a few breaths. "He was always stern and hard on me. From what I remember of my mom, though, she would try to overwhelm me with love and goodness. I remember the times she tried to teach me acceptance…" He trails off, his eyes distant and detached, lost in his memories.

"What happened to her?" I ask quietly, my heart going out to him. Even if I never knew my parents, there's a kinship in missing them, even if it is just his mom.

"For the longest time, he said she died in childbirth." Pax blinks rapidly, frowning. He grabs the pendant between his fingers, a nervous tick similar to mine. "When I told Father they were bringing the Great Karasi in to help Clint, he lost his damn mind. He was already ornery over the Magic communities, but that sent him over the edge. He couldn't understand why Magics were given special treatment and why King Darius thought another Magic could save his son."

He pauses, his frown deepening with a scowl. "He said, 'Magics can never be trusted. Look at your mother. She left with your sister like a thief in the night.'"

I startle, pulling my head back. "Wait. Your mom's a

Magic? Does that mean you're—"

He shakes his head, cutting me off. "I mean, yes to her being a Magic. But I didn't inherit that gene, I guess. I think she somehow knew my sister did, so that's why she left with her."

"How do you know you're not a Magic?" I ask, trying to see if I notice any traits about him that could lend to that heritage. He *is* really tall, probably the same height as Remy...

And that's when I realize the black gem around his necklace is hematite.

He shrugs, waving his hand up and down his body. "Look at me, Reva. Do I look like a Magic?"

"Not all Magics look like it," I explain, my eyes glued to his necklace. "If you've ever been faster or stronger than others, or you noticed you healed from things quicker than others or could last longer in knight drills and exercises than others... Those are all enhanced capabilities a Magic has."

His eyebrows twitch in the middle, like something has come to his mind.

I don't want to completely divert from the story and send him down an identity crisis spiral, so I briefly keep the hematite necklace comment to myself and squeeze his forearm. "It doesn't matter right now. You said your mom left with your sister?"

He nods, eyes flashing. "She had been pregnant, which is why I believed Father when he originally said she died in childbirth. I think I was mostly angry at her for

FATE DEMANDS SACRIFICE

leaving me behind than for you being Magic. How could she? She clearly left with my sister because she was afraid of my father's prejudice, but she was okay with leaving me behind with him.

"I was consumed by the idea that she was selfish. And, if my own mother was selfish, then my dad was right: all Magics cared about was themselves, and they didn't care who they hurt in the process."

My heart breaks in my chest, a harsh sting. I can't fault him for who he became or how he reacted when, for so many years, the only goodness he had ever known after his mother left were the Hespers and Fin. They accepted a Magic, betraying what he'd learned about someone who was supposed to love him but left.

"I got so angry at King Darius, Tariq, and Elly for blindly trusting you. It made me even angrier that Tariq left, acting like his sabbatical could still happen when a stranger was coming into our home. After I saw you for the first time, I knew I'd lost Fin to your charm."

Warmth floods my cheeks, so I look out onto the water, the island off the coast just barely visible in the midnight blue sky.

"Everything was just so suspicious to me," he continues. "I didn't trust your intentions, especially as the so-called apprentice of the most powerful Magic for the Gods know how long."

I clear my throat. "So, I've changed your mind then? About Magics and… Well, now Sirians?"

I feel his gaze lock onto me. I turn my head, meeting

those deep depths. He raises an eyebrow, his forehead wrinkling, as his eyes flick between where my Mark is hidden and back to my eyes.

"I hate to admit when Tariq is right." He stares at his boot, toeing a lump of pebbles. "I needed to see you work; I needed to actually get to know you. Watching you with Clint and seeing how much you genuinely love him changed everything for me.

"Learning you were Sirian also solidified it for me. You had all this power… And you chose to save Clint and Elly back in the spring. If you were evil incarnate, you could've easily taken this castle just by surprise alone, not to mention two god-powers."

"So, you changing your mind had nothing to do with winning Elly back?" I tease, smirking.

He frowns again, sadness hidden behind that hard exterior. "I've disappointed and hurt her."

"She believed in you when everyone else seemed to have given up, though," I explain, rubbing my hands on my skirt. "She loves you and knew the man she loved was there."

His eyes flash something deep and beautiful. "I've never told…"

"And what better time than now?" I cock my head to the ocean, where Elly stands at the edge of the water. "If you want to finally prove you trust me, go tell her."

Determination levels his brows and his stare. He lurches off the ground and rushes across the pebbled beach. From where they stand, Fin and Tariq frown, eyes

FATE DEMANDS SACRIFICE 225

trailing Pax as he jogs over the rocks to Elly. They both flicker their gazes at me before watching the events at the shore.

When Pax is a few feet from her, she must hear his footsteps because she turns on her heel to face him. She frowns, and it looks like she mouths his name. His back is to us, so I don't know what he says as he grabs her face in his hands, but shock flashes across it before melting into a soft smile. Her hand reaches up to grab his wrists, and at the same time, he yanks her to him.

When their lips collide, it's like watching two separate flames of fire intertwine. They meld into each other's bodies, his hands still holding her face as she runs them across his arms and down his back. And her face as they kiss?

Peace.

Fin's whooping snaps my attention away from my best friend and her knight. He claps his free arm on his thigh as he shouts. Tariq is clapping, too, but his eyes are latched onto me.

"What a way to end the night, you two," Fin yells with his free hand cupped on the side of his mouth.

"It's picturesque, isn't it?" Tariq elbows Fin's ribs as he starts walking toward me and the fire. "The sunset and kiss on the beach? Something tells me you had a hand in that, but it feels very unlike you to be a hopeless romantic."

"Me?" I squeal, pointing my finger to my chest. I gawk at him momentarily as he nears, but then I shrug and pout. "I have no idea what you're talking about. I'm also offended you don't take me for a romantic."

Tariq deadpans, but it's Fin's voice that carries on the salty breeze. "I mean, you're not."

I scoff, throwing my middle finger up in his direction as he walks beside Pax and Elly, who are hand-in-hand. Elly busts out laughing, leaning her weight into the arm that grips hers.

"Good Gods." Tariq picks up the empty wine bottle, wiggling it in Elly's direction. "Did you two do this?"

"And what if we did?" She stops mid-stride, fixing her hands on her hips. I chuckle as she extends her head to the sky, her words slurring just enough to be noticeable. "I'm older than you."

Tariq glares at his twin, and I watch in fascination as a real conversation seems to happen silently between them, entirely different from the one I saw between him and Pax the other day.

"Would you two quit?" Fin snaps playfully, helping Pax gather our supplies onto his horse. "Reva, could you…" He waves his hand over the blanket.

I catch the odd, detached tone in his voice, so I narrow my eyes into thin slits as I dramatically slap my hands on the ground and boost myself up—

Only to nearly fall flat on my face as the world pulses in my vision, all the wine I'd drank with Elly rushing straight to my head. I tilt with the horizon, bracing for the rocky beach, but luckily, a firm grip catches my elbow to help me.

FATE DEMANDS SACRIFICE 227

"Looks like you'll be riding back with me." Tariq laughs when I glare at him, but I swear I'm seeing two of him, and *that* conjures way too many enticing thoughts into my brain. "Yeah, you're riding back with me."

"I can ride myself—" I cut off, but the words are already out, and Elly doubles over in a fit of giggles as I catch an eye-roll from Pax.

"Wouldn't that be interesting," Tariq mutters, bringing his horse closer. "Maybe it can be our topic of conversation on our short ride back."

After helping me up onto the horse, Tariq mounts it and wraps his arms around me to grab the reins in his hands. They hang loose in his grip while the other hand snakes around my waist and starts lazily tracing a circle on my hip.

A fire ignites in my lower stomach and burns in my core. My body instinctively lays back against his warm embrace, closing my eyes against his caress, his hard chest, the lull of the horse…

"Are you comfortable?" Tariq whispers against my ear, but I can hear that damn smirk in his voice.

I snap my eyes open and cautiously twist my head to look behind me. I open my mouth, but I'm at a loss for words when I realize how close our faces are. I first notice the lower lip I just want to bite, but then my gaze moves to his eyes, and I spot a dark blue ring around the amber irises.

"You have blue in your eyes," I whisper, unable to stop my mouth before thinking about what I say, and my hand lifts to barely brush his beard. He startles, clearly stumped by my observation, and I bashfully turn forward again, holding my hand in my lap as my cheeks burn like my core.

Tariq clears his throat, then resumes his hand movement on my hip. This time, though, his fingertips trail across my waist, drawing a path that circles just above a very sensitive point between my legs.

"If we're dishing out strange compliments," Tariq mumbles behind me, his chest rumbling with the low volume of his voice, "You smell *incredible*."

"I—what?" I straighten, which is a mistake because it plunges his hand lower, just grazing the warmth gathering. I feel his fist clench as his body stiffens, but he relaxes as he places his hand back on the curve of my hip.

But I can't just leave well enough alone, especially as something firm rests against my lower back. I smirk to myself as I adjust my hips on the saddle, even if it isn't needed, eliciting a low grunt from the man at my back. I bite my lower lip as I arch my back a little and rub against him, more deliberately this time.

"Reva," Tariq growls, his fingers digging into my skin. I repeat the movement, slower. "Woman—"

Tariq quickly switches the reins into his left hand at my waist, and his right hand unabashedly slides up the front of my body to squeeze my throat, pushing my head back to meet his gaze as my gasp is cut off.

"I have no problem flipping you around and fucking you on this horse," Tariq grumbles low, his lips pressed

FATE DEMANDS SACRIFICE 229

to my ear. "But something tells me you've forgotten we would have an audience."

I swallow hard against his hand wrapped around my throat, remembering exactly who is traveling behind us back to the castle. With a quick squeeze and kiss to my temple, Tariq releases me from his hold, and I sit upright again.

We don't say anything for the rest of the ride back.

When we get to the castle's courtyard, we all walk in together, with Fin, Pax, and Elly leading while Tariq hangs back with me. The rest of the group keeps walking, lost in their conversation when Tariq and I stop in front of my door.

"This is where I leave you for the night," Tariq says, bowing slightly with a dip of his head. "Sleep well, Starfire."

He turns on his heel, and just before he walks away, I find my hand grabbing his. He hesitates, staring down at where our hands are locked before slowly dragging his burning gaze back up to my face.

"Yes?" he asks, an eyebrow raised.

My mouth opens, and it stays like that momentarily as I fight the war in my head.

Gods, I want nothing more than to invite him in, let that hand dip exactly where it was going, kiss that stupid, arrogant mouth of his—

Instead, I swallow once before whispering, "You smell really good, too."

Tariq's eyes flash something unfamiliar as they pulse,

but he relaxes into a smile with a breathy chuckle. He raises my hand to his lips, gently brushing them against my knuckles.

"Goodnight, Reva." He tips his head back before releasing my hand and walking down the hall where our friends have long since disappeared.

Chapter 16

I sit in front of Elly's vanity as she uses a cosmetic wax to slick down my hair pulled into a ponytail on the top of my head. My long, raven-black hair waterfalls from the band holding it up in uniform waves.

"Would you stop scrunching your face?" she snaps between clenched teeth, using a wet cloth to wipe any residue off her hands. "You're going to crease the powder on your face before the night has even started."

"I don't understand why I need any of this anyway," I scoff, fiddling with my hands as she retouches the bronze powder. "If it'll fall off by the end of the night, why waste the time to put all of this on?"

Elly presses her lips together, stepping back to observe her handiwork.

She had already completed her own cosmetic touches before me, with mauve powder on her eyelids, a coal-colored substance on her eyelashes, glittery powder across her cheekbones, and ruby red rouge on her lips to match the stones in her necklace. While her hair spirals down her back in perfect ringlets, the sides are pulled into a braid to the back of her head to expose her face.

232   K.M. DAVIDSON

I twist my head, which somehow seems heavier with this ponytail despite it having the same amount of hair as always, staring at my reflection in the mirror.

Since my skin tone is deeper than Elly's, she had to get me my own cosmetics to match my complexion. My eyelashes have the same black pomade as hers, making them appear extended, but my eyelids have a chocolate brown powder on them, dramatically enhancing my golden hazel eyes. She used the same brown powder in the hollow of my cheeks to accent my cheekbones, but I refused any sort of rouge on my lips.

"I think we're ready for dresses." Elly claps, running over to where two attendants wait with our gowns for the evening. "We're going to be the *stars* of the show." She inconspicuously wiggles her eyebrows at me, and I roll my eyes.

It takes us both a moment to put our dresses on without breaking a sweat, but Elly manages to finish before me. As the attendant continues securing the six buttons up my back, I let Elly have a moment to examine herself in the full-length mirror before saying anything.

"You look like an actual Princess," I awe quietly, startled by how regal and ethereal this dress makes her look.

Most of the dress is made from pale pink tulle, flowing graciously from where it hugs her waistline. The cut in the front is rather scandalous, with sheer fabric down the middle of her chest in a deep V that exposes most of her cleavage and past her sternum. From her waist and

FATE DEMANDS SACRIFICE 233

climbing up her shoulders, a thick, ivory applique shaped like birds and stars overlapping each other covers the tulle. Two birds are perched in front of the shoulder caps, and the tulle extends down her arms in loose balloon sleeves with the same applique scattered across it.

And sitting on top of her head is a gothic bronze crown embedded with black gems and rubies to match her necklace.

"While I might not enjoy planning these events," Elly sighs, adjusting her sleeves. "I do love a reason to get dressed up."

She gathers the bottom of her dress and rotates away from the full-length mirror to get a better look at me. I'm not sure why my heart pounds in my chest, reverberating up my throat.

"Reva," Elly whispers, her face softening. "You look absolutely beautiful."

"Not regal this time?" I try to laugh, but it comes out like a whimper instead.

And then I catch my reflection and the air leaves my body.

The color choice is superb, making *me* look like a princess. The champagne gold color immaculately complements the olive tone of my skin, not to mention that every inch of what appears to be a silk-like material is covered in glitter, reflecting the light in the room like flashes of stars. With a heart-shaped neckline, only one shoulder has a strap that extends from my waist and across my breast, where it splits into two, the second strap hanging loose on my arm. There is a slit hiding on the left side, only visible when I walk or move a certain way, reaching high up my thigh.

Standing in this dress, I realize how thin and lean I had been because of my life in Eldamain: arguably malnourished, drinking in excess, and traveling miles by foot. Since being in Mariande, I've filled out in many places, and I even glimpse muscle on my thigh.

I've always known I was pretty with my full lips, contrasting hair, eyes, skin, and rather round breasts, but I never thought I could *feel* beautiful. I knew men were attracted to me sexually, but I don't feel that way right now.

For once, I feel like I could be loved by someone.

"You outdid yourself, Elly," I croak, clearing my throat. The rush of emotions is overwhelming.

"Oh, Reva, please don't cry," Elly grumbles, trying to suppress her own tears and smile.

"I'm sorry," I mumble around my tears, fanning my face with her to dry it. "I just don't think I ever envisioned anything like this for myself. I never saw a future for me, just an existence. For once, I can see a real life in front of me."

As long as we aren't all killed first, hangs in the air between us silently, unable to vocalize that with the two attendants still here.

A knock on the door startles all four of us, but based on the clock above Elly's fireplace, it's time for us to get going. A whole new anxiousness flutters in my chest and

FATE DEMANDS SACRIFICE

235

stomach like frantic butterflies. I rest my hands over my sternum, hoping the touch and pressure will calm them down. With my head bowed, I wait for the attendants to open the door for us.

"Your Highness," one of them announces, fully swinging the door open. "May I present the Crown Prince Tariq and Prince Clint, accompanied by Sir Pax Forde."

The boys all file in one after the other, Tariq pushing Clint's wheelchair in as Pax follows close behind them. Tariq quickly utters something to the two attendants, and they bow before taking their leave.

"Princess Eloise," Pax greets, gently grasping Elly's fingers in his, raising her hand to his lips, and staring down her arm. "You are absolutely stunning."

No amount of powder could hide the blush that springs up Elly's neck and cheeks.

Either Clint or Tariq clears their throat, having moved closer into the room. I carefully grasp my dress and move around the lovebirds, which causes my leg to peek out from the slit. I instantly lock eyes with Tariq's, and they devour me as they flicker from mine to my thigh and back up again, a smirk climbing up his lips.

"We all match!" Clint interrupts gleefully, throwing his arms out to either side of him. I turn my attention to him and he lifts an eyebrow with a smirk identical to his brother's as he asks, "What do you think?"

For once, Clint is the teenager he's supposed to be, and it brings joyful tears back to my eyes again.

His slacks and dress shirt are both white, and the top two buttons are undone. His formal suit jacket is the same champagne gold as my dress, with a silk floral pattern across its entirety, besides the lapels. He wears a crown similar to Elly's, except more masculine in design, with two bronze ravens on the front.

Frustration and what I have to admit is excitement war in me as I register Tariq is wearing the exact same jacket as Clint—which means his jacket also matches the color of my dress.

What furthers that warming emotion from my chest into my arms, where I swear I'm losing feeling in my fingertips, is that Tariq is wearing a black dress shirt with two top buttons unclasped and slacks. But when I turn my head a certain way, the fabric shifts in color ever so slightly with a tinge of midnight blue...

Making it appear the same color as my hair.

"You look so incredibly handsome, Clint," I finally manage as his face studies me intently. I smile at him and walk forward to clasp his hands, holding them to my waist. "We're going to be the talk of the evening, that's for sure." I let my gaze snag onto Tariq with that statement, who has nothing but mischief dancing in those eyes.

"Let's not be fashionably late, now," Tariq teases, sweeping his hand toward the door. My eye catches on his crown, which has a little more grandeur than Clint's and made of a brighter gold. "Ladies, lead the way to the grand staircase."

FATE DEMANDS SACRIFICE 237

"How will Clint be getting down the stairs?" I ask, holding my dress in my hand.

As we exit Elly's room, I look back at Pax. His formal military uniform is a smidge flashier than usual, with brighter gold buttons and designs down the front and a richer maroon coat.

"Once we get to the top of the stairs," Pax explains. "I'll fold the wheelchair and carry it down. We were hoping you could walk with Elly while Tariq carries Clint down. We don't want him testing stairs yet."

I nod enthusiastically, catching a glimpse of Elly's smile spread across her face. I can't help but reflect that sentiment, excitement and nervousness battling it out in my chest.

We round a corner where the ceiling opens to the foyer and grand staircase, a low din of chatter echoing off the marble flooring and walls lined with royal tapestries. As we line up before the stairs, Elly sneaks up beside me, looping my trembling arm into hers.

Dozens of people are dressed in formal gowns and suits, now looking up at us as their voices slowly fade into silence. At the bottom of the steps, I catch a shade of auburn hair in a military uniform with one hand clasped behind his back and the other curved in a sling, facing the crowd of people acknowledging us.

"Ladies and gentlemen," Fin's voice projects a notch deeper and more authoritative than I've ever heard him before. "I present to you the Crown Prince Tariq and Prince Clint Hesper of Mariande, escorted by Lieutenant

General Sir Pax Forde of Mariande."

My head snaps to the boys as they descend the steps together, Pax trailing behind Clint and Tariq, the former cradled in his older brother's arms.

I whisper into Elly's ear as we wait, "When was his title reinstated?"

"After the bonfire on the beach," Elly whispers out of the corner of her red-tinted lips. A sly smirk tugs at the corners. "After we made up."

"Oh," I chuckle under my breath, straightening my shoulders back. "You mean after you—"

"Now, escorting the Princess Eloise Hesper of Mariande—" Fin's voice suddenly jerks our attention, making my heart plummet to my ass and my pulse thrum in my throat. "I present to you for the first time, the Royal Healer of Mariande, the Great Reva."

"Oh, I'm going to kill him," I groan through clenched teeth as Elly fails to suppress her laugh, throwing her head back.

We traipse down the steps in synchronization as the audience applauds our descent. My hand still trembles in hers, but I keep my eyes trained on Fin, remembering a time when there wasn't a giant brick wall between us, and he said I could look at him if I ever got nervous.

That moment seems like a lifetime ago.

We finally reach the bottom of the steps, where Tariq, Clint, and Pax are already waiting for us. Pax takes Elly's other arm and loops it through the crook of his as a guest instantly descends upon her.

FATE DEMANDS SACRIFICE 239

I slink closer to Clint's wheelchair, regarding him and Tariq with an eyebrow raised. "So, what happens now?"

"The same thing that just happened to Elly will start to happen with us," Clint grumbles, crossing his arm over his chest. "The other royals and leaders of the various countries will swarm like flies and tell us how much we've grown and how handsome we're looking and if we have our eyes on any ladies and suck our dicks—"

"Clint!" Tariq and I shout simultaneously, earning a few cautious glances from some nearby attendees.

I keep my lips sealed, pressing my palm to my jaw to avoid clenching it. Tariq steps in as the older brother and royal, "Not here, Clint. You may feel on top of the world right now, but that does not excuse you for being rude."

"Yes, sir," Clint grumbles, unfolding his arms to clasp his hands between his legs.

"Besides," Tariq says, extending his head forward. "It looks like it may be that time of the evening when the King and Queen snag you until the dancing begins."

I follow his line of sight where King Darius and Queen Lucia are nearing with Fin, Eamon, and Anya in tow.

King Darius is as dashing as ever, his graying, dark blond hair slicked back underneath a bright gold crown with tips that extend to the sky, glistening with red rubies. He sports black slacks, a velvet, forest green suit jacket, and a white shirt with a black bowtie. Even in her wheelchair, it is easy to see Lucia's dress is stunning on her. Made of sleek silk, the same shade of green as the king's jacket, the lace neckline reaches high up her neck, and the sleeves are tight down to her wrists.

Anya and Eamon also match in a lighter shade of green than the king and queen. The top half of Anya's dress is made entirely of sequins with a small gap in the middle. Eamon's suit jacket and pants match, making his emerald green eyes stand out. Standing beside Fin, it's uncanny how identical they look.

"Reva," Lucia greets, her smile wider than normal with her platinum blond hair pulled into a firm, low bun. "You are incredibly stunning tonight! That color on you is perfect."

"I have to echo the queen," Eamon agrees, his hand clasped over his wife's, who is gripping tightly to his bicep.

Anya stares at me with wide, glistening eyes, her mouth slightly propped open. She doesn't move or make a sound as her gaze roams over my face before latching onto my necklace. Her already-fair skin blanches, her hand trembling at the base of her neck.

My stomach turns, and I wonder if she knows what a hematite necklace could mean.

"I have to repeat what my son said at dinner," Darius interjects, snapping Anya out of her trance. "You look regal."

"Thank you, Your Highness," I bow, a small smile playing on my lips. "You both look amazing in your matching outfits."

"Lest people forget we're a married Queen and King

FATE DEMANDS SACRIFICE   241

with three lovely children," Darius chuckles, clearly showing how much the matching outfits matter to him. "I know we haven't had the chance to talk since you've been working diligently with Clint, but I just want to say we are forever indebted to you. It appears you've discovered the remedy to heal him."

My mouth goes dry, but I am able to nod through the tightness in my chest. "It wasn't easy, but I believe we can only go up from here."

"Excellent." Darius smiles, exchanging a brief glance with his wife. "I want you to enjoy yourself tonight—all of you kids."

"We're going to help with Clint tonight so you lot can enjoy yourselves," Eamon adds, unlocking Anya's grip from his arm.

Darius turns his attention to Tariq. "Son, you don't sleep, so if you'll be up all night, at least enjoy yourself. Try not to discuss politics too much or spend the evening strengthening alliances."

"I can't help it when my good looks and dazzling charm form the alliances themselves." Tariq shrugs, passing Clint's wheelchair over to Eamon as Fin's gaze burns into my skin.

But I avert my gaze, unable to behold whatever sits in those emerald eyes.

Tariq leans into his mother, kissing her on the cheek quickly, then firmly shaking his father's hand.

Anya interrupts Fin striding towards Tariq and me, "Finley, dear. Would you mind accompanying us for some time tonight? We've barely seen you, and I'm feeling a bit faint."

"Of course, Mom," Fin says quietly, his shoulders deflating slightly.

Darius gives me one final wink before they wheel towards a small gathering on the opposite side of the foyer.

"Starfire," Tariq says under his breath, startling me. My hand flies to my chest, but I spin on my heel to find an outstretched glass of bubbling champagne. "A night of revelry. What do you say?"

"Not too much debauchery," I mumble, accepting the outstretched stem.

We clink glasses before taking a few sips of the sweet and tart liquid tingling on my tongue. Tariq gestures for me to follow him with his finger before offering his elbow. I let him guide me into the mess of people to learn who could be an enemy and who could be an ally.

***

After watching the performers reenact the Creation of Aveesh in the Grand Ballroom, we finally meet back up with Fin, Elly, and Pax as the party is ushered outside. Stepping out the doors, we enter the courtyard where there is a string quartet in the center, poised on a risen platform. The entire circular enclosure is lit up with torches along the perimeter, reflecting different colors on

FATE DEMANDS SACRIFICE 243

the ground from the stained glass windows they're placed in front of.

So easily, the gray stone castle has been transformed into a romantic ball, where indeed, the moon *glows* full above us, stars neighboring it in the dark night sky.

"Isn't it lovely?" Elly grins, content. "This is my favorite season to celebrate. It's springtime, the sky is clear, the air is warmer, and everything is just brighter."

"Your springtime is definitely different from Eldamain's springtime." I finish my second glass of champagne before instantly accepting the new one Elly snagged from a steward passing by. "We go from cold, wet winter to humid, sopping spring. Everything melts so quickly."

"Where I'm from," says a deep voice with an accent reminiscent of Aithan's. "You would think it is already summer."

All of us whip around quickly, startled by the intrusion.

The stranger behind us appears to be in perpetual deep thought, bushy brown eyebrows drawn over golden hazel, almond-shaped eyes, almost like my own but a little darker. His dark brown hair is cropped particularly close to his head underneath a very simple bronze crown—almost like a band—along with his groomed beard.

"Oh, gloat all you want, Prince of the Desert," Tariq grumbles, waving his glass under the nose of the stranger. "Some of us are still thawing out."

"You have been gone long enough now." The man smirks at Tariq, holding out his hand. "Yet you still complain about the heat."

Tariq chuckles, accepting the outstretched hand and embracing the man like they're close comrades. As he does, I notice the two women flanking either side of him.

"Prince Ruhan—" Tariq clears his throat, gesturing to our small group. "You know Princess Eloise and Sir Pax. I would like you to meet our Royal Healer, Reva."

"Just Reva?" Prince Ruhan eyes me suspiciously, but there is a glisten in those bright eyes.

I squat into a small curtsy but confirm. "Yes. Magics are prone to choosing one name to keep their identities secure."

"I am aware," he says, though not unkindly, shrugging one shoulder. "But something tells me that is not why you are simply *Reva*."

I can't help but frown, blinking at Prince Ruhan. He stares at me in an uncomfortable, heavy silence, an all-knowing, subtle smile on his lips. Fin takes an impending step closer, and Tariq's eyes snap onto the movement.

"Brother," says the young woman to his left. "We are guests in their home. Let's not intimidate their Healer."

"My sister is right," Prince Ruhan admits, bobbing his head with a hand to his chest. "Where are my manners? I am Crown Prince Ruhan Citali of Riddling, and this is my betrothed, Lady Qita Paddock." He grips the hand of the woman who did not speak.

FATE DEMANDS SACRIFICE   245

She simply bows her head before slowly removing her hand from Prince Ruhan's, and I have to guess 'betrothed' is another way to refer to an arranged engagement.

"I'm Princess Naja Citali of Riddling," the one who spoke introduces, extending her hand to me. "It's nice to finally meet you. It sounds like Princess Eloise had much to say about you whenever she wrote to Prince Tariq."

Princess Naja. Elly mentioned a while ago that Riddling was trying to set up an engagement between Tariq and Princess Naja, and I'm confused as to why he would refuse because she's beautiful like the first day of summer.

While there are some similarities between her and Prince Ruhan—the nose, eyes, and skin tone—there are more differences. Her hair is parted down the middle, flowing across both shoulders, a lighter, chestnut brown compared to his. Her crown is more silver than gold, wrapping around her head. Her face also seems longer, and her one eyebrow is elevated higher than the other in curiosity as she studies me right back.

"It's nice to meet all of you," I finally answer, meeting each of their eyes except Lady Qita, who's staring at the ground. "I have just started meeting a lot of royals and people in general, if I'm being honest, so please do not take any offense to my decorum… Or lack thereof."

"Smooth," Pax grumbles under his breath, quiet enough so only Elly and I can hear it.

Elly quietly sputters on her drink.

"I appreciate the warning." Prince Ruhan's features soften slightly, and his shoulders loosen. "Where is it you come from?"

"Eldamain," I answer, tilting my head to the side. "As I'm sure you've heard, I wasn't privy to my parents and their heritage."

"Fascinating." Princess Naja squints, scrutinizing. "If I had to guess, Miss Reva, you have quite a bit of Riddling heritage in you. I wouldn't be surprised if one of your parents was from our country."

Prince Ruhan wraps his hand around his betrothed as he turns away. "I hope to meet again, Miss Reva."

They bid farewell and we wait until they've walked a healthy distance from where we're gathered before I lean into Elly.

"So are they an ally yet?" I question, one eyebrow raised.

She twirls the liquid in her glass momentarily before taking one swig. Then, she just shrugs. "It's still only a maybe. They're difficult people to read."

Tariq's gaze is still trailing Prince Ruhan and Princess Naja, but I catch the muscle tick in his jaw, barely perceptible unless you watch him like I do. When I follow Tariq's line of sight, Prince Ruhan bows his head at Tariq with a wide grin before extending his glass.

Chapter 17

Clint manages to dance through an entire song with me, keeping one hand clasped in mine and the other wrapped firmly on my waist. We rock side-to-side, and Clint even puts a little flare into it when the speed picks up for the chorus. Since we can't fully partake in any twirls the other partygoers are participating in, he dips our hands down and up dramatically as he laughs.

By the time the song ends and everyone applauds, Clint is breathing heavily, and his hands tremble in mine. I glance to the edge of the undesignated dancefloor where Fin waits alone with the wheelchair, his eyes glittering in the glow of the torches. I nod once at him, then twitch my head to Clint, who is now gripping my hand and waist rather tight, leaning his weight into me for support.

We purposely didn't move far from the outskirts of the crowd, but Clint wanted to at least walk a few steps toward me to awe everyone.

And awe them he did.

Lucia must not have known he'd been gradually walking because the tears that sprung to her eyes when she saw him standing and walking on his own nearly brought me to tears. Those closest even applauded as we clasped hands together before the song began.

"You did awesome, kid," Fin congratulates, both of us taking an arm each to lower him into the chair. "Talk about an entrance."

"I'm exhausted now," Clint sighs, leaning his head back with eyes shut, blond hair flowing back. "I need to at least last to the fireworks. Then I'll sleep like a baby."

"How much longer until the fireworks?" I ask Fin, scanning the crowd for our friends. I spot Elly, Pax, and Tariq huddled by one of the torches, cackling about something.

On cue, Tariq turns his head, and his eyes instantly latch onto mine, glowing.

He winks.

"Probably another hour or two," Fin winces, shrugging. He bends over to speak in Clint's ear. "Do you think you can make it?"

"As long as we don't go over to Mom and Dad," Clint says quietly, his eyes flickering over my shoulder.

I follow his gaze, pretending to search for someone even though it's hard to miss the king amongst the crowd, especially since people give a wide berth around Lucia and her chair.

Darius and Lucia are talking to two individuals I have yet to meet tonight, and that's honestly shocking to me at this rate. The woman has a kind face, maybe the same age as Lucia and Darius, but even from this distance, her eyes are vacant as she clutches her glass. Her smile doesn't

FATE DEMANDS SACRIFICE 249

quite reach her eyes, only the top row of teeth showing, as though it pains her. Chestnut brown hair flows down her back, streaked with gray. On the other hand, the man beside her has a harsh face with permanent frown wrinkles on his forehead, in the corners of his eyes, and even at the edges of his mouth where he's spent a lifetime pursing his lips.

The longer I stare, the more a strange tension builds in my chest, clogging my throat.

"The royals are all so very serious, aren't they?" A wraithlike voice interrupts my gawking.

I startle, my hand flying to my chest. I twist on my heel to the woman who has joined Clint, Fin, and me.

Roughly the same height as me with a more petite frame, her dress is similar to mine—slit and all—except it's black velvet, and her single sleeve reaches her wrist in a black, sheer mesh with silver beading. Her ash blond hair is straight and long past her waist, and her full lips are painted with red rouge darker than Elly's, but the dramatic combination of her dress and lips makes her sea-green eyes pop.

The boys eye her with wariness, although Fin has an added observation.

"Reva," Fin clears his throat, grabbing my attention. The woman slowly turns her head to him, raising an eyebrow. "This is Sidra... What is it you're calling yourself these days?"

"Countess, Earl, Lady," Sidra shrugs her exposed shoulder. "These days, formalities are scoffed at. A first-name basis is always more than enough."

"Reva," I reply, dipping my head. "I'm not sure if I should bow or curtsy to that, but I'd venture you don't want either."

Sidra rolls her eyes, waving her delicate hand in the air. "It only ever matters to royals, and us Magics are lucky if we can get them to call us by our first name."

I blink, tilting my head to the side. I'm not shocked by her declaration with those piercing eyes, but there's something else about her I can't quite place that is alluding to an *otherness*. "You're a Magic?"

Sidra nods once but doesn't take her eyes off mine. "It seems we have that in common, Reva."

"Well, I hope you find Mariande to your liking then." I let my eyes flicker over her, something uneasy pressing on my chest as though it's trying to get in. "We have quite the Magic community, and I hope your experience with the Hespers has been better than other royals. I've found they're quite accepting."

She pinches her face, a muscle ticking in her jaw, and I almost feel the jealousy humming from her, low and dark. My lower back tenses uncharacteristically.

"Yes, you are fortunate," she mutters, resetting her face into a neutral mask. "In Teslin, we have to fight tooth and nail to make a name for ourselves. I climbed the ladder and now own nearly every brothel and pub in Rian. Some of us aren't lucky enough to be rescued by princes."

My eyebrows shoot up just as a hand presses to my

FATE DEMANDS SACRIFICE

lower back, and by the scent wafting from him, I know it's Tariq before he speaks.

"Sidra," he greets from behind me, and I don't miss the questioning tone that hovers at the end. "I didn't think anyone from Teslin would be attending the Glow Ball. My apologies for not greeting you sooner."

She shrugs, flicking a single strand of hair over her shoulder. "I was just telling your Healer I don't require a fuss. But I accepted the offer, even if the Corvuses declined the invitation. Someone has to represent that cesspool of a country."

"I thought you nearly owned every building in Rian?" Fin narrows his eyes, his non-sling hand gripping the handle on Clint's wheelchair.

"They give me their coin." She whirls her attention back to me, her tone even as she says, "It doesn't mean I owe them my loyalty."

I am startled again, especially as Tariq's hand stiffens against my lower back.

"Anyways…" She throws back the remainder of her wine. "I came to meet the Magic who managed to slide her way into a royal position. I would congratulate you, but we'll see how long your station lasts once your young friend is cured."

Without another word or a chance for us to rebuttal, Sidra slings her hair over her shoulder and struts away, her hips swaying in the black velvet.

"Oh, Gods," Elly's voice interrupts as she and Pax approach. "She met Sidra. We leave her for a moment, and the snake slithers in."

"I don't understand." I twist around to face the group, my gaze landing on each one until I find Tariq still watching where Sidra went. His normal princely mask has vanished entirely, revealing the malice blazing in those eyes and his jaw clenched. While what I think is anger radiating from Tariq is jarring, I remember our conversation about anxiety and his alluding to the pressure he faces. I slowly brush my fingertips against his, a featherlight touch. He startles, his eyes flickering down to where I'd touched his hand to my face, his jaw relaxing and eyes softening.

"Sidra is just otherworldly." Elly lazily swirls the wine in her hand, oblivious as anyone else to what just transpired. "And not in an angelic way, but a demonic way."

"Gods, Elly," Pax says, chuckling into his hands. "I think we need to cut back on the champagne." She snaps her head at him, glaring.

"What Elly means is," Tariq drawls, fully recovered as he levels his twin with a glare. She straightens her shoulders. "Sidra owns a lot of controversial establishments in Teslin. The brothels and pubs she owns tend to give way to a lot of debauchery. The Corvus family of Teslin doesn't really run their city, so she gets away with many things she shouldn't."

"Her area of town is essentially Teslin's Magic community," Fin interjects, glancing briefly at Clint and hesitating. "Oh, what the hell. He's thirteen. There is a

FATE DEMANDS SACRIFICE 253

lot of assault happening in those places that the Magics inflict on the mortals. They rob them, harass them, drug them, and take advantage of them."

"That's awful," I frown, glancing at Tariq. "And this Corvus family? Are they a royal family or a lordship?"

Tariq sighs, shaking his head. "They're royal. They just don't seem to care very much. They're rather gluttonous, and I would bet money Sidra has some sort of agreement with the king, the princes, and the *entertainers* she employs."

"The only good thing about the Corvus family is the princess, Jenae," Elly explains. "She's very timid and keeps to herself, but from what I understand, she spends minimal time in public."

"Why doesn't she do something or step up?" I ask. "I don't mean that in a negative way—"

"I don't think she's had the freedoms Elly has to know where to begin. She's also the youngest with two older brothers." Tariq rolls his neck, but his eyes flicker toward someone moving toward us.

Darius smiles at each of us, his hands clasped behind his back. "When I see this group huddled together like this, I never have a reassuring feeling."

"We're behaving," Elly confirms, closing her eyes and lifting her chin like a child.

"Clearly," Darius deadpans, but then he directs his next statement to the rest of us. "I'm going to take Clint from here. Your mother, Fin, kidnapped Lucia, so I probably won't be seeing her for the rest of the evening."

"Typical," Fin chuckles, lightly pushing the chair over to Darius with one hand. "Let me know if you need help later getting him to his room for bed."

Darius scowls at Fin playfully, ignoring his offer as he leans over the wheelchair. He murmurs something into Clint's ear that makes him laugh as they roll away.

"We've got trouble," Pax grumbles. "Again."

I follow Pax's snarl, and I never thought I'd see him look at someone the way he used to look at me. At the same time, I'm slightly offended he loathed me that much when we first met.

Even from this distance, the stranger's sharp facial features stand out against his slicked-back, white-blond hair. He's nearly as tall as Fin but lankier, with little substance underneath his all-black tux. He's already surveying our group huddled by the torch, attempting to break the conversation he's having with the man and woman I saw talking to Darius and Lucia before.

"Oh, shit," Elly blurts before downing her glass of champagne. She gathers her skirts in her hands. "Not today. Pax, please escort me."

"My pleasure, Princess," Pax agrees, his eyes lingering with trepidation as he places Elly's hand in the crook of his elbow. He guides her away as the guy swaggers over.

As he nears, the same heavy pressure I'd felt with Sidra returns, and I can't decide if it's coming off him or from around him. Shockingly, my powers bubble underneath my skin. I follow Elly's lead, gulping down the rest of my drink to try and stifle it. Tariq side-eyes me, but I quickly

FATE DEMANDS SACRIFICE

255

shake my head.

"If it isn't the Crown Prince of Mariande, home at last," the man bellows as he shortens the distance between Tariq, Fin, and me. He falls in the torch's glow beside me, and I notice his turquoise blue eyes have small brown speckles like a robin egg.

The Korbin eye color.

"Prince Keiran Korbin," Tariq greets, but he doesn't bow his head. Instead, he tilts it to the side with a slight bob, assessing him. "On behalf of the Kingdom of Mariande, it's a pleasure to host the Etherean Royal Family."

"Mm," is all Prince Keiran manages, his eyes skating over to Fin. "Sir Finley, correct?"

Fin presses his lips together but bows at his waist while maintaining eye contact.

Prince Keiran's eyes bounce back to me with excitement and something far darker than I'd care to glimpse. He smiles, asking through clenched teeth, "And who is this delicious *creature?*"

Everything in me wants to recoil, disgust sweeping over my body at the scratch of his voice and hunger burning in those flat eyes as they trail from my toes to the top of my head.

Instead, I curtsy, slightly bowed.

"Reva," I answer. "The Royal Healer of Mariande."

"So, it's true." Prince Keiran grins with tight lips, a cat sizing up a mouse. "The witch."

I chance a glimpse at Fin and Tariq.

Fin stares Prince Keiran down with flared nostrils, the deep pink of his lips barely visible they're pressed together so tightly. Those eyes are like searing, melted emeralds. On the contrary, Tariq only acknowledges Prince Keiran with a raised eyebrow, forever assessing.

The Prince of Etherea follows my gaze to the boys, weighing Fin's reaction.

"Oh, how lovely," Prince Keiran chuckles darkly. "It seems she has come to entertain your knights, Prince. This one isn't very pleased with me."

Tariq snaps his head to Fin, eyes blazing. "Take a walk, Sir," Tariq commands sternly, a prince to his knight.

Fin reels his glare at Tariq, his free hand clenched in a fist. The awkward tension between the two settles onto my shoulders, wrapping around me like a wool blanket as my gaze bounces back and forth from Fin to Tariq.

"Your Highness—" Fin starts, but Tariq cuts him off by raising an eyebrow in warning. Fin straightens like an arrow, bowing to Tariq until his chest parallels the stone ground.

I hold my tongue and try to keep a neutral face as Fin rights himself and stalks off in the same direction Pax and Elly went.

"What a display," Prince Keiran drawls blandly. He picks at something invisible under his fingernail with his thumb. "So, where is that siren you call a sister?"

"You mean the Princess of Mariande," I correct, clasping my hands in front of my waist and trying to hold my tone steady. Prince Keiran's eyes flash something awful, his hand slowly falling to his side. "Isn't that the *sister* you're referring to?"

"Indeed," he responds, barely acknowledging me as he redirects his attention to Tariq.

"I am flattered, Prince Keiran," Tariq responds, again tilting to the side. He places his hands behind his back, naturally puffing his chest out. While Prince Keiran may be taller, Tariq makes up for it in sheer virility. "Considering the Princess and I are twins, one would think you consider me a siren, too."

It takes all my willpower to keep my eyes from shooting wide, holding back the smile threatening to break across my face. Instead, I cough inconspicuously, tightening the grip on my fingers and not looking at the Prince of Etherea—even if the anger is pulsing off him, that heavy pressure building.

"I hope your family has not forgotten the proposals my father and I have placed before you," Prince Keiran warns, taking one step closer to Tariq. My power simmers with my anger, and I hold my breath to keep it from coming out in flames. "It would be wise to consider them before it's too late."

"And what would be the consequences of our tardiness?" Tariq challenges, standing his ground.

Prince Keiran smirks. "We are all of ripe marrying and childbearing ages, Prince Tariq." He takes two steps back. "Both your sister and yourself should be married soon or at least entering into some sort of agreement. The

Kingdoms talk." With one last glare at me, he twirls on his heel and walks back the way he came.

"I have a lot of questions," I blurt, angling my head to Tariq.

I thought maybe I'd find his gaze latched onto Prince Keiran like every other encounter we've had where Tariq seems to be contemplating as he watches people walk away. Instead, I find him gazing down at me, his facial features softened.

"I have to apologize on Fin's behalf—" Tariq pauses, blinking. "Again."

"Why?" I frown, folding my arms across my chest. "Because he wears his emotions on his face?"

"Normally, that's my favorite quality about him." Tariq rubs his chest with a pained expression. "He knows better than to do that around Keiran."

"I know Etherea is *bad* bad," I explain, squinting. "But how bad are we talking?"

"They tried to kill you, Elly, and Clint just a few months ago, Starfire," Tariq whispers, barely audible as he scans around us. "This isn't the place to get into this, but let's just say he and his father will do everything in their power to get the Mariande throne, even if it comes to weakening us by attacking knights and Healers. They know what Fin means to my family, which means if they can hurt him in some way without outright killing him, it'll hurt our family."

The pieces click in my head, at least why it's such a big deal that Fin showed how angry he was at the comments toward me. He showed his greatest weakness is me, which puts a target on my back because they could come for me to try and hurt Fin. In turn, hurting the royal family.

As if being a Magic Royal Healer wasn't enough.

CHAPTER 18

After Tariq was pulled away to talk with another royal, I find myself observing the people of Mariande and its visitors. There are so many different people talking and smiling with one another, it's startling to see such a community. My gaze sweeps over the crowd, catching something—no, *someone*—reflecting light from a sconce. I snap back to find Jorah watching me, tipping his glass in my direction. I frown with a half-grin, giving a small wave.

The Hespers invited another influential Magic, so I wonder how many more are openly conversing with the mortals.

As the music slows, the pale pink of Elly's dress catches my eye as she guides Pax by his forearm to the crowded dance floor. Auburn hair glistens in dim light, and Fin stands beside a few other castle employees to my right, his gaze searching.

I don't want to deny him to his face, so I slip through the crowd that's making its way toward the dancing space. I beeline for the archway I know will lead to the grassy area surrounding the gardens on the opposite side

FATE DEMANDS SACRIFICE   261

of the castle walls.

Once my heels hit soft grass, I exhale a breath of relief, catching my reflection in a nearby window. Luckily, my salve has survived the night so far. The breeze drifting off the coast sweeps my hair that's fallen out of the hair tie from my face, cooling my warm body from being in such a confined space with an absurd amount of people. The music travels from the courtyard, and I wonder if it's audible from the closest rows of homes a mile away. I close my eyes, imagining what the families living there are doing if they aren't here. I keep the bottom of my dress in one hand, swaying with the rise and fall of music like the waves of the ocean—

Until a presence steps in front of me, blocking the breeze. My eyes snap open in time for them to grab my free hand and hold it between us.

Tariq's warm eyes radiate under the moonlight.

"A dance, Starfire?" he asks, an eyebrow raised as he bows at the waist. I stop swaying, hesitating. "Are you going to deny the Crown Prince?"

"It may help level that ego," I mutter, but he still waits, bent at an angle. I glance around us, searching for any sign of other people around.

"Everyone is occupied." Tariq grins wickedly, peeking up through his eyelashes.

I can't make contact with his burning gaze, my fingers aching to brush back that rogue strand of hair curling along his cheek. "You have a reputation to uphold, and dancing with your Magic Royal Healer isn't going to help that."

"You know I'm not one for the royal semantics." Tariq waves his hand, adjusting upright. "Besides, my reputation didn't seem to matter much when you tried to seduce me on a horse."

I flare my nostrils, irritation simmering. "Shouldn't you be asking a certain princess for a dance?" I challenge, but I regret it as his eyes dance and his smile spreads across his face.

"Do I detect... jealousy?" Tariq steps closer, peering down at me. I shift my weight on my feet. "You truly don't have to worry about that. Now, Reva, don't make me beg because you know I will. Can you spare me a dance?"

I don't think I could ever get used to my name on his lips, especially the way it drops at the first syllable and rises at the end.

Like the question I am.

I whisper my response. "Okay."

Excitement sets his eyes ablaze, his hand still holding mine. He shifts his grip, sliding his other hand onto my waist and around my back. He gently pulls me into him until our chests are pressed against each other, rising and falling in synchronization. I lift my head to him, raising an eyebrow. His eyes dip briefly to my neck before nodding once and gliding us into the dance.

We drift through the garden, the flowers and bushes now in full bloom around us, yet his eyes never leave mine. His muscles shift under my hand, which rests on the

FATE DEMANDS SACRIFICE 263

side of his bicep, and my heart swells with the rhythm and the steady pressure on my waist. I match his every move, allowing him to lead but never relenting total control.

He pushes against my waist, and I gracefully twirl away from him, my skirt parting the slit and wrapping around my ankles. He tugs on my arm, and I fold myself back into his body with my arms crossed in front of my waist. Tariq clasps my hand, sealing me against him. My back molds into his chest and stomach, my senses heightening as my body hums.

We sway side-to-side with the music, but I'm unsure whether this is dancing anymore. Being caged against him like this, every point of contact sends a shot of lightning through me: his firm stomach and his hips pressing into me, his biceps flexing with every movement.

He lowers his head, and his nose trails along my skin from the base of my neck all the way to the edge of my jaw. My body goes molten in his arms, my head falling back on his shoulder.

"You were made for the night." Tariq's breath fans my face, his lips dangerously close to the corners of mine. "You shine—dare I say—like a star?"

I chuckle, a calm contentedness sweeping over my body. "My, my, Prince. How you have a way with words."

He moans, his chest rumbling behind me. "Forgive me, but what can I say? You are astonishing."

I peel open my eyes and twist my head, Tariq's lips

grazing my cheek. His hands slacken, but I'm still encased in his embrace. I pivot around and he keeps his hands clasped onto my waist. I rest mine gently on his chest, and my breath comes quickly, my breasts swelling with every inhale. Despite the dip in the cleavage, his eyes never leave my face.

One hand lifts between us, and he places it under my chin, tilting my head back. His other presses me further into him, my back naturally arching. I grip the lapels of his jacket in my hands, praying we don't fall. My heart hammers against my ribcage in time with the beat of the music. Every part of him touching me is like pinpricks sending signals through my body, igniting me from within.

"You know what I want more than anything in this entire world?" he whispers.

I barely breathe now because I know. Our faces are only an inch apart, his breath a warm caress against my lips.

I should pull away before he asks and put more distance between us, but I can't even form a cohesive, responsible thought. All I manage is, "What?"

"For you to let me kiss you, Starfire," Tariq whispers, his eyes falling to my lips. He swallows. "Will you let me kiss you, Reva?"

My mouth parts open, my entire body tightening in anticipation. I've spent the last month avoiding this, but *Gods* if that damn lower lip doesn't call to me the same way his scent does.

FATE DEMANDS SACRIFICE 265

So, instead of saying *no, this is irresponsible, or* even *what about our friend*, I say, "I thought you'd never ask."

"Fucking finally." His face lowers the rest of the way without hesitation, lips colliding. My stomach flips and my body slackens further into him. His mouth dances with mine, tracing my lips so thoroughly I taste whiskey lingering on his tongue.

Both of his hands trail up and down my body, over the swell of my breasts, into the dip of my waist, and around the curve of my ass over my dress. He leaves a path of burning, tingling desire in his wake.

This kiss. It melts the world away, and it's just Tariq and me under the glistening stars.

I could stay like this forever, and I swear I hear drums pounding in tune with my heart.

We both pull away, and I open my eyes to lights flashing across his face. Fireworks rise across the horizon from somewhere south of the castle, exploding in the sky.

My mouth props open in awe, but Tariq grips my chin between his thumb and forefinger, pulling my attention back to him again.

We don't need words now.

I fling my arms around his neck, allowing this bliss to devour me. Tariq squeezes my waist to steady me and I let his mouth guide mine like he guided me in our dance, and I can't get enough.

It's like I didn't know I was drowning, but Tariq was the air I needed.

Loud booms echo off the castle walls, startling us apart

again. We smile with our foreheads pressed together.

Maybe it's the way the fireworks make his eyes glow like the starfire he claims me to be, the few glasses of champagne I've had, or sheer stupidity...

I take Tariq's hand in mine, my dress in the other, and I drag us to the castle.

"Reva?" Tariq questions, but follows me, nonetheless.

Traipsing through the grass, we approach the nearest door and pause before it. I reach up on my toes and kiss him, sparks floating across my skin.

When I pull away, he is the one to push the door open. With a mischievous wiggle of his brows, he tugs me behind him, and my smile broadens like a thief who's taken a gem that doesn't belong to them.

As we dash down the hallway, I realize we are headed for the stairwell leading to what I assume is Tariq's room.

A room I have yet to visit.

My heart balloons as though it'll explode like a firework, my powers tingling at my fingertips. The booms outside rattle the paintings on the walls, the only witnesses to the Crown Prince and Royal Healer flying up the stone stairwell.

We skid to a halt in front of a door that reminds me of Clint's room. Tariq faces me with his shoulder flush against the door, dangling the key in front of me like a pendulum on a simple, silver chain. His hand reaches for mine, holding it palm up and laying the key in it.

"I want this to be your choice," he whispers, huddled together in front of his door. I can't look away from him

FATE DEMANDS SACRIFICE 267

and those gleaming eyes. "Whatever happens, we play by your rules. You say the word, and I'm all yours to do as you please. You say the word, and this ends."

Nothing. Tariq offers me nothing at this moment, and that is everything. Friendship, but something else entirely. Something I get to choose, dictate, and rule—something I'm not used to. For once, I get to decide what happens.

I decide fate.

And I will not deny myself when Tariq gives so freely.

I don't take my eyes off him as I fumble with the key. He doesn't break contact either, but his hand grasps over mine to guide it to the lock. The intimacy and tension pulse between us, and anticipation rolls in my stomach again and tightens.

The lock clicks.

I jut between Tariq and the door, my back pressing against the wood, his chest rising and falling quickly. He places both hands on either side of me, pinning me and taunting me as he leans down towards my face. He places gentle, fleeting kisses on either cheekbone.

My eyes flutter, my body relaxes into the door, and one of his hands lowers to the doorknob. In one movement, he twists it and shoves the door open while using his other hand to catch me against him, his arm curved around my waist.

I cling to his lapels again—for stability, for comfort, for *this.*

His mouth drops to my neck in the darkness, overwhelming me with nips, licks, and kisses. I hear the door shut behind him, so I use one of my hands to flick a flame into the fireplace against the wall. It erupts in a woosh of light and heat, quickly settling into a soft glow. His eyes snap to the fireplace, and a devious glint in his eye darkens into lust. He finds my gaze again and strips me bare.

"This damned dress needs to come off," he growls against my lips. "Now."

I huff a breath of laughter, nearly melting into a puddle on the floor. I take one of his hands gripping my waist and guide it to the six buttons holding the dress together. His fingers find the first, releasing it from its clasp. With each button he undoes, I take a steadying breath, gathering my nerves.

When the last button is free, I step away from him, holding my dress up. Tariq's hand hovers in the air between us. I slide the dress over my breasts and down my hips, and it gathers in a pool of champagne around me.

Tariq's eyes drag from the top of my head all the way down to where the dress lays on the floor, then back up again to meet my gaze. The predatorial glint in his eyes makes my knees quake.

"Absolutely beautiful." He shrugs off his suit jacket, and—in one long stride—there is just an inch between us.

He crouches, those strong, calloused hands gripping the back of my thighs. Effortlessly, he lifts me against him,

FATE DEMANDS SACRIFICE 269

and I wrap my legs around his waist. I lower my face to him, kissing his lips like he's a taste I crave.

He doesn't hesitate, and we make our way towards his bed. The mattress presses against my back as he gracefully lays me down, my legs hanging over the edge. I watch him with hooded eyes as he meticulously unclasps every button on his shirt, undressing *for* me.

When he peels off his shirt, my mouth drops open.

A Crown Prince trained for war stands before me, but one who has yet to see that war. Perfect, sun-kissed skin stretches across the swell of muscle on his chest, flowing into a lean, toned stomach with a deep V trailing below his waistband, followed by a speckling of dark blond hair.

When I lift my eyes to him, I barely breathe.

"You keep looking at me like that," Tariq smirks, his body tensing. "And this won't last as long as I'd like it to."

I reach my hand out, suspended between us. He leans over me, trapping me with both hands on either side of my face, my hand flattening against his chest. I let it wander down his body, following the path laid there for me by the Gods themselves. I hit his waistband, and he shudders under my touch. Biting my lip, I tug on his belt, and he lets me undress him now, watching my every move.

When his pants and undergarments fall, his erection holds my attention before he lowers himself to his knees between my legs. My breath hitches at his touch as he peels off my undergarments. He clasps both legs in his hands, and I'm mesmerized by his hands slowly sliding up my thighs as he gently spreads them wider.

This man knows damn well what he's doing, and the thought makes my skin buzz.

My breath quickens as he kisses between my legs, the only warning before his tongue flattens against me, dragging all the way up before flicking my clit.

I throw my head back onto the sheets and arch my back at the electric shock lancing through me, but his rough hands grab my hips, pinning me to the bed. He plunges his tongue inside me, curling it upwards and dragging it back out against my inner walls. My hands find his, and I dig my fingernails in as the pressure builds.

When he replaces his tongue with two fingers, a moan escapes my lips, my hand flying over it as he kisses the sensitive skin on the inside of my leg. Just as my body starts to tremble, he lifts himself and hovers over me.

I open my eyes, his hand removing mine from my mouth and pinning it next to my head. That stupid smirk is plastered on his face as he guides his other hand toward my mouth. "I want you to taste how wet you are for me."

I keep eye contact with him until they're an inch in front of my face, then I wrap my lips around his two fingers down to their base, dragging my tongue. I slowly pull back to lay on the bed and his fingers slide out, smirking when his eyes darken.

He crashes his lips into mine with a low groan, and my taste mixes with the champagne and whiskey. He removes one of his hands to press himself at my entrance, shifting his hips.

FATE DEMANDS SACRIFICE 271

My eyes flutter shut, but Tariq stops me, saying, "Look at me, Reva." I lock my eyes with those amber depths again, and he growls, "Good girl."

He stares down at us as he slowly sheathes his length, filling every inch of me. A deep, pleasure-filled sigh falls from my lips that he captures with his own.

He pulls out nearly his entire length before pushing back in as slowly as he did the first time, antagonizing and teasing me, drawing out every spark pulsing through my veins. I squirm underneath him, clenching my teeth together as I'm unable to contain my want—my *need*—for more.

Just as he's about to slide back in, I lift my hips, squeeze his sides with my thighs, and arch my lower back, raising an eyebrow in challenge. Understanding registers on his face, along with unrelenting lust and a half-grin. With my hips propped wider, he plunges in quicker than before. When he hits the back walls, he gives his hips a jerk, which has him pressing a sensitive nerve.

The sound that escapes both our lips is animalistic.

I grip his face with my hands, slamming my lips back onto his. I can't get enough of him, taste enough of him, feel enough of him.

I want to consume him.

I want *him* to consume *me*.

One of his hands sweeps up my waist, over my shoulder, and straight to my neck. Tracing his thumb along my jawline, he removes his lips from mine. He tilts my head back, and he licks my neck from my collarbone all the way to my chin.

The feeling that has been building within me releases, and I shatter into a million pieces. My whole body pulses and trembles as he draws out my orgasm, and I can't contain the pleasure-filled gasp that flies from my lips. My hands slip to the back of his head, and I twist my fingers into his soft hair, tugging roughly at the long strands.

Tariq's release follows mine then, his head falling into the crook of my neck. We both stay like this for a moment, catching our breath. The sensation that washes over me is foreign, reminiscent of falling into a freshly made bed after a long day away. Eventually, he moves from me and extends his arms to carefully help me from the side of the bed.

Gods, we didn't even make it fully *onto* the bed before devouring each other.

"Do you need anything?" he asks with a hoarse voice, running a hand through his disheveled blond hair. "The bathing chamber is through that door if you need to…"

"Yep," I manage, my mind foggy. I head to the chamber to relieve myself and clean up.

I take a moment to study my reflection in the mirror, my Mark glowing but fading with each passing second. My mind replays his hand on my neck and his mouth on my legs, and I have to breathe through the returning arousal.

I just had sex with the Crown Prince of Mariande.

Who also happens to be my best friend's brother.

And the best friend of my former… interest?

FATE DEMANDS SACRIFICE
273

I press my lips together as the realization of the line I've crossed settles in.

"I hate to break it to you," Tariq chuckles from the bed. "But no matter how much you stare at it, the Mark isn't going anywhere."

I roll my eyes, eyeing his shirt on the ground near the door. I stalk over, snatching it and using it as a robe. I hold the two ends together with my hands, the hem of it just brushing against the top of my thighs.

Tariq lays in the bed, the sheets covering everything from his hips down. One hand props the back of his head against the headboard, the other patting the space next to him.

"You can't just stand there like that in my shirt and not expect me to invite you back into this bed," he adds.

"I don't know if it's a good idea if I stay the night," I admit out loud, playing with the sleeve. "What will people say when I leave here in last night's dress or this shirt?"

Tariq thrums his fingers on the bed beside him, but I can't quite read the emotion in his eyes. No matter how much I want to lay beside him curled up for the night, I know I can't. And he did say this was all my choice.

"Would you like me to walk you back then?" Tariq asks, his excitement slightly dimmer than before. The back of my throat burns, and my heart screams no, but I nod. He unfolds from the blanket, different cotton slacks hanging on his waist.

"Can you help me get back into my..." I stare at the

heap of fabric on the floor.

Tariq smirks with a soft chuckle, making his way over to me. I let the shirt slip off my shoulders, using all my self-control not to look at his reaction to the movement because I'm afraid that will lead to another round, and I definitely won't be able to leave after that.

Instead, I unfold the dress, holding it open and stepping into it. I slip my arm into the one sleeve and position it before glancing over my shoulder at Tariq. He silently approaches my back, buttoning each one as though we were going back in time.

But that's not what I want. Regret is not what I'm feeling.

It's more of a hesitation—a foreboding. I can't place the weight in my stomach as we put my dress on to make the walk of shame back to my own room.

"You're too quiet, Reva," Tariq whispers, his breath brushing the nape of my neck. "You're thinking too hard."

"I can't offer you anything," I whisper, facing him. He wears a neutral mask, per usual. "I don't know how. I don't know what this is or how we do this—"

"I told you." He grabs my hand and sandwiches it between his own. "This goes as far as you want. You just tell me when to stop, and this won't continue. Whether this is just our friendly banter or a little more happening—whatever—it's in your hands."

"But what do you want?" I ask, the question falling from my lips unintentionally.

FATE DEMANDS SACRIFICE 275

I try to read him as he grabs a simple tunic from the back of a chair, but his face has been trained his entire life to hide his emotions unless he wants people to see them. I know there are plenty of times he's let the mask slip for me, but this is not one of those, and I have a feeling it's to protect me.

"It doesn't matter right now, Starfire." He nods once, leading me to the door. "But you must allow me the honor of escorting you back to your room like a proper gentleman."

"One would argue some of the things that occurred in that bed were not proper," I mutter, loud enough for him to hear.

He throws his head back, that boisterous laugh that always lightens the heaviness in my chest echoing in his room. He opens the door and checks both ends of the hallway before ushering me out with his hand on my lower back.

"You never cease to amaze me, that's for sure." Tariq's devilish amusement flickers at the corners of his lips, relaxing the tension in my shoulders.

I let him walk me back to my room, and he even places a fleeting kiss to my forehead before hesitantly walking back down the hallways with his hands in his pockets, my heart swelling with each beat as it echoes his footsteps.

CHAPTER 19

For more reasons than one, I knew I had to talk to Elly about what happened last night.

Even though Tariq's her brother, she had already expressed she didn't care what he did or what I did, as long as I didn't go into grueling detail. She'll want to know how far it went, but I know she wouldn't want to hear about how dominating Tariq is in bed.

I find her hunched over a map in our usual meeting spot, a couple of books lying open beside the large piece of parchment. They seem to serve a dual purpose: to study the contents and keep the map from curling back up.

"I brought breakfast," I announce, waving the bag of muffins as she snaps her head over her shoulder. I chuckle at the dark circles under her eyes. "Late night?"

"And early morning," she grumbles, curling her lip at the muffins. "I had myself a very good time last night, both on the dance floor and in bed, but I am suffering for it this morning."

"Why didn't you come to my room?" I sink into one of the chairs at the opposite table, pulling out my muffin. "You know I have multiple cures for too much alcohol in

FATE DEMANDS SACRIFICE 277

my arsenal."

"Well," Elly drones rather dramatically, straightening. She twists toward me, arms crossed over her chest. "Pax knew I had over-consumed and, to prepare for the inevitable, he figured we could stop by your room after we left the dance floor because we saw you leave…"

My teeth stop mid-bite into my muffin, eyes widening as I avoid her intense stare.

"When we went to your room, you weren't there." A small smirk climbs its way up Elly's cheeks, an evil sort of grin. "So, we moved on and decided I'd come by in the morning. I was late for a meeting, so I couldn't stop by… But the question stands, Reva. Where were you last night?"

I unclench my jaw from around the muffin, placing it back on the table. While I eventually planned on telling her, I didn't think we were about to get into right now.

"I did leave the ball," I explain, holding my hands out. "I went to the garden… And Tariq followed." Elly's eyebrows shoot up her head, but there's that glint in her eye she gets when she wants to know something. "And then we kissed—"

"Reva!" Elly squeals, but I hold up one finger at her, and her jaw immediately drops. Her voice deepens as she croaks, "*Reva*… Did you two—"

"Have sex?" I ask, but I pause for dramatic effect before nodding once.

"Holy—" Elly takes a deep breath before shouting,

"Shit!"

"I had sex with the Crown Prince of Mariande," I groan, slamming my head into my palms. "And he offered to do it again. Multiple times."

My hands block my vision, but with her moment of silence, I guarantee she's staring at me with a calculated face as she asks, "What do you mean he offered it again?"

I drag my hands down my face, peering at her from above my fingertips. "He's essentially offering me friends with benefits on my terms. I decide how far it goes and when it stops."

Elly's amber eyes widen slightly, her head twitching back a notch with one eyebrow curled. "Tariq said that?"

I squint at her, frowning. "Why are you startled by that?" Her face recovers and takes on a neutral mask. I shake my head. "Oh, no. You can't just go all Princess of Mariande on me. What's so shocking? Do I need to be concerned about him seeing this as a declaration of love?"

Elly rolls her eyes and purses her lips with a scowl. "Tariq is not naive to a purely physical relationship. It's just interesting to me he's offered you complete control." It's my turn to scowl at her, but she waves me away. "Don't go taking that personally. I mean, it wasn't a mutual discussion that when you're both done with this, then it'll end? He said specifically you?"

"Yeah," I say, dragging out the word. "I'm pretty sure he said just me."

Elly shrugs before twirling back around to look at her map, leaving me to stare at my muffin on the table.

FATE DEMANDS SACRIFICE

279

I've had enough purely physical situations and one-night stands. I'm also not oblivious to the magnetism between Tariq and me since we met. I would go as far as to say real feelings are developing between us beyond caring about each other as friends.

At least on my end.

That realization makes me viscerally blanch at the muffin, my mouth dropping open and my heart stopping in my chest.

I actually have genuine feelings for Tariq, the *Crown Prince* of Mariande.

A strangled squeak falls from my ajar mouth, and I vaguely register Elly glance back over her shoulder.

"Do you speak to muffins now?" Elly asks, snapping my attention back to reality. "What just happened?"

"I like your brother," I admit aloud, albeit quietly. I meet her identical eyes. "I mean, I *like* him, Elly."

Elly frowns and opens her mouth to say something, but the library door opening and shutting—followed by three very familiar voices—has her snapping it shut and glaring at me with a warning.

"I told you they'd be here," Fin says, rounding the corner. He stops right at the aisle's exit, frowning at the state of Elly's table. "What are you doing?"

"Research." She shrugs like she's telling him the time.

Pax nearly slams into Fin's back, stopping himself with an arm on his good shoulder. He spots the map and books, pausing momentarily before shaking his head and looking at me.

"We all have important information to discuss," Pax says as he, Fin, and finally Tariq emerge into the open area. "It's about what the Elder said—the Dark Sirian base."

I press my eyebrows together, but my face immediately relaxes as Tariq sits directly beside me.

We haven't seen each other since last night, and it takes some calm breathing to keep from blushing in front of everyone. As Fin takes an interest in Elly's research, I meet Tariq's burning gaze with a raised eyebrow. The corner of his lip twitches imperceptibly before he slouches into the chair. He crosses his arms over his chest, purposely flexing his biceps and chest underneath his tighter-than-it-should-be tunic.

I roll my eyes at him.

"Were you guys able to look at those maps I gave you?" Elly asks, dragging an extra chair from another table to place herself between me and where Fin has decided to sit across from Tariq.

"We did," Tariq confirms with a nod. He keeps his eyes on me, occasionally flickering between Pax, Elly, and Fin. "When you told us the Elder mentioned a base somewhere between Etherea and Teslin, we found it very odd because The Raven's Wood is between those two countries. If someone were looking to train Sirians in their power, whether that be Dark or Light, we've learned discretion is extremely key."

"You once told me the Darkness was like a disease that infects," Fin jumps in, leaning forward and caressing his slinged arm. "That evening they attacked Saros, I watched their power ricochet just like Light would, so the forest would be noticeably affected by them if they were gathered there."

"Are there any towns on either side?" I ask, my attention snagging on the small rolled parchment Pax pulls out of his uniform pocket.

He rolls it out in the middle of the table. I stare at the drawing of the southern half of the Main Continent and find The Raven's Wood they're talking about, just as Pax says, "In Teslin, Sado and Rian are roughly the same distance to the forest, but there is no designated village closer to it. Rian would not be a place to be inconspicuous since it's a hub and a pirate town."

"There's this city here." I point at a village marked *Lolis* on the map on the Etherean side. "Is that an inhabited city?"

Tariq and Fin lock eyes briefly before Tariq explains, "Lolis is no longer inhabited. It used to be a sort of underground hiding city for Magics until Etherea demolished it nearly thirty-five years ago."

"I see." I rest against the chair, folding my hands in my lap. "Is there a chance they would pick that city for that reason?"

"If they're using it, we think it's only one of their bases." Pax lifts his eyes to meet Elly's. "While the idea that they could have two bases or more is a problem, there's something arguably worse about Lolis being one of them."

Staring at the map, I already know what he's going to say.

After meeting Prince Keiran last night and now learning Etherea wiped out a Magic community living in their country, there's no way Etherea would let Magics—let alone Sirians—lay a foot on a single blade of grass again unless...

"You think Etherea has already allied with the Dark Sirians," I vocalize, gauging Tariq.

"As of right now, it's a best guess." Tariq reaches out, nearly grabbing my hand in his. He plays it off by smoothing the map out. "Everything is starting to become too coincidental. We have more Ethereans making noise in Saros, then they infiltrate our military right before you come here. They openly attack the castle, and then the minute I come home, there are Dark Sirians assaulting the Magics in our city. Now, they hear the Sirian movement's Elders are in town and choose to act on a whim?"

I draw my lip into my mouth, gnawing at it between my top and bottom teeth. Tariq's thumb twitches, lightly stroking the side of my hand. I drag my eyes to Elly, and from her downturned eyes and blanched skin, I know she's thinking the same thing I am.

"If Etherea's allied with them, they're going to use their military," I sigh, rubbing my temple. "I need to tell Lightning."

"Tell her as soon as you can," Tariq insists, holding each of our gazes. "We need to meet with the Elders...

FATE DEMANDS SACRIFICE 283

All of us."

***

Given how much the mass has shrunk, I give Clint a little break and let him work with some of the nurses employed to move his body and strengthen his limbs. I alert Lightning with a message that I'm ready to train with her more seriously.

I meet her downstairs at the usual time, and she gets right to work with me. It doesn't take long to register the strange distance between us that wasn't there before.

We're completely silent during our warm-up jog and stretches, and she doesn't taunt me like she usually does when my control starts to slip. She works me through commands on running, jumping, lunging, sliding, and twisting—all while wielding the Light.

Granted, I can't use massive amounts of power because I don't want to bring the castle down, but practicing with my level of control is still applicable here.

"We're going to need a better place for me to train eventually," I interject, trying to claw a conversation out of her.

"Ideally, you would come back with me to the Sirian community," she says, her voice and face drawn tight. "But I know you won't leave the Hespers, even if Clint were completely healed."

I glare up at the ceiling, blowing out a heavy breath.

"Just get it out, Lightning. What did the Elders say?"

She stands with her hands clasped behind her back, reminiscent of how Pax and Fin commonly stand on duty. She stares at me with those beady, hauntingly bright eyes, cutting through my tightening chest.

"They think you're too blinded by the kindness the Hespers have shown you," she blatantly admits, unmoving. "They especially think you're sleeping with the prince, so your credibility to judge their trustworthiness has gone out the window."

I omit I have now slept with the prince, explaining, "I don't think I'm blinded, Lightning. I truly believe they all mean well. Even Pax has come to enjoy my company. If I can convince him to trust Sirians, I think I could convince King Darius."

She blinks rapidly at the mention of Pax, dark brown eyebrows drawn together. "He accepts you now? I thought he despised you?"

"Confined quarters can make you like someone, I guess." I shrug, rubbing my arm. "He said it was because he saw me healing Clint without owing Mariande anything, and when he saw me wield the Light to save him... It just clicked that maybe everything his dad has told him wasn't the truth."

She snaps her head away from me, staring at a nearby wall. She presses her lips together before continuing, "It's not as simple as you'd like to think... Not with convincing the Elders that Mariande can be trusted, and I doubt it's as simple as you think to convince your king."

FATE DEMANDS SACRIFICE   285

I take a few steps closer to her, wiping sweat from my forehead as I breach the topic I need to discuss with her. "Aithan said you all believe there is a base between Teslin and Etherea… What makes you believe that?"

Lightning grunts as she gestures for me to follow her lead, sitting cross-legged on the floor. As I carefully lower to the ground, Lightning explains, "We have various methods of gathering intel, and after a few interrogations, some village scoping, and some sea trips, we narrowed it down to this weird in-between spot on one side of The Raven's Wood… We just haven't figured out where."

I take a deep inhale, preparing for what I have to admit. "I told Tariq and Pax about that bit of information."

"You what?" Lightning gapes at me, her eyes faintly glowing in the dim room. "Reva, I swear to the *Gods*—"

"Hear me out!" I shout back, raising my hands between us. "Mariande keeps a keen eye on Etherea's actions because they don't trust them. I thought maybe they knew something about a location in that area that none of you could figure out, especially if you mostly hide out everywhere."

Lightning purses her lips tightly, her nostrils flaring. "You better have found something good."

"I wouldn't say good is the right word." I wince.

I tell her verbatim what the boys explained to Elly and me the day before, drawing the map as best as possible in the sand from my memory. By the time I've finished my narration, any brightness that naturally emanates from

Lightning is snuffed out, eyes dull. She examines the sketch on the ground, her eyes flitting between where I've drawn Sado, Rian, the forest, and Lolis.

"That would explain their resources," Lightning whispers, her head still bowed to the ground. "We know they have pretty impressive boats and are relatively nourished. We just thought they had some sort of powerful or wealthy connection. We never considered a kingdom would side with them."

"If someone has something to offer that's nearly priceless to them…" I shake my head, staring at the nearest sconce on the wall. "People will put aside their morals to get what they want. I'm sure whoever is leading the Dark Sirians appealed to the King of Etherea and added a dash of power flex for fun."

"We need Mariande, then." Lightning finally meets my eyes. "The Elders are going to want to meet with a representative."

"It will have to be Tariq and Elly. He wants all of us to meet collectively."

"Of course he does," she groans, twisting to stand up. "And we can't say no to the Crown Prince of Mariande, can we?"

I chuckle darkly under my breath because, Gods, does that resonate with me—just on a different level.

"I'll send word to the Elders and figure out what they want to do from here," Lightning explains as we make our way to the stairs. Before we start the climb, she whirls on me, gripping my shoulder. "For what it's worth, Reva,

FATE DEMANDS SACRIFICE 287

I see you trying to step into this role. You're doing great for someone who hasn't known a world beyond her front door."

I scoff, but the tightness in my chest loosens, and the self-doubt quiets. "Thanks, Lightning. You're not too bad yourself."

"Oh," she grins wickedly. "I'm well aware of that, but I trained for this. It's clear you were born for it."

CHAPTER 20

"We have to expect the Sirian Elders will want to meet on some sort of common ground," Tariq mulls over with Pax by the window in Clint's room. I continue to mix the ginger and turmeric tea I've been giving Clint every morning to fight inflammation. "The bottom line is they don't trust us, so we have to show them we are willing to meet on their terms throughout this partnership."

"So, they won't want to meet in Saros." Pax rubs the stubble along his sharp jaw. He balances his elbow on his crossed arm, his hand flourishing between them. "You think they'll want to meet somewhere deeper inland?"

Tariq shakes his head, crossing his arms over his chest as he leans against the window frame and gazes out the window. I hand Clint his tea, noticing Tariq's biceps strain against his tunic as he shifts. Someone clears their throat, and I snap to Tariq's face.

He smirks at me, raising one eyebrow. My cheeks burn, and I widen my eyes, tucking my head down to face Clint, who is *snickering* into his tea. I gently bop him on top of his head, pointing my finger at him with a glare

FATE DEMANDS SACRIFICE

289

in warning as he glowers over the rim of the cup.

I sit beside Clint's outstretched legs, waiting for him to tenderly sip on the tea, scowling at it with a scrunched face. I try to divert his attention, "Is this how you always know so much about the inner political workings? They use your room to talk business?"

Clint nods, swallowing and then curling his lip. "It's always a combination of Tariq, Fin, Pax, and Elly talking about things happening in the countries. I know all about the betrothals, who likes and hates who… All the drama, Reva."

"You do love your drama," I chuckle, remembering when Clint asked me about the ongoings of my life. I take the now-empty teacup from him and place it on the nightstand. He inhales slowly through his nose, holding it in before releasing it from his pursed lips. I regard him with my hands held up. "Are we ready to do this?"

Clint shifts in the bed so he's lying flat on his back before asking, "Are we going to be able to get rid of it completely today?"

I clench my jaw, grinding my teeth together before tilting my head. "It should be small enough, so we'll see what I can do here. I'm not sure exactly how to zap something so small."

"Well," Clint clears his throat, shutting his eyes. "Only one way to find out."

I notice the silence in the room before I even conjure the starfire power. I apply gentle pressure to Clint's stomach and peer over my shoulder at Pax and Tariq, who watch me with still faces. Tariq and I lock eyes, and he encourages me with the smallest nod.

I close my eyes like I do every time I've shrunk Clint's mass and wrap the shield around it like a blanket. The cell cluster can't be bigger than a plum now, quivering at the iridescent blue aura.

The Energy strikes like lightning. Following each attack, the mass emits a high-pitched screech, ringing in my ears with a low, pulsing hum that blocks out any noise from the rest of the world. The cells' hostility is more potent this time, and the lashes are met with more resistance, like trying to cut through rope. I vaguely sense my brow furrowing in my corporeal body, and the force I hit the mass with next is like winding my arm back to whack it with a baton.

The noise from the mass now is low and guttural, rattling in my skull and reverberating against my teeth.

You will obey, that ethereal voice echoes through the chasm in my head, the strange place I go to envision the mass and my shield.

Instead of the high-pitched ring that has answered before, thousands of gritted voices yell in unison, like an army charging into battle. Somewhere far away, a warm, wet sensation touches my upper lip, a metallic taste dripping into my mouth.

I shake the distraction away, refocusing on the mass enclosed within the walls of my shield, quaking in rage before me. I try to yank back the baton of Asteria's god-power again, but when I dive in, I'm met with a

FATE DEMANDS SACRIFICE   291

wall resembling a thick curtain pulled taut. I try to push through it, but it's nailed shut.

The necklace, a husky voice like Karasi's says, but it's not quite Karasi. It's disembodied and modulated, almost forced.

But when the necklace is mentioned, my body centers on a blistering heat spreading from the point on my chest where it typically rests, as though it were branding me.

Remove the necklace, daughter, the voice resounds again, echoing from one ear to the next.

I hesitate, feeling my brows press together again. My name is called in a question somewhere in reality while I'm shoved out of my body, and my vision wavers between watching from above Clint's bed and sitting within my own mind.

Quickly yanking the power out of the young boy's body, it rolls up under the skin in waiting. One hand stays pressed against the boy while the other trembles, grasping for the necklace and yanking it off with a snap.

"Reva?" the Unintended King asks again, taking one step forward.

Ignoring the predatorial advancement, the tainted stone is thrown to the ground. The hand returns to the boy, and the starfire unleashes.

I'm suddenly pulled back into the battle with the mass just as the line between the gold-tinged Sirian Energy and the blue swirling of starfire fades like smoke. The blue god-power invades the Energy until nothing is left but the white-blue glow.

This time, I don't need the shield.

I glare at the small number of clustered cells left in Clint, who have gone silent as though they now understand who—or what—I am and have accepted their fate. Just like I release the Light when I finish practicing, I will the mass to release itself back into existence. The mass glows a vibrant blue before separating into smaller and smaller light orbs until there isn't a trace of it left.

I gasp as I plunge back into reality. I'm instantly aware of the fatigue that settles into my bones, my vision wavering. When I lift my hands from Clint, it's like trying to drag them through water.

"What the hell was that?" Pax whispers harshly from the window.

My blood races through my veins like liquid ice. I blink past the nauseating pain, trying to move from the bed, but every part of me cries out, my body panicking at just the touch of clothes on my skin.

"What's happening—" Tariq is cut off as a cross between a scream and groan is ripped from me when my foot touches the floor. "Reva!"

Gravity weighs heavily on my shoulders, and I collapse to my hands and knees. I cry at the pins and needles pressing into the point of contact on the floor and shooting up my arms and legs. My whole body screams at me—or maybe I'm screaming at it.

I sway to the side as my vision rolls back into my head, and I plummet into a cold that burns me from the inside

FATE DEMANDS SACRIFICE 293

out.

***

After hearing Karasi's voice, I thought she might come into my dream again. Instead, it's like I blinked and appeared in my dim bedroom, the curtain over my window drawn closed.

My senses slowly return to my body. The first two things I notice are I'm not alone in my bed and my cloak is wrapped around me underneath the blankets. I may be sleeping on my side toward the window, but I don't have to look to know it's Tariq who has an arm tucked under my head, a leg draped over mine, and a book resting on my shoulder. His scent wraps around me like another layer of protection, my anxiety calm but my heart still racing.

"How are you feeling, Starfire?" Tariq asks, his voice gravelly. He clears his throat as he flips a page.

"Are you using my shoulder as a table?" I question, unable to hide the disbelief in my voice.

He chuckles, the sound rumbling against my back. "I wasn't about to leave this room when we all thought you were dying, but I also had to entertain myself, considering you've been unconscious for a few hours—"

"A few hours?" I shout incredulously, lurching from the bed to sit upright. I instantly regret it, though, because a sharp, stabbing pain hits both of my temples, my vision

294   K.M. DAVIDSON

tunneling.

"Calm down," Tariq insists, tossing his book aside. I'm stunned as he eases me back against the pillows, his arm staying behind me as the other rotates me toward him. We lay with our faces just inches apart. "You had quite the... episode. We're not sure how your body is going to respond."

"What happened?" I ask, searching his face.

I don't find his confident, princely mask underneath the dark blond stubble or loose strands of hair. While his face is relaxed in relief, small frown lines are peeking out from his forehead and at the corner of his lips as his eyes study me right back, albeit more frantically than I look at him. Whatever happened must have spooked him because he doesn't hear me, so I slide my hand up and cup his cheek. His eyes stop searching, landing on mine.

"Tariq," I say quietly, repeating, "What happened?"

"I feel like I should be asking you that question," Tariq sighs. He grabs my wrist in his hand and brings my palm to his mouth, placing a gentle kiss in the middle. I melt, reminded of the burning cold I felt before I passed out.

"The mass," I whisper as Tariq tucks my hand under his chin. "I got rid of it entirely. Clint no longer has it in his body."

Tariq's eyes widen, his eyebrows climbing up his forehead. "You're positive?"

I nod, the side of my face rubbing against the pillow. "It was fighting back harder than before, but there was

FATE DEMANDS SACRIFICE

just so little left. I was trying to slam it with the Asteria god-power—"

"The starfire," Tariq interrupts with a wink and a slight tilt of his lips.

Something about that tickles the back of my mind, but I narrow my eyes before continuing, "As I was saying, I was trying to wield the *starfire,* and it was like I came to a wall in that power. But it wasn't like I'd used it all… I couldn't access the true extent of it."

"Is that why you ripped your necklace off?" Tariq asks, his face relaxing. "You didn't say anything, but your facial features were moving like you were having a conversation only you could hear. You were frowning, and blood started dripping from your nose."

I recall taking the necklace off, but something deep inside my gut tells me it wasn't really me who took it off, as if my arms were attached to a string like a matinee doll, and something else was the puppeteer.

"Yes," I answer slowly, not sure how to explain what happened in a way he'd understand. Tariq barely lifts his head from the pillow to peer down at me, but he doesn't push. "I heard a voice again, and it sounded like Karasi, but I don't think it was… It told me to take the necklace off. After I took it off, it was like a door opened, and the Light wasn't there anymore. It was just the starfire."

"I thought the hematite necklaces were symbolic," Tariq says, squinting at me. "I didn't think they actually had a purpose."

"Elly said they were given to demi-gods and their

descendants to keep them grounded, to keep them from yearning for power beyond." I wiggle my head dramatically, pulling my hand from underneath Tariq's chin. "What if it was blocking my god-powers' full capabilities?"

"You're telling me you're even *more* powerful than you've demonstrated?" Tariq awes, his eye lingering on what is probably my exposed Sirian Mark. "I've got to tell you, Starfire... You are nothing like I ever thought you'd be when Elly first told me about you."

I glare at him momentarily. "I've rarely taken my hematite necklace off my entire life. Even when I have taken it off, it's never been when I try to use my powers. I've also actively avoided that blue-tinged power for years because of Karasi's reaction to it... Which is saying a lot for that woman."

"We should have Elly look into the hematite necklaces further," Tariq explains, twisting onto his back and staring at the ceiling. He rests his free hand on his stomach, the other still trapped underneath me. "Maybe she can ask Jorah about it, too. After all, he is a jewel and stone expert, not to mention our new intel that he's part of some underground Sirian system."

Speaking of an underground system, I make a mental note to ask Karasi about this next time she decides to appear in my dreams, considering she was alive while the Sirians roamed Aveesh as free people.

"Do you know why you were shivering?" Tariq asks, his voice quiet. He's still gazing up at the ceiling, his

FATE DEMANDS SACRIFICE   297

eyes distant and muted. "You kept saying 'it hurts' and trembling. No matter what I did, it didn't help. I put your coat on you, I got under the covers with you… Elly kept saying we should get a Magic we trust, but I told her you wouldn't want another person finding out about you."

"You what?" I whisper, unable to answer his question. The thought of him so close to me after using my powers—

"You were cold to the touch." Tariq turns his head to me, scanning my face again. "Your veins were glowing blue underneath your skin, from your elbows down to your hands. I threw one of the blankets from Clint's room over you and brought you here…"

My heart clenches in my chest as he recalls the events, but I can't focus on what he's saying about Elly panicking. All I can think about is that he helped and touched me while my powers were still active, seemingly without a second thought.

Having been told my entire life my powers were something to control, something to fear, something to keep under wraps, my heart sings at the fact that someone who has never experienced Sirian Light before barely bats an eye as I wield it.

The warmth spreads through my chest, extending to every limb. "You carried me."

He startles slightly, a small and quick shake of his head, as his eyes round out. "That's what you're taking from this? That I carried you—"

I don't let him finish because I can't stand how my

chest won't stop expanding the longer I look at him, threatening to burst. I grab the back of his neck and pull him into me, squeezing my eyes tight as I press our lips together. His body stiffens momentarily in shock, but then he releases a content moan against my lips.

His hand slides over my waist and behind my back, easily yanking me closer against him so there is not an inch between us. My lips move in time with his, tracing every dip and bow of his mouth as his tongue tangles with mine. His taste washes over me, drowning out any doubt about who I am, where I'm from, and who I can be.

Because I don't give a damn as long as I'm right here with him.

Tariq's hand slides down the curve of my ass, drawing under my thigh until he grips the back of my knee. He hoists it over his hip, angling his body so his thigh presses between my legs. A groan escapes my own lips as my hand tangles in his soft locks, happy to find it free of his usual bun. Tariq's hands continue to roam my body frantically, as though he were making sure every part of me was still intact.

"Reva," he mumbles against my lips like a prayer.

With one leg already looped over him, I press my hand to his firm chest and break away from his swollen lips. His face is flushed, those beautiful, glowing eyes searching mine for something.

I use my perfectly placed hand to push him back onto the bed, taking advantage of the angle I'm at and straddling his waist. His hands fall onto my hips where

FATE DEMANDS SACRIFICE   299

my legs bend, tucking his thumbs into the crease. His hard length strains against his pants beneath me, taunting me. I tilt my head back as I roll my hips against him.

The low rumble that omits from him sends a jolt through my very core.

I don't waste any more time, snapping my eyes to his as I gather my long dress into both hands. Tariq smirks, helping me grab the fabric and throw it over my head. As he balls it up and tosses it to the side, I fumble with the buttons on his slacks, my heart hammering against my chest with bated breaths. He lifts his hips from the bed enough for me to slide his pants out of the way, his cock flinging free.

I don't even bother with my undergarments, simply pulling the strip guarding my entrance to the side. I take his member in my hand, marveling at the smooth skin running along the vein that stretches from the base. I stroke up and down the shaft once, twice, peeking up at Tariq through heavy lashes. He watches my hand, his lips parted slightly as his chest heaves up and down. His eyes flicker to mine, those burning orange hues swirling and setting me aflame.

I raise my hips above him, positioning him and startling myself at how slick I am. I easily sink onto his full length, throwing my head back again as his cock hits deep inside me.

"Gods, Reva," Tariq moans, his head pressing deeper into the pillow, his hands gripping my thighs.

I angle my body, running my hands up his defined

stomach, stopping when they're resting on his broad chest. I put pressure against him, lifting my hips again before slamming back down and rolling my hips.

"*Fuck,*" Tariq grits against his teeth, drinking me in as his gaze follows the path of his hands up my waist and over my ribs to cup my breasts in both hands.

I press my lips together as I ride him in a steady, tantalizing rhythm, reveling in the moans and sounds I can elicit from the Crown Prince below me.

Tariq locks my neck in his grip, slamming his lips on mine and nipping at my lower lip. He mutters against them, "How much can you take, Healer?"

Something carnal stirs deep in my stomach as I whisper, "I'm at your mercy, Your *Highness.*"

An unfamiliar but exhilarating darkness swirls in the depths of his amber eyes. In a swift movement, he effortlessly pulls me off of him and flips me onto my stomach. He kneels behind me on the soft mattress and—with a quick rip—tears my underwear off. He positions my hands and knees before he sheaths himself inside of me down to the base, ripping a satisfying moan from me.

"You like that?" Tariq mutters against my ear. "Let me show how good I can really make you feel."

Both of his hands grab my waist, adjusting one of his legs so it's propped beside me. He thrusts into me at an angle, his hips rolling down and up as he hits one of those bundles of nerves repeatedly.

It doesn't take long for my walls to squeeze

FATE DEMANDS SACRIFICE

301

around him and spasm, my body trembling with warm pleasure. The sensation continues deep within me as his movements slow. His soft lips place fleeting kisses up my spine, the gentle touch like small zaps of Light.

We fall onto my bed beside each other, panting. I curl into his chest and let him engulf me in his embrace. He tucks my head under his chin so my nose presses against his neck, his pulse racing in tune with mine. I can't help but nip at the sensitive skin there.

Tariq chuckles low in his chest, his hand tracing the same trail he kissed up and down my back. "You're insatiable."

"You said it yourself," I whisper, bending my head back to look at him. "Now that I've touched you, I don't think I can stop."

"Using my words against me?" He smirks, his eyes drooping lazily.

I shrug, pursing my lips. "You said whenever I want."

"Greedy little thing." Tariq pulls me closer into his chest. "Ruin me, Starfire. Take whatever you want from me."

CHAPTER 21

*T*he setting in this dream is unfamiliar to me, yet something tickles at the back of my mind.

Unmistakably, the Black Avalanches loom in front of me, the same oily thickness that has plagued them over the last two decades swirling there. The Abyss is just as thick as it was when I left, but the shadows snake through the peaks like living entities.

I stand in the middle of an empty square surrounded by stone buildings adorned with different signs indicating the type of establishment lying within. My steps crunch the tiny gravel below my feet with each step I take deeper into the large village, surrounded by structures and monuments on every side of me. If I had to guess, this place is as big as Saros, or at least near the same size.

"Incredible what time will do to a place," Karasi's voice echoes around me, clearer than the other day when I'd helped Clint.

I twirl on my heel to find her poised, her hands clasped in front of her.

Except she looks nothing like I'm used to.

Her marigold eyes are the same piercing color, observing

FATE DEMANDS SACRIFICE

303

me as always. The dullness behind them tells me the same Karasi I know and love looks upon me now, but based on the image she presents to me, she could be my age.

Long black dreads entwine with bronze circlets and coils, dangling down her curvy figure. A bronze band wraps around her head, following her hairline and disappearing underneath the many strands. Her ebony skin is free of wrinkles, smooth across her forehead and the corners of her eyes, especially with her stoic expression. Beige clothes hang from her shoulders, wrapping around her arms and tied with a thick, bronze belt at the waist.

I never realized we were the same height without her hunch.

"So, this is the Great Karasi the world first knew," I manage around the thickness clogging my throat, still surveying her. The twitch of her lips is the only answer I get. "What is this place?"

Her head scans our surroundings, those snake-like eyes squinting in deep thought. She tilts her head to the side, contemplative. "It's only fitting it would be this memory." Her gaze locks onto mine. "You now know this place by a simple name. But long ago, it was known by another throughout the land, run by a family deeply influenced by your god-power."

"This is Main Town?" She can only be referring to Asteria since Dionne came from Riddling, not to mention the Black Avalanches behind me.

She nods once, the plethora of bronze and gold jewelry she wears tinkling. "A little less than a thousand years ago. Shortly after, the Sirians suffered at the hands of the Korbins."

304 K.M. DAVIDSON

At the mention of the Sirians, I remember the incident with Clint and my hematite necklace. Elly still hadn't been able to find anything about when Magics started passing out hematite jewelry to demi-gods and what the true purpose was, and Jorah had been occupied recently. "Karasi... I healed Clint."

"I know, aster." She smiles warmly. "I knew you would."

"I heard your voice," I explain, stepping toward her. "You told me to take my necklace off. When I did, something happened to my powers. They were easier to wield, but the burning I got from Asteria's power intensified. It was unbearable. What does it mean?"

Something clouds over her eyes, muting their color before they return to normal. She presses her lips together before admitting, "She told me she was going to use my voice to appeal to you."

My heart stops beating in my chest. I want to ask again who she's referring to, but I know she can't. The earthquake in the dream last time was clear. Whoever watches me doesn't want me to know.

At least not now. "Why?"

Karasi shakes her head, her dangled earrings clanking. "My mother told me never to wear hematite pieces at a young age. She said they would mute my abilities, the ones I inherited from her, despite being the child of a demi-god.

"I always had a feeling the hematite was meant to keep a leash on the abilities of the demi-gods. Why is beyond my knowledge and was a decision made far before my time. I was the final child born directly from a demi-god, although there were plenty of descendants of my cousins."

FATE DEMANDS SACRIFICE 305

"So, it doesn't keep me from 'yearning for more'?" I ask, an eyebrow raised. She scrunches her nose and curls her lip at that. "Why did you let me wear it all this time?"

Her face falls, her head turning down to avoid my gaze, a rarity. "I always knew who your god-powers came from, just as I knew it could not be my role to teach you how to wield those powers to their full capacity. I encouraged the necklace because I knew it was just as I said: a leash.

"Leashes can be taken off." Her head raises, a small smirk tugging at her lips. "I knew one day you would be ready for your full powers, and you would no longer need the hematite necklace to keep them at bay."

"When I took it off, the starfire overcame the Energy," I explain, something flickering out of the corner of my eyes. I turn my head toward the nearest building, but it stands as it usually does.

In ruins.

I glance around me quickly, noticing Main Town is now restored to what it looks like in the present day.

"Asteria's power has always been an enhanced variation of the Light." Karasi smiles, grimly. "This power you call starfire is your Energy. The hematite is just able to separate it from your natural Sirian heritage. I'm sure the more you wield the starfire, the more your body will acclimate to it and no longer feel its effects." She takes two steps closer to me. "But remember, while your starfire is unleashed without your necklace, so will be the firepower."

"So, hematite is still useful when I'm not using my powers." The stone structure in my peripheral flickers again, *slowly fading away until Karasi and I are surrounded by pure white…*

Nothing.

"You are the most powerful Sirian to walk Aveesh since Asteria herself," Karasi blurts, startling me. I snap my head forward to find her just inches from me. She snatches my hands, squeezing tight as if she fears them slipping away.

Her normally yellow eyes have a milky film over them, her voice taking on an airy quality. "The powerful must be few for balance to remain. Fate will demand sacrifice."

That statement lands like a blow to my chest as the wind picks up around us, distant screams echoing through the nothingness we stand in.

I can't tear my eyes away from her. Those stunning, bright irises return, rising from behind the clouds in her eyes like the sun. My heart clenches in my chest as she raises a hand to cup my cheek, swiping a tear away.

"Why am I crying?" I whisper between us as she raises her other hand to grip my head between both of them.

She gently pulls me toward her now that we're at the same height, placing a tender kiss against my Mark. The fleeting touch spreads from the six points like a feather dragging along my skin.

When she pulls away from me, she looks like she did when I left her: gray hair, wrinkles, and pudgy body.

"You know why, aster," she whispers back, a tear of her own escaping. "The Stars have called you back home, my little orphan, but do not forget who you are." Her bony finger jabs my chest directly above my heart. "Do not forget all those who

FATE DEMANDS SACRIFICE   307

have loved you."

Tears silently slip down my cheeks, racing each other to the ground. I stand frozen, watching her walk toward the expanse of white, her footsteps soundless.

As my vision tunnels and the deep black closes in, Karasi whips her head over her shoulder. She gazes longingly at me, those luminescent eyes growing dimmer with the darkness until they are the last thing I have left in my dream.

★★★

I'm trembling from head to toe as I journey to the dining room, where I'm supposed to meet Elly for breakfast. I threw on something simple and quick, rubbing a generous amount of salve on my forehead before heading out my door. I even went as far as to wear my necklace for safety, to keep the power simmering in my veins on a leash.

I round the dining room doorway just as I finish braiding my hair, locking eyes with Elly from across the room. She hunches over an open book; a spoon pauses halfway to her mouth.

"Reva?" Elly asks, laying down her spoon in her bowl. "You look like you've seen a ghost. What in the Gods' names has happened?"

I can't keep it to myself any longer. I throw myself into the chair in front of her, the words tumbling from my mouth in a hushed voice in case any intruding attendants or castle dwellers pass by.

I explain to her how Karasi has appeared in my dreams, part of the many gifts she inherited from whom I could confirm was her mother, Sybil. I divulge every detail of my conversations with Karasi, from the settings of the dreams to the ominous *she* Karasi continuously referred to.

By the time I finish the most recent dream, I'm shaking profusely, the liquid in my teacup sloshing over the sides.

"Let's take a few deep breaths," Elly insists, laying her hand flat across the table. "You've been dealing with a lot between the new layer of your gifts and what we've realized with the Sirian movement. Just relax a little bit, drink some tea, maybe a glass of wine, and we can start jotting down the different moving pieces to help us know exactly what we're looking at here."

A small chuckle flutters off my lips at her wine comment, a smile pulling at my lips.

"That's better." Elly grins, sitting back in her chair triumphantly. "Why don't we eat breakfast—"

A thunderous boom rattles the dining room walls, jerking my and Elly's attention toward the courtyard and my heart stopping dead in my chest. Knights shout incoherently, their voices rising like a chorus. A handful ramble past the dining room, hands gripping the swords strapped to their belts. Elly and I exchange a brief glance before lurching from our seats and running in the same direction as the knights.

FATE DEMANDS SACRIFICE 309

The courtyard.

We nearly collide with Pax and Tariq, whose frantic faces probably mirror our own.

"Did you hear that?" Elly asks Tariq, gripping his forearm. "What was that?"

"That's what we're trying to figure out," Tariq grumbles, flustered. His eyes are wide and wild, scanning Elly and me.

"It's best if none of you come," Pax insists, twirling to block Elly, Tariq, and me in the doorway and our only path to the courtyard. I peer over his shoulder to find two dozen knights surrounding a blurred figure.

A flash of black has my heart slamming against my ribcage, the blood rushing to my head.

"If it's what we think it is," I hiss at Pax under my breath. "You're going to need me."

A familiar vibrato carries over the commotion, and my heart skips a beat. "Khonsa above, I thought you all were supposed to be accepting of Magics."

"Let me through, *now*," I demand, using a bit of the Energy to shove Pax's thick arm from the doorframe. He swears, nearly falling sideways from the sudden loss of balance.

The knights' voices are nearly deafening as they echo off the stone walls, but all silence as Tariq shouts above them, "Give the man some room. Let the Healer in."

I barely register the knights parting a line directly in front of me as my eyes connect with a set of bright purple ones that belong to the man crouched defensively before me, black leathery wings flaring out behind him. He slowly inches to full height, towering over every knight around him. His hair is windblown and longer than the last time I saw him, but his beard and curled mustache are impeccably groomed as always.

Remy's mouth twitches up at the corner. "Talk about making an entrance, huh?"

There's no stopping the tears I've been fighting since we said our vague goodbye. I extend my gaze to the sky, take a deep breath, and run towards Remy's outstretched arms, those tears streaming down my face and falling behind me. He cautiously steps toward me just before I leap into his arms, his hand bracing against my shoulder blades as the other holds my head against his chest. I bury my face into his collar.

"Gods, girl," he mumbles into my hair, but I hear the sob he chokes on.

Once my feet are steady on the ground, he pulls me back to examine me thoroughly. Gripping both shoulders, his eyes scan every inch of me. The smirk from before turns into a full smile underneath his beard as he removes one hand from my shoulder, cupping my cheek.

"Is it possible you've gotten more beautiful?" he asks with genuine awe. "You are glowing."

"Probably," I giggle through the tears, trying to grasp what remains of my sanity.

Standing before Remy, it's like I never left. The only difference happens to be the biggest; we're standing in the middle of the Castle of Andromeda in Mariande.

FATE DEMANDS SACRIFICE   311

My smile falters, and Remy instantly catches it. He glances over my shoulder, smiling at the remaining knights, but it doesn't quite reach his eyes. When his fake smile falters, I follow his line of sight to find Elly, Tariq, and Pax all standing in the doorway.

"Is there somewhere private we can talk?" Remy asks, his eyes pinned on all three of my friends. "It's about Eldamain."

I frown, trying to read his expression.

But when he finds my eyes, they've darkened in hue. "And Karasi."

***

"I'm sorry for the unexpected arrival," Remy begins, sitting beside me at the long table in the strategy room. He slings his arm over the back of my chair, leaning into it. "I was under the impression you all were more open to my kind, considering one lives under your roof."

"No insult to you." Tariq stands behind Elly, who sits directly across from us. "While that may be, we also don't expect Magics to drop from the sky with large wings in the middle of the day, either."

"If you think those are large," Remy mutters, eyeing Tariq far more intently than I'd like him to.

I jab him in the side before clearing my throat. "Everyone, this is Remy, who you all have heard of to varying degrees. Remy, these are my friends."

"Prince Tariq," he introduces, his hand patting Elly's shoulder. "And my sister, Princess Eloise."

Remy extends his hand to Elly across the table, putting his weight into it. She accepts with a smile, which elicits an eyebrow raise and a tilt of the head from Remy. There is nothing but mischief in those purple eyes.

"Filthy Magic," I grumble under my breath, glaring at him. He just hums, side-eyeing me with his lips pursed.

Fin and Pax introduce themselves appropriately, offering Remy a small bow, which has him recoiling from both of them with a scowl. The anger simmers in Pax, and I wonder if he should even be here for this discussion.

Remy slowly scans the group, his gaze bouncing from one person to the next, occasionally flickering to me with reservation. He looks to Fin last, who frowns at the attention, glancing at me with a question on his face.

"They know about you, don't they?" Remy blurts, uncurling his arm from behind me to fold over his chest. "Gods, I feel like you might have more to tell me than I have to tell you."

"In due time, Remy," I sigh, rubbing my temple. I twist in my seat to face him more, searching for a sign of what's coming. "You once told me the last time I saw your wings would be the final time, yet you just revealed them to a host of Mariande knights. I have a feeling whatever you have is more important and urgent."

My palms are instantly sweating when Remy looks up at me around a strand of hair hanging in front of his forehead. His eyes loop around the table again before

FATE DEMANDS SACRIFICE 313

landing back on me.

"Main Town was attacked," Remy says calmly, but those demons dance in his eyes and shadow them. "By Dark Sirians."

Elly gasps, her hand flying to cover her mouth with a slap. Tariq's hand slowly slips off the back of Elly's chair, his face slacking and the light winking out of his eyes. Pax and Fin are both swearing, and I'm sure if I looked at Fin, he'd be shades lighter from his own experience with the Darkness.

"How bad?" I whisper. Tariq takes trepid steps toward a map on the far wall. Even from where I sit, I can see where Main Town is marked, which is not far from Karasi's hut at the edge of Orion's Lake.

"We could barely defend ourselves," Remy snaps at no one in particular, running a rough hand through his disheveled hair. "A couple of homemade incendiary cocktails had them scattering after we blew up a few of their friends, but not before we lost people... Roughly half the town."

"*Half* the town?" I squeal, jumping from my seat. It clatters to the ground behind me, echoing through the room. "You can't be serious?"

"Some of the regulars from The Red Raven and some you've done business with. Willem and Dahlia are okay, but Rol went down."

My bottom lip quivers as I fight the tears gathering in my eyes. My stomach drops before I even ask the question because I already know the answer.

I blink once, slowly, before asking, "What about Karasi?"

Remy swallows harshly, pinning his eyes on me. They're downturned as he whispers, "I'm so sorry, Reva."

The room falls into a deep, heavy silence, my chest caving in on itself as something inside me starts screaming.

Except on the outside, my lips stay pressed into a thin line with the slightest pout. I close my eyes, breathing in and out, trying to calm the beating of my heart, which is just as loud as the guttural scream ringing in my head.

"Reva?" Elly whispers, her voice distant. "We're here for you. You know that, right?"

The drawing of Orion's Lake taunts me from across the room, blurring.

"She just needs to process," Remy explains quietly, his hand wrapping around my wrist. I blink back the tears. "Karasi may have been difficult, but she did her best to be a mother to you."

Mother. A corner of my heart breaks off and shatters on the ground. I swallow the lump in my throat blocking my airway, a single tear escaping as the lump falls to the pit of my stomach.

I nod once, swiping the tear away. "I need to go there."

"Eldamain?" Remy frowns, shaking his head. "There's nothing you can do for them now, Reva. It's just damage control and laying the dead to rest."

"Not them," I explain. "I want to go to Karasi's—my

FATE DEMANDS SACRIFICE 315

house. I should be the one to go through things, and we should have a ceremony, and we need to figure out what to do with the house, or it's going to be…" I trail off, my voice disappearing on a quivering breath of air.

"We'll go with you," Elly interjects, slowly rising from her seat. This time, she directs her attention to Tariq, who's still standing by the map. "Clint is doing incredibly and is healed, and there are plenty of Magics here that can help should someone get hurt."

"I don't want to leave Clint here alone." Tariq gnaws at the inside of his lip. "Or our parents, for that matter. If the Dark Sirians are openly attacking towns, they're getting ready to fight back."

"I'll stay," Pax jumps in, stepping closer to the table. Elly and I frown at him, but he focuses on me. "It's not that I don't want to support you as a friend, Reva, but it would be best if I didn't join you. I know I've been more accepting, but that's a lot of Magics to be around. I don't want to involuntarily do or say something to offend them during their mourning."

"That's very considerate of you," Remy says kindly, even if he tilts his head to the side.

"Thank you," I whisper.

Pax nods once, and Elly moves to wrap her arms around his middle.

"So, us four, then?" I ask, meeting Fin, Elly, and Tariq's eyes and stopping on him. The longer I stare at him, the softer his eyes turn, peeking out from underneath his mask.

"I'll fly back to Eldamain to let Dahlia and Willem know," Remy says quietly, laying a hand on my shoulder. "I'll meet you all back there, okay?"

I don't react until Remy yanks me into him, wrapping me in his arms like a cocoon. The first sobs escape me, followed by a swift torrent of them that rack my body. All I can do is cling to the back of his shirt, fisting the fabric in my grip as he smooths his hand down my back.

Acute pain accompanies the crushing in my chest returns as I inhale around another sob. My entire body wants to battle the truth, grasping at the air like I could pull the world I'd been living in just moments ago back to me. The desire to change this fate pierces me like an arrow, and I would bargain my soul for another outcome.

But what sinks its claws deeper than any pain is the realization that my life had started tipping long ago...

And I no longer know which way is truly up.

CHAPTER 22

The silence in the carriage that accumulated over the last two-day trip shifts restlessly as we pull up to the edge of our plot on Orion's Lake. My old home grows closer with every trot of the horses' hooves. The scenery I used to see every morning passes by outside the window, stirring memory after memory in my mind.

A quivering breath trembles from my lips, and a soft hand clasps over mine. I peek at Elly beside me.

"Take it one step at a time," she whispers, leaning her head against my shoulder. I shut my eyes against the emotions rising in my chest, but no tears are left. "As slow and steady as we have to."

I just nod once.

We pull up as close as we can, the figure on the porch obvious from his height and stature. I lean forward, rapping the wall of the carriage. "We're good here."

Either Fin or Tariq pulls on the reins, the horses protesting as the boys' voices rumble in conversation. I swing the carriage door open and leap out.

The snow is gone now, and the land is filled with towering green grass that bends in the breeze. It reaches my thighs and makes its way under my skirt, tickling my legs. I march through the overgrown grass, the familiar scent of the Black Avalanches rushing down, reminding me again of when I met Remy. This time, the burnt oil lamp smell is stronger than ever, stinging the back of my nose.

"It's not pleasant, is it?" Remy calls, noticing my grimace. He twitches his head towards the Black Avalanches. "Take a gander."

Standing at the bottom of the porch, I turn slightly west to find the Black Avalanches towering eerily in the distance. While their peaks are still snow-capped, they're shadowed by the tendrils of black that swirl around them like a smoke ring, as though someone smeared black paint across the landscape, distorting their view.

It reminds me of how they looked in Karasi's memory in my dream, except wilder.

"I think I need to see them before we leave," I explain, taking the few steps up the porch, the wood creaking under my weight. "Karasi showed me them in my dream for a reason. I want to know what it feels like."

Remy scoffs, picking at a splinter on the wooden beam. "If that's what you think needs to be done, I'll take you over there."

Tariq, Elly, and Fin approach the hut. The Hespers skeptically study the exterior of my old home while Fin looks like he's lost in memory as he stares at me with glistening emerald eyes.

Too many memories here.

FATE DEMANDS SACRIFICE

319

Remy extends his arm to me, eyes wary. "Let's go inside. We need to talk about some things that are better said privately."

We trail behind Remy in a single file line, and when we cross the threshold, I'm hit with a wave of overwhelming nostalgia that turns my blood to ice.

If our home hadn't been a rundown shack before, it certainly is now. After I left, Karasi barely lifted a finger. Shelves are emptied of potions, herbs, and mixes, and cobwebs hang from the corners of the ceiling. Flat surfaces have a layer of dust on them, disrupted by an occasional smear from a cup or bowl. The indent on the couch where she always sat is deeper than before, and her shawl drapes over the arm where her cane now rests.

"Was she not here when she was attacked?" Tariq asks, stepping up beside me.

"She stopped calling for us, stopped answering our visits," Remy explains, sitting on one of the chairs at the kitchen table. He diverts his gaze from the couch, and on the table in front of him is a small box with a tiny metal latch. "Despite that, Willem, Dahlia, and I came when possible. We rotated shifts, making sure she had food and water and was nourished. Dahlia was staying with her the most, and I know she will have more to tell you when she arrives. She had convinced Karasi to go into town the day of the attack."

A chill runs down my spine, raising the hairs on the back of my neck. The dream had been in Main Town, even if it was during a completely different century.

"I'm sure you have just as much to tell us," Remy says, tapping the box. "But there are a lot of things in here you need to see."

"What is it?" I ask, sinking into the seat next to Remy with my eyes pinned to the unfamiliar little box.

"That's a loaded question," Remy chuckles darkly, slowly sliding it across the wood to me. "It's something Karasi once told me you'd need to see when she wasn't around anymore."

"Why?" I urge, bouncing my leg.

"All I know is your father left the contents of this box with Karasi when he dropped you on her doorstep."

Fin softly swears under his breath at the same time Elly sucks in air between her teeth. My heart leaps into my throat, and I can't tear my gaze away from the box. For nearly twenty-three years, Karasi kept this from me.

A final gift from my father.

Time stops, and I don't know how much passes when a seat creaks directly in front of me, pulling my attention from the box. I slowly lift my head to find Tariq across from me, his warm eyes pinned on me and his eyebrow raised in question.

"Are we doing this?" he asks quietly, the conversation only meant for him and me.

I blink once, then nod. He inclines his head, urging me to open it. I reach out with an unsteady hand and press the latch. With a click, the box cracks open, and as I raise the lid, a slightly musty scent drifts out. I flare my nostrils.

A letter sits on top with my name written in what can

FATE DEMANDS SACRIFICE   321

only be a man's handwriting, the edges yellowed. I pick it up with a delicate touch, noticing another letter beneath with Karasi's name in the same handwriting.

"Read it," I say aloud, meeting Tariq's eyes again as I thrust it toward him. He frowns, but shock flashes over his face. I explain, "I won't be able to read it. I'll stop at the first line. I need you to read it to me."

"Okay," he agrees, someone shifting on their feet near the door.

Tariq carefully handles the letter as if it will disintegrate in his hands. He opens one fold at a time, staring at the writing before beginning.

"Hello, my—" Tariq pauses, lifting his eyes briefly off the paper to meet mine. "*Aster.* That's the old Etherean language."

"Fucking Karasi," Remy grumbles.

"Karasi called me that," I whisper, clarifying for Tariq.

He nods in acknowledgment before starting over, "Hello, my *aster*. I know I will be long gone by the time you read this. For that, I apologize. I find I'm doing a lot of that lately with these death letters, but I need you to know… If there were any other way, I would have died trying to find it. Gods, I'm probably going to die anyway.

"But I've followed my instincts, which have led me to some inn in Eldamain, about to drop you off with the Great Karasi. Maybe it was you who led me here with your mother's beautiful face and that Mark that is always trying to give us away."

Tariq's eyes flicker up, checking on me. I just stare, waiting as something restless inside me threatens to burst from my chest to devour the letter. He clears his throat. "There's so much I want to say, Reva. There are so many pieces of advice I should lend to you. A father's wisdom, I suppose. Except I was never known for being all that bright. That was always Em's job. But hey—what I lacked in brains, I made up for in good looks and charm."

I press my lips together, staring at Tariq with incredulity. The way the last sentence sits perfectly on his lips is almost uncanny. He hides his smile, barely, as he continues, "Be the best person you can be. Make smart decisions. Don't fall for the first guy you meet. Let your heart break and shatter. Love with everything you have at any chance you get… These are just a few things your mother would probably say.

"I miss her more than anything, and I wish you would have had the chance to know her. You are already as beautiful as she was, and it breaks my heart sometimes." Tariq pauses again, his face softening with a small twitch of his lips. "I did not give you up willingly, Reva. I gave you up because you were safer without me. You will be able to change this world. I have a feeling you will be stronger than I ever was, and for more reasons than one."

Tariq flips the page over, his eyes briefly scanning the rest of the page before landing on something that makes his eyes widen drastically—larger than I thought possible. I swear he holds his breath.

He glances over his shoulder at Fin, tilting his head

to the paper. Fin leans forward, resting a hand on Tariq's shoulder, and his face mirrors him, his mouth dropping open.

"What?" I half-yell, glancing between them. "Finish it."

Tariq glances at me one more time, really looking at me, before finishing the letter. "I never thought I would have a Sirian child, but I do not regret the choices your mother and I made that landed us in this position. We chose this path, knowing it could lead to one or both of our deaths. In this case, it's both. As long as you survived, it would always be worth it.

"I hope you know love like the kind we wanted to give you. So much love we always had and always will have for you." Tariq places the paper down on the table. "It's signed Jedrek Carraphim."

A sob breaks out of me, a tear spilling down my cheek. So many things in that letter leave me empty and raw, like I've been ripped down the middle, and every part of me scooped out.

I had a family that wanted me to have the world and accepted me for my Mark, but they had to make the worst decision because of it. I even have a last name: *Carraphim*.

But that first name Tariq said rings a bell, pulling me out of the haze of my overwhelming emotions.

"Reva," Fin whispers, standing beside Tariq as they both look at me with awe and shock written on their faces.

"Wait," I sniffle, blinking rapidly. "That name…

Jedrek. Didn't your father say…"

Jedrek, Eamon, and myself grew up side-by-side…My right and left-hand men… Bryna was his wife.

We believe they were killed some time back.

"It's him, isn't it?" I manage, my throat clogging and my vision tilting.

"Yes, Starfire," Tariq smiles softly, almost a wince. I barely register Remy reaching into the box to pull out the second letter. "Jedrek and Bryna Carraphim were our parents' best friends. They vanished almost twenty-three years ago."

"The 'Em' he mentioned must've been my dad," Fin tells Tariq. I barely hear them discussing the timeline of things and how little they really knew about Jedrek and Bryna's—my *parent's*—disappearance. Their voices are distant, like they're underwater, as I stare into the box.

"Is there another letter in there?" Remy asks, his voice distant and faded. Tariq and him glance into the box. "His letter to Karasi said there were two letters with hers. She must have delivered the third…"

My sanity and control slip through my fingers like smoke as I replay one of the last things Karasi said in my dream.

The Stars have called you back home.

My parents were from Mariande.

A pounding headache spreads from my Mark and races around the crown of my head. I place my palm against it, rubbing hard enough that I know the salve is coming off. Remy and Elly's gazes both latch onto me as

FATE DEMANDS SACRIFICE

325

I unclasp the necklace from where it burns around my neck.

The necklace from my mother, Bryna.

"Reva," Elly drawls in warning.

I snap my head up at her, and she steps back against the wall. Out of the corner of my eye, I recognize the red glow of embers sparking off my fingertips.

I startle from my chair, rushing outside.

Everyone calls out to me, but I can't breathe. I need air and water, and the house is too stifling. My power presses against my skin, trying to break out as it thrums with every thought, sweat beading on my forehead.

Karasi is dead.

My last name is Carraphim, and my father was a knight of Mariande.

Gods, I'm so sick of hiding. I'm so sick of learning who I am in whatever bits and pieces people feel are convenient to reveal on their own timelines.

I am a Sirian, the most powerful since Asteria, a demi-god descendant of the Goddess, Danica.

And my name is Reva Carraphim.

I scream at the top of my lungs, the sound vibrating my whole body as it scrapes my throat. I shoot my hands out to the nearest tree, a stream of molten fire bursting out of both hands, hotter than anything I've ever experienced. Sweat trickles down the back of my neck and into my eyes, blurring my vision as it mixes with the remaining tears. I keep screaming, and the power keeps coming. The tree begins to *melt* under my power.

It melts until it's a pile of black, crumbled rock and ash-white tree bark.

I yank my power back in like a hooked fish on a line, that snap reverberating underneath my skin, throwing me backward from the force of it.

"Reva!" someone shouts, grass shifting as they approach. I lay on my back, staring up at the blue sky. Streaks of pink spread across it as the sun begins to set.

A shadowed face blocks my view.

"Do you feel better?" Tariq asks, hand outstretched. "I'm not going to regret this, am I?"

I sigh, accepting his assistance.

He tugs my hand, launching me back onto my feet. I stumble into his arms, lightheaded and winded. Spots cloud my vision, but Tariq's strong arms hold me steady.

Instinctively, I lay all my weight into him, pressing my temple against his shoulder. For a moment, he's an immovable brick wall, but it doesn't take him long to slowly curve over me and gently place his chin on my head.

"I can't do this anymore," I mumble against his arm, closing my eyes as I let his sweet, woodsy scent drape around me. "I haven't just lost Karasi. I've lost so much more. I've lost a father and a mother, the person I could've been. What am I supposed to do?"

"Gods, do I wish I had the answers for you, Starfire." He tightens his grip around me, mumbling into the top of my head. "I really do, but all I can tell you is I know the feeling of the world being thrown onto your shoulders

FATE DEMANDS SACRIFICE 327

and losing parts of who you thought you were supposed to be. But you know what?"

I almost whimper at the loss of his warmth as he peels away to grab my face and tilt my head back so our eyes meet. He bends down until I think he's going to kiss me in front of everyone.

"You are not alone in this. You have an army of people ready to rattle behind you in whatever you need. You have a family here, and you have us in Mariande." His thumb strokes gently across my cheek as he studies me. "I would go to war if it meant I could alleviate some of your pain."

I swallow the lump in my throat, burning raw from the firepower and screaming. I nod my head in his hands, and he smiles, content.

"Out of all the hiccups you've had as a child," Remy's voice booms across the lawn. "This is by far the one thing I won't be able to fix."

I finally pull away from Tariq, giving him one last look of appreciation before walking back towards the house to where Remy, Elly, and Fin stand on the porch with another person.

"Dahlia," I breathe.

***

We all scatter about the hut, but that's not saying much for how small it is. Remy, Dahlia, Tariq, and I sit around the table while Elly and Fin take the couch, leaving Karasi's spot open. If I close my eyes, her presence still lingers there, so I don't blame them for huddling together on the other two seat cushions.

Dahlia holds the glass of liquor I quickly whipped up from memory, both hands curled around it like a mug. Her brick-red eyes stand out against the dark purple and blue circles deep underneath them. Her black hair is pulled tightly into a low bun, a few pieces falling in front of her face and sweeping against her cheeks.

"I don't want to talk about the day she died," Dahlia says, breaking the silence. "I'm sure we can talk about the attack later. It was the days leading up to her death that were unnerving. She was strange in the end."

She clears her throat, throwing back a quick swig before continuing, "I would argue you can feel her wisdom and age without knowing how old she really is. It wasn't just how she looked, but how she held herself and the aura she radiated."

"She was a force to be reckoned with." Remy nods, leaning back in the kitchen chair with his ankle resting on his knee.

Dahlia shakes her head, refusing to make eye contact with me. She looks down at her glass, continuing, "You would think she regressed. The way she looked and her face just changed. It was suddenly like she was young again, like a new Magic coming to realize how powerful she is."

"It's common with very old Magics," Remy explains

FATE DEMANDS SACRIFICE 329

to everyone. "I've seen it before."

"Remy," Dahlia's head snaps to him. "You don't realize how old Karasi was. We joke about it, but she knew things that no one knows. She spoke of events that have been lost to history."

"Reva and I discovered how old she was," Elly jumps in, her eyes briefly meeting Dahlia's. She quickly explains the books we found, the math, and my dream where Karasi confirmed it.

"The old hag wasn't lying then," Dahlia scowls, her eye twitching. "It was like she needed to tell us before it was too late, revealing her age to you and dumping her history lesson on me."

"What did she tell you, Dahlia?" I ask, frowning.

Her eyes snap onto me, pinning me to the spot. "The Korbin Legacy," Dahlia announces. "The real one."

Out of the corner of my eye, Elly shifts forward on the couch to get a better view of Dahlia. Her and I have had countless discussions about what may or may not have happened regarding Alrik Korbin and the fall of the Sirians, but it's only ever been speculation.

"Are you saying the one we know isn't real?" Tariq pries, leaning back in the wooden kitchen chair. Remy eyes him suspiciously.

"Most of it is real." Dahlia smooths her hand over her hair and takes another swig. "But there is so much that's been hidden. The stories we recognize as truth were just lies spun to benefit Alrik Korbin."

"Why did Karasi feel the need to tell you this?" Remy

asks. "I can't imagine how this could be involved with anything."

"It's everything," she breathes. Elly stands slowly from the couch, drawing our attention to her.

"It would make sense," Elly says, shuffling towards me. "Reva and I have had a few conversations. We know the Abyss is linked to the Dark Sirians, but months ago, we came across an old account of the Abyss. We theorized that it and the Darkness didn't exist before Alrik Korbin."

"So, he created the Abyss?" Remy frowns. "He wasn't Sirian, though."

"His daughter was," I add, switching my gaze back to Dahlia. I repeat, "What did Karasi tell you?"

Dahlia stares off to a random point in the kitchen, her finger tapping lightly against the glass she grips. "I don't know exactly how old she was when the events of the Korbin Legacy happened, but old enough to remember and have a connection to the Korbin family. She heard firsthand the events and atrocities Alrik committed. Because that's what they were. He committed genocide."

"The Sirians," I whisper. "*He* killed them?"

"With his own weapon," Dahlia whispers, shaking her head.

A heavy, visceral silence falls over the room as we process what Dahlia is saying. Based on something Karasi has told her, it wasn't the Sirians who destroyed themselves, but somehow Alrik was able to use a weapon to destroy them himself.

And I know who that weapon was because I guessed

FATE DEMANDS SACRIFICE   331

as much when Elly and I made our discovery.

He used his own daughter to destroy the Sirians.

"As you all know, Alrik Korbin was the firstborn to the Royal Sirian Family of Etherea," Dahlia recalls, her gaze distant. "But he wasn't born with the Mark, and that was extremely rare, especially since his two younger siblings were born with it. Karasi said it was evident that despite being the Crown Prince, his parents did not favor him.

"When it came time to marry, it seemed Alrik purposely chose a female of non-Sirian descent, which only worried and agitated his parents more. The public thought he'd want to throw some sort of *honor* back on his name by raising the chances of having Sirian children, but it furthered the strain between himself and his family. This fueled his hatred towards them and Sirians as an entire race of beings. He wanted them out of everything."

Dahlia takes a deep, unsteady breath, lifting a trembling hand to sweep the hair from her face.

"Alrik married his four oldest sons to the other royal families by offering them something they needed. Teslin caught onto what Alrik was doing and decided to just kiss up to Etherea."

"So, this part of the story stays the same," Tariq observes, scratching his stubble. "Sure, there is more insight into why Alrik wanted to do what he did, but it's not all that different."

"This next part is where things get complicated." Dahlia raises her gaze from her glass, meeting Tariq's.

"Before he can get the ball rolling, Alrik has a daughter—a Sirian daughter, Tyra. For a long time, no one saw the child. People thought she passed in childbirth. Karasi knew someone close to the family, and she said Alrik was pushing Tyra away and hiding her. He threatened her if she ever used her powers, which had never been done before. One day, she snapped.

"Shortly before Tyra's first public appearance, the Sirian and Magic community started to hum. Something was happening in the Black Avalanches. A strange, thick substance, almost an entire being in itself, was living within the shadows of the mountain range. It hung in the air and just seemed to pulse. They started to call it the Abyss."

"We know punishing Sirians and causing them to fear their powers leads to the Darkness," Elly juts in, crossing her arms over her chest. "He was punishing her for her powers. She was terrified of herself. The Abyss and the Darkness were first created with Tyra."

"And that became Alrik's greatest weapon," Dahlia adds. The pit in my stomach sits heavy.

"Tyra was his weapon?" Tariq asks, brow furrowing.

"According to myth, the Sirians started turning on each other and wielding the Darkness," I explain. "This caused people to start fearing them in the first place because of this rumored, hidden, evil power."

"It was a lie," Dahlia chuckles, a breathy sound. "Alrik used Tyra and her Darkness to massacre these different Sirian colonies as a way to practice her powers. No one

FATE DEMANDS SACRIFICE 333

knew she was Sirian until she was much older, so no one suspected a thing."

"The Arcane Island," Remy whispers, but that feeling of being far away happens again, my pulse echoing in my ears. "Good gods... Are you saying—"

"Alrik created an elaborate heist to use Tyra in destroying the Arcane Island," Dahlia confirms, pressing her lips together. "He used that poor child and her fear and her need for acceptance to murder nearly an entire race. After the devastation of the island, it didn't take much to convince the public Sirians were a danger to themselves and the world.

"Mariande was not easy to sway until the sudden and rapid deaths of the Sirians caused unrest on their borders. Eldamain was a little more difficult because they and The Clips had male heirs, and Alrik only had one daughter. By the time she became of age, Eldamain had already married their son off. So, Alrik had Tyra kill them, and they framed his siblings."

"That's why his siblings have always been coined as the culprits and the masterminds of all the uprisings within the Sirian colonies," Tariq realizes, sitting straight as a board. "They were publicly executed because of that. People used to say *that's* why Alrik wiped out Sirians because his siblings were these cruel Dark Sirians."

"Karasi couldn't tell me if Alrik planned all that in the end or if the events that unfolded from the moment Eldamain married until the end were just luck on his part. But the murder of the royal family of Eldamain caused the collapse of their kingdom, and Alrik all but gifted the country to The Clips along with Tyra as part of that agreement. The rest we know."

Dahlia is right. From there, Tyra's husband learned of her Sirian Mark. She tried to attack him, and he killed her. He revealed to the world she'd been part of the rebellion with her aunt and uncle, all underneath Alrik's nose.

But clearly, that's a little far from the truth when she was single-handedly responsible for killing almost an entire race under the ruse of a rebellion that didn't ever happen. All because her father sought to wield her as a weapon to his means.

"What is history turns into myth," Elly whispers, rubbing her arm. "What is myth turns into fear."

The only thing that isn't a myth is that an untrained, Dark-wielding Sirian girl wiped out an entire island of trained Sirians, so what can a host of potentially trained Dark Sirians do?

"I still fail to see how this has any relevance," Remy murmurs, twisting the ends of his mustache.

Tariq leans forward in his seat, resting his arms on the table. "Knowing the truth about what happened back then, the last time the world experienced Light *and* Dark Sirians, will help us defend the Light Sirians to the world."

Remy snakes his gaze to me, squinting. "Are you telling me you're just going to out yourself to the world for shits and giggles?"

I shake my head, but Tariq answers instead, "There is a reason the Black Avalanches are host to the Abyss again, and you've seen them yourself. The Dark Sirians are back, and war is coming."

CHAPTER 23

Eventually, Willem arrives at Karasi's, and he, Dahlia, and Remy explain what happened when the Dark Sirians attacked Main Town.

Apparently, they popped out of nowhere, torturing Magics with the black vines that flowed from their hands. Remy said it was too easy for them to spear person after person, running them through with the Darkness until their victims' veins mimicked those black tendrils. What made my blood run cold was that Dahlia believes Karasi had been targeted. She said it was like the woman who attacked her knew who she was, and there was no doubt in my mind that Karasi knew who this woman was.

Now, Dahlia and Willem sit with me and Tariq while Remy assists Fin and Elly with setting up our tents. I tell them everything I've been through, my version of what happened in Saros—Sirian Elders and all—as Remy playfully argues with Elly about how a Princess shouldn't be lifting her *pretty little finger*.

"So Mariande supposes they're empathetic to Magics," Willem blurts. His cigarette hangs lazily from his lip, the second bottle of spirits I whipped up in honor

FATE DEMANDS SACRIFICE

of Karasi tight in his hands.

"We are not empathetic," Tariq answers, pursing his lips with a small frown, as if he were confused Willem would insinuate that. "The mortal folk can't imagine the suffering Magics have been through as a result of hundreds—if not thousands—of years of transgressions.

"What we can do is make it better for you to live amongst us. To have lives and conduct the jobs you wish to have. We simplify transitions and provide the Mariande military's support to help."

"Do they actually help?" Willem asks incredulously, bouncing his leg. "Or will we find many are like the men in your castle who have harassed and attacked Reva?"

"There are small groups who are reluctant to this change," Tariq answers coolly with a shrug. "The infiltrators from Etherea attacked the castle months ago. Any of our knights employed who can't handle the change are being educated, reprimanded, and—or—relieved of their positions."

"So, it's not entirely safe for Magics." Willem chuckles darkly, extending his arm to prop himself back. He reels his attention on me as he waves his hand around. "And they are the *only* ones who know about your Mark?"

"Besides Jorah, the Sirians, the young prince, and the knight I've mentioned," I admit, sighing. "He's been slow to warm up, I can't lie about that. When he thought I was a Magic, he treated me worse than now."

"Probably because he's scared you'll set him on fire

with a snap of your fingers," Dahlia snorts, using her glass to gesture toward the now-demolished tree on the property.

I glower at her, curling my lip. She smirks triumphantly.

Like I never left.

"The bottom line is," Tariq interjects pointedly, making eye contact with all three of us. "You don't have to hide. Not anymore. And with Reva in the castle, at least recognized as a Magic, people are even more open."

"All of your cities have Magic colonies," Dahlia drawls out. "Yet we have not heard anything from them. They know how many reside here, so why wouldn't they reach out?"

"Like he said," I jump in before Tariq can answer. He tenses beside me, barely perceptible, but he doesn't stop me from taking the lead here. These are my people, and I know what they need to hear. "Slow building, Dahlia. Too many Magics at once would frighten mortals, let's be real. They'd see it as a threat and a takeover.

"And Tariq isn't going to say this because he's assessing and trying to understand you, but that would cause retaliation. Magics who are there already know that, too. That's why they're gauging how their presence is influencing the locals. They're helping prepare for more to come. Eldamain may be a big hideaway, but there are still others gathered across the continent in hiding who have never had the means to get here and need homes. You have homes for now."

FATE DEMANDS SACRIFICE

339

"For now," Dahlia questions, lowering her glass from her lips. "What's that supposed to mean?"

"You were literally *in town* when it was attacked," I laugh in disbelief, shaking my head. "You don't think they'll come back?"

"You have options," Tariq explains. "Should you want them. You are welcome within Mariande's borders, where you'll not only have protection from any ornery individuals but also from the Dark Sirians."

Willem presses his lips together tightly, wobbling his head back and forth mockingly. Tariq's nostrils flare ever so slightly, but that's the only indication his composure is breaking. He covers it by rising from the log.

"It's an offer." He smooths his pants. "Do with it what you will."

He walks away from us to join Fin and the others, offering Elly assistance in gathering some of the supplies into one of the tents.

Trying to navigate this political side of things is a different world than I'm used to. When I was talking with the Elders, I shouldn't have used Tariq's first name, and I probably shouldn't have interrupted a Crown Prince talking matters of business with Magics, but this is my family. Talking to them like they're representatives of a foreign land will not get us anywhere. Tariq knows he can personify an image of a king, but I know he can't act like one with those like Remy, Willem, and Dahlia until he is one.

Maybe even then.

They've watched kings come and go from thrones in multiple countries. What's one more?

"You're in deep shit, aren't you?" Dahlia giggles, elbowing Willem beside her. He smirks through the fading light, his eyes still glued to Tariq's back. She presses, "You are falling for the *Crown Prince* of Mariande."

"Do you mind?" I snarl. She laughs, cackling like the evil witch she is. I press my lips together and take a deep breath before saying, "This is not the time. I am not here to be taunted and teased."

"We have months to make up for," Willem shrugs, reaching his hand over the fire with the bottle in hand. "Loosen up, Reva."

I ignore his offer. I flare the fire so it licks against his skin and the bottle. He hisses, yanking his hand back. I meet his eyes, not flinching from the anger there.

"You are acting like children," I lecture, flicking my eyes between them. "Karasi is dead." I choke on the last word. "I've lost yet another person in my life."

"You seem to be replacing people just fine," Dahlia retorts.

I flinch, caught off guard. "No one is replaced." I gawk, digging my nails into the palms of my hands.

"Your new life with the royal family would suggest otherwise," Willem adds, throwing back whatever hot drink is left in the bottle. He winces against the gulp.

"My new life isn't some glamorous dream," I bite back, my voice rising. Dahlia's eyes widen at my tone.

FATE DEMANDS SACRIFICE 341

I roll my lips together, collecting my temper. "Don't think I went there to work on the young prince and revel in my riches from the Hespers. I have been dealing with far worse and a lot more than I signed up for. I've been trying to figure out how the hell I'm involved in the grand scheme of things and how I can master *two* god-powers.

"If you haven't noticed, I'm a Sirian, but not just any Sirian. The powers of Dionne *and* Asteria run through my veins, so I've got more than just the Light."

I shoot up from my seat in front of the fire, the flames leaning towards me as if bowing to their God. Willem's eyes train on that motion, his eyes flashing something distant and revered.

I move around the log, glaring at them one last time. "I have to figure out who is wielding the Darkness, and how and why. But before I continue to do that, I'm going to mourn the only mother I've ever known. I don't know when the next time I'll be able to return will be. *If* I'll be able to come back at all."

I march over to the tents, leaving them to their thoughts. Remy drops a sack of clothes but I ignore him, raising my eye at Elly. She offers a pained smile but gestures to one of the prepared tents.

I yank the flap open and throw myself inside. A small cot and crate of clothes sit at the back, a lantern dangling from the top. I flick my finger, and it flares to life.

This firepower is a lot easier without the necklace on. Sitting at the edge of the cot, I dig my elbows into my thighs and shove my head into my hands. I grab two good fistfuls of hair, taking stifled, deep breaths to try and calm the boiling temper growing hot inside me.

I knew I shouldn't have made them that drink. This group always gets volatile when they're intoxicated and upset, and they've lost Karasi, too. They've known her decades longer than I have.

It still doesn't excuse them for lashing out at me for it.

Maybe I should put the necklace back on.

Someone clears their throat at the entrance of the tent. I sneer from between my fingers.

Remy chuckles as he steps into the tent. The flap sways behind him as he takes several steps to stand next to the cot. He gestures his hand next to me, asking, "May I?"

I nod, rubbing my hands down my face. He silently sits beside me, slinging an arm over my shoulder. I lean into his embrace, savoring the moment.

"How are you doing, kid?" he asks, pulling a breathy laugh from me. He rubs his hand against my arm. "I know it's been a lot, but I think you're doing pretty damn well."

"I'd be inclined to disagree." I look up at him, meeting those striking purple hues. "It feels like I'm tearing in half."

"Aren't we all," he mumbles, glancing at the crate of clothes. "I have to admit, Dahlia did catch onto something I noticed even when I flew into Mariande. Her approach was a little half-ass backward, but what do you expect

FATE DEMANDS SACRIFICE 343

from her?"

"If you're talking about Tariq," I say quietly. "Then this discussion ends here."

He smiles broadly, his mustache climbing up at the corners. He presses, "You would make a fine match. The way you two are already in tune with one another—"

"Remy," I groan, pulling out from under his arm. "There are too many variables for me to digest where I stand emotionally with Tariq. I could think of several reasons why it would not work out. I don't have time—"

"For happiness?" he interrupts, all humor and teasing vanishing from his sharp features, his eyes frantic. "I know you think you may have to carry the world on your shoulders, but for the love of the Gods, Reva, do not forget to find happiness in it all. Let yourself have love, no matter how short it might last."

He tucks a stray hair behind my ear, pausing to caress my cheek. "Otherwise, you'll look back one day and regret all the moments you spent resisting it when you could have been relishing it."

I close my eyes against his unnaturally smooth hands.

"You deserve happiness and love, Reva," he continues, barely a whisper. "Without it, there is nothing to fight for... nothing to die for."

"It's strange coming from you," I say, not unkindly. I open my eyes to find his face in a battle of emotions. He smiles, and while his eyes are downturned, they're filled with deep happiness as he rubs a thumb along my cheekbone.

"I'm old enough to have loved at least once, girl," Remy sighs, swallowing whatever he's feeling. "Don't be so shocked I know what I'm talking about. I may not be Karasi, but I have a few words of wisdom up my sleeve."

I study his face, the too-sharp features and glowing purple eyes always so startling. I try to envision Remy having the love of his life and what he or she may have looked like.

What would they have been like? What happened to them?

If the sadness in his smile is any indication, nothing good, yet I know plenty of moments in my life where I saw genuine happiness radiating from Remy. A lot of those moments when he looked at me.

I smile, flinging my arms around his neck. He hugs me tight, taking a deep breath.

"I've never thanked you," I whisper against his shoulder, still holding on. "For always being what I needed."

"And what was that?" Remy asks, not letting go.

"A friend," I answer confidently. "But more importantly… A father."

His breath hitches slightly before he tightens his grip on me. I pull back in time to see the silver of tears lining his eyes recede.

"Just because I learned who my parents are won't ever change that," I admit, even if that statement stabs the knife deeper into my chest.

"I'm honored," he says, holding me in front of him.

FATE DEMANDS SACRIFICE

345

"And Gods, I've missed you, kid."

I wouldn't be able to wipe the smile from my face even if I tried. "I've missed you, too."

***

Karasi's funeral was more than I could bear. Those left from the massacre of Main Town must have all come to pay their respects, appearing in small groups to lay an offering from their House: sea shells and strips of fabric for the House of Argo, various flowers for the House of Nemea, and different types of crystals for the House of Echidna.

I stood beside her funeral bed, silently thanking the Gods Dahlia had already dressed and wrapped Karasi in the traditional way of Magics rather than an open casket like mortals practiced. I couldn't imagine seeing Karasi's graying skin or expressionless face as she lay on the slat.

After a child with hollow, magenta eyes gazes up at me as she places a bundle of forget-me-nots directly above where Karasi's lips would be underneath the dressing, I excuse myself, clutching my necklace in my hand and relishing in the edges of the circle biting into it. I keep my head down, watching my feet step one in front of the other until I reach the bank of Orion's Lake, the soft sound of water rolling against the edge of the grassy shore.

Despite the hollowness in my chest, I can't seem to

take a big enough breath without it being accompanied by a sharp sting. I feel like it's been this way since the final dream Karasi appeared in, her final goodbye.

Seeing her as a younger version of herself made her more *mortal* to me. I never thought she was born into this world looking the way she did when I was a child, but to think she did have different stages of her life starts to put one thousand years of existence into perspective. I was a blip in her existence, a mere twenty-two years to over one thousand.

And yet, I was her greatest journey.

My heart clenches at the thought I may never know all her stories. I never knew if she had ever loved, if she ever had a chance to have her own children, if she had actually been to every continent, or how many different kings and queens, dead and alive, she knew…

The version of Karasi I knew was one of many.

Grass swishes quietly behind me, pulling my attention away from the endless blue horizon. I peer over my shoulder to find Elly trudging through the blades, her dress gathered in both hands.

"At first, I thought maybe you'd want to be alone," Elly explains softly, rubbing a hand up and down her arm. "But then I thought even if you wanted to be alone, it could help to have someone stand beside you."

A smile twitches at the corner of my lips, but it doesn't break beyond that. Even if I don't say it, having Elly beside me does bring a sense of calmness to my raging mind. I've never had a true friend like Elly before—not

FATE DEMANDS SACRIFICE

347

one that I got to choose.

"Our parents were best friends," I say aloud, my voice fading at the end. My eyes burn at the edges, blurring the vision of the lake before me. "My parents would have known you and Tariq, probably interacted with you two, even if you don't remember."

"We would've been almost two by that point," Elly muses. Out of my peripheral, I see her head turned towards me.

"How different my life would've been." I let out a breath of disbelief. "Is it bad that's all I can think about right now?"

"You get to handle this however you need to, Reva." Elly's hand brushes mine limp at my side, locking our pinkies together. "You just lost someone very important to you, and you just learned who your parents are after never knowing. It doesn't sound like it, but it's a lot to take on… On top of everything else."

"I just have so many questions, and I keep spiraling from one to the next until I find myself jumping to another train of thought." I slowly turn my head to her, genuinely asking her, "If my dad didn't trust one of his childhood best friends with the knowledge he had a Sirian daughter, should I ever trust your father?"

Her face is downturned, but there's a subtle furrow of her brow. "I can't speak for your parents. But they had to have their reasons. My father didn't open the Magic communities until after Jedrek and Bryna disappeared."

"Everyone has reasons," I grumble, snapping my head

back to the lake. "And who was the woman who went with my mom to Jorah? Was it your mother or Anya?"

Elly sighs heavily, not in annoyance but as if she's absorbing every word I say.

"What would my life have been like?" I repeat quietly. Pax and Elly grew up together, friends to lovers in the deepest sense. "Would Fin and I have worked because he'd have grown up with my powers? Or would I still have found myself pulled to Tariq? We could've had decades together as best friends—"

"This is where I'm here to stop you from spiraling too far down the path of *what if*," Elly interjects, grasping my hand. She tugs lightly on it so I'm forced to face her, then slips her other hand into mine. "You can't live on what ifs and what could've been, Reva. I would've loved to have grown up in the castle with you like I did with Fin and Pax. I would've loved to watch you have the same battle over Fin versus Tariq as we got older the way you are now.

"But Fate didn't give you that life." She releases her grip, raising her hand to tuck a stray strand behind my ear. "All I can thank the Gods for is that you made it home to us, one way or another. And I'd gladly take you now rather than never having the chance to meet you."

The breath I take quivers in my lungs, a rogue tear slipping down my cheek. When I meet Elly's glistening eyes, I giggle at the tears I find rimming hers, too. She brushes them away before yanking me into her warm, soft embrace.

FATE DEMANDS SACRIFICE

"What are we going to do?" I whisper against her golden blond hair, my hands splayed across her back.

"We can't tell my dad and mom who your parents are yet." I feel her hand twisting around a strand of my hair, still holding onto one another. "They'll probably get suspicious about why your parents ran and start digging. It's not the right time."

I think again about the woman who escorted my mother to Jorah. Whoever she was, she had to have heard him when he confirmed my mother's dream. We peel off each other, still locked at arm's length, gripping forearms.

"The woman who went with my mom to Jorah…" I bite my lip, looking over Elly's shoulder toward the direction of The Red Raven. "When I first met Eamon, he kept asking me questions about where I was from and who my parents were. I think he even said I looked familiar. Then, Anya kept sneaking glances at me at the dinner we had. At the ball, she acted like she'd seen a ghost."

"You think they already know who you are?" Elly asks, her eyebrows arching.

I press my lips together, contemplating momentarily. "I think there's a possibility they know but haven't acknowledged it. Anya even stared at my necklace at the ball and got visibly ill."

"From what I know, Anya and Bryna were friends before they married Eamon and Jedrek," Elly explains with a shrug. "At least from what they've explained. If Anya was close with your mom, she probably would've recognized the necklace."

"I think I need to talk to Fin's parents." I throw my head to the sky. "It's a huge risk telling them, but if they have recognized me and haven't told your parents, there's something to that."

"You know I'm here for you, whatever you want to do." Elly loops my arm through hers, turning us toward the water again.

We stand like that until the sun sets, heads resting together as we watch the water change color with the sky.

Chapter 24

After a rather heated argument between Fin and Tariq on why it was preposterous that the Crown Prince would want to come on a horseback ride to the Black Avalanches, Remy made the executive decision, stepping in as the legitimate adult.

Fin and I would ride the two horses that carried our carriage here from Mariande while Remy flew overhead to guide us toward the mountains. From there, he could see from above if any suspicious individuals were lurking around it.

We set a steady pace with the horses, riding side-by-side in an uncomfortable silence. It's the first time Fin and I have been alone since we argued after he was injured by the Dark Sirian. His gaze keeps catching above us on Remy's hovering figure high in the air, his dark, leather wings making me realize maybe he is more bat than man.

"I thought you said Remy never used his wings?" Fin asks, his eyes still watching Remy warily.

I snort as I follow his line of sight, marveling at how Remy can keep his body parallel to the ground, wings flapping like a bird's. "He usually doesn't. I never really knew why he kept them hidden or didn't use them. I have a feeling it has something to do with his past, but I never pushed."

Fin gives his head a final shake, staring at the peaks looming in front of us. He curls his lip, rolling his shoulder. "I can feel it from here."

"You can feel it?" I snap my head to him, furrowing my brow. "We thought only Magics and Sirians could feel the Abyss."

His eyes are glued to the black tendrils slithering at the base of the nearest incline, wrapping itself around and through various boulders. "I wonder if it's because, just for a moment, it had a hold on me. When it…" His hand raises to where his shoulder has been healing, no longer in the sling.

"I wouldn't be surprised," I whisper, tearing my gaze from him. I instantly feel his eyes searing into me like a brand. I peer at him from the corner of my eyes to find him studying me, his hands flexing around the reins. "Is there something you'd like to say?"

Out of the corner of my eye, he clenches his jaw and faces the Black Avalanches nearing rapidly. "Is it worth it anymore?"

I startle, whipping my head toward him. I glare, screwing my mouth into a half-scowl and half-frown. "What's that supposed to mean?"

"No matter what I say to you, Reva, you don't want to hear it," Fin sighs, scanning the peaks as Remy lands

FATE DEMANDS SACRIFICE   353

just in front of a tendril, sneering at it. "There's nothing I can say to convince you I don't hold any resentment for your powers or the fact you're Sirian. You've made up your mind there, and I just feel like I'm fighting a losing battle."

My face morphs, drooping with my heart. "That's not… I don't think you resent me, Fin. I just think you're conflicted. You care about me, and you like the idea of me, but the reality is who I'm becoming is a different person than you—or I—envisioned when we first met."

Fin shuts his eyes, indicating the end of this conversation. I stay seated on my horse until Fin dismounts his and walks over to the side of mine.

I take a deep breath before swinging my leg around the side and jumping down from the horse. I stumble on the uneven ground, though, and Fin grabs my waist to steady me. I grip his forearms in a gentle squeeze, reluctantly gazing up into his eyes. The sadness in those dull green hues spears through me like the Darkness that stabbed him in Saros.

"So, what are we looking for?" Remy interrupts, cutting into the strange stare-down between Fin and me. We both detach from each other, our arms sliding away.

"I'm not looking for anything specific," I explain, carefully walking through the rocky gravel toward Remy, where a path cuts through the bottom of two peaks. I nearly lose my balance, so Fin grips my hand and helps me over the uneven ground.

"Well, whatever you're waiting for it to do," Remy

pauses, peering over his shoulder. "I can't stand this feeling, so let's make it quick."

When Karasi, Remy, and other Magics described the Abyss, I conjured an imaginary sensation, but it's far worse than I thought. I don't know if it's because it's been getting worse or it's difficult to put into words.

The air is different, thicker than the humidity before a storm without the dampness from the rain. It's dry, burning the back of my throat like smoke from a fire despite no heat source. In fact, sharp gooseflesh rises on my arms, but the temperature is no different than at the hut.

"It's difficult to think around," Fin explains, squinting. "It's like being in a steam room with hot coals, but—"

"Without the heat," we say simultaneously, glancing at each other warily.

"You can feel it?" Remy questions, side-eyeing Fin suspiciously. I wave them both away as Fin divulges his theory about his wound.

While I've never ventured this close to the Black Avalanches, the sensation is naggingly familiar. I step one foot onto the natural path that leads far into the mountain, my hand slipping from Fin's.

"Reva," Fin drawls, his tone warning. I urge him to quiet with my palm facing him.

An uneasiness presses against my chest, not just from being by the mysterious mountains and the Abyss. It hums, low and dark, pulsing like it's breathing. My lower

FATE DEMANDS SACRIFICE

355

back tenses, and I audibly gasp, the feeling reminiscent of something I've experienced. In my mind, I can almost see a pair of eyes, but they're just out of reach, like trying to peer through a sheer cotton curtain.

"Reva!" Remy yells, snapping me out of my thought process, and with that goes the memory I tried to grasp. "You alright?"

"Yeah," I answer quietly, blinking.

Rocks crunch and Fin gently tugs my wrist as he approaches me, frowning. "What's wrong?"

"There's something familiar here," I explain in a hushed tone. "This feeling… I've had it before."

"The attack in Saros?" Fin shrugs, squinting up at the closest peak.

"Maybe," I agree, even if I know that's not what it is. But without a genuine idea of who my mind is pleading with me to remember, I can't vocalize anything yet.

"I hope you got what you needed," Remy interjects as Fin starts helping me back out of the rocky terrain. "But let's get the hell out of here. I don't know how you can stand it, Reva."

★★★

The entire ride back, I keep running the familiar tension in my body through my mind over and over again, hoping I'll remember something—*anything*—from either the assault on Saros or when those knights attacked the castle all those months ago.

But the farther from the Black Avalanches we get and the closer to our old hut, the more my head feels scrambled. I grip the reins tighter and tighter in my hands, the edge of the leather strap digging into my palms.

"Hey," Fin calls from his horse as we approach Tariq and Elly packing up the carriage. My eyes flicker to the fresh dirt pile underneath my mangled tree before returning to Fin. "Don't beat yourself over whatever you're battling right now."

"I can see them in my head," I try to explain, fiercely shaking my head. "But it's like there's a film over my memory, and I can't wash it away."

"You've met a lot of people in the last few months." Fin offers a half-smile with a tilt of his head. "It'll come to you."

You'd think working at The Red Raven for years, I'd have a great memory of placing faces and events. Remembering patrons was different because the likelihood of meeting them again if they weren't regulars from Main Town was slim. At the Glow Ball alone, I'd met so many different people, including the royals from other kingdoms…

The eyes flash in my head again, but I shove that down because there is no possible way that is who the Abyss reminded me of.

It wouldn't make sense at all.

"Did you find anything?" Elly calls as we gallop up

FATE DEMANDS SACRIFICE

beside the carriage, and Remy plops down from the sky. Tariq's eyes snag onto me as he walks over to the side of my horse.

"We got a feel of the Abyss if that's what you mean," Fin explains as he jumps down from his horse. I cling to Tariq as he helps me dismount.

"What do you mean 'we'?" Tariq asks as he hesitantly releases my waist, taking one step back.

"After he got stabbed by the Darkness, it seems he can now feel the Abyss," Remy jumps in, tossing his loose waves over his shoulder as he rolls his head to Elly. "And here I thought I was special, being a Magic and all."

Elly gives him a cheeky smile, one I would consider flirtatious. Tariq scoffs loudly at her beside me, which has her startling and staring at him with one of those weird, silent communication looks they get between them.

"Anything else helpful?" Tariq turns his attention to me, an eyebrow raised.

I press my lips together momentarily, debating if I should bring up the tickle of an idea that has been forming. "I'm not sure yet."

"Yet?" Tariq urges, leaning into me. "So, there's something in that pretty little head of yours?"

"I mean…" I trail off, my face morphing into a scowl. "My head is not little."

Tariq eyes me with an expression I would interpret as, *You really want to challenge that?* I can't help but wonder if we've begun to develop our own silent form of communication.

"Well," Elly interrupts, clearing her throat. Tariq and I snap our gazes at her and Fin, the latter with a small wrinkle between his brows. "We've got some travel time to mull over and discuss what you felt, but we really should be getting back."

After some grumbles of agreement, Tariq, Elly, and Fin walk to the carriage with the horses, but I linger behind as Remy quietly steps one foot in front of the other until he's beside me. I turn to face him fully, craning my neck to look into his face.

He hunches over to lower his height. "So off you go again, saving the world?"

I clear the emotion from my throat, briefly throwing my gaze over my shoulder at my home for what will probably be the last time. If I stare hard enough, I can see the ghost of a small child building a snowman.

"It's who I am now," I whisper, inclining my head to him as I throw my shoulders back.

"I'm not surprised, really," Remy admits, smiling softly. "I always knew you'd be part of something great, whether or not I knew the prophecy."

I frown, blinking back tears. "You know the prophecy?"

He nods slowly, staring off as he watches Tariq and Fin reattach the horses to the carriage. "You'll need to know it one day, but I'm following Karasi's advice for now. She said I couldn't reveal it until you met the one wielding the Darkness... The one who is responsible for all of this."

FATE DEMANDS SACRIFICE   359

"What if I already think I know?" I admit quietly enough I know he'll hear with his enhanced abilities. If I can vocalize it to anyone right now, it may be Remy.

He turns those sad eyes back to me. "I mean head-to-head, Reva. Even if you think you know, they'll reveal themselves to you."

My mouth goes dry. I don't want to wait for them to come to me. I would rather show up at their doorstep.

And do what exactly, I have no idea.

"So you're going to stay here?" I ask, gesturing to the hut. "Start doling out prophecies to those who come looking for the Great Karasi. You can be the Great Remy."

He laughs at that, throwing his head back. "My time to make something of myself came and went decades ago, kid. I say we just let this place go with time. People will realize eventually she's gone."

The statement clenches my heart in grief's grip. I gaze upon the hut, considering sending it up in flames.

But Karasi deserves something to commemorate her dedication to the world, even if they never knew how much her prophecies kept it moving.

"I wasn't kidding when you first left," Remy interrupts, grasping my hand. "If you need me for anything, Reva, you know where to find me."

"I could say the same to you." I smile, swinging our arms back and forth like a pendulum. "You'd be faster than me, anyway."

He chuckles low, squeezing my hand. "Well, just

know you can send word on a raven. They seem to find me pretty well no matter where I go."

"Is that a metaphor, or are you serious?" I laugh, imagining sending a message by bird carrier.

His grip tightens in my hand as he yanks me into his embrace. He holds me to him, petting the back of my head. I close my eyes at the tenderness, pressing my forehead and nose into the hardness of his chest.

"When you need me, Reva," Remy mutters into my hair, tugging on a strand. "You send for me. I'll be there in a heartbeat."

I swallow the tears back, leaning back to take one last good look at him before I leave for Gods know how long. He bends down, placing a rough kiss on my forehead.

"Go do incredible shit, kid," he mumbles against my Mark, giving my shoulders one last squeeze.

CHAPTER 25

I sit by the fire at our stop with my shawl draped around my shoulders. My hand hovers above the heat, my necklace clutched in my other. The flames dance effortlessly on top of the logs, waving and twirling with the swipe of my arm or flick of my wrist. I stretch my fingers as wide as they can go, and the flames spread in five separate streaks of fire.

Without the necklace, wielding my god-powers is drastically different. Instead of dropping into that pit of molten fire at full speed, the power rose to me when I called it to light the pit Fin created with rocks and twigs. It's ironic that the stone used to keep a leash on the power happened to make it more difficult to reach and control.

"You look like you're getting along with fire now." Fin stands above me, staring down with a smirk that has his dimple peeking out from under his stubble.

I chuckle, leaving the fire alone and tucking my hand under my shawl. "Maybe I've got my party trick back. Just in time to meet the Elders again."

Fin gestures to the ground beside me with an eyebrow raised. I nod once, patting the cool dirt ground.

He plops down with a low grunt, extending his legs out in front of him and reclining his arms back.

"Look at us," Fin says, but there is a tinge of nostalgia in his voice. I side-eye him, forgetting how light can make those emerald depths endless. "Talking about Elders, openly wielding your firepower, trying to conquer an ancient Darkness… Who knew when I first showed up at The Red Raven and said the fancy little saying that we'd be here almost five months later?"

I fight the smile tugging at the corners of my cheeks. "Are we seriously reminiscing by a fire right now?"

"It just got me thinking about that first stop we made after I took you from Karasi." Fin shrugs his shoulder, locking his gaze on me. "You dismantled a knight within a day."

"I dismantled you the minute you showed up on my doorstep," I tease, shoving him to the side. He laughs then, some of the tension between us from earlier subsiding. "It's not my fault you're the most casual general of sorts. You were dropping Elly and Tariq's nicknames like you weren't talking about the Crown Prince and Princess of Mariande to a total stranger."

"You did what?" Tariq jumps in, sitting opposite Fin and me.

Fin's grin only broadens at the look Tariq gives him, and I'm reminded these two have been friends since they were children.

And here I am, sitting between them.

"Now that we all know Reva pretty well," Elly pauses

FATE DEMANDS SACRIFICE 363

as she sits beside her twin, popping the cork off the liquor we snagged from Dahlia. "What was it like retrieving our Great Reva?"

"And where is this nickname coming from?" Tariq adds, his gaze sweeping to me over the flames. "Fin called you that at the Glow Ball."

"It's a nickname I refuse to let stick." I point at Tariq, glaring. "One nickname is enough from you."

He narrows his eyes playfully, one corner of his mouth quirking up.

"Well, at The Red Raven, Reva had her posse there," Fin explains, waving his hand toward the direction we just traveled from. "Who now we all know. I thought they would jump me when I said that stupid saying my dad told me about. Then, when I showed up on Karasi's doorstep, I thought Reva was the Great Karasi because she answered the damn door."

I laugh, throwing my head back at the memory of Fin's face when I opened the door. Knowing him now, I have a good guess of the thoughts that went through his head at that moment.

"You were gone for quite a long time, though." Elly frowns as she blindly hands the bottle to Tariq. "Where did you and the other knights stay?"

"Well, we had to figure out which pub was the right one, and I wanted to make sure we wouldn't be received with too much hostility," Fin explains, gesturing for the twins to pass the bottle our way. "I also didn't anticipate Karasi offering Reva in her place as the Royal Healer, so

I had to make that split decision in a day."

"Dad said whatever it took, right?" Tariq winks at me over the fire. "He was desperate to find someone to help Clint. Hell, we all were. Now look at us and our *Magic* Royal Healer who hasn't been met with too much more resistance, if I do say so myself."

"Unless you count people from the other countries who still use more derogatory terms or jealous Magics—" I stop reaching for the bottle from Fin, the encounter with Sidra and Keiran replaying in my mind, as well as the skin-crawling sensation that overcame me at the Black Avalanches.

"Reva?" Elly asks, her voice distant as both of their eyes flash in my head, coupled with the odd feelings I got around them. "What's wrong?"

I can't ignore the nagging within me anymore, so I blurt, "I think I know who is part of the Dark Sirian movement."

Tariq and Elly balk at me, both of their regal masks falling with a snap of a finger. Fin leans forward to look at me. "You *think* you know?"

"The feeling I got," I say as I rise from the ground. I draw my shawl tighter as I pace around the fire between Tariq and Fin. "I know what I felt at the Avalanches had nothing to do with the attack on Saros. When I met them, I thought I was just so overwhelmed with the people and the ball, but I *knew* something wasn't right about them—"

"Who are you talking about?" Tariq urges, standing and grabbing my shoulders, eyes searching.

FATE DEMANDS SACRIFICE

365

I swallow as my eyes meet his, then flicker to Elly and Fin. "It's Sidra and Keiran."

Elly chokes on the sharp gasp of air she takes, sputtering around it. Tariq's studies me, tipping his head back.

"You're telling me," Tariq pauses, his voice even, "The *Crown Prince* of Etherea, one of the most powerful and cruelest countries, is a Dark Sirian and has partnered with Sidra, a Magic con artist from Teslin?"

"Reva," Elly begins after recovering from her initial shock. "If Keiran was a Sirian, I don't know he would have survived his birth. His father would've killed him upon entering the world."

I hesitate momentarily. Considering all we know regarding the Dark wielders and what we just learned about the Korbin legacy, I'm more confident than I have been. "I'm sure if we lived during the reign of Alrik Korbin, we would've said the same thing."

Tariq takes a step back from me, exchanging a look with Elly that holds so many words, but I know they're considering this possibility. They study one another, their similarities uncanny as the wheels in their head start turning, and their heads twitch imperceptibly.

"We did hypothesize that Etherea could be involved if there's a chance the Dark wielders are hiding in Lolis," Tariq muses, turning to Fin and reflecting my train of thought. "Sidra has access to a wealth of power in Teslin, including their own community of delinquent Magics. If Karasi created an underground network for Sirians with

Jorah in Mariande, Sidra could've done the same thing with her influence on the Magics in Teslin."

"Wait," Fin juts in, jumping from his spot on the ground. "Are we actually entertaining the idea that *Prince Keiran* is a Dark Sirian? He despises Magics."

"And King Alrik despised Sirians." I turn to Fin with my hands up. "The Etherean family still carries the Korbin last name, and King Alrik was King of Etherea before his sons became kings in every other country. What if Alrik told his sons how he used Tyra as a weapon?"

"So Keiran's the weapon this time?" Tariq catches on, squinting toward the direction of Etherea. "King Ciar is pulling the strings, then?"

"I didn't get to meet the king at the Glow Ball." I shake my head, trying to find a hole in our theory, but the longer I think about it, the more it pieces together. "It's a lot to work out for something I just realized throughout the day, but we already were sure Etherea was involved. Now, we have at least an understanding of to what extent. One way or another, the Korbins are involved. Again."

"You said you knew something was weird about them?" Elly asks, bouncing from Fin to me to Tariq.

"The same oppressive feeling I had when I stood by the Black Avalanches was very familiar to what I felt when I met both Keiran and Sidra," I explain, waving my hand at Fin.

"I had already been attacked in Saros by then," Fin says, crossing his arms over his chest. "I didn't feel anything from either of them when we encountered them at the Glow Ball."

I pause, sharing a momentary glance with Tariq. "Maybe it has to do with my starfire power or being Sirian. I don't know, but I can't pretend I didn't have the same feeling."

Fin and Tariq stare at each other, but they exchange a gesture that makes me believe they'll talk about it together later.

Tariq rubs his forehead, his eyes distant. "Let's all get some rest. We can get on the road extra early so we don't leave everyone at the castle longer than necessary."

"Fucking fantastic," Fin grumbles, rising from his spot by the fire. Elly's skin has paled a shade or two as she stares at the flames. Fin lightly caresses her arm, snapping her out of her trance as he adds, "Etherea? Do we realize how bad this is?"

"We thought they had to have someone supporting them," Tariq says, but I can hear a slight slip in his usual demeanor.

"But Keiran?" Elly whispers, shaking her head. "If this is true…"

We all exchange one final glance before Fin and Elly head to their tents. As I dim the fire to a dull glow, Tariq slips a gentle hand around my waist just as Fin's tent flap shuts behind him. I lean into his embrace instinctively, resting my head against his shoulder. He presses his lips to the top of my head before resting his cheek against my hair.

"You did good, Starfire," he mumbles, squeezing my waist. "Something tells me you've been sitting on that all day, though."

"I didn't want to be right," I whisper, sinking deeper into his warmth. "Karasi, my parents, now this?"

Tariq pulls back, hooking his thumb and forefinger under my chin and tilting my head in his direction. "You're not alone, Reva. Not while you've got all of us."

"All of you?" I question, his eyes still glistening in the dark.

"Especially me," he whispers, barely audible. Foreheads touching, he adds, "As long as you want me."

***

On the last leg of our ride home, Tariq and Fin's conversation about the possibilities of Etherea and Teslin's royal family being involved flitted in through the open window of the carriage. At one point, they even theorized if The Clips were somehow involved, too.

Apparently, Etherea has had such a firm grip on the balls of those two countries since King Alrik made aggressive power moves over a thousand years ago.

Inside the carriage, Elly and I discussed my dreams with Karasi again, identifying what could possibly have been part of the prophecy that she revealed and who the 'she' was who Karasi kept referring to. We came up with a few possibilities for the unknown woman.

FATE DEMANDS SACRIFICE 369

If it's to be believed that our souls pass onto the beyond when we die, then that ruled out my mother, which left us with three other options.

The first was Asteria herself. We don't know what happens to demi-gods when they die or pass on, whether or not they join the souls of mere mortals and beings of Aveesh in the afterlife. No doubt she'd want to see what became of her bloodline.

The second option would be Dola, the Goddess of Destiny and Fate, considering fate has had *such* a hand in leading me on my path. It would also explain why the earthquake happened when Karasi tried to tell me more than they wanted her to.

The final person is Danica, the Mother of Sirians herself. After all, this path I'm on could lead to the rise of the Sirians again, whether that be the Light or Dark. Who knows if a Goddess cares which one it is, especially after what happened to her children?

The carriage rolls into the courtyard well past sunset, the sconces lighting the enclosure just enough to see. After the door swings open, Elly accepts Tariq's outstretched hand, jumps from the carriage, and instantly stretches when her feet touch the gray stone.

Once Elly steps away, Tariq extends his hand in front of the carriage door to me. I ignore it but instantly regret it as I stumble down the steps. I yelp, but Tariq lurches forward to catch me in his arms. Tangled in them, my hands grip his forearms. I gaze up at him, and he's glaring down at me as if to say, *How'd that work for you?*

A loud thud echoes off the stone walls around us. I snap my attention toward it, my eyes connecting with blazing green ones.

Fin spins on his heels, leaving behind one of the crates as he mutters something under his breath, stalking off towards the door. I shrug out of Tariq's arms, chasing after Fin with clumsy, rushed steps. I squeeze through the side door just before it can close in his wake.

Fin is nearly halfway down the hall before I can get close enough to shout, "Finley!"

He stops mid-stride, pausing as he runs a hand through his hair. Then, he twists around to face me fully.

Even with the feet of distance between us, his face reveals so much emotion, just as it always does. As he tries to avert his gaze, I catch the flash of agony. His lips are set in a firm line, but even those have a slight downturn at the corners. His shoulders slump forward as if they may collapse on themselves.

I may have avoided this conversation for too long.

"Talk to me, Fin." I take a few steps closer. Fin stares into me, those green eyes rimmed with silver. "Are you okay?"

"I thought I could do this, but I just need time, I think," he sighs, adjusting his uniform. "Maybe I'll be okay, then."

"I know there's been a lot going on," I explain, splaying my hands out in front of me. "And I know we've been having a bit of a tough time lately—"

"It's not that." He offers a broken smile, his dimple

FATE DEMANDS SACRIFICE 371

hidden.

"Fin," I plead, pulling my hands into my body. I reach for my necklace, fiddling with the hematite pendant. His eyes track the movement, glazing like he's lost in a memory. "I'm sorry things aren't working out…"

He swallows, his attention still locked on my necklace. I stop playing with it and lower my hands in front of me.

"You know, I think I knew this thing between us was fading a while ago." He finally raises his focus to me, his cheeks flushed. "But I guess I never expected it was because the girl I'm in love with started falling for my best friend."

The world falls away around us as my vision tunnels. *The girl I'm in love with…*

My mouth opens in shock, but no words come out because I don't know what to say. I knew Fin cared deeply about me, but I always thought it was because he liked me a lot and cares deeply about everyone he allows close. Maybe I had brushed it off too much, especially the last month and a half, as I slowly pulled away while he continued to reach for me repeatedly.

"Fin," I start to protest, at least the part about falling for his best friend, but he glares at me.

"I know you by now, Reva." The grin that spreads across his face looks more like a grimace. "And I see you and Tariq. I see the way you two look at each other, and what's *fucking infuriating* is that I can't even be mad!" He throws his arms out on either side of him. "Any woman would be lucky to have him, and Gods, if anyone is worthy of you, it's him."

"We don't have each other, Fin." My voice is soft, barely above a whisper, as the back of my throat burns. A tear slips down his cheek, and what is left of my heart shatters into pieces on the floor.

"But don't you?" Fin closes his eyes, shaking away the tears that continue to gather. My chest concaves on itself. "I could hear you two talking last night…"

A tear falls down my cheek now, and I can't breathe.

"You may not realize it, but you have him, Reva, just like you have me."

"Finley—" I try again, but he holds up his finger, using his other hand to pinch the bridge of his nose.

"You know damn well without question," he swallows, wincing again. "That I would give you the very shirt off my back if you asked for it—my very skin and blood and bones—to keep you safe and happy." He takes two steps closer but stops himself. "If that means walking away right now, you have to let me. You need to allow me to let you go."

He shakes his head, then retreats a few steps before twisting away from me and disappearing down the hall. Each click of his boots against the ground creates a splinter in my chest that grows, cracking like ice on Orion's Lake.

I'm stuck in place, nailed to the floor by every word he uttered. I blink rapidly, a final tear escaping down my cheek.

FATE DEMANDS SACRIFICE

And just like that, we are strangers again.

CHAPTER 26

I work alone with Clint in his room, helping him walk from one end to the other. As his balance and leg strength improves, he puts less and less weight on my arm. I have to say, he's even put on a little bit of weight, and I've already noticed his voice keeps cracking when it gets too high-pitched.

He's finally starting to go through puberty now that his body can absorb the nourishment it gets.

"You're really quiet today," Clint observes, peeking at me from the corner of his eyes while angling his head toward his feet. "Do you want to talk about it?"

For the last two days, outside of silently working with Clint, I've kept myself secluded in my room. The moment Fin walked away, a strange numbness swept through me, and I've found it difficult to do anything but go through the motions.

"Just a lot going on, kid." I try to smile, but I'm sure my closed-lip grin looks like nothing more than a wince.

"I know you lost Karasi," Clint says quietly, stopping in the middle of the room. He cautiously twists to face me. "And then you find out about your parents, the stuff

FATE DEMANDS SACRIFICE 375

about the Darkness."

I clench my teeth together, my jaw flexing.

Clint offers a small smirk, shrugging. "I know the look on your face."

I raise an eyebrow, the rest of my face stoic. "What look?"

"When you're giving up," Clint admits, taking my other hand so they're clasped between us. "How many times did I try to give up, but you never let me?"

Something twinges in my chest at the memory, one from months ago when he had his first terrible reaction. The second was when he nearly died.

"I will not let you give up, Reva," Clint whispers, squeezing both of my hands. "So, you can stare blankly at me all you want, get lost in thought when mixing my teas, and ignore my jokes. But you're not allowed to give up on me. Not yet."

I roll my head back to look at the ceiling, biting on the inside of my lower lip to keep the tears from flowing again.

They never stop, do they?

I bring my head back to stare at Clint, lolling it to the side. I take his head in both of my hands, tilting it up so I can look into those glittering, amber eyes.

The way he ogles at me with the smallest smirk, I know he's going to look so much like his older brother as he starts to age and grow into himself. The hair at his roots is even growing in a darker blond than the platinum lengths, framing his face in choppy layers.

"I'm very proud of you," I whisper, swiping my thumb along his cheekbone. "You're an incredible kid."

He shrugs nonchalantly, the smirk growing into a cheesy grin.

A quick knock on the door is the only warning before it creaks open, and Elly pokes her head in.

"You busy?" she asks, looking directly at me. I shake my head, gesturing for her to come in as I help Clint back to his bed. "Lightning finally got back. She's in the library and says we all need to talk right now."

"Did you tell her about Eldamain?" I ask, letting Clint swing his legs on the covers without my assistance.

"She said she heard, and I filled her in briefly on the bits we know," she explains, shrugging. "She also said she heard back from the Elders. They've delivered their terms."

"Call for one of the nurses if you need anything," I instruct Clint, tossing him a new book. He catches it with ease, grinning from ear to ear when he sees it's a title on Sirians I snagged from Karasi's. I point my finger at him. "Do not let anyone see that. Lunch should be coming soon, so keep your ears open and shove it into your little hiding spot."

"Ay, ay, captain!" He salutes with a roguish grin, eliciting an eye-roll from me.

Elly and I walk side-by-side to the library, traveling down the hallway toward the stairwell. She loops her arm into mine, our shoulders brushing together as we step one foot in front of the next.

FATE DEMANDS SACRIFICE 377

"How are you doing?" Elly asks, her voice soft and low. "It's been a few days."

I think about my conversation with Clint, a ghost of a smile fluttering on my lips. "I'm actually doing better than I was this morning, I think. Per usual, Clint seemed to brighten my day a little bit more."

"I'm glad." Elly smiles, her eyes dimming gradually. "Fin came to me yesterday and explained what happened between you two."

"Oh, Gods," I groan, throwing my head back. "What did he say?"

She presses her lips together, tilting her head to the side. "It was going to happen, Reva. I know it's not the best feeling, but you do have to give him some time."

"He said I have to allow him to let me go," I whisper, the phrase pouring more salt into my wound. "I hurt him. I put the conversation off for too long."

"Probably." Elly shrugs, waving her free hand around us. "You warned him other things were distracting you. Most of the time, we only saw him outside his new shift, meeting about something dire. There's never a good time to bring up that conversation."

"I think it just really hurt him to know about Tariq," I admit, shaking my head. "Are Tariq and I that obvious?"

Elly fights a smile, the corners of her lips twitching as she stares at the door in front of the library. I follow her gaze to find Tariq reclining against the large double doors with his hands in his pockets, one side of his mouth tilted up.

"When you look at each other like that," Elly whispers in my ear. "It's written on the damn wall."

"I've been waiting for you," Tariq shouts at us as he props the door open, but he looks at me when he says it, and something about the tone in his voice has my knees quivering.

"Don't think about doing anything remotely inappropriate in this library, Tariq Hesper," Elly snaps, pointing her finger in his face. "You defile those books, and there will be hell to pay."

Tariq raises both hands in surrender, keeping the door open with the toe of his boot. Elly continues to glare at him as she passes the threshold until she's forced to look forward. Once she does, Tariq leans down so his lips just barely brush against my ear.

"Challenge accepted," he mumbles.

I gasp, slapping him on his stiff chest, which only pulls a boisterous laugh from him. I march off to find which direction Elly has scurried off to, but Tariq's grip on my wrist has me pausing.

"Hey," he says quietly, scanning my face frantically. "Are you okay? I haven't seen you in a couple of days."

I nod, pressing my lips together. "I just needed some time to sit with myself and with everything. It's all still so fresh and raw."

"I'd expect as much." His thumb brushes along the inside of my wrist. "If you want to talk, whether you want advice or to just yell at someone, you know where to find me."

FATE DEMANDS SACRIFICE 379

My chest warms, the tenderness in his grip caressing my heart. Something inside me wants to shove down this feeling swelling in my chest, both from guilt and fear, but at the same time, the other half of me doesn't want to shy away.

You deserve love and happiness, Reva...

I use his grip on my arm to urge him closer to me, which he obliges, raising an eyebrow. I slowly lift to the balls of my feet, gently brushing our lips together.

"Thank you," I say against them, my skin lighting up as he snakes his other hand around my waist.

"That wasn't a challenge!" Elly shouts from down an aisle. I smile against Tariq's lips, that warmth blooming in my chest as he reflects it.

"Come on, Starfire." Tariq places his hand on my lower back, ushering me down the aisle Elly's voice came from.

Lightning is already waiting for us at the tables within the library where we usually congregate. She sits in one of the chairs, shoving against the table with her training boots and balancing on its back legs.

"Do you mind?" Elly scoffs, folding her arms across her chest. Lightning scowls and plops down on the floor with an echoing thunk.

"So proper," Lightning chides, that devilish smirk plastered on her face. "I thought I said only Reva."

"If we are going to discuss an alliance with my army, whether you plan to deny us or not," Tariq interjects, pulling out a chair at the opposite table and gesturing for me to sit. "Then I should be here to discuss. I suggested that Finley and Pax also attend, but apparently, you were vehemently against that."

Lightning sneers at the mention of Fin's name, but when Pax's name falls off Tariq's lips, something dark shadows those piercing eyes.

I narrow my eyes, tilting my head.

"Fine," Lightning concedes, folding her hands into her lap. "I haven't been able to tell the Elders about your theory on the Crown Prince of Etherea and this Sidra you mentioned since I just learned today, but your theories on Etherea being involved before were enough to convince the Elders they would need to form a mortal alliance."

"I would argue that if they knew exactly how intimately the royal military of Etherea is involved," I snort, folding my arms on top of one another on the table in front of me. "Then the Elders would have no choice but to ally with another kingdom. Your best bet is Mariande, considering I have an in with some of the family members."

Lightning levels me with a glare. "That being said, they refuse to meet here again."

"So, where would they like to meet?" Tariq asks patiently, relaxing into the chair. He spreads his legs wide under the table, his knee brushing mine.

"They want to meet on neutral territory." Lightning's gaze flickers from Elly to me. "They want you all to meet roughly a dozen of those who will be able to fight. But we're not about to reveal where our colony is to you, and

FATE DEMANDS SACRIFICE 381

bringing a dozen healthy, skilled Sirians into Mariande, where the Elders were attacked last time, is not the safest idea. Not until we have your guaranteed protection."

"I can understand that," I agree, nodding and glancing at Tariq. He blinks, nodding along. "So, what is neutral ground then?"

A chilling smile crawls up her cheeks as she reels her attention to Elly. "It is common for royal children to take sabbaticals to benefit their positions, is it not?"

Elly frowns, pouting. "Yes," she drawls, glancing at Tariq and me from the corner of her eyes. "Why? Do you have something in mind?"

Lightning shrugs, that smile relaxing some. "I know geography is one of your specialties, and you study the many ancient maps in this library. You've also been very invested in the Gods, demi-gods, and the various religions of Aveesh. One would argue, particularly these last two or three months."

"What are you getting at?" I ask, but I have a hunch I know where this is going. Lightning catches that registration on my face.

"Let's say you hypothetically come across a very, very old map hidden deep within this library's wards." Lightning reaches under the table she's sitting at, tossing a rolled-up piece of parchment that's seen better days on top. Elly flinches at the brutality. "And that map shows you the exact location of the hidden Arcane Island."

Tariq and I simultaneously swear under our breaths, lurching from our seats. The three of us meet at

Lightning's table, huddling around the parchment as Elly delicately unfurls it from the ribbon wrapped around it.

"Gods," Tariq awes, huffing. "It's almost right off the coast of our own damn country. How has no one caught this traveling from here to Riddling or from Eldamain to Riddling?"

"Rumor says it's veiled by a mist only the Light can penetrate." Lightning shrugs as if she's explaining how to find the dining hall.

"Okay… so we all meet at the Arcane Island." I flourish my hand over the map. "How do you suppose we convince King Darius to let us all go?"

"Who's *us all?*" Lightning crosses her arms over her chest. "I can convince them a maximum of you three."

"Our father won't let Elly and I go to some long-forgotten island alone." Tariq points at the map. "Not without an entourage. He'd have no problem sending Fin and Pax with her as her guards, but it might take some convincing to allow me to go, especially since he'll be down two Lieutenant Generals without Pax or me."

"With Clint healed," I add, extending my head. "I won't have a problem going with Elly. As far as he knows, I've been taking self-defense lessons with Tariq, and I'm the Royal Healer. We should have medical personnel when traipsing about a seemingly uninhabited island."

Elly chuckles under her breath at that remark. Her eyes are still scanning the map in awe, studying beyond the small drawing of the island.

FATE DEMANDS SACRIFICE 383

"Like I said, it can only be you three," Lightning argues through clenched teeth, her eyes frantic as she plants her hands on the table and rises from her seat.

"I'm sorry, but there is no way the Crown Prince and Princess of Mariande and their Royal Healer are traveling to meet your Elders unprotected," Tariq demands, a more authoritative side peeking out as he stands straight. I avert my gaze to the map to hide the inappropriate blush warming my cheeks. "It's nothing against the Sirians but everything against pirates, Etherean spies, and Dark Sirians.

"The five of us—six if you are to travel with us—is still a very small entourage for what we're trying to do here." Tariq's eyes are studious, and I know what it feels like to be under that magnifying glass when he's reading you. Something flickers across them, almost like recognition. "Is it Finley? I know you two have some sort of spat with one another."

"I couldn't honestly care less about your *soft* knight," Lightning sneers, pacing away from the table and back again.

"Do you want to be alone with Elly?" I guess, but even that seems ridiculous the minute it leaves my lips. Both Tariq and Elly startle, confusion written on their faces. I shrug, frowning.

"I told you I like women one time," Lightning mutters under her breath.

"You like women?" Elly asks, staring at Lightning like she's seeing her for the first time.

"This is really not the time," Tariq chuckles darkly, rubbing his temple. "Well, that just leaves—"

"Pax," I interrupt, but my voice is barely above a whisper. Again, at the mention of his name, Lightning's eyes deepen in color, her face softening, and finally—*finally*—I realize why something about her facial structure and the way she holds herself has always tickled at the back of my head with familiarity.

My heart pounds in my chest because there's no way their stories have any similarities other than mere coincidences. But the more I piece them together, the more the whole picture forms.

Because the more I stare at Lightning, the more I realize she looks a lot like Pax.

"You're his…" I trail off, wondering if I'm the only one who knows Lightning *and* Pax's history. "What's your real name, Lightning?"

Those are *tears* I see in her glowing, ice-blue hues.

"My mother was known as Cypress," Lightning admits, her head falling to stare at her hands as they intertwine around each other. "But her mortal name was Abelia, and my father is Russ Forde."

"What," Tariq chokes out as Elly's hand flies to her mouth, trembling.

"You're—" Elly pauses, taking a few tentative steps toward Lightning. "You're Pax's *sister*?"

Lightning nods, her gaze lifting. "My real name is Seneca Forde."

Seneca.

FATE DEMANDS SACRIFICE

385

"Oh, Gods," Elly gasps, twisting to face Tariq and me. Her hands are clenched over her stomach. "He's lived his entire life wondering what ever happened to his mother and sister."

"He what?" Lightning—well, Seneca— whispers, her face falling.

"What are we going to tell him?" Elly asks us, but I don't know what I'm supposed to do here, and I recognize the irony of the situation.

For once, I know something about someone's life that they don't, and I don't know how to tell them.

"Please don't tell him," Seneca pleads, reaching for Elly's hand. "If he has to come with us to the Arcane Island, I'll be the one to tell him. I will tell him the way I need to."

"He'll lose his mind if he knows we know before him," I admit, because there have been plenty of times I have.

"How do you think he will react when he finds out his sister is Sirian?" Tariq chuckles, side-eyeing me. I point my finger at Tariq, pursing my lips.

"This isn't a joke," Elly snaps at us. "You two are insufferable."

"I'm sorry, Elly," I sigh, throwing my hands out. "I'm really spent at this point with surprises. For once, this has nothing to do with me, so I will just let this play out."

Elly grits her teeth, flaring her nostrils.

"Alright, let's get serious for a moment," Tariq concedes, placing his hands on the table. "You're Pax's biological sister, the one who was taken from him and his father by your mother nearly twenty-three years ago. I'm guessing it was because you were Sirian, and we all know or are at least aware of how Russ Forde is as a person."

"He forced our mother to conceal the fact she was Magic when he took her from her home in Riddling," Seneca explains, rubbing a hand against her chest. "He tricked her into leaving, and when they returned to Etherea, he was cruel. Mother said the Etherean military found out he had wed a Magic and didn't care if it was because it was some cruel, twisted game for him. They kicked him out."

"We knew he was relieved of his position there," Tariq admits, mulling it over as he nibbles on the inside of his cheek. "I will say we didn't know the truth."

"My mother knew what to look for when she was pregnant with a Sirian. When she realized what I was, she had to get out, even if that meant leaving Pax behind. She figured he'd be better off since he was already starting school beside you two." Seneca sits in the chair she'd been in, running a hand over her braided silver hair. "She couldn't take care of two kids alone."

My gaze bounces to Seneca, Elly, and Tariq before settling back on the map between us.

"Well, you sit with how you want to tell *your brother* you're his long lost sister," I direct at Seneca, but then I wave my hand over the map. "But he won't let Elly come to the islands alone, so you have to figure it out. Until then, we need to devise a plan that will have King Darius

FATE DEMANDS SACRIFICE

agreeing to let all of us go in the first place."

Elly scoffs in disbelief, shaking her head. "So now what? Where do we go from here, Tariq?"

We all look up to the Crown Prince of Mariande hunched over the old map on the table. He clicks his tongue against his teeth, his eyes flitting across the parchment as they glisten, the wheels in that brain of his turning as he mulls everything we've learned.

"This is what we're going to do," Tariq begins, nodding to himself.

And I listen to Tariq explain the plan with a sense of foreboding, that breath of fate tickling my spine as I sit on the precipice of who I was and who I'm about to become.

EPILOGUE

The young woman strolled across the ballroom floor, the long train of her dress dragging behind her like a serpent's tail. She snagged a glass of champagne from a nearby servant, clutching it precariously between the tips of her fingers.

She spotted her target observing his party from the edges of the bodies pressed together, fixated on the half-naked women dangling from the ceiling in strands of pearl-white silk. His boisterous laugh traveled across the room to her, his mouth gaping like a fish out of water. The men surrounding him in a complete circle leaned into the empty middle or onto one another's shoulders, beside themselves over their conversation.

The young woman inclined her head, holding it just high enough to be deemed important but not too high that she would be untouchable. She raised the glass to her lips, tipping it back, a splash of the fizzing liquor flowing into her mouth. She swallowed, allowing the bubbles to settle in her stomach before a smirk tugged at her cheek, red lips twitching.

She approached the circle of men, standing directly

opposite her target, peering between two of his comrades' heads.

At first, his eyes grazed over her, but they returned sharply. She met his robin-egg-blue irises, bowing her head while still holding contact. He tilted it, a slight flex of his neck muscles.

She held his stare, slowly stepping one heeled foot in front of the other, working her way around the half circle to him. His eyes trailed her the entire way, and he only acknowledged his friends with a smile and nod.

Because she commanded his attention now.

She shimmied up to his side, standing directly behind the other man next to him. She held the glass in front of her waist, clasping the champagne flute between all ten fingertips, shoulders pressed back. She stared off into the crowd, appearing to be searching for someone.

"My lady," her target greeted, leaning into her. His bourbon-tinged breath skated across her collarbone. "Are you looking for someone?"

"Mm," she hummed, side-eyeing him. "I was, but I've found them. I was told to make my acquaintance with the King of Etherea."

"And yet you look off into the crowd as if he's not standing directly beside you," he chuckled, amused. "Does making your acquaintance involve an assassination attempt?"

She carefully turned her head toward him, raising an eyebrow and scowling. "Pardon my manners, your Highness, but I don't believe the people who want you dead are *that* bold."

Those pale eyes traveled from her exaggerated cleavage and up the length of her neck until they locked onto her gaze. A wide grin, full of glowing white teeth, spread across his face, mischief twinkling. "Touché, my lady."

They detached from each other simultaneously, their faces turned back to the entertainment and crowd of people gathered. His friends stayed close by, but they no longer circled him. The woman and the King of Etherea now stood alone, shoulder to shoulder.

Too easy to persuade a vulgar King for a moment alone.

She let him ponder silently and waited for him to break the tension between them. She knew his mind would claw to decipher who she was and why she would be told to make his acquaintance.

When she tipped her glass back for another swig, he finally asked, "So what brings you here tonight, my lady?"

"Business," she answered, the glass poised below her lips. She took a small gulp before shrugging and adding, "Of sorts."

"Is that so?" He turned fully flush toward her, slipping his free hand into his pant pocket. He swirled his half-empty glass. "What sort of business would a beautiful, young woman like yourself require from the King of Etherea?"

"I have a proposition for you, your Highness," she admitted, grabbing her dress in one hand as she set her own unfinished drink on the tray of a servant passing

FATE DEMANDS SACRIFICE

391

by. She faced the King so they were standing before one another. "I believe I have capabilities, knowledge, and power that would be of great use to you."

His eyes narrowed skeptically. He sucked on his teeth before tapping the lip of his glass to his temple, stepping into her. "You know, you have my attention if that was your goal tonight. You saunter over to me from across the room after watching me for the better half of the evening. Then, you act as though you might slip poison into my drink, but you make your presence known. You stand before me now, a young woman in—oh, I'm guessing—her early twenties, insinuating you could be indispensable in numerous ways. Am I to think you are telling the truth and worth a private audience, or am I to continue thinking you are here for an assassination?"

Men are so predictable.

She pressed her lips together, leaning her head towards her shoulder. She took her own step into the King of Etherea, her breasts brushing against his chest. He inhaled sharply, his gaze glancing down her cleavage. She took a deep breath so they swelled just a little more.

"Your Highness," she began, watching her hand as she plucked an invisible lint ball from his lapel. She pet him, her hand lingering momentarily along the smooth jacket. "My goal was not to grab your attention. In fact, my goal tonight is to make a business transaction, which I know will happen. Besides, if I wanted you dead, it would be fairly simple for me, which is part of this transaction."

She trailed her eyes up, lifting her head to study his

face, but kept her own stoic as she continued, "You are correct to assume my age, yet I hardly believe how that has anything to do with business when I have the power a man of *your* age could only dream of. So yes, King Ciar. I believe I am worth more than a private audience."

He gawked, awestruck by her performance.

And why wouldn't he be? She knew every card to play, from getting into this event to gaining his attention. She went as far as to wear his favorite color on her lips and body.

Maroon.

"Walk with me, my lady." King Ciar smiled, holding out the crook of his elbow for her to take.

She delicately slipped her hand into it, allowing the other to rest against his forearm. He guided her towards one of the concealed doors in the back of the room, exchanging a nod with the guard in front of it.

"You obviously know who I am," King Ciar chuckled, extending his hand to allow her entrance into the narrow hallway before them.

She confidently walked under the doorframe, waiting for the door to shut behind them. Pinning her bright, sea-green eyes on him, she produced a handkerchief from between her breasts, wiping the salve from the middle of her forehead to reveal the six-pointed Mark. The color drained from his face as she called the Darkness forward, and she knew her pupils had swallowed the color surrounding them.

"They call me Sidra."

The story continues in Book 3

ACKNOWLEDGEMENTS

Here we are at the end of Book 2 in The Sirians Series, and what a ride it's been so far.

I want to thank all of the fans out there because if you're reading this, this means you read *Darkness Comes Again* and enjoyed it enough to read Book 2. So, thank you from the bottom of my heart for believing in this story and where I want to take it.

Next, I have to thank those who have been around since the very beginning when I had just a few hundred followers and a lot of ambition to get to this point. Ya'll are really something else and know how to keep a girl going.

To my family, who has stood by my side every step of this journey, from the moment I said I was *finally* going to publish my book to reading all my smutty chapters—you guys are the real MVPs and know that you all have a place in my story.

To my fellow author friends (that's right, I'm coming for you): There are so many to name, but I first have to start with the ones that willingly read Book 2 at the Alpha stage. Thank you for always laughing with me, for giving the best advice, and overall just giving me a space to vent about book-related struggles and life happenings. You are all a gift I cherish, and forever hold a place in my heart.

Next, this goes out to the Beta and ARC readers: You are the best hype team I could ever ask for, and the fandom you've created has truly made this series what it's becoming. I finished writing Book 2 in 6 weeks because my ARC readers' reviews from *Darkness Comes Again*—you fueled the characters and the motivation to write. So, thank you from the bottom of my heart.

Brian… Your talent as an artist has helped me reach those (like myself) who judge a book by its cover before you even read a synopsis or see the tropes. I can't wait to see what we can do with the rest of the series. Sophie… Thank you for making this story the best it can be, encouraging the feral moments, and sticking with me through the wild twists I have planned, even if they break your heart.

And, of course, to all my friends who have supported me along the way, your support feels like one in a million, and I'm blessed to have you all in my life. From letting me ramble to shouting about me from the mountaintops (I'm looking at you, Kristyn), you all are what I've always needed.

Saving the best for last… Jake. Thank you for all the morning brainstorming sessions that led to developing this universe beyond the Sirians Series. And thank you for understanding that I'm in love with my own characters.

About the Author

K.M. "Katie" Davidson is an adult fantasy author. Her authorial journey began as a young writer creating YA fantasy novels in composition notebooks and publishing them on Wattpad. After getting her Bachelor's in Creative Writing and Master's in English Literature—and abandoning 20+ book ideas—she finally sat down in 2023 and finished her debut novel, *Darkness Comes Again,* Book 1 of the Sirians Series.

Outside of writing and reading, Katie is a Content Marketer. She loves dance parties with her husband and dog, hiking, traveling, entertaining conspiracy theories (none more than aliens), collecting more rocks, and buying old copies of books published over 100 years ago.

For exclusive sneak peeks, character aesthetics, and more news, follow K.M. Davidson on social media: @kmdavidsonbooks

Printed in the USA
CPSIA information can be obtained
at www.ICGtesting.com
CBHW061137241024
16330CB0002\6B/209/J